NO
GODS
FOR
DROWNING

NO
GODS
FOR
DROWNING

HAILEY PIPER

Copyright © 2022 by Hailey Piiper
Cover and jacket design by Mimi Bark

ISBN 978-1-951709-80-8
eISBN: 978-1-957957-11-1

Library of Congress Control Number: available upon request

First hardcover edition September 2022 by Agora Books
An imprint of Polis Books, LLC
62 Ottowa Road South
Marlboro, NJ 07746
www.PolisBooks.com

For J, forever.

VALENTINE

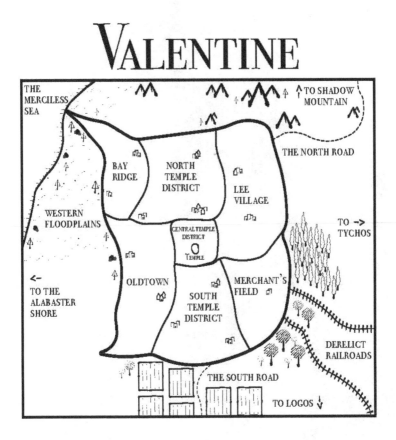

THE HOLY LAND OF AEG

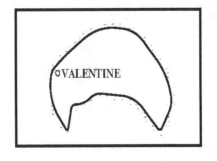

PART ONE

A
NINE-POINTED STAR

CHAPTER I

In the beginning, men were prey, and in the end, they would be prey again.

Lilac Antonis couldn't wait that long. She had listened for the approaching pair from her corner, hidden behind barnacle-crusted crates, their wood stinking of old seawater. The dark shack hugged her while minutes crawled, as if in this forgotten pocket of Oldtown, she would go forgotten, too.

"You sure this is the place?" a shrill voice asked, as a reedy chicken of a man—Flip?— shoved open the shack's door. "Don't see Vince."

A sturdy shadow followed, had to be Marko. "It's the place," he said, and then raised his voice. "Barton, where you'd get?"

Lilac had never hurt anyone before, not on purpose. Not the way she would today. Minutes scurried now, impatient. She couldn't let the men get their bearings straight, let their eyes adjust, let them realize there was no Vince Barton here like they thought.

Pale outside light curled at the edges of their silhouettes as Lilac crept out, painting Flip in a ratty old suit and tattered derby. Beside him, Marko wore more practical clothes for the coming rainy season, a wool coat and thick brown fisherman's pants tucked into galoshes. He tugged a pocket watch from his coat, its chain clinking, and Flip leaned over to check it too.

They were ordinary men. Flesh and bone. Mortal.

Lilac swept in as quiet as poison and slammed a smooth stone into the back of each man's skull in turn. Marko went down first; Flip next. Too hard a blow, and they would never wake up. Lilac would've counted that as mercy.

But there was no goddess of mercy, and Lilac had no time to waste on made-up gods when she needed the real thing. At least one of these men should hear and understand.

Flip smelled off in a way Lilac couldn't put her finger on as she bound him in a discarded fishing net. Marko smelled sharp, like he'd been drinking, and that explained a few things. He would sober up once he woke. Lilac bound his wrists and ankles in thick rope. Everything in the shack once belonged to fishers, and when she finished tying the knots, she could only smell saltwater.

The beach rushed in from the back of her mind, the sunstruck sea twinkling in memory, but Lilac shook it away. She refused to dredge up the past, as if she had organized and prepared for nothing. Her plan would work. Life would go back to normal—no, better. Her life would know miracles again.

She took deep breaths as her nerves reminded her how wrong this might have gone had she been slower, or louder, or had either man carried a gun. Better to focus on the work ahead. She had never done this before, but she would have to do it again and again until her task was finished.

Marko stirred, grumbled, and raised his head off the floor. He spotted Flip ahead of him, wrapped tight in the net, and tried to reach out. The ropes held firm. He started to fuss, and the bindings chewed at his wrists, a waste of blood. Lilac couldn't stall any longer.

A solitary candle lit the patch of wood floor where Flip's net slumped against a wall. Marko struggled beside him. Lilac slipped into the light on tender steps, the floorboards rough on her bare feet. These days, a priestess of the old covenants was more likely to be a homeless beggar than sustenance for any long-gone bloodthirsty god. Some were even thieves, smugglers, and black market merchants like these two men.

"Vince, that you?" Marko asked. "Why you dressed like them robes?"

A featureless black robe covered Lilac's naked body, so shapeless and flowing that it made her figure hard to see, especially in the dim shack. She turned her head in slow inches toward Marko. The soft candlelight outlined her harsh nose, curls of auburn hair, and skin too olive for Vince's pallor.

"A priestess?" Marko strained at his bindings again. "Where's Vince? Did you kill him?"

Lilac froze mid-step—they cared about each other. Honor among thieves. Her idea that one of the men should hear her reasons had been naïve. She should have finished this before they woke up, before she heard them care. Best to end it before they showed themselves as any more human. She breathed in the shack's sea-stink and thought of the beach, and a sickness in the waves, and the reason she had to hurt these people today.

"In the beginning, men were prey," she said, and her voice came stronger than she'd expected. She was no stranger to the holy Verses of Aeg, and maybe her throat knew scripture enough to ignore her quaking muscles and jittery nerves. Was she really going through with this?

"Can't you hear me?" Marko asked.

"We scurried over small islands," Lilac went on. "Simple beasts without voice or thought, food for the glories of the seas, and those hungry seas surrounded us." She sidled toward Flip, his derby lying a few feet away. "But then came the blessing. The heavens opened, and the Dawn Gods descended on the world to save us."

Marko kicked at the floor, and a growl tinged his voice. "You need to answer up, lady. Vince. Barton. Where's he at?"

Lilac knelt over Flip's net—no stirring—and stroked her fingertips across the corded rope. "The Dawn Gods pushed back the seas with their heavenly might. The many islands of the archipelago joined in the united Holy Land of Aeg, and so did the many peoples become one."

"Will you stop reciting the fucking scripture and answer me?" Marko kicked again.

Lilac's fingers wove through the netting and into Flip's hair. He looked at peace as she yanked his head from the floor. Sticky blood matted his neck.

"Not content to merely preserve us in those dawn days, the Dawn Gods taught us to better ourselves, and so came the gifts, one from each of the seven. They taught us to build fire and grow food. They taught us to speak, heal, construct, create." Lilac's eyes at last slid toward Marko. "They taught us law."

Marko shouted now. "Let him go! Vince is expecting us. Don't you understand?"

"But we can't all learn law." Time was up—either Lilac went through with it, or she surrendered to the end of everything. She shook her right arm, and a silvery dagger slid down her sleeve, into her palm. Its blade curved into a sharp teardrop.

"Gods," Marko whispered. "Wait one minute."

Listening to him would be easy. Lilac could drop the sacrificial dagger, untie these men, and walk away. She could catch a bus to the coast and watch the frothing tide roll in, and wait for the rains to drown the city, and hope there was still a god somewhere across Aeg who cared about mortal life, blood or no blood to offer. Everyone she loved could vanish upon the beach in her thoughts and turn to twinkling seawater. No faces, no voices, only empty funeral pyres washed out by rainfall.

If she didn't call the gods, who would? If she walked away now, she would accept the end. Maybe not in thought, but in action. As if she consented to that terrible day four years ago.

She couldn't accept that. Ever.

Her dagger's tip chewed down Flip's neck, carved his chest, and drove into his heart. Red rivers spat across the wooden floor, staining his fallen derby. The shack's saltwater stink drowned in a bitter copper odor. No more scents of beach and ocean, only blood.

The shack smelled of a goddess's temple.

Marko hammered his booted heels against the floor. His ropes held. He began tossing his head back and forth, teeth gritted, drool slinging down his stubbly chin. "No," he grunted. "Gods, please—"

"Yes, call to the gods." Lilac dragged her free hand's fingers through Flip's blood. The coppery stink thickened, and she thought of priestesses, daggers, and a nine-headed holiness filling the temple. "All for the gods. All for Logoi."

Marko leaned his face toward his knees. His words rushed out. "Listen, there's been a misunderstanding. Clearly Vince sent us to the wrong house, or we messed up the address."

Lilac stood from Flip's body and crossed him on tiptoe. His growing puddle of blood dogged her heels. She reached her free hand to the wall above and smeared a red shape across the dingy planks. A dot, a line, a point, a curve, another, another. She'd drawn this sign a thousand times since her childhood in the temple of Logos.

"Listen," Marko said again. Drool struck his fisherman's pants. "You were in the middle of something important, and we intruded. We were wrong, I see that now. We're—I'm sorry. You hear?" He paused, a detail catching his attention, and then panic drained into shock.

Lilac's hand slid from the wall, but no blood dripped from her fingers. She almost felt her pores dilate, her skin acting with countless mouths to drink up the red fluid. She didn't mean to, never meant to. Couldn't be helped as a matter of birth.

"Gods, you're one of them? A descendant?" Marko leaned back, wide-eyed. His mouth hung dark, and sweat dotted his skin.

Lilac couldn't prolong this. Suffering was not the point. "In Logos, beneath the eyes of Many-Headed Logoi, to break the law in her city is to surrender your life to her."

"A mistake!" Marko snapped. "You got Flip; you don't need me. I won't tell."

He was right. He wouldn't.

Lilac lunged across his knees and drove her teardrop dagger into his chest. And again, to make sure. Suffering was not the point. He quit thrashing and shouting, quit everything, and slumped to the floor.

Sticky redness again soaked Lilac's fingers. "Wheel of resolve, turn for me, all which I've done and said. Bring it home and hearth to be, for all the living and the dead."

Quickly now, her skin was thirsty. Both men dead, one having heard his sacrificial purpose, no more feeling to them, she went for the harsher work of cutting open their torsos and spilling tubes and lumps onto the floorboards. She used Marko's coat to shove the pieces into an offering mound, and—

Why was she crying? In Logos, these men would have been killed long ago.

But Logos was far away, and Logoi was gone. That was the point of sacrifice. Lilac didn't have the luxury of caring that Marko had worn his coat because the rainy season made it cold outside, and he felt cold, he'd been a person who felt things, and now his soul had walked away.

If she walked, too, she would have to accept a damned future, where men would be prey in the end. She would have to accept that day at the beach.

Her robe slid from her body, smoother than a snake shedding its skin. She had watched Logoi's priestesses bare themselves for the goddess countless times. When they painted red dots along their bellies, chests, chins, they had all the time in the world.

But they had been ordinary mortals. Lilac's skin was thirsty, and she had to hurry. Dots, streaks, crossing everything until her skin echoed the nine-pointed star she'd painted on the shack's wall.

The star on her skin would vanish in moments. Lilac hoped its fleeting nature echoed life's brevity, or made some other sacrificial meaning. She had only pantomimed it in the past.

She crossed her ankles and aimed her feet at each other. She then raised her arms overhead, crossed her wrists, and steepled her fingers. Crimson trails forked, merged, and webbed down her body.

"I call to Logoi the Many-Headed!" she shouted. "I call to Logoi, Goddess of Reason."

The blood began to fade. Every sip eased her exhaustion, but the narrow window for ritual rattled her nerves. Her body needed sustenance; her skin would take it. Faster now.

"I call to Mother Logoi, find these offerings worthy of your attention and your return. Look upon this symbol of the bounty we would feed you. Accept this sacrifice, and wipe clean these men's souls. Accept their deaths, their blood, and come to feed upon them. Return to us, and save us."

Lilac's trembling arms slid down her sides as the prayer broke from dutiful to personal.

"We need the gods' help, like a daughter needs her mother," Lilac whispered. "I love you."

No blood stained her skin. The floor's puddle would congeal around the offering mound of innards, Marko's coat, and Flip's derby. Wherever Lilac stepped, bare floor would show through in the shape of her footprints. And what about her soul? No one would see the blood on her hands, but she would know.

Too far a fate to worry about. She hurried into underwear and threw the covenant robe over her body again.

Had it worked? Not right away, and she couldn't pretend two men's deaths were enough. No use crying for gods unless she was willing to slit a few throats. And if her sacrifices didn't work, she couldn't be caught either.

She dragged a small drum of oil from the shack's corner, placed here before the men arrived, and splashed the walls and bodies and floor. She then drew an oily line from the shack's center to its door, where she set the candle.

Best to leave the sacrifice for as long as possible in case the nine-pointed star drew Logoi's eyes. Best to hope she saw it at all.

CHAPTER 2

In the beginning, men were prey. The first line of holy writ floated unbidden into Captain Arcadia Myrn's thoughts each time she went knocking on doors in Oldtown, like a sinister good morning. The Dawn Gods promised mankind would never be prey again, and yet the later Verses of Aeg promised they would.

The line echoed again as Arcadia climbed from Oldtown's dirt street up short stone steps toward a tired wooden door, hoping to give the former prophecy power over the latter as best she could.

After a few knocks, a gaunt young woman answered with an exhausted scowl. She wore a gray button-down and slacks, her hair tied in a blue kerchief.

Arcadia tried a smile. "Arcadia Myrn. I'm captain to the evacuation team, or you might better know us as your local flood fighters."

Five agents in loose sea-green uniforms stood behind her. She made sure to be first in the line of fire, whether the resident who answered the door greeted the evacuation team with an unkind word or a snub nose revolver. Every knock was a sales pitch. Arcadia sold the promise that she had each Valentine citizen's best interests at heart in exchange for a little trust and cooperation. Her smile shined eternal.

"We're here to help," Arcadia said.

The woman in the dim doorway chewed at her words. "More

Logos than local. I thought you people were supposed to be rougher around the edges. For baby-snatchers."

Arcadia ran a hand through the bristles of her buzzed-cut hair. People in the city of Valentine had been skittish about the presence of officials from Logos since Commander Thale led them north ten months ago. Especially in Oldtown. Arcadia wanted to soften those concerns, but she cut an imposing figure, tall and muscled, and there was little her gentle smile could do about that.

Sell it, she told herself.

"We're not here to snatch babies, ma'am," Arcadia said. "We're here to evacuate the neighborhood before the rains, buffer the sea-facing barricades, and defend against the glories if necessary. We've only taken children, along with their families, to the refugee housing on the city's east side. Will you let us help you?"

"You have knives somewhere in those pretty uniforms?" the woman asked.

"Yes." On the left side of Arcadia's utility belt, beside her two-way radio.

The woman tugged her kerchief. "And guns?"

"Yes, ma'am," Arcadia said. On the right, a black six-round revolver across the line of pouches, but never meant for people, only to stop glories. Arcadia had quit the Logos police force and their cruelty going on a decade now. Flood fighters, the evac team—their job was to help people out of Oldtown and then beat back the rising tide. To call on Commander Thale and the occupying police from Logos would only make matters worse. But to Oldtown residents, flood fighters and police officers came cut from the same Logos cloth.

"Can't really do anything to stop you then, can I?" the woman asked, and let the agents inside.

Seeing one of these Oldtown homes meant seeing them all. Worn stone walls, aged wooden doors, cramped damp rooms, a grimy kitchen, barely passing the fire code—less a concern during the rainy season. Bread and wild greens would make up the brunt of most meals. Holes in the outside walls, left gaping for the summer dry season, would be plugged with wool and wooden boards by week's end. The rains were almost here.

There was only one bedroom, where parent and baby slept together. The crib sat beside a window, as it often did in these houses. Today, Arcadia found a baby inside.

"How'd you know we were still here?" the mother asked.

"We check everyone," Agent Cassis said, behind Arcadia. Dark hair raked her shoulders. "Every house."

"No wonder you're taking so long." The woman was right. At this rate, the rains would fill Oldtown before the evacuation could finish.

Arcadia let a hand dangle into the crib, above the sleeping baby. "He's sweet. What's his name?"

The mother stepped beside Arcadia. "Junior."

"After his father?"

"After me. June Green."

Arcadia smiled at her again. Dire times, a friendly face, and sometimes you had to appreciate the weirdness of the world. "Do you have any relatives to stay with?" Arcadia asked.

"Think I'd live in Oldtown then?" June asked. "I don't mind stomping in the mud. I don't have much, but I got good boots."

"I bet." Arcadia also bet that June knew mud and cold weren't the worry this year. Oldtown would flood, worse than ever before, and no other district of the Valentine city-state sat closer to the sea. "We have a truck idling outside with three other nice families from this neighborhood who haven't left yet. Soon, it'll take them, and you and Junior, to the refuge in Lee Village, where you'll be taken care."

"Until when?" June asked. "The end of the rainy season?"

Until the evac team can be sure the levees will hold the coast, Arcadia thought, but she kept that to herself. She squeezed June's

19

shoulder and hoped she understood this wasn't forever. Maybe she would also understand that Arcadia knew the hardship of leaving everything behind. She had done it more than once, in more than one way.

June seemed to crumble under Arcadia's gentle touch. "I've been here every rainy season. Oldtown floods. We get by."

"I know," Arcadia said, desperate to sound sympathetic. "But not this year."

Twenty minutes later, Agents Cassis and Leander escorted June and Junior down the steps, locked the door, and guided them into the truck. No rains yet, but the world outside June's house looked as gray as her stone walls, and as worn, too. So many Oldtown houses had been rubbed raw by rising water, their guttered rooftops beaten down by time. What a difference ten years of seasonal flooding could make. Oldtown used to be a decent enough part of the city, no worse than the South Temple District. Everyone who could afford to move had since found nicer parts of Valentine.

The rest who couldn't—and that was plenty—were Arcadia's responsibility.

Cassis stood at the truck's hood and turned a crank until the engine roared to life. Somewhere in the racket, Junior began to cry. After another couple of minutes, Arcadia heard him laugh. They really were nice families. They would be fine. If only there were a way to make the neighborhood safe instead of emptying it, but there wasn't time.

Agent Ilene Summers jogged toward Arcadia. "Captain, truck's almost filled up. You want to radio in another?"

Arcadia glanced in the back, where June, Junior, and a few other locals sat on covered benches. "We can fit one more family. On to the next house."

Doubt squeezed her guts. Should she have listened to Ilene, brought in another truck? As if that would change anything, somehow trick the rains into waiting until she could convince every holdout in Oldtown to clear this section of the city.

Instead, she walked to June's next-door neighbor, climbed the short steps, and knocked on the door. No one answered, and Arcadia sent her agents circling. Cassis reported light from inside one window. Likely someone was home.

Arcadia tried the knob—locked—and ordered two more agents, Bryce and Athas, to fetch the ram. They shouldn't have needed to break a door down unless the insides had swollen with floodwater pressure, but what if someone had left a child inside? Arcadia had to make sure.

The agents carried up the wooden column with a hard flat helm, their faces a little too excited. Captaining the evac team at times felt like herding a litter of puppies who'd confused themselves for watchdogs.

Arcadia covered her face against a laugh. "Not too rough, you two. Break the lock, don't shatter the door."

Heave, ho, the battering ram knocked once and popped the door's lock. A dim doorway smiled sideways from the frame. No sunlight inside, each curtain drawn shut, but there was light. A candle, by the look of its dancing glow.

Arcadia brushed past her agents and pressed the door open another inch. "Anyone home?"

Silence. An empty house? She couldn't know without stepping inside, not when so many people in this neighborhood took evacuation orders as a challenge and flooding as a test of piety. They would hide and risk death by sea without ever leaving land.

Arcadia leaned her head through the open door and let her eyes adjust to the darkness. Where was that candlelight coming from? She scanned the gloomy shelves and countertops, the end tables and couch, the damp red carpet.

Except there was no carpet. The front door's gray daylight and the meager unseen candle reflected in a wide pool of shimmering blood. Dark streaks spread up the walls and over furniture.

Where there was blood, there were bodies. One lump coated the sofa, another propped against a wall. Was there a third? Arcadia couldn't tell; these people had been cut open, their pieces scattered and piled, and the house was too dark. Had the glories been here? Were they still here? Arcadia let one hand fall to her revolver's butt while the other hand shoved the door open.

She realized too late where the candle stood. It had been placed within reach of the door, and its opening knocked the wax column and flame to the floor. Fire snaked down the hall, into the living room, and across the house's innards. Arcadia had been too distracted by the blood to notice oil on the wooden planks.

Now flames ripped at walls, furniture, bodies. No more darkness in this house, but too much light, ringed with crimson-painted surfaces.

Someone had dotted the wallpaper with nine gooey splotches and then drawn rough lines between them until the blood formed a star. Its arms stretched cruel and slender, their peaks representing the faces of Nine-Headed Logoi, Goddess of Reason, who had long ago founded and then abandoned Logos.

Bodies, fire, and her star. Like the old days. Like Shah.

Arcadia flinched from the doorway and stumbled backward onto the steps. She needed to sit. Concerned hands patted at her, aswirl with worried words. Who spoke, Cassis? Ilene? Leander?

"Captain Myrn, you hurt?"

"God, it's burning."

"There's people inside!"

"They're already dead, Athas."

"What do we do?"

"We're flood fighters, not firefighters."

"Get to that last house and call them then," one voice snapped. Definitely Ilene.

Arcadia should have given that order. She was their captain. One hand ran across her bristly scalp, and then both closed over her face. Where was she again?

"Someone get around, find a back window, see if you can smear that star," Ilene said. "Valentine firefighters might get the wrong idea otherwise, blame us." She lowered her voice and squeezed Arcadia's arm. "Don't worry, captain. We've got it."

Clomping footsteps dogged down the steps, around the house. Arcadia wanted to tell her flood fighters to be careful. To tell Ilene she was doing a good job. They all were. Everyone was doing their jobs, protecting Valentine, while Arcadia sat useless to the side.

Yes, exactly like the old days. Like Shah.

Chapter 3

"You're a mess, Myrn."

Arcadia nestled into a too-small wooden chair. A similar chair sat next to her, empty.

Commander Rhoster Thale sat behind his paper-piled desk at the back of his cramped office. A blue police jacket draped his burly shoulders, and a grimace cut through his scraggly brown beard, flecked with gray.

"Know why I've called you?" he asked.

Arcadia wanted to say she didn't. Thale had little reason to call her, she wasn't police anymore. The flood fighters only followed his lead in any way because he'd brought them along with his officers from the Logos city-state to take charge of Valentine. If Arcadia had any say, she would never see him again.

But she had none and said nothing.

"Your team didn't report you." Thale reached under his desk and brought up a brown decanter and shot glass. "No, your agents said you directed them smoothly, perfectly. That's what tipped me off. No such thing as perfect in these situations. I see the red in your eyes." He splashed amber-colored Mercai into the glass and slid it Arcadia's way.

She knocked it back as if ordered.

"Being captain means taking responsibility, even for a government agency as soft as the flood fighters," Thale went on. "The evac team is important, but I struggle keeping you in charge. At your best, Myrn, you excel, but at your worst, there is no one worse."

Arcadia slid the glass back across the desk. It struck a sheet of paper and bunched the corner.

Thale eyed it, as if he might take a shot, too. "Next time there's trouble, calm down and do your job. Seaside evacuation's stalled enough without your little breakdowns. Call us police you despise so much next time you find a crime scene. No more fits, got it, Myrn? Shah was ten years ago. Get over it."

Always bringing Shah into the conversation, as if Thale hadn't murdered people back then, back there. Did he remember? All he seemed to recall was when he'd given Arcadia an order, she'd frozen stiff.

Never mind that she alone lived without Shah's blood on her hands. The shame remained. She was unreliable. Was that a conscious decision or by her nature? Inherently insubordinate or inherently moral, she was useless to Thale. He should have been relieved when she quit the police and chose to fight floods and glories.

Yet she was a failure on that front, too.

Thale returned the glass and decanter of Mercai to the underside of his desk. "I hope you get on with your life someday. You can be better."

Arcadia wished she could say the same of Thale, but he was a consistent creature without variance or degree.

"Firefighters saw Logoi's star," he said. "Thoughts?"

Not if Arcadia could help them. "Drawn as well as anyone could with blood."

"The meaning, Myrn. Why would anyone draw it?" Thale leaned back and folded hands over his broad chest. Stiff blue cloth rippled at his shoulders. "Three dead smugglers. Probably knew each other, or had some common acquaintance. In Logos, they'd have been hung from the Racks, but these Valentine people, they have soft hearts. Executing criminals won't pass here."

Was Arcadia supposed to pity him for having no goddess to feed? All the gods were gone, cruel and sweet alike. Where did any of this put Arcadia? Evacuation was her business; homicide was the police's. Her boots ground against the stuffy office's floorboards.

"If locals think we killed those men, they may drive us out of the city," Thale said. "You didn't see anyone?"

"Only the dead," Arcadia said, affect flat. And the fire. And the sign of Logoi, as if Arcadia had returned to Shah. As if she still walked Logos streets and sometimes spotted Logoi's procession of to-be-executed criminals.

As if they weren't all so far from home.

Thale's desk phone jangled tinny bells. He gritted his teeth and snatched up the earpiece and staff. In Logos, he'd had funds for a secretary. But then, he'd had a larger office, and bigger bookshelves, and wider windows. Now he had to make do with a refurbished ground floor apartment bedroom, one segment of the apartment building Logos police had commandeered as their headquarters. For Valentine's own good, so it was said.

"Thale speaking." His face soured worse somehow. "One officer, or a squad? I need details in writing. No one sets foot inside unless it goes up in smoke, hear me?" He jammed the earpiece down and eyed Arcadia. "Why are you still here?"

Arcadia couldn't be sure why she'd come at all. She eased out of the chair, towered over the desk, and then turned to the door.

It burst open before she could touch the knob. A blue-uniformed police officer barreled into the office. Over his heart, a brass badge in the shape of a nine-pointed star gleamed in the lamplight.

"Commander," the officer said, gasping. "There's been another murder."

Thale glanced at the phone. "They called your office first? They just told me about the Bay Ridge house."

Bay Ridge, northeast section of Valentine, slightly higher in elevation than Oldtown to its south.

The officer raised an eyebrow. "You mean Cyprus Street, commander?"

Cyprus Street ran east and west through the city, but Arcadia guessed the address in this case would be somewhere in Oldtown.

Thale squeezed the bridge of his nose. "Give me a minute."

"South Chambers, Cyprus, Bay Ridge," Arcadia said. "Three murder sites. How many dead altogether?"

"A minute," Thale snapped.

The Oldtown house had kept meaty piles, three bodies, but there could be more in the other locations. A couple dead smugglers didn't concern Thale, but multiple homicides spread across the western part of Valentine? That would make the Logos police look incapable.

To look the way he made Arcadia feel—Thale couldn't accept that. He glanced over his office, beard spreading as he opened his mouth to speak again.

The jangling phone cut him off.

CHAPTER 4

Four multiple homicide locations. Arcadia never learned how many victims between them. Thale had kicked her out quickly after the next phone call. She was yet another element of unwanted chaos he'd needed gone.

She should have gone home to rest. These days, that meant Radiance Hotel, where she and other Logos exiles had been staying the past ten months since their arrival in Valentine. There were worse places to call home in this city.

Like Oldtown, where Arcadia went after leaving Thale's office. Not right away; she stopped at a diner to settle food beside Thale's alcohol. She then took a cab to South Chambers Street, June Green's neighbor's house, its insides now charred.

Leander and Cassis stood on the stone steps. "Keeping watch until local help arrives," Cassis said.

"Couple of Valentine private detectives," Leander said.

No wonder he and Cassis were waiting. Logos police never had investigators of any kind under Logoi's rule, and their move to Valentine hadn't changed that practice. Thale must have needed time to write a contract and phone for professionals.

"Do you know their names?" Arcadia asked.

Leander scratched his head. "Alexander Something and Something Gilly?"

Alexander Stathos? Arcadia should be so lucky. "Go home, you two," she said.

Cassis set her teeth, nervous. "Commander Thale said we couldn't leave until the detectives met us."

"You don't follow him; you follow me," Arcadia said. "Thale himself told me you're my responsibility, and I'm looking after you. Get some rest."

Cassis glanced at Leander, and then back to Arcadia. "But who'll look after you?"

They were too good. Thale could call them soft as mud in rain, but Arcadia knew each agent had earned their sea-greens. They were here, weren't they? Thale had a city to run, but every member of the evac team faced accusations of being interlopers, tyrants, baby-snatchers. They faced scowls and fists and pistols. Someday they might even face the glories.

"I'll be fine," Arcadia said. "Alex is an old friend."

Cassis and Leander left, each step reluctant, but they didn't have a disobedient bone between them. In that way, they were better than Arcadia.

She sat on the cool stone steps and listened to the city. Distant car horns and bustle rumbled from nearby neighborhoods. She imagined she could hear the ocean, but coastal wind drowned out the beach to the west. No fire crackled through the open door behind her. With the flames doused and Logoi's star smeared, the bodies alone no longer echoed Shah. At worst, Arcadia thought she smelled them, but there was too much soil and dampness in the air to be certain.

Her pocket watch showed 6:30 by the time another rusty gray cab rolled down South Chambers Street and paused outside June Green's house. The driver popped out to give his engine a turn with the crank, while two men stepped from the cab's groaning back doors onto the muddy street.

The first was a young stranger in a lengthy brown trench coat, buttoned to his sternum, a burgundy tie tucked inside. Beneath a broad tan fedora, his hair was a wild patch of tawny weeds, streaked here and there with strawberry red. His slender white face flashed an uneasy grin.

Arcadia had known the other man for over twenty-five years, both little more than kids when they first met in training at the Logos barracks, long before either had quit the Logos police. Alexander Stathos had been a scrawny, quiet thirteen-year-old then. Today he was a forty-year-old man and wore an unbuttoned black trench coat, its sides flapping free from his black tie, white buttoned shirt, and dark vest that puffed out at his middle. A black fedora with a white band hid most of his oil-dark hair, which he kept shorn short despite having left the Logos police six or seven years ago. Arcadia knew too well that such habits died hard.

"You guys want I should idle?" their cabbie asked, prying the crank from his engine. "Getting dark, and this neighborhood can be pretty rough."

"So can we," Alex said, his voice taut and confident. He paid the driver. "Besides, we'll be a while."

His wild-haired companion watched their taxi slip down the street. "Nice guy, that, such a love," he said, energetic in ways Arcadia couldn't remember feeling since adolescence. "Must come from South Temple District, not here. No one ever says their own neighborhood's the worst."

This young stranger's accent, the way it curled, and his face, a pale complexion atypical to the olive tones of Arcadia, Alex, and most people of the Holy Land—a man from West Amberdan, maybe? The sun shined fainter there. Arcadia wondered how long ago he'd come to Aeg's shores. The last ship from overseas had vanished many years back.

"Arcadia!" Alex strode near with a giant's smile. "What are you doing out here?" His arms squeezed tight around her.

Arcadia gave him a ferocious hug. "It's been too long, Lexi."

The hug broke, and so did Alex's smile. "Please don't call me that around—"

"*Lexi?*" The wild-haired man popped up beside Alex. "That your codename back when you were in the police? Did everyone call you that, or just her?"

Alex clapped the other man on the back. "This apology counts for all further interaction you two will have, so I'm only going to say it once—I'm sorry about him. Meet Detective Cecil Gillion. The other half of Ace Investigations."

"Lovely." Cecil whipped a paper card from his coat pocket to Arcadia's hand.

"Ace Investigations, Agents in Matters Public and Private, Civil and Criminal," Arcadia read aloud. This didn't make sense. "Don't your type spy on covenant traitors, cheating spouses, business deals?"

"Not much care for witches, cheaters, and cutthroat dealings these days," Cecil said. "We're Thale's dogs now. His fault for not having detectives of his own."

Arcadia slid the card into one of her belt's pouches. "It wasn't his decision. Logoi wasn't interested in investigations." The goddess of reason had only wanted her sacrifices in criminal blood, no questions asked.

"Well, if she wants to gripe about it, she can—" Cecil's expression faltered. He bowed his head to Arcadia. "Apologies, love. Meant no offense. I'm not all that properly versed on your city-state, and Alex here, he's not one to tell tales. Not to me, at least."

"Let's say I left the badge for a reason," Alex said. "Several reasons. Hard to forget the last time I tore off the uniform."

Arcadia knew the feeling. She never wanted to wear blue again. Not after Shah.

"Anyway, Cecil, meet Arcadia Myrn," Alex said. "The best friend you could ever have."

"Thought I was your mate," Cecil said, but his smile was back and aimed at the steps. "Arcadia, the love, the wonder, anything we can do for you?"

Arcadia thought neither would ever ask. "I want to see inside. With you."

Alex glanced to the dark doorway. "You're sure?"

Cecil clapped his hands. "Terrific. I'll lead. We got four of these troubles tonight, and this is only number one, so let's not keep the dead boys waiting." He slipped up the steps past Arcadia and pressed open the front door.

Alex followed him. "Broken into, huh?"

"Evac team did that," Arcadia said, trailing them inside. "Our discovery. Thale kept the exact addresses for the other sites to himself, but I knew someone would come eventually. Thankfully, it's you."

The house better resembled how Arcadia had found it before the fire, its secrets hiding in darkness, until Cecil sidled along one wall and thrust open the curtains.

Dusk's frail light cut through the gloomy house in orange-yellow slats, enough to show Arcadia the furniture, the walls, and the bodies. Red-tinged, charred in places, their torso cavities gaping open in ugly dripping mouths. She missed the darkness already, but the site lay calmer than it had this afternoon. If only sunset could get rid of the burnt-flesh smell.

Cecil gagged into his coat sleeve. "I'm thinking knife wounds, but what scraped the rubbish from their guts?"

Alex tipped a chair, glanced at a corpse's head, and then set the legs in place on the damp floor. "Calling it now, a team effort."

"Yes, they surely died as a team," Cecil said.

"I mean the murderer." Alex stroked his jaw. "Or murderers."

Cecil knelt over a body slumped against the wall. The skin had melted into the blackened stone. "One man could do this."

"One man did this in four places, in one day, in different parts of town?" Alex asked. "I don't think so. Limited time and energy."

"It's a big stretch of neighborhood, but it's all on the west end."

Cecil grimaced at the body. "It'd be tiresome work, but it could be done."

Alex turned to Arcadia. "What's your impression?"

Arcadia looked over the still bodies, their charred skin and clothes. "They're dead."

"Makings of a true investigator," Cecil said. He opened one palm and held it an inch from the body beneath him. "Don't expect I'll feel anything off them. Stabbing says emotional involvement, but fire is cleansing and messes everything up." He lowered his hand and winked at Arcadia. "Know what I mean?"

She shook her head. Cecil seemed an oddball; that was the best she could gather.

"Cecil's what we in the detective business call a cheater," Alex said. "Mildly clairvoyant. A descendant."

Arcadia studied Cecil again as he stood. He seemed too carefree for a descendant, but then, how was a god's mortal child supposed to behave? Red dashes stroked his light hair, the color a sign of godliness—it was possible.

"Which god?" Arcadia asked.

"See that?" Cecil asked, grinning. "Bring a fine gent to a lounge, a lady to a murder scene, dainty or stuffy or a big muscly beauty like yourself, they always want to know which god. Imagine I said Tychron, huh? No one would show me a good time then." He adjusted his fedora. "Poke the branches of my family tree, you'll find Lyvien, God of Instinct. I try to stay humble."

"Except when you're asking those gents and ladies to dinner," Alex said.

Cecil waved a hand. "It's nothing, really. Descendant gifts aren't a leaf to the great tree of a god's holy power. Special enough to be full of myself, but mortal enough to die."

"He'll get emotional resonance, event fragments, sometimes a person's thoughts." Alex neared Cecil and clapped his back. "Occasional thoughts of his own, too."

Arcadia couldn't help laughing. Cecil seemed good for Alex. Cecil laughed, too. "She don't believe us."

"I believe you," Arcadia said. "But I thought descendants would've left Aeg with the gods."

"How long ago?" Cecil asked. "Grandfather Lyvien popped off from the Holy Land way ahead of the others. Abandoned Aeg before it became a fad." He reached out to Arcadia. "Here, love. Your hand."

Alex sighed. "I wouldn't do that."

If Ace Investigations didn't work out, these two should start an act, head to Dialos and get into the talkies. Arcadia's mirth faded as she remembered no one sent films of any kind out from Dialos anymore—for all she knew, the Sunshine City was gone. She held out her hand.

Cecil pursed his lips in thought, and then said, "I see true love in your future."

Alex tugged Cecil's arm. "That's enough. We have work."

Cecil bowed out of Arcadia's reach. "Now you see what makes me the greatest detective in the Holy Land. Descendant, optimist, romanticist—"

"Arcadia, I don't think you're here to learn the finer points of investigation." Alex pulled a pair of rubber gloves from his coat. "And we have better places to catch up than over a trio of dead bodies. What did you need?"

Good old Alex, always sharp. Arcadia had worried she'd have to dance around her request another hour. "The other murder houses."

"Planning to visit them ahead of us?"

"I have someone I might ask about them," Arcadia said. "She's quick, like you. My only job is to make sure this area's empty before the dry season ends, but I want to help. She could offer that."

Meager sunlight shifted. Somehow the room's gore had grown more grotesque as dusk deepened. Arcadia had already seen too much of knife wounds, nine-pointed stars, reminders of Shah—useless things. Locations would help more, accounting for time, distance, and human ability.

"I'd bring the info to her," Arcadia went on. "Rather than bring her here. This is dangerous."

"Is it?" Cecil asked. "Oh dear, I might be in the wrong line of work."

Alex drew a small notebook from his trench coat, flipped between two pages, scribbled on one, and tore it out. "Thale gave me the addresses."

Arcadia gripped Alex's shoulder. "I appreciate it. And you might, too."

"I'd love that." Alex pocketed his notebook. "We really need to catch up. Barring bad weather or murder calamities tomorrow evening, we should head out for dinner. I might have Cecil in tow, but I'll keep him on his best behavior, for what that's worth."

"It's fine. I might not be alone, either." Arcadia managed a smile against the gloomy room. "There's someone I want you to meet."

"Beautiful." Alex fitted gloves over his hands. "Now, if you have what you came for, might be a nice time to leave."

"Unless you want to see this get intimate." Cecil drew out his own pair of rubber gloves.

Arcadia turned from the living room of horrors. "Have a good night, Lexi. See you tomorrow. Catch up."

She told Cecil it was nice meeting him and he would make a fine detective someday, which made Alex laugh. She then stepped out the front door, back into a world that made a little more sense.

But only a little.

CHAPTER 5

Murder was tiring work. Lilac blamed her sluggishness in turning over these last couple hotel rooms on running up and down Valentine's west side with a dagger and a prayer. She'd spent the day nervous, hiding, dragging, tying, cutting, crying, pushing, piling. Hotel maids had to hide their exhaustion, which meant she was failing basic professional housekeeping. The blood she'd drained during the rituals should have kept her from this bone-deep weariness, but her arms moved like truck tires in Old-town mud.

She thought about her orations to now-dead men and wondered if their killing weighed on her spirit instead. How much power did the soul have to drag on muscles? Nothing she'd heard in Logoi's temple covered it, not for descendants. If she weren't a goddess's child, she could spill her veins in buckets and cleanse every wrong from her soul, but no such luck. Descendant blood was useless to the gods. And it wasn't like they were here anyway.

Mother Logoi hadn't returned.

This hotel room's tenant, Mr. Barrow, tapped his foot and checked his pocket watch, again and again. If he wanted Lilac to leave, she could, but the room wouldn't turn itself over. She was halfway crawling through a sheet change when another maid popped through the room's doorway.

"Visitor," Marcy said. "Aren't you off-shift anyway?"

"After this hall," Lilac said. "If it's Cecil again, he'll have to wait." Even the words went snail-slow off her tongue. She had little strength for work, let alone for friends to drop by unannounced.

"She's definitely not Cecil."

Lilac perked up. *She* was here.

Marcy elbowed Lilac away from the bed, her dull black uniform swishing at each jab. "Go on, I've finished mine. I kept a lady waiting once, and she wasn't there when I got around to her. Don't make my mistake."

Between room swaps, shift switches, and every convenient rescue from hotel guest royalty, Lilac owed Marcy a couple dozen favors. She gave quick thanks, promised Mr. Barrow he was in good hands, and slipped out the door.

Another maid, Bristol, passed in the hall, adjusting her hair's white kerchief. "What's that smirk?" she asked, matching it.

"Marcy is a goddess in disguise," Lilac said. She hadn't realized she was smirking; her lips felt as heavy as the rest of her.

Bristol winked and then disappeared around a corner. Her shift was only beginning.

Before Valentine began to crumble, Radiance Hotel had catered solely to wealthy travelers. The vaulted ceilings, vibrant gold-colored carpets, and silver sconces had been for their benefit. With the gods gone ten years now, travel having shriveled to nothing between Aeg's city-states, and the government's State House having fallen apart, the elegance was shown largely to the occupying forces from Logos: police officers, admins, and agents of the flood fighters.

Agents such as Captain Arcadia Myrn, who waited outside her room. She loomed over Lilac, her tan eyes bright with wonder as if Lilac were as precious as one of the movie stars whose photos lined the lobby walls.

As if Lilac wasn't a murderer.

She freed long tangles of auburn hair from her white kerchief.

"Evening, Captain Myrn. How can I help the powers that be to-day?"

Arcadia scratched at her bristly scalp. "I don't have a clever answer," she said.

"Don't worry, I do." Lilac stood on her toes and kissed Arcadia's soft lips.

Warmth spread through Lilac's face and lightened the spiritual weight from her muscles. If she returned to Mr. Barrow's room, she could feel rightly annoyed like usual. Arcadia had broken through the numbness with her slight smile, the awkward shifting of her big lovable figure. Ultimately, each bloody sacrifice meant keeping her and everyone else alive a little longer. Her nervous, earnest demeanor made all the day's work worthwhile.

"What did I do to deserve a sweet distraction like you?" Lilac asked.

Arcadia held up a large, rolled-up paper. "I need your help."

So, Lilac hadn't earned Arcadia's attention yet, but she would. She took Arcadia's arm in both hands and let Arcadia pull them into her hotel room. She lived in a half-suite, furnished with a bed, bathroom, and table like the others, but also a sitting area, its own telephone, and small kitchenette, perks of a flood fighter captain on a long-term stay.

Her determined footsteps rattled the furniture as she approached the table. Unease and worry haunted her posture. Fine, there was business, but there was also a woman who needed a break.

"Get out of your greens and I'll run a bath," Lilac said. "While you're in, I'll set the stove."

"Lilac." The stoic way Arcadia said it grabbed Lilac's attention. This was near the end of a rough day, but not yet the end.

Arcadia unrolled her large paper across the tabletop, revealing a map of Valentine. Oldtown took the west and southwest sections, Bay Ridge to the northwest, the middle column formed the

North, Central, and South Temple Districts, Lee Village the east and northeast, and neon-lit Merchant's Field opened the city toward farmland in the southeast.

"I need your help," Arcadia said again.

"You'll relax after?" Lilac neared the table. "Let's get you helped then. What is it?"

"Can you find these addresses?" Arcadia pulled a torn notebook page from a belt pouch and laid it on the map's corner. "You know the city better."

Most wanderers from Logos had only come a year ago or less, after Valentine's government collapsed and someone had the bright idea that Valentine needed assistance from their southern neighboring city-state. Lilac had left Logos a decade back, its purpose gone when her divine mother abandoned Aeg with the rest of the gods. She hadn't run straight to Valentine, but the city had become her home in time.

She'd had nowhere else to go.

"The city's hard to read, all the streets kind of narrow," Arcadia said. "I need an overhead on these crime scenes."

The map seemed vast if you looked close enough, but was intimate to Lilac. These weren't words on paper. They were Marko and Flip at Bay Ridge, the Montey Brothers on South Chambers Street, on and on, blood spilling, organs piling, the stink so strong even in memory, Lilac had to press a hand against her nose here in the hotel.

And the needling thought came: *Does Arcadia know? Is this a trap?*

Lilac avoided Arcadia's eyes by closing her own and shutting out the world. The moments stretched the way Logoi had taught her, giving Lilac time to jam together puzzle pieces of information. No, Arcadia was unaware. Yes, Lilac could help without helping. She opened her eyes and smudged each site with a pencil, as close as she could tell when the map only gave street names.

"Do you see a pattern?" Arcadia asked.

Lilac only ever saw patterns. She guessed that was really why Arcadia had brought this work to her. Without knowing Lilac was a descendant, Arcadia had picked up on this meager gift of fitting pieces of the world together.

"If you mean why each location's important, I have no idea." Lilac slashed pencil across map, connecting the dots. "But overhead view? I see an X. But you could see that when I put the dots down."

Arcadia's finger traced the lines. "The place between them? I thought it might be more complicated."

"It might." Lilac planted her thumb at the X's center. "The distance between seems similar, maybe deliberate, but put a bunch of dots on a map and it's easy to make an X, a diamond, triangles, spirals."

Arcadia placed her hand on the small of Lilac's back. "That's why I brought it to you. Your smarts always impress me."

"I don't know smarts, but the patterns show clear." Lilac tucked her chin in one hand. "One spot might be crucial, buried in the others. I would need to see crime scene notes, photographs, whatever your police know."

"*I* don't even know what the police know." Arcadia stood away from the map. "The evac team isn't officially involved."

"Then why are you unofficially involved?" Lilac asked.

"I found the South Chambers site. Thale will put money toward this, for the good press, but he won't really try." Arcadia looked away. "We could do more for Valentine than pretend to care."

Lilac hadn't meant for any of this to land on Arcadia's shoulders. She reached for Arcadia's face. "No wonder you quit. You're too good for that man." She pulled Arcadia down into a gentle kiss and then slipped back. "You can relax now, yes?"

Steel nerves eased from Arcadia's frame. "Yes."

"Get undressed then." Lilac hurried off to run a warm and frothy bath.

When she came back, she found Arcadia lying naked across the broad bed, its cotton sheets wrinkled. Her momentum had stalled, no more work to do, and lethargy had wriggled in. Her eyes glazed over, disinterested in the world.

She'd ended up like this before. Lilac would be cooking a chicken-and-leek stew, or getting the bed made, and she'd find Arcadia frozen at a window or stuck at the bathroom mirror in a staring contest with her reflection. Whatever future Lilac glimpsed in those eyes, their gaze now and then wandered from firm ground and twisted toward dark piers and darker seas.

Sometimes Arcadia got lost.

And sometimes Lilac blamed herself for letting the hotel room go still and quiet. Logoi's temple had been a place of peace and reverence, but she was only one of Lilac's mothers. These days, Lilac shared an apartment with her other—mortal—mother, Simone, who filled their home with endless chatter. The stillness that crept casually into Arcadia's room sometimes reminded Lilac of the temple's solemnity. She didn't mind basking in it.

There was no peace in the quiet tonight. Lilac had put worse shadows into Arcadia than the shock of finding murdered men. Today had stirred a deep and mysterious memory, echoes of a past Arcadia kept to herself. They weren't the kinds of lovers who dragged bad memories into the present. Lilac doubted this evening was the time to change that.

"Up, now." Lilac could only make a suggestion. She had only so much muscle, while ox bones stacked Arcadia's frame. She didn't budge.

"Will you stay?" Arcadia asked, her voice faint.

Lilac had plans, but glancing at the open map across the room and then back to Arcadia, those plans might need a few hours' delay. This situation was Lilac's fault. She would have to make it work.

"I'll stay," she said.

She shut off the lamp and crawled onto the bed. Arcadia was a creature of stone and iron, but Lilac knew how to find that elusive softness. She lay behind Arcadia and stroked her scalp, fingertips brushing short hair, until Arcadia's muscles melted loose.

"It was a bad day?" Lilac asked.

Arcadia's voice came lifeless. "It was."

"And it ended. Don't think about it, don't dream about it. Everything will be fine." Lilac said it like she was sure, and hopefully she was right. She hated lying to Arcadia.

CHAPTER 6

A gray cab waited outside a small house in Bay Ridge, the only hill within Valentine's city limits, as Alex and Cecil approached the front door. During the day, Alex might have looked west and watched the waves, but daylight had left and he could only tell the distant sea began by where the stars disappeared from the dark sky. His feet hurt, his eyes stung, near the end of a long evening and yet not the end.

"Might as well check this one yourself," Cecil said, clapping hands down his trench coat. He seemed ready to throw the evening away. "Lot of good I've done. Not sure my skillset's matched for getting fresh with broiled corpses."

"This house will suit you better," Alex said. "It's the only scene where no one knocked over the candle, wasn't set close enough to the door. Everything's raw."

"Will it smell any better?"

"Better? No. *Different* is the word I'd use." Alex pressed open the front door and aimed his flashlight.

The odor hit first, and he and Cecil coughed in unison. The house was more a box with high aspirations, its single room crammed with barrels and crates, their wood warped by seawater and crusted by barnacles. Ragged fishing nets dangled from the ceiling.

"Old shipping house," Alex said. From back when ships still

came and went between Aeg and other continents.

Cecil ran a hand over the nearest crates. "Spices, once upon a time. Fish, but that might be from the sea, not the cargo."

Alex's flashlight beam struggled where crate shadows met dark gore. Congealed blood painted a footprint pattern across floorboards, and red-brown streaks marked the far wall, their shape as familiar to Alex as his parents' faces—Logoi's narrow-limbed star. Beneath it, one body lay bound against the wall. Another lay tangled in a fishing net.

"Poor blighters have been dead a bit." Cecil approached the tied-up body. "Might even be where our killer started."

That would explain the candle-to-door error. First blood could be a treasure trove of mistakes.

The ceiling sagged near the shack's center, as if it might bite down on the crime scene and swallow it from the world. Oil's stink breathed from the walls, mixed with scents of copper and rot. The murderers had meant to burn this place like the others, but they'd failed.

"If you're covering your tracks, it makes more sense to set the fire on your way out the door," Alex said. "Why leave the bodies to burn only when the candle runs down or gets knocked over?"

"Set a fire, someone'll check it," Cecil said. His hand hovered over the body bound in a fishing net. "By the time Arcadia found the South Chambers Street murders, our killer had already finished the rest."

"Smart. Got a means of death?"

Cecil nodded to the netted corpse. "Slashed throat. Didn't need me to tell you that. Actually—" He opened his hand.

Watching him work felt vaguely voyeuristic, like Alex might be spying on a private holy rite and not a quirk Cecil flaunted every chance he got.

"Our killer stabbed their hearts. Gutted them, too. We got organ piles here, like Arcadia's site." Cecil's hand drooped to his side as he strafed the pool of blood. "Strange feelings I'm getting. Fear, but also love."

Alex gazed at the organ mounds. He saw no love here. "Think the killers knew these two?"

"Not personal love." Cecil aimed his palm at the air, the ceiling, everywhere. "Lingering, unfocused is all. And then check the floor marks."

Alex saw no distinct patterns except the footprint-marked blood. No godly signs besides Logoi's star.

"Here, bloody half-footprints," Cecil said, pointing down. "And above, finger smudges. The positions, they're all crossed strange. I'll try to show you."

Cecil was younger and spryer than Alex, but he was no dancer. Still, buttoned up in his trench coat, he made his best effort to cross his ankles, stand on the toes of his ragged boots, cross his wrists overhead, and steeple his fingers.

No, it couldn't be.

Cecil settled onto his heels and dropped his arms. "Not quite it, but you get the picture, eh?"

Alex did get the picture. He found his mouth hanging open and shut it.

"What?" Cecil asked. "Is this a lewd posture to you?"

"Entirely the opposite," Alex said, astonished. "A sacred stance I've seen a thousand times."

"Really? I never have."

"You wouldn't. Not in West Amberdan, and certainly not here in Valentine."

From the far wall, Logoi's vicious nine-pointed star glared into Alex. He'd left Logos long before Thale dragged his entourage to Valentine, and though Logoi had abandoned continent, city-state, and people first, Alex felt judged, as if he'd betrayed the goddess of reason. He'd seen the stance when inducted into the Logos police in the temple at age seventeen, performed by a dozen priestesses in solemn veneration to Logoi, there and all over Logos.

"No one's trying to frame the Logos police as the murderers," Alex said. "This has nothing to do with Valentine. It's a sacrifice to Logoi."

Cecil turned to Alex, incredulous. "Someone's trying to summon her?"

"It explains the candle." Alex gestured at the door. "The murderers want their offerings left out as long as possible, the evidence only ruined at the last moment."

"Why ruin it at all?" Cecil asked. "Wouldn't make sense unless they knew me, knew I might pick up on something."

"The way you just did?" Alex asked. "You're not exactly private about your gift."

"Doesn't fit your theory." Cecil strafed the blood puddle again, careful it didn't touch his boots. "Keeping me in mind is smart, but summoning Logoi this way wouldn't work. A sacrifice has to be willing, else the gods get nothing for it. No miracle juice. This murderer's too smart not to know that."

Alex rubbed his jaw, a nervous tic he'd picked up in the barracks as a kid and never lost. "I can't be sure. Logoi had loopholes, logical shortcuts, stating anyone in her city was subject to her laws, and to break her laws was to surrender your life to her."

"Nonsense," Cecil snapped. "She could tell herself that all she liked, but a god knows when they're getting juiced up by a sacrifice, I don't give a damn how many poor people she had you lot hang from the Racks. If they didn't intend to die for her, it's nothing doing."

Even if Cecil was right, the murderers believed they could summon Logoi. A few cutthroats in Valentine were outliers, but in the Tychos city-state to the east, this kind of radical human sacrifice was the norm. Maybe the same belief had spread to Korenbalas and its steel mill and quarries, and to Diomarch and its vineyards, and every inch of Aeg between. Valentine might be the last peaceful city-state in the Holy Land.

"This might be happening in Logos, too," Alex said. "Someone should get their HQ on the horn, or take a drive south and back before the rains." The room's smell festered in him, and he doubted it would leave before morning. "Surprised it took so many years for anyone to get this desperate. The gods chose to leave for their own reasons, meaning these murderers have as much chance of calling one to Aeg as a god has of calling a Dawn God."

A nervous laugh shook through Cecil. "Alex, my dear, brilliant, clearly exhausted colleague, it's past midnight. Let's take a breather. Drink, sleep, puzzle the pieces tomorrow."

"Fair enough." Alex hardly had to think about it. He doubted the murderers would slaughter anyone else before morning. Today had to have been long for them, too.

He and Cecil shared a cab to a bar, ate dinner, and went their separate ways. Cecil headed off to his apartment, Alex to the Ace Investigations office. He didn't mean to fall asleep at his desk, but he did it four times a week lately, and it always left a crick in his neck.

Just as well. Had he gone home, he would have missed the phone's raw jangle—one of its bells was missing. He hefted his head toward the staff's mouthpiece, and one clumsy hand tugged the earpiece close.

"Ace Investigations, Detective Alexander Stathos speaking." He listened. "One more time? I'm a little groggy." He listened again. "I'll be there. Thanks."

He'd been wrong about the murderers' exhaustion last night. Three more crime scenes.

More sacrifices.

CHAPTER 7

That damn phone. A perk and a curse of the hotel's better accommodations. Its ringing shook Lilac awake, and she slapped an awkward hand at the nightstand to stop it. Last round, get your calls in before the rains come. Never could tell when the lines might blow away in wind and hail, or if the year had finally come when the sea would sweep in and break the Holy Land into an archipelago for the first time in five thousand years.

Rhoster Thale cursed through the earpiece. Lilac let his bluster slip over her skin, unabsorbed and barely heard, eyes closed as she let the patterns fit together. She'd been out late, more work to be done, slept late, and though she had the day off, Arcadia did not.

When Thale finished shouting, Lilac told him Captain Myrn would be on her way, and he hung up. He talked to everyone on the hotel staff with the respect he'd give an ant, and she thanked the gods he slept elsewhere. Then again, if the gods hadn't left, they would all be back in Logos and she would only have to see and hear him if he stepped into Logoi's temple. None of that had mattered in ten years.

Lilac slammed the earpiece back on the phone staff and slapped Arcadia's arm. "Wake up, doll. Daylight's burning."

Only somewhat true—day was here, but a gray haze had overtaken the sky. Lilac supposed she should be grateful to Thale for waking her. There was no rain in her dreams. Only fire.

48

"Burning," Lilac said again. "I dreamed of a burning tree."

Corded muscle stirred beside her. "A past life?" Arcadia asked, yawning.

"Maybe." Sometimes people dreamed of stains on their souls. Lilac couldn't imagine why she'd dream of a tree on fire. A symbol for a dying family? A rodent fleeing a forest fire? Was she Noema the Sick in a past life, she who'd burned the last gift of the Dawn Gods, the Holy Psychopomp Tree? Likely it didn't matter. Better to focus on the work ahead. New stains for her old soul.

"Arcadia, shower," Lilac said. "Now."

"Yes, right away." Arcadia stretched catlike along the bed and then hopped off toward the bathroom. A quick wake-up was one of many habits she couldn't shake from her police days.

The pipes thumped to life, and Lilac hurried to sort out the rest of Arcadia's morning. A phone call, a flood fighter uniform readied, the kinds of small details someone might see as inconsequential, but they would make Arcadia's day easier, and so every piece mattered.

Lilac found Arcadia at the bathroom mirror post-shower. No staring contest this time, only trimming her bristly hair with a pair of silvery shears.

"Keep doing what you're doing." Lilac planted a mug of coffee beside the sink basin. "I've handled everything else."

"Everything else?" Arcadia asked. Her eyes didn't leave the mirror. "Why?"

"You're late. Sip your coffee while I get you dressed." Lilac worked clothing over Arcadia's limbs while she sipped and snipped. "Thale wants some report filed and then for you to hit Oldtown. Cab's coming, it'll have your breakfast from Gold's Bakery down the block. There's an extra sweetened roll in case Thale needs sweetening. The driver has directions, so hop in and go. You'll hit HQ before he knows it."

Arcadia set her coffee down, stared into Lilac's face, and then looked herself over. She was entirely dressed except for her boots.

Lilac admired her work too. "I clean you up nice, huh? Even got the belt latched right." She gave a playful tug. "Today will be better, I promise."

Arcadia stretched to full height. "I couldn't do this morning without you. Thank you."

"Thank *you* for keeping the city safe." Lilac kissed Arcadia's cheek.

Arcadia pivoted to kiss Lilac's lips. "Don't clean my room while I'm gone. You clean up after every slob here. The least I can do is look after myself."

"You do know I don't clean every room in the hotel, right?" Lilac asked.

Arcadia held her face. "I want to do something for you."

"Dinner is nice." Lilac bounced an encouraging eyebrow. "My place."

"That's you doing something for me."

"It really isn't." Lilac patted Arcadia's cheek. "The rains will be here soon. Keep those glories out, Captain. We'll never be prey again, right?"

Arcadia tugged her sidearm to be sure it was latched to the belt, grabbed the map she'd brought in yesterday, and then headed out the door.

Lilac lingered in the doorway. Had she arranged last night's sacrifices right to keep them out of the evac team's path? The pieces lined up in her head. Next came the rest. She was off from hotel work today, but more work awaited, and no one else would make the hard choice to do it.

She was nearly finished.

CHAPTER 8

A distant commotion grew to a two-man shouting match as Arcadia strode down the sky-blue police headquarters hall toward Thale's closed office door. She recognized both voices.

"Why not?" Alex shouted.

"Because it's bullshit!" Thale snapped. "Your empty-headed partner guesses at murder masquerading as sacrifice, and you believe it, no proof, no sense. Tychos might be up to the neck in mounds of corpses and skulls, but not here. Not Valentine."

"Until now," Alex said.

"Prove it." The door quaked. Thale must've slammed a fist on his desk, and Arcadia slipped back in case either man stormed out the door. "I brought the police, flood fighters, and admins, but Logoi's covenant stayed behind."

"We've all stayed behind." A chair scraped—Alex getting up? "The gods left, but we're still here. Will you at least put out a word to Logos command? One phone call before the rain ruins the long distance."

Thale groaned. "Don't expect anything."

"Fair enough."

The door creaked open, and Arcadia had no way to dodge down the hall without looking obvious. Alex emerged wearing the same black trench coat as yesterday, still unbuttoned, his fedora in one hand.

He eyed Arcadia, shut the door behind him, and leaned against the wall. "Fun working here?"

"I don't work here," Arcadia said. "I came to file evac reports before hitting Oldtown."

"Is it really quitting the police if you still have to see Thale?" Alex asked.

The question made Arcadia's skin feel soiled. "I could ask you the same. You've been brusquer with him before."

Alex eyed Thale's door and then started toward the lobby. "One of the benefits of quitting was I could badmouth Thale all I pleased. Now he's a client and I'm tongue-tied. Story of my life, right?"

Arcadia held in a laugh.

No amount of smashing down residential walls could hide the lobby's origins as a couple of apartments fused into a reception area. Bars blocked doors in the under-street level, but anyone could see they were once bedrooms. The Logos police could scavenge this building's flesh, but its bones showed through.

"A summoning," Alex muttered, as if finishing some conversation with himself. "You think countries overseas wonder why our gods showed up, same as we wonder why they left?"

"Maybe." Arcadia hadn't thought about it. Aeg had so many problems, there was no room for other countries' feelings on godly exile. "They don't have to make pilgrimages to the Holy Land to see the Dawn Gods' children anymore. I'm sure they're pleased."

"Can't imagine anyone's happy wherever Tychron resettled. Or Logoi, for that matter." Alex fitted on his fedora. "But what do they care, right? No one survives the crossing anymore without a god. In the other countries, everybody's likely forgotten us."

Same as the gods, Arcadia kept to herself.

Alex gave Arcadia's arm a reassuring pat. "You'd better file your reports before Thale's head bursts. He's already in a tiff over last night's murders."

The morning's brightness faded. "More?" Arcadia asked.

"Three sites before dawn. You want addresses?" Alex pulled his notebook from his coat and tore out a page. "I had a feeling you'd want them."

Arcadia took the paper, but she wasn't sure where they fit on her map. Besides, an X couldn't have more than four points, five if you counted where the lines crossed. Seven sites defied Lilac's pattern.

"I can give you victims' names, but Thale won't let me see their police files." Exhaustion haunted Alex's face as he pocketed his notebook. "He couldn't care less, anyway. This is all for show, to say he tried, keep *The Valentine Herald* and local radio off his back, not that it helps. *Herald* especially, seeing they've already coined a moniker: the Valentine Butcher. Like there's only one killer and not two or three." He leaned close, his fedora's brim hiding his eyes, and lowered his voice. "They're offering sacrifices to Logoi, trying lure her home under her old *whoever breaks the law and so on* loophole. But they're murders, not real sacrifices."

"To break the law in her city is to surrender your life to her." Arcadia hadn't meant to recite those words, but she'd heard them hundreds of times, usually when someone was about to wear a rope necklace. A bad taste filled her mouth as she tucked the notebook page into a belt pouch.

"This isn't her city, and she's not here," Alex said, and then he leaned back. "I'm meeting Cecil to investigate, for all the good it'll do. Dinner tonight, yes?"

"Tonight, Lexi." Arcadia remembered that she'd made plans with Lilac, too. Would it be better to cancel with Alex, or invite him and Cecil to Lilac's apartment? She needed a moment to decide, but without another word, without thinking, she pulled Alex close and hugged him.

Alex chuckled into her shoulder. "What was that for?"

"Because—" Arcadia started, but she didn't know how to finish. Because she needed it. Because they were old friends. Because some violent nerve told her this might be the last time.

CHAPTER 9

Despondent clouds lingered from morning, unwilling to let the narrowest ray of sunshine into Valentine. The gloomy weather made knocking on Oldtown doors all the more important. Rain any day now, the radio said. Any minute, really.

As if Arcadia's team could meet such a vague deadline. She doubted a week would be enough to clear out Oldtown, door by door, with a handful of agents.

All for show, Alex had said, suggesting Thale believed in appearances over substance. After the show, then what? While Oldtown residents holed up in their flooding homes, was Arcadia's team supposed to reinforce the western barricade, run sandbags, gun down glories in the name of humanity?

Doubtful. Doomed.

Arcadia let Ilene and the others hit the next house while she waited at the truck, her city map spread across the hood. Logos had been a plan before anyone cut its first marble slab, carefully lain in ordered squares, but Valentine was more a hodgepodge of villages that shared streets and a temple than a proper city. To apply Logoi's logic here had to be a daunting task for the murderer.

Arcadia stared at Lilac's pencil-drawn X and tried to un-see its imposed order. Only the even spacing between the dots kept their pattern from breaking into chaos. The same points could form nearly half of a nine-pointed star. Arcadia looked from Alex's notebook paper to the map and made best guesses at streets and corners. Last night's scenes followed the western edge of the city, again through Bay Ridge and Oldtown. Arcadia marked them with a broken half-pencil. If what she suspected was right, the last two murder sites needed to appear on the northeastern corner and the eastern edge of Oldtown, along the borders to the North and Central Temple Districts.

Ilene appeared from the house beyond the truck, holding the arm of a gray-haired woman with a stooped spine. "One step at a time, ma'am," Ilene said. Bryce waited in the doorway behind them.

"Don't see what all the fuss is," the woman said. Her left leg was made of wood below the knee.

Arcadia folded the map along what would be the star's center and poked her pencil through paper, making two holes. She connected the dots again, ignoring the X, and the nine-pointed star formed beneath her pencil as if the map had come drawn that way.

Alex was right. Someone wanted Logoi, and badly. They might as well have rigged a neon sign to scream *Come home, Goddess*, but blood would do better. The map now showed two potential crime scenes and likely more than one murder apiece.

Or they might be nothing.

Investigation and evacuation alike were all for show, for Thale to say he tried. He talked a lot these days. *At your best, Myrn, you excel, but at your worst, there is no one worse.*

What if Arcadia could actually get something done?

"Overreacting baby-snatchers." The elderly woman neared the truck, her face pinched in a scowl. "I'd get on just as well at home."

"We're here to help," Ilene said. She'd almost led the woman to the truck's bed.

"Help?" the woman chirped. "Help me two years ago when them fishy scum took my leg. They don't scare me no more, no, miss. I'll swim in the sea, and I'll do it naked. Give them something to choke on." The sky rumbled as if roused, and she glanced up. "You can choke, too, you worthless storm."

Was Arcadia the reason the evacuation was going so slow? Too much time and effort spent selling the effort rather than making it happen? Maybe Thale was right—barely a captain, borderline useless. People would die because she was too soft.

She had pledged herself to Logoi's service for induction into the Logos police at age seventeen, and then weeks after, with the temple empty except for goddess and priestesses, Arcadia had sworn her soul to Logoi's will for a miracle of transformation. Both instantaneous and everlasting, painful and painless in a way Arcadia couldn't describe, it had been a strange hum that made her tremble from head to toe until she was changed exactly as she'd asked. A body less like her late father, more like her late mother, inside and out, the way Arcadia had always dreamed.

Arcadia, Logoi had said then. *You swore. Do not forget.*

And Arcadia hadn't. Over two decades later, half-in and half-out of the police, she was thankful to the goddess for a miracle of wholeness. Her old shape was a frail memory, but her gratitude held as strong as Logoi's miracle itself. Even having quit the police ten years now, there was no forgetting the goddess, her generous power, or the allegiance owed and all it entailed.

Maybe Thale had understood that much.

Arcadia waved to Ilene. "Do you have this?"

Ilene flashed a worried glance between the elderly evacuee and Arcadia. "Do I *what*?"

"I need to run a quick errand," Arcadia said. "Can you handle the team until I get back?"

Ilene rubbed her shorn hair, a habit she might have picked up from Arcadia, and then stood straight. "Absolutely, Captain. Anything for you."

"An hour or less, promise." Arcadia started from the truck. "Hopefully it's nothing."

"Take Athas with you," Ilene said. "Or Cassis."

Arcadia eyed Ilene. She couldn't know what Arcadia meant to do, but why else suggest taking an agent along?

"Keep everyone with you," Arcadia said. "Keep momentum." *Do a better job than your captain has,* she wanted to say.

Ilene asked no more questions. "Yes, Captain." She turned to the others. "Next house, come on. You heard the sky. It's getting as impatient as I am."

Arcadia stuffed Alex's note into a belt pouch and carried the map open in front of her. The possible northeastern Oldtown site touched the North Temple District, built stronger than Oldtown, ruined State House aside. This put the scene nearer to the police headquarters, risky both for murderer and Arcadia alike.

The eastern site was closer, between a local music lounge and an abandoned diner, not far from the temple plaza. A likely place for sacrifice. If Arcadia arrived first, and people were still alive, she could warn them, and sure it might be nothing, but—

A raindrop tapped the map where the North Road led from the city's edges toward the Grave of the Holy Tree, and beyond that, Shadow Mountain and its hills. Another drop struck the eastern river, Valentine's border with the Tychos city-state.

The rains were here. Soon storms would rage across Aeg and bring with them rising rivers and swelling tides. The glories would surge over the western beach, levees, and floodplains, up to the stone barricade, Oldtown's last stand against the sea.

It should never have come to this. People needed the gods. Thousands of years of divine protection, and then all of a sudden, nothing. No warning, no explanation, only the trickle of emptying temples as the gods abandoned Aeg. The Holy Land seemed no longer holy, and as in the beginning, men were prey. What exactly had Logoi and the others thought would happen? The glories had been slow coming, maybe uncertain the gods weren't trying to trick them, but after ten years of incursions along the coasts, they were ready.

Small wonder a desperate soul had turned to human sacrifice. Surprising it hadn't happened sooner.

It wouldn't work. If Logoi wanted to come home, she'd do it. Any god who returned to Aeg now could have anything they wanted. The only god, goddess, or godex in the Holy Land would be loved from coast to coast.

So why leave?

Arcadia glanced from her map to the hollow homes to either side of the street. They looked no less weary than if they were full of people. She walked another twenty minutes until she came half a block from a corner house, the intersection of Lelys Street and Copper Avenue where a dot showed on her map. New raindrops streaked its paper.

The house was white stone, a wooden door, slender windows, only one floor. There might be someone inside. Alive? Dead? If Arcadia pressed the door open without knowing, a candle might knock over and the scene would echo Shah like yesterday.

But she might save someone's life.

An hour or less, Arcadia had promised, and she couldn't keep that promise if she spent the day pacing the sidewalk, her mind spinning in circles. The house's wooden door faced the derelict corner, visible from both streets, waiting for her. She only had to knock.

But why? This wasn't her business, not her occupation anymore, not even her city.

That was the problem. Valentine wasn't Logos. You weren't supposed to murder people in Valentine. Even Thale knew that, and he'd stained his hands with more blood for Logoi than anyone. The goddess of reason had abandoned her city of Logos, and now her people had abandoned it, too. Valentine was home, and why should some pious murderer get to stain it this way? These people mattered.

Captaining the flood fighters meant helping Valentine's citizens. Arcadia wouldn't watch this city shrivel into another blood-soaked Logos if she could help it. To interrupt one murder and save one life would be a start.

She folded her map, approached the door, and knocked.

Chapter 10

"To break the law in Logos was to surrender your life to Logoi," Lilac said. "Every execution was a willing sacrifice. There was an old parapet, remains of a castle from the Holy War, called the Racks. A bloodless death, hanged by rope, so not a drop of blood would be wasted. All for Logoi."

Lilac doubted Darien Chontos was listening. She'd knocked him down, bound him with rope, and he hadn't moved or spoken since. Barely alive in this narrow living room, most of its furniture gone, the rest toppled, the stone house abandoned. He was making it easy, and she wished she'd started with him when her task began yesterday.

Or maybe today felt easy because she'd killed so many people in the last thirty-plus hours. Her stained soul might have grown numb.

"Every person's life is precious." Lilac hunched beside the net and drew her teardrop-bladed dagger. "Do you understand? It's why the Dawn Gods came to us from the heavens, why they told the gods to look after us when the heavens called them back. Every life, every thought and feeling, every memory and intent. Sacrifice has no power unless something of value is lost. Something precious."

Darien remained unmoving. His fallen spectacles lay beside

his head, one lens cracked. No matter; he wouldn't need them anymore. Was Lilac helping him understand, or taunting him? She couldn't tell, had no precedent. Those executed in Logos came to the temple already dead.

Once Logoi had absorbed their blood, she'd made miracles. Human lifeforce let gods do the impossible. Healing bodies, changing them, revitalizing land, fighting back the sea—Aeg needed such miracles. Now.

But cruelty was pointless. Time to finish. "You are precious," Lilac went on. "Your life means something. Your death will bring a goddess to the Holy Land. In return, when your soul slips into the Between, this sacrifice will wipe your soul clean. Reincarnate purely, and be better for it."

She stabbed through Darien's pinstriped jacket and into his heart. Blood burbled across his shirt and onto the wood floor, and Lilac got to work.

Logoi had loved the concept of a day. Each was a raindrop in time, but within, everything could change. Lilac had seen it. One day, Logoi was there, and the world made sense. The next, Logoi was gone. Yesterday morning, Lilac had never sacrificed anyone. Today?

Today, the Holy Land was falling apart. Tomorrow, Logoi could return. What a change one day would make. If Lilac performed her ritual. If the star across Valentine lay complete. If Logoi noticed.

Lilac was about to soak her fingers in Darien's blood and give this star its final point when a fist knocked at the door.

At times, her descendant's gift overwhelmed her. Every object, person, and place held a legion of individual possibilities, their combinations infinite. She could easily become paralyzed with indecision, almost like having no gift from her mother goddess at all.

Worse, she could panic. Her fingers stroked the blood, desperate to draw a quick nine-pointed star, but her hands shook and her breath hitched.

Another knock. If the police had found her, they wouldn't be patient.

She'd been sloppy, blood soaking not only her skin, but the sleeves of her robe, purchased only three weeks ago when she'd thought up this plan. Her skin would drink, but the cloth was stained. Passersby would notice.

At every prior sacrifice, she'd left the scene to linger, the blood waiting to be drunk in by a goddess, and only set the oil and candle to burn upon discovery, no sooner. She wouldn't have let them burn at all, but a certain friend had a certain gift from his godly grandfather, rendered useless by flames.

Had the cleansing fire ruined her ritual? She couldn't be sure, but she couldn't risk Cecil Gillion figuring her out. She was no genius, no priestess, only the scared daughter of a goddess and a mortal woman.

"Mother Logoi, please," Lilac whispered as she dumped oil and threw down a match. "I miss you. Mom's here, too, and we need you."

Smoke billowed through the room. Lilac launched toward the back window and slipped over the sill, onto an alley's sole-scraping pavement. When she turned to close the window and trap the smoke inside, she noticed a red stain on the outer wall's white stone.

A little souvenir from Darien Chontos.

Lilac rubbed at it, but the effort only smudged the stain. There wasn't time to clean. She turned down the alley and ran as fast as she could.

CHAPTER II

Arcadia smelled the smoke before she spotted it, and the scent knocked her off-balance. Smoke mixed with flesh. In a funeral pyre, olive branches, sweet oils, honey, and wax hid the scent of a burning corpse.

This was raw. Arcadia's gut lurched as she doubled over and let her map drift to the sidewalk. Her crude geometry had checked out, guided by Lilac's even spacing, but kicking down this door to prove it would echo yesterday's uselessness and prove Thale right. This *Valentine Butcher* would get away, and the evac team wasn't here to clean up Arcadia's mess. The memory flashes came so strong sometimes, this past decade seemed an illusion, the world having clearly ended at Shah.

Her hand covered her mouth and nose. *Focus now. Focus on anything.*

The murderer wouldn't linger inside a burning house, but they had to have set the fire. Arcadia had disturbed them—they hadn't waited for someone else to knock over a candle like at the other sites.

Meaning they couldn't have gone far.

Smoke climbed from behind the house and sent Arcadia dashing along Lelys Street and into a network of alleys. A red smear marred the stone beneath one half-open window. Raindrops streaked across it, but the storm had come too late to wash away the clue.

Arcadia followed another alleyway. No more bloodstains. A careful murderer, smart and patient and ruthless, but also imperfect, like all people.

The alley opened onto another street, and across the lanes someone in dark robes stepped into yet another alley. Covenant clothing, the kind of getup Arcadia expected a zealot might wear while making sacrifices to the gods.

Arcadia plowed into the street ahead of a screeching buggy, and didn't stop to look if any more cars were coming. There wasn't time now that her knock at the door had blown the element of surprise.

Pursuit had always been a risk. That was why Lilac had an escape plan, with a safe goal at the end, and she was following it.

But she had never expected her pursuer to be *Arcadia*.

Captain Arcadia Myrn would be hard to evade. Worse, if she'd already seen Lilac's face, running would be meaningless. She already knew where Lilac lived. The past was a secret—Lilac's godly second mother with it—but home was the present and Lilac hadn't seen a reason to keep it hidden.

The alley ended in a forking road and a trading post of stone walls, covered awnings, and produce-stuffed market stalls. Lilac darted left, rubbed her bloody sleeve on a white corner wall, and then dashed right, around the trading post, between it and another building. The ruse might not throw Arcadia off for long, but every moment counted. That would have to be good enough until—

Stabbing, merciless pain.

Lilac bit her lip not to scream as she hobbled against a flaking wall. Some careless littering piece of shit had smashed a beer bottle, and now a green glass shard jutted from Lilac's right sole, jagged and painful.

She pinched the pointed end and tugged. Skin stretched, clinging to the glass, a hard curve with mean teeth. Blood spit behind it. Lilac was going to leave a trail, and there was nothing she could do about it. Gods help the drunk who'd shattered that bottle if she ever found them.

How to get away? How to stop this? She closed her eyes. Ignoring the world's shapes and colors sometimes made thinking easier, but pain pierced the blackness, and thoughts drowned in glass-dotted blood.

Arcadia had to be close.

Lilac leaned onto her left foot and stepped gingerly on her right toes. Slow progress was still progress. If only she could've bathed in Darien's blood, she might have eased the tension from waiting for him, recovered her strength from striking him, and forgotten the stress of cutting him open. Being the goddess of reason's daughter, her perfect jewel, could only get Lilac so far. Logoi's daughter, yes, but Simone's daughter, too, and Lilac was only a descendant, not a goddess. Mortal was mortal.

Enough. Lilac couldn't outrun Arcadia, whose boots would protect her feet from broken glass. No more worming and weaving through alleys; Lilac turned at the next corner and hobbled for the city's center.

The alley was dark and full of trash. If the Valentine Butcher meant to ambush Arcadia, there were plenty of places to hide.

No one came slashing. Arcadia made one turn, a second, and spotted another red smear on the wall to one side of a trading post. People in slacks and dresses carried their baskets and bags beneath a wooden awning, protected for now from the gentle rain. How long it would stay gentle, no one could say.

Arcadia approached the smeared wall. Victim's blood, or murderer's? No way to tell, but Arcadia doubted anyone else had left so fresh a stain. She started down the street.

A muffled shriek froze her in place. Another woman, Arcadia was certain. It came from behind, back around a corner from the trading post.

She followed, and found bloody droplets, broken glass, and a trail of red smudges on the pavement. The murderer had been injured for certain—a taste of her own medicine. Arcadia stomped past the broken glass and followed the trail until it swept and curved, as if the murderer had begun hobbling in a circle. Another distraction? This killer in priestess clothing might've cut herself to throw Arcadia off. She'd been heading northward until she realized someone was following, and now she'd started due east.

Of course. Where else would a priestess go, murderer or not, but the largest and most famous building in the city? Dead center, from which every neighborhood spread, a place with doorways facing every direction and letting out to all sides of Valentine. If the murderer made it, she could escape to anywhere in the city, and Arcadia would have no idea which way to follow.

Unless Arcadia got there first. She quit chasing the red-smudge circles and headed east.

At the center of the city, core of the Central Temple District, the grand temple loomed over every rooftop. An open cobblestone plaza stretched around its edges, where long marble steps greeted every visitor and climbed up and between gargantuan white columns. A pearly dome capped the temple, sheltering covenant and visiting faithful across the vast marble floor.

When Valmydion, Goddess of Prosperity, still lived in her city of Valentine, residents from the fishers of Bay Ridge to the pin-stripe-suited elite of the State House had knelt at the altars here. A hundred loyal clergy once attended Valmydion's edicts, led her people in worship, and cut themselves for their goddess.

These days, the temple stood godless and empty. Occasional passersby might seek shelter from bad weather or offer a pointless prayer, but there were no more miracles here.

No one haunted the steps as Arcadia climbed. She paused to catch her breath at the top, where raindrops patterned her uniform, and she hoped the moisture hadn't damaged her revolver or two-way radio.

The murderer didn't have to come inside to break for another Valentine neighborhood, but Arcadia thought she would. A pious priestess would crave every scrap of divinity, even in the temple of another goddess. Arcadia had to hope. She ducked beneath a thirty-foot marble archway and into the temple.

Ancient murals colored the domed roof's underside with depictions of Valmydion's deeds. In one image, the painting of her plump likeness bargained for peace during the Holy War while her cousins quarreled, their miracles tearing reality asunder. Behind the gods, the glories saw their chance to take back Aeg from their former prey. In another mural, beautiful Valmydion helped her people hold back the sea when the glories came again, thinking they had their chance when six of the Dawn Gods had returned to the heavens and the seventh had transformed forever.

Always the glories, eating at the edges of human history since before time. When the rainy season came, the sea followed, year after year, forever. Only the Dawn Gods and their divine children had kept back the tide. Empty temples left only stone barricades, sandbags, and firearms to resist oceanic terror. How long until human efforts failed?

How long before the Holy Land again broke into an archipelago upon the unholy sea?

Marble seating filled the temple's ground floor. Flat altars climbed here and there where members of Valmydion's covenant once bled to feed her miracles, and the altars grew more numerous and clustered toward the center, where they encircled her pillared seat.

No one but Arcadia stood in the temple. No sounds but the slow patter of rain across the roof.

Twin staircases ascended inner walls, leading to a ring of suspended seating above the altars. Arcadia could get a better view from there. She started climbing, step after step.

Logoi's temple was less extravagant, but then Logoi the Many-Headed was a different kind of goddess. Without her, the agencies of Logos continued to function. She had built them to last. Without Valmydion's presence, Valentine crumbled—even her temple, Arcadia realized as a chunk of staircase broke off underfoot and plummeted to the far floor. A misstep would send her falling after it, and not even the Holy Land's best surgeons could save her broken body then.

Four walkways stretched from the upper ring of seating, where the faithful could sit if the temple floor crowded over. Arcadia crossed one walkway toward these seats and peered over the walkway's side to watch the ground floor. No sign of life.

Perfect. Arcadia couldn't have asked for better.

She wiped one arm across her brow and her hands on her uniform's pants. In all the running around, she hadn't noticed she was sweating so hard. Best to take this one moment at a time. She drew her revolver, hefted it, and slid one slick finger over the trigger guard.

This was a temple of prosperity, which meant good things for those who came here, and yet being abandoned, those who came here might no longer prosper. Arcadia couldn't guess which way fate might fall. She popped the revolver's cylindrical chamber and gave the bullets a quick glance. She might need them. In fact, she was sure of it.

A tremor worked down her hand, and she almost dropped the gun. Its barrel should aim at the sea. It wasn't meant to shoot humans—only glories—and even then Arcadia had never faced one, never shot anyone, not even in Shah. This felt wrong.

But what else could she do? This murderer cut people apart, spilled their guts into offering mounds, and burned the corpses. The Valentine Butcher might not be inclined to surrender.

This was going to get ugly. Arcadia popped the chamber back

into the gun.

Its click echoed toward the high ceiling. So did the sticky scuffing of a foot on marble, as if someone had stopped quickly out of surprise. Someone whose foot might be damp with blood.

Arcadia held still. The murderer had snuck into the temple and crept below, and Arcadia was lucky to have not revealed herself until now. The murderer would have no idea where Arcadia hid since the echo had carried throughout the temple. She slipped along the benches and glanced down, careful to keep her footsteps gentle.

The priestess was a shifting black shadow among stone seats, cautious but limping. She still intended to use the temple to disappear. Arcadia stepped toward a walkway.

Marble sank beneath her boot, and she jumped back.

The walkway sagged like burlap and collapsed toward floor, altar, and murderer. Broken marble chunks exploded across the temple. Their fragments crushed seats like brittle glass and shook the outer columns, the temple quaking with rage at Arcadia and murderer alike. The largest walkway piece smashed Valmydion's seat, and then the center of the temple floor caved into an enormous round sinkhole.

White powder swallowed the temple's insides from floor to roof, masking the world from Arcadia's sight. She waved her free hand, but the swirling debris didn't care. Even the ceiling murals were hidden.

Dust clung to Arcadia's clothes and gun as the thunderous crash echoed. No scuffing footsteps or breath. Pieces of the floor flaked into the temple's vacuous underbelly. Water damage must have weakened the catacomb ceilings, their shelves filled with the ash-loaded urns of dead clergy. Those remains would now mix with crushed marble.

Arcadia followed the remaining upper ring of seats and edged toward an unbroken walkway. The debris cloud was dissipating and yet seemed endless. Was the murderer alive or dead below? Arcadia needed to see.

Footsteps and coughing broke the trembling din, but now the echo was on the murderer's side. She must know someone had caused the collapse. She'd be running now.

Arcadia peered at the ground floor. Her hands were so slick, she was afraid she'd drop her revolver and have to watch uselessly as the murderer sauntered victorious out of the temple.

A black shape clambered through the white dust at the new pit's edge. Crumbling chunks slithered into the hole at each step. Arcadia couldn't force the murderer to stop from up here by word alone.

No, she would have to end it now.

She aimed her gun. Sweat ran between her eyes. No stalling, no more nervous thoughts or flashes of Shah and its fire and blood, its clacking submachine guns and their miserable disc-shaped ammo drums full of death. Alex had stood there, not in his fedora and trench coat, but in the blue police uniform, his badge gleaming a firelit nine-pointed star.

Myrn, fire! Both Thale and Alex had shouted that night. Pull the trigger and spill blood. *All for Logoi.*

Why couldn't Arcadia do it? Pull, and this would be over, now, she had to do it now. Never mind she'd never done it before this unending moment.

But why? Never before, so why now?

When she was seventeen, she'd told no one in advance about her private meeting with Logoi or the raw miracle of transformation—except Alex. He'd met her outside the temple after, to hold her while she cried and laughed for joy. When she told her old squad later, they'd congratulated her, told her she was closer to the goddess than anyone, that she was loved, and they'd taken her out for drinks and music and more.

But no one held her that night when she cried for her future.

She loved herself, and her changed body, but Logoi would own Arcadia from that day on, and that unrepayable miracle would dominate her soul in each terrible act to come. Every miracle cost blood, and no god granted them lightly. Divine assistance carried a price.

But now Logoi was gone. And exactly what had Thale done that mattered? What terrible acts did Arcadia owe him that he deserved a seat in her mind?

Fire at will!

A decade-old order, but he'd practically taunted her into this moment yesterday. Called her useless, the evac team soft, said she should move on from Shah, but what did that mean? Reenlisting with the police? She probably only chased the murderer in the first place thanks to Thale's needling words in the back of her head, an infection that preyed on her nerves and thoughts.

Arcadia had been his cudgel in Logos from age seventeen until age thirty—until Shah. A decade later, forty years old, was she going to let him take her again?

Myrn, fire!

No, she wasn't. This past decade was not an illusion. She was no longer a tool for Logoi, or the badge, and this flood fighter gun had always been for glories, never for humans. Thale could be his own weapon for a change and leave Arcadia be.

Myrn, fire at will!

Her thumb ticked up the revolver's hammer. Let the bullet sleep in its chamber.

Marble cracked behind her, another weakness found in the temple's structure. She turned to see if the whole seating ring was about to give way.

This moment, too, felt unending, Arcadia trapped in mid-turn as she realized details she'd overlooked.

Deducing where the murderer would go hadn't mattered even since the beginning of her pursuit. The Valentine Butcher had never looked back when entering the temple, surviving the crashed walkway, fleeing. Like she knew something her pursuer didn't. Arcadia had tenacity, but determination or not, she was alone.

Calling it now, a team effort, Alex had said yesterday, as if trying to warn her. *Murderers.*

A figure stood from behind the seats—a man with pale skin, blond hair, and the grayest eyes. He smiled at Arcadia.

And then he shoved her, before she could finish turning to him, before she could find her footing and stop his hands. When he struck her, the revolver flew from her sweaty palms. She never saw where it went.

She only saw the man's face shrink as she plummeted to the bottom of Valmydion's temple.

PART TWO
BEFORE

Chapter 12

They wanted to see the beach.

Lilac had thought over every way a beach day might go wrong, but the twins had asked a hundred times. For a pair of three-year-olds to ask for something, again and again, and stay sweet and polite was nearly a miracle. On some level, taking Sara and Daphne seaward almost seemed logical.

In those days, no one understood the severity of the problem. The gods had left the Holy Land, even the stragglers had been gone six years. Lack of leadership bred chaos across Aeg, but the people of Valentine were patient. Some holy purpose beyond mortal comprehension had surely drawn the gods from Aeg to other continents, maybe even a heavenly need given by their Dawn God progenitors. On the scale of immortality, six years was nothing. Best to assume the goddess of prosperity had left to pick up bread and milk, be home before supper, love you all.

The Holy Land was falling apart, but on the west coast near Valentine, there was peace.

Because of this, no one yet understood the danger. Perhaps even the threat had hesitated, uncertain whether the gods might return by surprise.

Lilac took her daughters to the beach. She wanted to go before the sky turned gray for the rainy season that year, while the wind was gentle and smelled more like the sea and less like a storm.

There were dangers in the calm season, too, but if Lilac wanted to avoid all risks in life, she wouldn't have had children.

A bus crossed the floodplains to the coast, where fellow passengers gathered on a nearby hillside for some purpose of their own, away from the water, as if they knew something was amiss. Lilac even thought it at the time, but having a mind open to endless possibilities sometimes muddied her instincts.

Sara and Daphne seemed almost reluctant themselves after having dragged their mother out here, but once they crossed the hill and saw white sand for the first time, Lilac wasn't sure she'd ever get them to leave.

No photograph could do it justice. Not even the sepia-colored picture shows they played at the movie house could truly capture the ebb and flow of the sea on silent, muddy reels. You had to listen to crashing waves in person, feel the damp wind on your face, narrow your eyes to the shining white sand, bright blue sky, and turquoise water stretching far as the eye could see. The twins ran a ways along the shore, the waves splashing at their little legs.

"Stay together!" Lilac shouted.

Sara and Daphne were laughing too hard to hear her, and she had to laugh, too. They held each other's hands; that would have to be good enough. Sara paused when she looked back and noticed their footprints were disappearing in the wet sand, and then she and Daphne backtracked, as if retracing their steps enough times would leave a permanent mark on the beach. After a few tries, they gave up and charged onward. Either they grew bored, or they realized even at three there was no such thing as permanence.

Neither looked much like Lilac. None of her auburn hair or olive skin, not like their dark-haired mortal grandmother Simone, and certainly nothing of their nine-headed grandmother Logoi, but they wore their father's features better than he did. Their light hair might turn green if they played in the water too long, something Lilac hadn't foreseen. She thought of their pale skin catching a green tint too and laughed to herself.

If only Logoi could see them. Her only grandchildren.

The twins had paused to gather seashells when Lilac heard a rhythmic splashing down the beach. Far to her left, black rocks shot up from the sea and lined the shore. To the right, the beach stretched until it hit a faraway rock wall—the sound came from this direction.

Something thrashed in the water. Lilac couldn't tell what from this far, under sunshine's glare, but it sounded distressed. She treaded across the damp sand, glanced back at the girls, and then kept moving. The wind carried Sara's laughter. Lilac had almost reached the presence before she spotted it clearly in the foaming tide.

It was a dolphin. A small, dying dolphin, whose tail jittered in the waves, a red gash torn deep in its side. Most marine mammals didn't want to strand themselves, but this one had come flopping onto land to escape a predator. Not fast enough; glorious claws had slashed flesh, exposed organs, and left the imprints of snaking limbs in the dolphin's hide.

One bottomless black eye stared into Lilac. *I didn't make it,* the darkness told her.

A bloodied dolphin was one of early mankind's most dire omens. Lilac shrugged it off with the cold denial of any modern woman faced with ancient superstitions. Old tales couldn't touch her. Those were ignorant thoughts from ignorant days, when humans couldn't write their own names before the Dawn Gods taught them letters.

But after denial came fear. Glories were real, their presence possible, and Lilac's mind could turn any possibility over and over until it became unavoidable.

She spun from the dying animal. "Sara! Daphne!"

The thing about children is, you only have to take your eyes off them for a moment. Lilac had spent a solid minute with her eyes locked on the dolphin. When she turned back to the beach, her daughters were nowhere to be seen.

She glanced back at the dolphin, into its black eye. *What are you waiting for?* it asked.

Lilac charged up the beach. Her footsteps made *slop, slop* noises in the wet sand and she remembered the girls, their footprints, their insistence on them. Misshapen impressions in the sand swept by. Ahead, foot-like shapes, and then full footprints on their way to losing shape. Every crashing wave erased the trail a little more.

And then the footprints were gone.

"Sara! Daphne, answer me!" Lilac put her hands to her ears and listened.

She heard them. They were laughing up ahead, and she charged again.

"Girls, come back here!"

Laughing, giggling, and then laughing again. They weren't going to think this was funny when she got them home. She reached the black rocks, each three times her height. Too smooth to grasp where they faced the sea, but their beach sides were rippled and climbable. One slip here would break anyone's neck, mother or child.

Lilac climbed anyway. "Girls?"

She didn't see them, but the laughter went on. Where, dammit? She slid along one rock, its rough surface cutting her palms and soles, and then hopped onto the next.

No one. Nothing. Below?

Lilac glanced between the rocks into a shadowy frothing darkness. Neither daughter knew how to swim, but they kept laughing, so they couldn't be in danger. They had to be clinging to the rocks. Why weren't they scared?

"Stay where you are," Lilac said. "Mama's coming."

She meant it. The descent would've been rough, the sea merciless, but she'd have done it to help her babies. She was halfway down the rock when her gift overtook her emotions, the pieces drew together, and she realized what was really happening.

Sara and Daphne could not survive that churning mess, not without broken limbs or busted skulls, and especially when they couldn't even swim.

Lilac clambered back to the rock's peak and closed her eyes. The laughter came again, but now she listened better, absorbed each detail in the sound as if laughter were a language. Both girls laughed in unison, the same way they sometimes spoke. A giggle next—Daphne. A bigger, boisterous laugh—Sara. And then they laughed in unison, exactly as before. The same sounds, repeated beat for beat, no variance in length, volume, rhythm. No saltwater gurgling or choking cries. Only the exact same laughter, again and again.

An imitation. A trick as old as omens. Thousands of years since the dawn days, and yet humans still fell for it because they loved each other so much.

Between the rocks, unseen glories mimicked the twins' laughter. They had no idea Lilac had their game figured out, and they had no reason to stop. Her face tightened the way it always did when she squeezed out tears, but she didn't sob.

She laughed. Giddier and louder than the imitations of her daughters. The girls had stayed together, exactly as she'd instructed. She never told them, *Don't let the glories get you*, fool's talk, ancient fears, no longer sensible in a modern world where the gods protected mankind.

Except the gods were gone. Humans were still here. The glories were still here.

Passengers from the bus trip found her at dusk, atop the rocks long after the glories had given up. By the time anyone climbed up and helped her down, her laughter had decayed to a dry cackle.

She told them about the glories. They had killed a dolphin, taken her daughters, and tried to take her, too.

News trickled through Valentine, unbelieving at first, yielding in time, a city-wide awakening to a threat the rest of Aeg had already accepted. The gods weren't coming back. Valmydion had left her people to drown, same as every god of the Holy Land. Men would be prey again, as they had been in the dawn days, as if the last five thousand years had never happened.

And didn't it feel like they hadn't? As if no time had passed? After all, the gods were gone. Lilac's children were gone.

Years passed before she found a reason to laugh again. Her name was Arcadia Myrn.

PART THREE

THE NATURE
OF SACRIFICE

CHAPTER 13

Vince Barton waited with an arm on the counter of Honest Hector's Pawnshop, Merchant in Items of the Mundane and Miraculous. Pawnshop, and sometimes a fence for goods of questionable origin. Vince's blond hair, pinstriped jacket, and black slacks wore a thin layer of white dust. If anyone asked, a passing car had crashed through a mound of sand and coated him. No one asked.

"I don't know, friend," Hector called from the back. "I'll dig through some of the old crates, but I don't know."

Always the same song and dance with Hector, predictable as the seasons. If Vince brought something valuable, well, Hector just couldn't be sure it was going to be worth much. They'd haggle, Vince would get cheated somewhat, Hector would pay a little more than he wanted, and they'd be back at it again next week. If Vince wanted something, Hector couldn't be sure he had one, and he'd search for a while before returning to the front counter like he'd found the blessed skull of an ancient god's mortal lover. Vince wondered if Hector was aware of his own behavior.

A bell rang above the pawnshop door as two men in dark robes stepped inside. Vince had been looking at his pocket watch, but he eyed the newcomers long enough to be sure they weren't here to stick up Hector.

No, only a pair of priests in their dirty robes. More accurately ex-priests, but really they never stopped being what they were, even when they found new jobs, which these two hadn't. They came in with the same garbage their kind always brought to pawn. Tree bark they'd promise had survived the burning of the Holy Psychopomp Tree, a radio they'd allegedly stolen from Tychron's temple, a marble chunk they'd swear came from the lost city of Aedos. Usually their holy robes and pages from the Verses of Aeg, torn out verse by verse. Anything they could sell to Hector, no matter its presumed holiness.

Vince was sometimes baffled that he alone had the world figured out. Couldn't people see? Everyone was something of a scoundrel, even those sworn to the gods.

And here came the biggest scoundrel of all—Hector, a big rough-and-tumble bearded fellow. He held a jeweler's eye in one hand and Vince's tiny, gold-colored prize in the other. Over his shoulder lay a black garment wrapped in wax paper.

He set the prize on the counter. "Worthless, Vince. I'm sorry."

Vince pocketed his watch with a smile. A decade from now, Hector would pull this same nonsense. "Really, Hector? I'm sure it's not entirely without worth. Let's put it at five hundred, yeah? Minus whatever I owe you for the priestess robe."

But Hector's face was grim. "I'm not trying to dicker with you. Not on this. Sincerely, bottom of my heart, I'm sorry and I hope you get even with whatever crook gave you this like it was worth a damn, because it's not."

Vince laid both hands on the counter to either side of his prize. "It's from a secret room under Valmydion's temple. Do you know what I did to get this thing?"

"Some priestly heirloom, maybe."

"It's a rare jewel."

Hector handed the jeweler's eye to Vince. "Take a closer look."

Vince held the glass-lensed cylinder to his face. His eyes weren't the best, he had to admit, but he was surprised he'd overlooked the stone's texture.

"It's a coralstone," Hector said. "Unusual color, and perhaps it was grown to curve, or cut this way by hand, but there's nothing valuable about a hunk of coral. Grew around something, maybe a pebble, then hardened. It's jagged all over, like you'd see on a reef, and note the tiny holes? Places for sea life to live and feed."

Vince saw them. He set the jeweler's eye on the counter.

"Look," Hector said. "I was going to give you a fuss about the priestess robe, since it's my last one and dearly precious."

"My ass," Vince said. "How many clergy have sold you the robes off their backs for grocery money?"

"Twenty for it." Hector shrugged, and the paper crinkled on his shoulder. "On account of us being friends."

"Fifteen," Vince said. "For good friends."

Hector passed the wax paper bundle across the counter. "I'm not a cheat, Barton. You know that."

Vince knew a few things about Hector but didn't share them. He stuffed the coralstone beside his pocket watch. Worthless. He supposed if he'd stroked his fingertip across the surface, he might've felt his prize's rough, porous surface and saved himself the embarrassment.

On the street, he checked the time again. He was supposed to be home already, awaiting Lilac's phone call. She would call more than once, but she'd be angry by the time he picked up.

He fortunately lived only a couple blocks from the pawnshop, a more regular stop for him than the farmer's market. Sometimes he reflected how far he could've gone in more respectable professions—law, politics, business, perhaps medicine—had he ever been inclined.

Better to know himself and make his surroundings comfortable. Having a place of power was not a privilege exclusive to the gods. No one else seemed to get that. Maybe Honest Hector, but few others, even associates Vince respected. Always grasping and clawing for something bigger, something better. They had needed little persuasion to draw them to the houses where Lilac waited, expecting to find a friend but finding her instead. None spoke to each other. None would know Vince had spent these past two days waiting in the temple for Lilac.

He wondered if there was some grand lesson his soul might learn from these events, but he thought not. People were a mess. No one else seemed to have figured that out.

Vince tossed the wax paper bundle over his shoulder and hurried down the street.

Home was a flat-roofed box of white stone, no different from most South Temple District houses. Best to blend in. His phone was silent as he unlocked the door and stepped inside. Still time. He laid the robe on a wooden chair and placed the worthless coralstone on top. Lilac could have it as a memento. Or an apology, whichever she liked.

He walked into his cluttered junk pile of a home, as stuffed with crates and barrels as the storage houses where he'd sent his colleagues, with only the central floor sitting clear. No one else should have been here, but there was a muffled crying from one corner next to the front door. A huddled-up woman sat in a covenant robe, coated in white dust, its bottom hem torn.

Vince's nerves settled. "Lilac."

She said nothing. The front door had been locked, but from the way she crept in and out of houses with calculated finesse, he should have expected her to know her way around a window.

"I'm fine, thanks, how are you?" Vince asked, heading for his rusty-edged stovetop. Lilac would want tea, and he could use some himself. "That could've gone better, I agree. You almost didn't need to say it. Could've gone worse, too. You'd like honey with tea, yes?"

Lilac didn't answer, but she'd stopped crying. If he could get her to laugh, everything would be fine.

He pulled the clay honeypot from a cabinet stuffed with old

cans and bottles. "You're angry with me. Stop denying it, I feel it burning my back." He filled a silvery kettle with water from the faucet and struck a match to light the stovetop. "Tea will be a few minutes. If I'd known you still wanted to meet up, we might've gone to your place, seen your mother. How's Simone doing these days? Does she know you're summoning up her ex? Ah, I see, a surprise. Love these chats, how verbose you can be when you really get going."

Vince studied Lilac's robe, a disaster wrapped around a beautiful, intelligent woman. She got the beauty for free from Simone. Both her intelligence and misfortune stemmed from Logoi.

"Bought you a new robe." Vince approached the chair by the door and patted the wax paper package. His fingers absentmindedly brushed the coralstone. "Pretty, yes? Called a coralstone, a temple relic or the like. Could be useful to you. Found it in that pit when I checked on your lady—"

He felt Lilac's eyes on him and stopped. Couldn't say why; it wasn't as if mentioning Lilac's new lover's death would bring that truth to fruition. It did that on its own by being the truth. They both knew what had happened. Lilac had to be turning the scene in her head, over and over, a coin she kept hoping would spawn a third side.

"You're thinking of killing me." Vince laid the coralstone beside Lilac. A strip of black fabric wrapped her right foot. "But you won't. Know why? Because killing me would be unreasonable."

He watched her face remain still, but that in itself was a reaction. He had her ear, if not her eye or heart. Lilac had just started killing people as of yesterday morning, beginning with Flip and Marko. Vince could reach for the woman she'd been before he came back to Valentine, before she'd concocted this whole Logoi-summoning scheme, and pull her through to the now.

"We've been dancing mad these past few days," Vince said. "A wilder week than when we met years back. But we had fun then, right? And I've been a big help in this whole summoning, haven't I? And not to put too fine a point on a rough day, but I just saved your life."

Lilac shuddered, and pale flakes rained from her robe.

"She was going to kill you, Lilac. She didn't know it was you, and we don't know if finding out would've lowered her revolver. I get you two were close—in ways you and I never got the chance to be—but she used to be police. What did you expect? Best we move right on."

Vince checked the stove—the kettle water hissed but did not yet boil—and then turned to Lilac again.

"I couldn't let her kill you," he went on. "And what, find me? Supposing I could explain I was sleeping off a night on the town, even then I couldn't explain all my colleagues' addresses and meet-up plans in my pockets." He reached into his jacket and tore out a crumpled chunk of notebook pages. "I let you kill these people. Some were—some thought we were friends. You want to talk sacrifice? What about that?" He tossed the chunk on the floor. The pages scattered.

Lilac said nothing.

"Are you still holding the twins against me?"

Still nothing.

"Answer, for gods' sakes!" Vince snapped. "How many times I got to repeat myself before it's good enough? I. Didn't. Know. You think I would've run off if I'd known you were pregnant? I didn't even hear about them until I came back. You think I would've missed them? That it might've changed anything? That I'd miss their funeral? How could I attend a funeral for people I didn't even know existed? Answer me that!"

Nothing. Lilac was a statue.

"Exactly," Vince said, catching his breath. "You know I didn't do it to you on purpose."

The tea kettle whistled and then screamed.

Vince turned to the stove to silence it. "You know it, Lilac. It wasn't my fucking fault."

He realized as he turned the gas off that the kettle's scream had muffled other sounds. The tap as Lilac's foot kicked the coralstone. The odd pad of her limping footsteps as she crossed the stone floor. He heard the coralstone smack the front door, but by then it was too late.

The dagger plunged into his back and, after he spun around, into his chest. She was sloppy about it, her clasped hands half on the hilt, half on the blade, cutting her fingers as easily as she cut through Vince's torso, their blood mixing in his jacket. Narrow gray stripes turned crimson.

He gritted his teeth, refusing to scream. That was a tea kettle thing to do, and he had his pride. He wouldn't hurt Lilac either, not physically. If she'd wanted to end him so he couldn't react, that would have been easy. He wouldn't abuse these final moments by being rude about his own murder.

She had calculated that, he was sure. She calculated everything. Maybe she had the world figured out too, in her own way.

Vince smiled as everything went dark.

Chapter 14

Lilac didn't kill Vince for revenge, and she didn't kill him out of anger, though she *was* angry. Revenge and anger wouldn't have sent her catching his body and lowering him to the floor, wouldn't have let her cradle him and say, "I'm sorry, I'm so sorry, it wasn't your fault. It was mine." And she didn't kill him out of some delusion his death would bring Arcadia back.

She killed him because he'd made a habit of raining chaos on her life. Had she no one left to lose, maybe she could have let him live, even after what he did to Arcadia.

But Lilac had plenty to lose. She could only mourn a moment before she set to work again. No reason to waste what Vince had given.

"To break the law in her city is to surrender your life to her," Lilac said.

She dragged Vince's body to the center of his cluttered den. Vince had believed there would be a world past all this, where the gods would return to their temples and rejuvenate Aeg. Maybe that was why he'd helped in Lilac's plan. In death, he could help a little more.

"May you find peace in your next life." Lilac tugged off Vince's jacket and cut her dagger across his arms, thighs, and gut. Blood spilled across the stone floor as his innards slopped into an offering mound. She avoided his face. Whatever they had been together that week years ago, and the different thing they had been this past week, he held a place in her heart. She meant to honor it.

She tore off her robe, ran her hand over the reddened floor, and drew a crude nine-pointed star on the nearest wall. Vince's blood dressed her naked skin in another star. Exhaustion eased from her muscles as her body drank him in. If only blood could ease heartache.

Lilac threw her arms over her head, crossed her wrists, steepled her fingers, crossed her legs at the ankles, and tried to stand on her toes to venerate Logoi.

Her right foot stung through its cloth wrapping and dragged her down on her heels. It would take longer to heal than she could spare right now. She ripped the cloth away and tried crossing her legs before raising her hands. The sting hit worse this time and dropped her to the floor.

She didn't have time for this. Vince's blood would lose potency, and already her skin had slurped it thin, joining his lifeforce with hers. She found herself kneeling to Logoi's star, far more submissive than she'd ever been as a descendant, as a daughter, but maybe right now Mother needed a display of humility and smallness.

"I call to Logoi the Many-Headed, Goddess of Reason." Lilac raised her hands. "Enjoy the bounty we would feed you. Accept this offering, be replenished, and return to us. To me. We need the gods as a daughter needs—like I need you, Mother."

Lilac's skin showed clean, the blood absorbed. Her prayer had been too wordy.

She didn't belong on her knees; a god's child shouldn't be made to pray like this. Never equals to gods, but never their submissive faithful either. Desperation had dragged Lilac down. No one should ever have been pushed to this point, but the gods were gone, and Vince was dead, and Arcadia was dead, and Lilac was at the end of her rope.

She turned from Logoi's star to Vince's growing pool of blood, where it flowed past his pocket watch, lost from his jacket, and against the gold-colored coralstone. Lilac grabbed it and thrust it overhead between lacerated fingers.

"Mother, I offer this relic of Valmydion. Take everything she left behind, and Tychron, Korenbal, Carimeldra, all of them. The other gods are gone, but their cities, temples, people—they're yours."

Lilac's fingers stung where they'd slipped across her own tear-shaped blade. Her foot ached. She tightened her grip on the coralstone.

"Silence isn't enough, Mother. I was a good daughter, your only child. I have killed so many people—I killed the father of my children for you. You never met your granddaughters, and they're dead, too, and that's my fault. Arcadia's gone. Do you want Mom, too? You didn't want her before, so I don't know."

Logoi's star dripped down the wall. Lilac laid a hand on the red smear, stood up, and pressed her forehead against the blood. She felt nothing but cold stone.

"What more can I offer you? I've stained my soul to bring you home, but you're not here. I don't know what's left to do. What else will it take for you to come back to me?"

Lilac sank again to her knees. A great expanse of nothingness awaited her, a lull of anticipation and then the dark seas rising and filling her nose, mouth, throat, lungs. She would be dead long before the glories began to eat her. And Logoi wouldn't care.

"Mother, please." Lilac clenched her teeth as tears rolled down her cheeks. "Please."

"Your despair is oppressive."

Lilac shot back from the wall and hit the floor.

A powerful feminine whisper slid through her bones. "Do not drop the coralstone, or you will lose my voice."

Lilac sat up and stared hard at the coralstone. She'd seen it for a sedentary lump the moment Vince placed it beside her, but now it thrummed in time to her heartbeat. A pulse shot down her fingers and through her arm, harder when she pressed her fingertips into the coralstone's pores, lighter when she relaxed her grip.

She swallowed before she spoke. Too much to hope, but she had to know. "Mother?"

The coralstone's warmth breathed across Lilac's skin. "Yes, my perfect jewel."

Only Logoi had ever called Lilac that. Her breath rushed out. "Mother, where are you? Are you talking through this thing? Is it your conduit? Vince found it in Valmydion's temple, but—"

Crimson light gleamed behind dark yellow pores. "It is my prison."

Lilac had never considered the gods' absence might have come against their will. They were immortal, invincible. A cold wave of shame washed through Lilac. This past decade, she'd blamed Logoi, despaired for her. Never hated her, but love had become hard.

But now it seemed the gods could be trapped. "Are there others imprisoned?" Lilac asked. "Other gods?"

"It may be so." The coralstone trembled. "I do not know from inside."

"Who did this to you?"

"I do not know this either. I do not know the state of the world outside."

Lilac gave a pained laugh. "The world's a mess. People are dying, the rain's coming, the glories—" She clutched the coralstone to her heart, pulse against pulse. There was too much to tell.

"I must mend this," Logoi said. "I must mend you."

"How?" What had happened to Aeg seemed beyond repair.

"When I am free, I will draw down the heavens." The coralstone throbbed so hard it hurt Lilac's sternum. "When you free me, we will mend the Holy Land, and then the world. It will be done the way you have reached out to me. I must feed to be free."

Feed. Logoi would need more blood. Lilac had no idea where

she'd find it, but that didn't matter right now. She'd learned more these past few minutes than in the past ten years.

"If I grow silent, seep mortal blood into the stone," Logoi said. "I am weak, but a small offering will work wonders. Make me strong and then would come the mending."

"Yes, Mother." Saying it after all this time almost made Lilac cry.

The coralstone quaked. "Until then, you must remain strong despite your suffering. Cry if you must, but do not lose yourself with tears. I cannot save mankind if you are broken."

"Yes, Mother." This time, saying it warmed Lilac's chest. She'd found her holy mother again, and all would be well.

"Bring my prison to a safe place. Rest, and then the work must begin." The pulse ceased.

Ten years. No communication, no sacrifice, no blood. Logoi had to be exhausted. What monster had done this to her? What if the other gods hadn't left the Holy Land, but lay trapped beneath each other's temples?

Lilac sat stunned, her hands shaking so hard she could believe the heartbeat had returned to the coralstone. Today had been an atrocity, but there was hope. Nothing she'd done had been in vain.

She blinked until her eyes cleared and then grabbed her dagger off the floor beside Vince. Someone else would have to arrange his funeral pyre; she had bigger problems. She took out her money from the ravaged covenant robe and pulled the other robe from its wax paper. Calling it new was a lie, and used would be a kindness; it smelled musty and had been patched in several places, but it was free of blood, dust, and the memories of what Lilac had done.

Stepping outside Vince Barton's gloomy house, onto a busy street of pedestrians and cars, she didn't see a world of circumstances and the chains of reaction that bound them. She saw a world on which no plan could be drawn, a space of shapeless potential and possibility.

"I wish Arcadia could see this," Lilac whispered. But Arcadia might have always seen the world this way. Maybe that's why she'd wanted to help people, no matter how impossible.

Home or the hotel? The hotel made the most sense, it was Lilac's cover for everything she did on the street and she had a shift starting in an hour, but home was a safer place to stash Logoi's prison.

She clutched the coralstone in her robe's pocket and hurried on.

CHAPTER 15

Lilac and Simone rented a second-floor apartment in the South Temple District, not far from Oldtown. The best they could do, and enough.

A thin rug lay in the center of the living room, where two soft chairs sat to either side of a wooden end table for the radio. The kitchen was clean. A bedroom hung off to the side, but Lilac rarely slept there anymore, not since she'd gotten rid of the twins' crib. Some nights she curled up on the floor or stretched across one of the chairs, other nights she rested in a hotel room. The past few months she'd spent some nights with Arcadia. Lilac kept a few of Sara's drawings on one corner wall behind the twins' wooden toy chest, which she now used as a makeshift clothing drawer. On another wall hung a movie poster for *Nights That Never Happened*— Simone's favorite.

Simone Antonis sat by the window in a wicker chair with the small radio planted on the windowsill. Gale Remi was singing "Miss You, Miss Sunshine" from the radio, a song of peppy melody and upbeat brass that every station would overplay half to death before the rainy season ended, just like every year.

Love you lightly, love you brightly,
I'll make your days all mine,
Miss you today, miss you always,
Miss, miss, miss you, Miss Sunshine!

Simone switched the music off when Lilac shut the front door, and the apartment filled with the tapping of rain against the window.

"Mom," Lilac said. "How about a hello?"

Simone's eyes stayed fixed on the radio. "Hello? But you've been here all day."

Lilac grabbed clean bits and pieces of her maid uniform from the closet and toy chest. Once dressed, she tucked Logoi's coralstone deep in the toy chest, hiding one mother before turning to the other.

"What did the two of us do all day?" Lilac asked.

"You slept late," Simone said. "We listened to the radio. Carter Rogos sang 'Misty Blue.' They played that three times. The news was all about the weather forecast and some trouble in Oldtown yesterday." Her gaze flashed to Lilac and then away. "The radio show was some lurid romance; I forget the name. I left a couple of times to help Eva hang her laundry, but I was only gone ten minutes. You and I bickered about whether that lecher you're friends with has an eye for you."

"Cecil? I think he's seeing a lounge singer. Or was." Lilac couldn't imagine having that argument. "Sounds uneventful."

"It has to be, sometimes."

Lilac approached the table and turned the radio on again. Static clouded a low saxophone. "And then I got ready for work."

Simone grasped Lilac's hands and studied her fingers. "You must've been sloppy cutting an orange for me."

Lilac drew her hands back. "And then what do I say if someone notices the other hand? That I passed the knife right to left and cut those fingers, too? It's ludicrous."

"It's kinder than what you've really been doing," Simone said, raising an eyebrow. "Very sloppy. Your mother taught you better."

That was funny, their past considered, but Lilac didn't laugh. "Mom, I—"

Her jaw worked without sound. How to tell any of today? How much to tell? Over fifty years ago, Logoi had poured a goddess's power into Simone, and then that mortal woman gave birth to a goddess's mortal daughter. Lilac had aged slower than most daughters, and while Logoi took an interest in her, the goddess of reason had no more use for Simone. One mother kept Lilac and banished the other. Simone left their lives for a time, but she went carrying baggage.

"Mom, I—" Simone echoed. "What?"

"Nothing," Lilac said.

She avoided glancing at the toy chest. Her mothers were sharing a dwelling for the first time in decades, but telling Simone would have to wait until Lilac climbed out of her grief. Arcadia was dead; Vince was dead. Lilac could mediate a reunion between Logoi and Simone someday, but not right now.

"I'm going to work," Lilac said.

As if Radiance Hotel could keep her from sinking. She would have called out sick, but to deviate from schedule might look suspicious should anyone suspect her of the murders.

Work carried its own weight. Between turning over rooms, Lilac spent much of her shift cleaning up after a lounge party for the people in suits and dresses with oversized hats and feathers in their hair. They had left, finished drinking wine, lighting mint smokes, dancing until they dropped. Maybe they were finished pretending the world could never end.

Lilac passed Arcadia's room again and again. How long until she broke down knowing this was entirely, inescapably her fault? She did her crying in a hotel restroom, under her breath.

The sky hung dark when she stepped out of a cab hours later, home again. She tried to look on the bright side. Logoi was here. She rarely spoke comforting words, but her presence would be enough. She was hope incarnate.

Lilac discovered more presences when she climbed her apartment building's outdoor steps to the second-floor landing. Simone chatted through the door, and voices answered. Had the Logos police found Lilac out? They would've certainly found Arcadia's body by now.

No point in stalling. Lilac opened the apartment door, where scents of onions and spices clouded her face. The oven hissed, and food sizzled on the stovetop, Simone at work in the kitchen.

Cecil Gillion appeared at Lilac's side, his smile big as always. "Lilac, love!" He pulled her into a quick hug.

She hugged him back. They used to be on no-touching terms when they first became friends, in case his telltale skin might notice he was getting nothing from her, until she learned of his gift's unreliability. Easy to chalk up never sensing anything from her to his own godly failures, which hit especially when he'd been drinking, and he was often drinking.

"What are you doing here?" Lilac asked. This didn't make sense. Cecil stopped by now and then, but Simone had never cooked for him.

"I didn't realize you knew each other," a gruff voice said.

Lilac let Cecil go and looked to the window where Simone had sat earlier. A forty-something man Lilac didn't know stood in a black trench coat. A fedora lay on the window's table beside Simone's radio. The man's hair was shorn short like Arcadia's.

"That's Alexander Stathos, my partner at Ace Investigations," Cecil said, thrusting his hands toward Alex. He seemed a livewire tonight. "I've never introduced him because I wanted you to like me, but I didn't even know here's where we were coming, and we were both already invited."

Lilac glanced to Simone, face full of questions.

Simone waved a carving knife. "Kick off your work clothes and come help me," she said. "Cecil's trying, but he's useless in the kitchen except for finding alcohol, and your guests shouldn't have to help their host."

Why were they Lilac's guests? What had she done? More importantly, what did they know she'd done? She studied Cecil—cheery and oblivious—and then Alex, who seemed to struggle with relaxing, but he might've been trying. This was wrong. The only person she'd asked over tonight was—

"I invited them," a familiar voice said. "Hope that's not crossing a line."

She sat in one of the living room chairs, too tall and carved to look comfortable, but she had been through worse today. That fragile smile—Lilac had thought she'd never see it again.

Arcadia.

CHAPTER 16

This face was a trap set for Lilac by Logos police or Cecil's stoic detective friend. The authorities somehow knew every wrong she had ever done, and they had fashioned some Arcadia looka-like to—what? Lilac couldn't find the pattern here. None of this checked out, not Arcadia's face, her dark jacket and cap, all of it impossible after what Lilac had done.

Arcadia's chipper demeanor faded in Lilac's shadow. "You're upset. I was supposed to come alone, but I brought surprise guests. That was rude of me, a mistake."

"No!" Lilac cried. "No, no, you're good, doll."

The trap was working; she'd already been lured into treating this Arcadia like the real woman, excited for her, calling her by a favored pet name. She even acted like a true Arcadia, a strange construct of gentle strength and firm presence. Lilac had invited Arcadia over, wanted to introduce lover to mother, and here reality acted as if that intent superseded the universal truth that Arcadia was dead. Was Vince a liar? What had this maybe-Arcadia said? Had Simone kept her story straight?

Or was Arcadia really here and impossibly alive?

Floorboards creaked as Alex left the window. "You're Lilac, right? Nice meeting you. How do you know Cecil?"

Lilac tried to pretend at normal, at least. "Counseling. Not for me, but coworkers, neighbors. Before he was a detective. We got to chatting and made friends when he was at the hotel fishing for new clients—not that I ever became one." Maybe she should have. She sounded stilted, her brain like a car driven over too many potholes, now falling apart inside.

"I was good at it, too," Cecil said. "Knew their troubles before they did. But investigation makes a better fit for my gift, and I couldn't properly annoy Alex otherwise."

"And we had common acquaintances, some of his exes." Lilac shrugged into a head tilt. "You know how he is."

Alex nodded; he did.

Better, more like herself, but Lilac struggled with the jubilant atmosphere as balanced between helping Simone in the kitchen and conversing in the living room. Every smile and laugh came forced, except when Lilac looked at Arcadia. No one seemed to know anything had gone wrong today.

What about Arcadia? Had she seen Lilac's face at the temple? What did anyone know? Lilac had figured Cecil might stumble into this eventually as an outside consultant, having blabbed his godly heritage to half of Valentine. Reason enough set the sacrifices to burn, only for Arcadia to show up at the end. Action and consequence dizzied in thought.

Lilac focused hard on her surroundings. Simone had gathered everyone around the small table between living room seats, too small for five adults. Lilac sat on the edge of Arcadia's seat, Cecil on the floor, and Alex stood at the wall, everyone with a plate of garlic-topped greens and seasoned roast chicken.

"Do I have everyone's situation straight?" Simone asked. "Arcadia, you fight floods, and Alexander, you investigate—things?"

"People, mostly," Alex said. He bit a forkful and hummed approval.

Simone aimed her fork around the room. "And we're all from Logos."

"West Amberdan," Cecil said with his mouth full. "Never got

down to Logos."

"But the rest."

Others nodded, Lilac with them, and then wondered if that was right. Motherhood didn't necessarily mean they'd both lived in Logos. Had Lilac now given something away? She should have calculated first, but even the inclination to sort out life's patterns seemed alien tonight.

"Both ex-police?" Simone asked, nodding to Arcadia and then Alex.

"Arcadia and I go way back." Alex patted at his coat. "As far back as the barracks. I take it she never mentioned me."

Arcadia shifted beside Lilac. Her discomfort seemed genuine. She and Lilac had chosen to only share yesteryear's untarnished memories, like Lilac's living with Simone, or Arcadia's second visit to Logoi for her miracle. No talk of police, or trauma, or twins. With the way the world was, Lilac couldn't blame either of them for immediate indulgence, no past, no future. A self-fulfilling anxiety, she reflected.

They might have seen each other in the Logos temple. Arcadia wouldn't have known. Clever Logoi had hidden her mortal daughter from attention in plain sight among the priestesses. When she was small, Lilac had played at the goddess's feet. Grown, she performed rituals with Logoi's covenant. Only a handful of elders knew Logoi had a mortal daughter.

Arcadia and Alex would have looked like any other graduating cadets at some forgotten ceremony, and Arcadia would have looked like a different person before her miracle of transformation. Strangers until they'd abandoned home. Unrecognizable teenagers.

"And you?" Alex asked.

"And me?" Lilac swallowed hard on a strip of garlic-soaked asparagus.

Alex aimed his fork. "Where'd you meet Arcadia?"

Simone leaned from her chair. "Oh, I want to hear this too."

"The hotel, where she works," Arcadia said. Was there distress in her voice, or was Lilac paranoid?

"Working turnover, you get to chatting with guests," Lilac said. "Arcadia didn't chat, but she wouldn't leave her room sometimes when I came to clean, stuck reading a book or—" She almost mentioned when Arcadia would get lost in herself, but she swallowed that. "She's funny. I'd need to dust her chair, and she'd get up and stand by the window. But then I'd need to clean the window. Or she'd sit on the bed when I had to change the sheets. Always chasing her around."

"Couldn't you have cleaned everything else and saved wherever she was for last?" Alex asked.

"That wouldn't have been the most efficient turnover." Lilac laughed, almost coughing. "There's a pattern. And there were reasons to get close to her."

Alex was blank-faced, maybe a shut door to romance and attraction. Lilac knew people like that, but he would have laughed, too, had he seen ridiculous Arcadia shuffling out of the way only to somehow get in the way even more, almost on purpose.

"I came to like chasing her around her room," Lilac went on. "Anyone else would leave, but she'd take up a new spot and go on reading. It's not a very interesting story, I know. After a couple weeks, I noticed I'd been coming to her room with the giggles. I couldn't remember feeling so silly in years. One day, I went in to start the turnover chase again, and she asked if I'd like to chase her to dinner and a show. I had to run it through my head a little, there were workplace considerations versus her being a cute and strapping flood fighter, and the long and short of it is, I said yes."

Alex didn't need to know the selfishness of that moment, how Lilac had felt she deserved a nice night for a change. Maybe she didn't, especially now, but she'd lived too long without laughter. Her heart and soul had needed that silliness and light, as if Arcadia had swept Lilac into both arms and showed her she could fly.

"Funny you tell it that way," Alex said. He'd cleaned his plate while listening. "That doesn't sound like Arcadia." He was prodding. Why?

"What sounds off?" Lilac asked. "Her boldness?"

"Her waiting. Must've been a good book." Alex glanced to Arcadia for a reaction.

Arcadia had cleaned her plate, too, and she stretched up from her seat to take both their dishes to the kitchen. Simone followed, saying something about a lemon pudding she'd stirred together quick and needed help with, and Cecil took her seat to finish eating.

The room began to spin. Why couldn't Lilac ease up and enjoy this? Why did everyone flash swords in their eyes and daggers on their tongues? How could Arcadia be alive right now?

"Arcadia's tough as they come," Alex said softly, as if answering unspoken questions.

Lilac wanted to see through him the way Cecil saw through most people. He'd never suspected she was a fellow descendant when he felt nothing from her, but she never asked how life felt when having his off-and-on gift, only absorbed what he boasted or complained about freely. The gift's frailty to drink and fire, his openness with others.

How did he see his fellow detective? Or Arcadia? Could he tell what stirred inside her tonight?

"If she never told you about me, she wouldn't have told you what happened our first week in the barracks." Alex kept his voice low, like he didn't want Arcadia to overhear. "I'll never forget that bare-handed Arcadia can be a beast when she means it."

The room found its gravity, and Lilac clawed into it. "A beast?"

Alex leaned deeper over the table. "Wasn't long after we met. She'd been conscripted like any orphan after her parents' accident, and mine thought I needed straightening up. Imagine the barracks, thirty-odd teenagers crammed into two rows of bunkbeds. Someone pissed Arcadia off enough for her to risk reprimand and step out the door that evening past curfew."

"Kids can be shits," Cecil said.

"Honest, I don't remember how the incident started," Alex went on. "And it didn't matter to anyone else until Arcadia came back in the middle of the night. I'd kept myself up crying, so I might've been the only one to realize anything was happening. The door opened, I assumed because Arcadia was coming back—she was—but then something clicked against the door as it shut. Some kid cried out, hit the ground. Another kid screamed, and everyone was awake then. Bed after bed, a figure flew hitting every other kid, everyone trying to figure out what was happening, everyone fighting back."

Lilac shut her eyes and found a storm of battling teenagers in the darkness.

"I thought to hit the lights." Alex pounded the table, clanking the utensils. "Didn't work. Arcadia had thought of it first. This other girl, Sybil Loris? She tried the door, but it wouldn't open. Imagine, everyone's stuck in the dark, clueless, but someone's beating the stones out of them all. A few of us gave up quick and crawled under the beds to cry it out."

"Never the fighter," Cecil chuckled.

Alex let out a big laugh. "We were practically children! But bless them, the others tried, and the racket dragged our sergeant to come checking. Didn't find out until after, but Arcadia had set a steel panel from the dockyard to fall against the door and jam it after she came in. Only someone outside could open up. She'd also pulled the plug on the lights. Our sergeant found kids strangling each other, beating each other, hiding under beds, but there was Arcadia standing over everybody, bruised and bloody, but victorious. In the dark, none of us knew who was a friend, but for Arcadia, everyone was the enemy. Whatever started it, no one messed with her ever again." Alex finished as Arcadia returned, small bowls balanced in her hands. Nothing in this gentle giant screamed vengeful teenager, but her barracks days were over twenty-five years ago.

Arcadia looked embarrassed now. "I would've liked if you hadn't told that story," she said, passing a palm-sized bowl of banana-colored pudding into Alex's hands.

"Sounds like you'll have to hurt him, love," Cecil said, taking his. "Go on, he's been cruising for it."

Lilac accepted her bowl and felt Arcadia settle into the chair, solid and genuine. How had she survived the fall in Valmydion's temple? Vince wouldn't have lied that he'd killed her. It would've been more like him to do the opposite.

"Were you afraid of her, too?" Simone asked. She must have been listening from the kitchen. She carried small clear glasses in her hands, some full of juice, others a thick violet wine, and passed them around accordingly.

"Certainly," Alex said. "That's why I made friends with her."

Simone ushered Cecil out of her seat and leaned toward Arcadia. "How long have you been fighting floods?"

"Nine or ten years," Arcadia said. "Only made captain when we came to Valentine."

She seemed pretty good at forcing out more than two-word answers when she wanted. Every night in the hotel had seemed so quiet. Were Arcadia to take Lilac back there tonight, they would slip into quiet again, and only the rain would speak for her. That didn't mean her mind was idle. Making chitchat might be another side to her—good. Lilac wanted to know Arcadia's every facet now that they had a second chance. Logoi was here. None of them knew it yet, but Aeg would carry on, glories be damned. There would be time for such second chances.

Logoi. Lilac glanced from the table to the toy chest across the living room.

The gods couldn't bring back the dead; it went against the laws of nature. Legend said some had tried anyway, during the Holy War when gods fought gods. Supposedly that was how cities like Aedos vanished into history and then myth, some enigmatic destruction helping eternal gods keep their secrets beyond human lifespans. But even if gods wouldn't resurrect mortals to those lives, what if Arcadia had survived her fall? Vince had found the coralstone beneath the temple after shoving her down. He might have gone to check if she was alive when he found the coralstone, but it had nestled beside Arcadia first.

Bleeding, dying Arcadia. Logoi was a prisoner, but not a powerless one. Blood fueled miracles, and the gods were no strangers to healing. While Vince had given Arcadia up for dead, Logoi could have mended Arcadia's wounds right there.

Lilac owed Mother thanks times a thousand.

She thrust up from the arm of Arcadia's seat. "Excuse me." She wanted to run for the toy chest, yank out the coralstone, kiss her godly mother, show everyone the new miracle. Even Simone couldn't hold her grudge against Logoi if she'd saved Arcadia's life.

Lilac instead drifted to the window and stared out at the stormy darkness. Here came the new age of miracles. People would believe the gods could come back, the dawn days were done, the glories were old troubles, best forgotten. They might start to think even the Dawn Gods would return from the heavens.

Anything was possible now.

"Nice radio," Alex said.

His sudden closeness made Lilac flinch. She glanced back to the others, still chatting in the living room. Cecil had taken Lilac's place near Arcadia. Nothing to be nervous about anymore. The day made sense, and the world would follow with it.

Lilac turned to Alex with a smile. "Not during the rainy season. We'll be lucky if it plays anything but 'Miss You, Miss Sunshine' until the growth season."

"Maybe there'll be new music someday," Alex said, laughing. He quieted fast. "You saw Arcadia yesterday, right? Was she bad last night?"

"She was bothered, but I didn't really ask." Lilac tensed, her legs eager to walk away from her memory. "I never ask." But she would ask next time. She couldn't waste this chance.

Alex glanced at the window glass, where raindrops danced down his and Lilac's reflections. "Has she told you about Shah?"

"No," Lilac said. "Is that a funny story, like the one about the barracks?"

"It isn't."

"Then it can wait."

Alex pulled his hands from his pockets and reached deep into his coat. "Did she tell you what happened yesterday? The murders?"

"A little." Nervous tingling crawled between Lilac's shoulders.

Alex pulled a wax paper bundle from his coat. Alarm bells rang in Lilac's head until she realized this had nothing to do with Vince's package. No covenant robe slipped loose. Instead, Alex withdrew a familiar folded paper.

"Arcadia's evac team lost her for a few hours today," Alex said. "Ilene Summers found this while searching, gave it to me when I came asking."

Alex unfolded a map of Valentine. A black X marked where Lilac had drawn it yesterday, but new dots stretched beside it, and someone had drawn a nine-pointed star between them.

Alex passed the map into Lilac's hands. "You've seen it before. I take it you're the genius Arcadia talked about."

"That's a strong word for changing sheets and cleaning rooms." Lilac pointed to the dots beside her X. "I didn't do these."

"But the X." Alex took back the map. "The other dots—I've asked Arcadia, but she's zipper-lipped. Where Ilene found this? The house was burning, another man dead."

"I'm not so smart then, I guess." Lilac wanted to retreat from Alex, his subtle flame, but that was exactly why she had to stay. He was prodding again, worse this time. She'd let her guard down, but Alex seemed unlike Cecil, who was much more cavalier in switching off-duty and on-duty. An investigator like Alex always watched, always wondered.

Alex glanced from the map's edge to the thin lines on Lilac's fingers. "Did I give you a papercut?"

Lilac glanced at her fingertips. The map's edge had slit through one of her dagger's cuts and reopened the wound.

"A little deep for it," Alex said.

"Cutting oranges," Lilac said, but the excuse was nonsense, and her teeth sank into her tongue.

Alex folded the map, stuffed it into its wax paper, and shoved the bundle into his trench coat. "Arcadia would make a good detective," he said. "She saw the pattern."

Lilac's thoughts traced Arcadia's pencil marks, the beautiful and cruel star of Logoi, unrelated to Lilac's pitiful X. Did Alex suspect her? Would asking for details seem suspicious? Or would it be more suspicious to ask nothing? She wished she understood him enough to know.

Deep down, he had to be curious. He could put patterns together as well as Lilac, and he wasn't even a descendant as far as she knew. The knowledge lay inside him, a baby bird ready to hatch and shout to the morning, *There's blood on Lilac's hands.*

Cecil shouted instead, tearing Alex's gaze from her. She turned, too, and watched Cecil pace back and forth in front of Simone's and Arcadia's seats, waving his arms.

"He was drinking on the way," Alex said. "I should've known he'd hit the wall." He stormed over.

Lilac followed, and her aching foot made her wonder if Cecil was the drunk who'd smashed the bottle in the alley, but if so, he was saving her now. Maybe all drunks balanced each other out, some cosmic scale more powerful than the long-dead Holy Psychopomp Tree.

Arcadia snatched twice at thin air before she caught Cecil's left hand and squeezed a cloth napkin to his palm. He quit thrashing, but now his feet stamped as if he needed to pace or else he'd drop dead.

"He's cut himself," Simone said, holding up a glass. A hairline crack ran down the side.

"What of it?" Cecil tugged his arm, but Arcadia held tight. "Food of the gods here."

Lilac strode past Alex, his hand covering his forehead, and took Cecil's free arm. "Gods don't understand food and water," she said. She took on the calming tone she'd used when Sara would scrape her knee, or Daphne would bang into a wall, which she used to do at least once a day. "If only we could have more of their power."

"A descendant's raw deal," Cecil snapped. "Get a couple hundred years, enough to watch generations, but you die. You get a little godly power, but it's like a leaf to a tree, and a wrinkled one at that. Might as well be any other mortal, then at least a god could heal this." He tried to wave his injured hand, but Arcadia wouldn't let go.

"You're still a big deal," Lilac said, reassuring as she adjusted his fedora. "We listen to you, you know? Like the gods used to listen to your grandfather's advice."

"If only he knew why they left," Alex muttered.

Not left, Lilac wanted to say. *Trapped.* But Logoi's circumstances didn't necessarily speak for every god. Lilac leaned into Cecil's face and smelled his breath, thick with rich scents from Diomarch vineyards, and plenty local too.

"Maybe since Lyvien left, the rest took a hint," Lilac said.

Cecil's eyes widened, as if he'd been accused of causing the downfall of Aeg, and then he scoffed hard, spraying spittle. "If my grandfather's wandering had any power over the rest, the gods would've left Aeg long ago, love. He never stayed put, and he was never a big deal, much as I love him. You want to talk important? That was way back when the Dawn Gods put their power into mortal women, no descendants mucking it up. You had guaranteed parent gods and child gods. Not that they'd known until that rascal Exalis dropped onto Medes."

A tremble worked through the room. Lilac had never heard anyone call one of the Dawn Gods anything but a blessing dressed in flesh and sunlight. Alex's hand hid his mouth, but his eyes narrowed like he was smiling. Simone set her jaw, and Arcadia remained expressionless.

Cecil puffed up. His tie had come loose from his coat. "But then Exalis takes Medes to him, and a couple months later, she knows she's got a little god on the way since the power's in her, and she ascends, you know? Mortal turned goddess. So out comes Aeda, and no one's ever seen a baby goddess before, never been one, and the other Dawn Gods go, huh, spiffy. And they find mortal women, too, and make all the First Children." He raised his free arm past Lilac's face and aimed at Alex, and then Arcadia. "Your Logoi, you know, she was a baby too. But who's her mother? No one thinks about it, no one wonders. The ascended parents never got cities, except what's her face because her children gave her land. They remember Savvas since so far he's the only ascended father, and Medes since she was the first ascended mother, but few others. Bullshit, isn't it?"

"I think so," Simone said.

"See?" Cecil asked. "We remember the babies. Aeda, being first of the gods. Korenbal, Godex of Strength, and who forgets them with a name like that? The rest of the First Children, Naetalia, Diomedron, Ethoc. And Logoi the Many-Headed, she was up there, too—you remember someone like her, big old dragon-looking goddess, hard to forget. Think she came out the womb with nine heads?"

Lilac gripped his arm and hoped the toy chest muffled his voice from the coralstone. He was her friend, and though miracles were useless on a descendant, she didn't want Logoi ordering someone else to hurt him when she returned to the world.

Cecil veered his cloudy gaze on Lilac. "Well, don't be shy, pitch in. You're from Logos too; you've got to have an opinion."

Simone cleared her throat. "I've never heard it asked, even in the Logos temple."

Lilac kept her grip on Cecil so not to squeeze Simone's hand for silence. Had she been drinking, too? Now wasn't the time to spill her sordid story of troubled youth, volunteering to Logoi's covenant, being chosen as the goddess's lover, only to never ascend since Lilac was never a goddess in the womb. Simone would have plenty of time to talk over abandonment when Logoi was free.

Arcadia tied her napkin around Cecil's hand and stood back. "We don't talk about Logoi so casually," she said. Her tone came so stern, for a moment Lilac felt Alex's barracks story writhing alive in the living room.

Tears glistened in Cecil's eyes as he looked over his hand. Crimson blotches dotted the once-white fabric. "But you know what I mean? We remember Logoi, but not her mother. Ascended goddesses fading off, like they didn't matter. City of Aedos puffs out of memory, like it never was. If someone immortal gets forgotten, what hope do the rest of us have? Not even leaves to a tree." He wiped the napkin's clean side down his cheeks. "Oh, I forgot myself. Dear me, need to keep it shut now and then. Alex, you tell me."

Alex fetched his fedora and pulled the front door open. "It's true; he needs to shut it more often." But there was amusement in Alex's eyes. On some level, he was fond of Cecil for moments like this.

They both thanked Simone for a lovely evening, Alex hugged

Arcadia goodbye, Cecil hugged everyone, even Alex, and then they tromped outside onto the second-floor landing, umbrellas bowing in the wind.

Simone retreated to the kitchen. Her shoulders seemed heavy after Cecil's tirade, and she needed time to collect herself. Too many thoughts about Logoi, likely. Lilac didn't protest. She needed time, too.

"Ms. Antonis," Arcadia said.

Lilac turned shakily and beamed up. "Captain."

"I owe you an apology. I've been pretending everything's fine tonight, and it isn't."

Arcadia lifted the black cap from her scalp and revealed a gash running through her bristly hair. It looked nearly healed, but Lilac couldn't imagine how bad it had been earlier today, having cracked against marble.

Arcadia tugged the cap back down. "I've had a day."

And Lilac was to blame, same as yesterday was her fault, and her daughters' deaths. Maybe somehow the glories were her fault, too, some grand retaliation against mankind for the sin of having eventually birthed Lilac. The hollow thought crossed her mind to blurt out everything because she was going to fix it.

But Logoi wasn't free yet.

"I'm sorry for your day," Lilac said. "Again."

"I went looking for trouble," Arcadia said. "And found it."

Lilac giggled as she pressed her face against Arcadia's neck, let steady breath brush her hair. Trouble found, yes, but also salvation.

"I know we've kept our pasts off limits," Lilac whispered. "I can't tell you about mine just yet, but you mean a lot to me. You picked me up from something I thought would hold me down forever."

Arcadia said nothing, but the same sense lingered in her weathered hands where they touched Lilac's arm and back.

"I don't want a shallow tryst anymore," Lilac went on. "Let's get our pasts on the table. Our futures, too. You need to know what you've done for me, how you mean so much, how I—" How broken she'd been, thinking she'd lost Arcadia today. "No one's promised a future. We decide if this goes on as frothy niceness, or if we mean it, and how deep we mean it. I don't want niceness anymore. I want everything. Your memories, pain. Everything. I want to know what broke you, and what made you whole. I want to tell you what happened to me, and how you let me laugh again."

"I'd like that, too," Arcadia said. "A new day tomorrow."

Lilac kissed Arcadia's cheek, watched her wish Simone a good night, and then saw Arcadia out of the apartment. She was too good for Valentine, for all of Aeg. If Oldtown sank into nothingness, she would take it personally and take it hard. Logoi's return would lift the responsibility off her shoulders.

Simone had nearly finished washing up when Lilac joined her in the kitchen. She snatched up a rag and began to scrub the stovetop of dried splatter.

"Nervous girl," Simone said, nudging hip to hip. "They were your guests. Didn't you want a break from the quiet?"

"I did," Lilac said, a little too forceful. She wouldn't characterize Simone's chatter as quiet, but this was the busiest the apartment had sounded since four people had lived here. Lilac hadn't noticed the stagnation until its breaking. "It was nice."

"You were scared I'd tell about me and Logoi, admit it. You didn't want them to know you're a goddess's daughter, too."

"I wouldn't want to give Cecil anything else to rant about." Lilac scrubbed harder. What a mess he'd been, but he was probably as stressed as everyone. Soon she'd solve all their problems.

"They have to wonder, you know?" Simone settled a dish into the sink and scrubbed another. "There's the slow aging. How old did you tell Arcadia you are?"

"I don't remember exactly. Thirty-one? Thirty-two?" Lilac hardly felt her age anyway. Spending most of her life in the Logos temple hadn't prepared her for the outside world.

"You'd better get your story straight, or she might suspect. You could dance around the girls' father, but women always know." Simone chuckled to herself. "How else is she going to reconcile your seventy-year-old mother?"

"Don't worry," Lilac said. "If she asks, I'll tell her you look old for your age."

Simone smacked Lilac's arm, but she had a smile on. Lilac did, too. Easier now that everyone had left. Hers and her mother's day-to-day life together could be cut into three eras the way Lilac saw it. First their reunion, when Lilac showed up at Simone's apartment, sick and hungry. Next, when the twins arrived. And then after the twins left them.

Logoi's return meant beginning another chapter in their lives. Something bright and new.

CHAPTER 17

Alex and Cecil crossed the street from Lilac's apartment. Too much of Alex's effort went into steering Cecil over puddles, too much of his attention on the suspicions orbiting his thoughts, his brain playing with a puzzle box made of knives and darkness. He didn't need to be descended from a promiscuous god of instinct to feel something was off.

"Should've called us a cab," Cecil said, stuffing his tie back into his trench coat. "Think a stroll will help me sober, or you wanted to walk?"

"To talk," Alex said. "How well do you know her?"

Cecil clutched his umbrella with both hands against a harsh gust. "Only just met her."

"Not Arcadia. Not Simone, either. Lilac."

"You said *her*, like I'm supposed to know who you're on about out of three women in there," Cecil said. "You barely spoke to your friend in there; that what you call catching up? No, scoping out my friend. Pessimistic, glass half empty, paranoid damn man you are."

Cecil was up his own ass when drunk, but usually the frustration never boiled onto Alex. Maybe Cecil had canceled a date for this dinner. Or broken a heart, the timing coincidental. He rummaged inside his coat, withdrew a tin flask, and took a sip. And then another.

Alex let him drink. "There now. Did you drink enough?"

"I never drink enough." Cecil gave a limp smile.

"How well do you know Lilac?" Alex leaned in. "You said you're friends, right? Acquaintances, or the real thing?"

Cecil cocked his head. "Getting weird on me. I don't like it. Already having a bad day, it turns out, so I can walk it off by myself if you're in a piss mood of your own."

"And she knows what you can do?"

"I was trying to get her into bed when we first met, so yeah, I told her."

No surprise there. "And does she know that fire cleanses your clairvoyance?" Alex asked.

Cecil's expression slackened. He was getting it. "Hang on. What's this about?"

"Thinking aloud." Alex led them across another street. "Would you call Lilac a smart woman? From Logos, right?"

"Oh, what?" Cecil scoffed. "Do you know how you sound, every smart woman from Logos—"

Alex yanked out a paper-wrapped map of the city and thrashed it open. Rain patted the paper. "Note this pattern?"

Cecil wiped at his face and peered over. "Same star as Logoi's."

"Except the X; it links yesterday's four murder sites, while the star connects them all," Alex said. "Lilac drew it, admitted as much to me. She played it off like she'd made a bad deduction, but Arcadia wouldn't have shared the case unless she trusted Lilac's intelligence, her judgment. Drawing the X should've steered Arcadia off."

"Alex, you're reaching," Cecil said.

"When I noticed Lilac recognized it, I noticed a couple other things. Cuts on her fingers, a slight limp. Signs of struggle, of chase. Where did the cuts come from? Cooking? It was both hands." Alex folded the map before it could get soaked. "Arcadia won't tell anyone where she went today, why she disappeared, but I've heard Valmydion's temple is a wreck, and no one knows what happened.

I think she was there. I think they were *both* there."

"You sound ridiculous." Cecil seemed to be sobering fast. "If Arcadia chased Lilac, why not tell?"

"Maybe she didn't see Lilac's face," Alex said. "Covenant robes have hoods. What if Lilac was a priestess back in Logos? Think, Cecil—why not leave the sacrifices to rot? Logoi never asked her offerings be burned; she wanted the blood. No reason to torch the crime scenes except to destroy evidence, part of which is any psychic residue you, and you alone, might pull from the surroundings. And Lilac? She knows you."

"Straying so far afield—" Cecil fought his umbrella against the budding wind. "And? That makes Lilac the murderer?"

"One of them?" Alex settled back. "Not entirely. Her physical condition's circumstantial. The map is most damning, but maybe she's not as smart as Arcadia thinks. Arcadia's secrecy might be shame or trauma, hard to tell with her. But everything together makes me suspicious, and we have no other leads."

"Worth checking." Cecil nodded, absorbing this. "Worth crossing her off your list."

"Sure." Alex gave a knowing smirk. "Besides, I'm Arcadia's friend. It's my job to approve of her relationships."

"Wait, are they sweet on each other?" Cecil asked.

Alex raised an eyebrow. "How are you a detective?"

Cecil paused at the next corner. The nearby iron streetlights seemed to wither in the thickening rain, and the distant ones became petrified fireflies. If the power went out, the storm would paint Valentine black.

"Thale has his hands full," Alex said. "Small wonder he passed the case to us. Police haven't got the smarts or skills for investigative work. They only know making trouble and then dragging that trouble for Logoi to eat. How else will Thale solve it but us?"

"Might not want it solved," Cecil muttered.

Alex turned, twisting his neck. "Say again?"

Cecil's shrug seemed labored. "Don't take me as any scholar on the man. Could be Thale hired us to look like he's busy. Mystery killer gets criminals off his hands in the Logos fashion, and with a Logoi-loving madman to blame it on."

Hadn't Alex ranted something similar to Arcadia this morning? *This is all for show*, suggesting Thale's apathy. But that he might be actively against solving the case? Alex shot the idea through his head. After years of Logos slaughter, and the catastrophe at Shah a decade back, he wouldn't put anything past Commander Rhoster Thale.

"I mean, what are we doing, mixed in this muck?" Cecil asked. "Didn't the man read our file? Catching unfaithful spouses, spotting underhanded dealings, all those fun higher callings we used to have in the State House. And then the whole building comes down, *bang*, whole clientele dies, and nothing makes sense anymore. Now here we are, hunting murderers."

"Policework probably gives Thale a skewed idea of what we do," Alex said.

"Well, his skewed idea of what we do is skewing what we do, too. I'd put him straight if he wasn't our only client." Cecil licked rainwater off his lips. "Every billable hour tastes wonderful."

Alex dodged past a man in a black robe, dashing through the rain. "I think tomorrow I'll get on Thale's case again."

"Sounds fun." Cecil nudged Alex's arm. "Want I should tag along?"

"Yes, using your best judgment."

"My best judgment?" Cecil laughed hard, and his little umbrella fell into a puddle. He picked it up and began to walk.

"But first I have something a lot more fun for you. Digging through papers kind of fun." Alex told Cecil what he wanted.

Cecil balked. "Crawl up my ass, why don't you."

"If that helps you sleep at night," Alex said.

"I'll do it, you shit, don't worry." Cecil pawed at his trench coat, either grabbing for his flask or checking it hadn't run off without him. "But I'm not going to like it."

"I'm very sorry." Alex placed a hand on Cecil's shoulder. He was such a bony man beneath all his clothes. Did he ever eat, or was alcohol his breakfast, lunch, and dinner?

"Save it, you wouldn't know if water was wet," Cecil said. "Proving you wrong on Lilac will make it all worth it."

Alex wanted to be proven wrong. He wanted it more than he wanted to speak with Thale tomorrow. He and Cecil passed the temple plaza and approached an avenue of the North Temple District holding upscale diners, the radio station, a lounge, a stage-house, and a movie house, along with a pile of offices. Ace Investigations was one of them.

Alex glanced at the theater marquee; it read *The One Smart Man* and no other shows. A comedy first released six years ago, but since the moviemaking industry folded up along with Dialos, its city-state of operations, no one could be too choosy.

"Want to catch a talkie?" Alex asked.

Cecil looked at the marquee and then to Alex. "I'd love that. You know I'm always up for a laugh."

CHAPTER 18

Maybe it was the mid-movie scene where the lead dangled from a high window, but after leaving the theater's black-and-white screen and parting ways with Cecil, Alex stopped at the office and made a phone call. He, too, felt himself dangling.

"Operator?" Alex hesitated. What would he do if his suspicions were right? Live with it, he supposed. "Long-distance call. I'll cover charges. Put me through to Logos, police high command. Their operator will know the connecting number."

"Right away, sir," the Valentine operator said, his tone friendly. A pause, and then several clicks. "Sir? There's no answer from Logos."

Alex drummed his fingers on the desk. "That was pretty quick. You gave them time?"

"There was no connection, sir." The operator paused, thinking. "The long-distance lines may have come down in the storm."

Alex glanced across the darkened office, where a frail streetlight shined through the rain-spotted window. Two days in, and already the interstate lines were down. What kind of season were they in for?

"Sir?" the operator squeaked. "Is there anything else I can do for you?"

Alex rubbed his jaw as if he could massage good ideas out of his mouth. "Long-distance call. Tychos, if you don't mind. Their government office or equivalent."

"One moment."

The line clicked a few times, enough for Alex to deduce the Valentine operator had connected with someone in Tychos. Word on Tychron's city-state these days said the people were less about answering phones and more about fortifying their central city with spiked walls and cadaverous decorations, while inside the temple, a drug-addled covenant sacrificed children to their lost god. In Tychos, they would call the Valentine Butcher a neighbor.

"Call connecting," the Valentine operator muttered. He sounded rattled.

Alex held the line until he heard giggling from whatever Tychos office he'd been connected to, and then he hung up. At least some long-distance lines still stood.

But not to Logos.

Alex would have to figure things out for himself. Seeing Arcadia in that apartment, her eyes aglow when Lilac sat beside her, he wanted desperately to be wrong. A word from Logos might tell him more.

An hour later, he rented a creaky-framed little car and drove down the eastern side of Valentine through southern Lee Village. Slow going around the foot traffic, but the city's center would be worse, and Oldtown was a mud trap. The car reached Merchant's Field, every storefront ablaze with neon. Alex turned at the South Temple District's edge, towards the city's southern exit. His fedora rode in the passenger's seat.

How long since he'd last seen Logos? Six years, easy, but maybe more. Logos hadn't felt like home since long before leaving the police and then the city-state.

The drive smoothed out once Alex passed the derelict train station marking Valentine's southern exit and rolled down the South Road toward its tollhouse. Beyond, the interstate highway linked Valentine to Logos. To the east, the grass spread wild against the city-state river borders, where five thousand years ago they had been separate islands. No other cars dotted the road, and only the rusted husks of train cars haunted the broken railroad. Each year there were fewer ways and reasons to travel between city-states. To the west, the floodplains waited to drown beyond the stone barricade that protected Oldtown. Everywhere you went, the same doomed story.

The rain slammed Alex's windshield harder, as if the storm knew what was about to happen and wanted to warn him. He eased off the gas a little to avoid coasting. He eased off entirely and slammed the brake when he reached the tollhouse.

The roadway gate was down. Three black-uniformed roadmen under midnight blue umbrellas funneled out of the small wooden tollhouse. The tallest roadman approached Alex's window.

"I don't feel like cranking the engine again, so don't make me idle," Alex said. "I'll pay and be on my way."

"Onramp is down, mister," the roadman said. He was maybe twice Alex's age, too old to be manning a tollhouse. "You should head back."

Alex raised his voice against the rain. "I'm heading to Logos. The lower road is still good, isn't it?"

"Not exactly." The roadman pointed south. "The rivers are flooded already. You can't see it now, but the water's foaming white. Soon it'll overcome the banks."

And the water would spread across Aeg, and the city-states would revert to the archipelago islands they'd been before the dawn days. The same problems every year since the gods abandoned the Holy Land—yet worse now.

"It's important I get to Logos," Alex said, as if that could part the waters.

"You won't be getting to Logos, sir," the roadman said. "I'm sorry."

Alex leaned out the window. "You're saying I'm not allowed to pass?"

"I'm saying, you're welcome to try, but we'll never find your body."

Alex let the rain trickle down his face and then ducked into the car. He reversed from the tollgate and headed back toward the city.

If a chill ran down his spine, he pretended not to feel it.

CHAPTER 19

Gray light woke Lilac in her soft chair, chosen last night in the hope of absorbing any warmth Arcadia had left behind. In a friendlier season, the morning would have shined warmer.

As she performed her morning routine, Lilac wondered if the streetlights would stay lit. This could be the worst rainy season in thousands of years. She changed her foot's bandage in a hurry. Vince's blood had healed some of the wound, leaving yesterday's glass a minor yet painful puncture. She was lucky not to have severed a tendon.

Beside the kitchen, Simone kept the bedroom door shut. She'd long ago stopped offering Lilac the bed for the night, and Lilac hadn't slept there in years. The living room seats were lumpy and uneven, but they were free of memories. The bedroom reminded her too much of Sara and Daphne, even in the dark.

The clothing-stuffed toy chest was easier to bear, especially now. The coralstone lay buried behind socks and stockings until Lilac's gentle fingers drew it out. Cool to touch, same as when she'd first grabbed it off Vince's floor.

She carried it to the window, where raindrops crawled lazily down the glass. Whatever stream of cause and effect stretched beyond even her power to calculate would reunite a mother and daughter, with the fate of the Holy Land between them.

Lilac crossed her legs, dropped to the floor, and placed the coralstone in her lap. "Mother?"

The coralstone gave off a faint heartbeat. "Lilac." Logoi sounded distant, her voice singing across a thousand miles.

"Are you starving in there?" Lilac asked.

"Starvation is not our nature," Logoi said. "But blood runs thin. Without more, only silence."

Lilac lowered her head, and tangles of hair wrapped around the coralstone. "Mother, thank you for saving Arcadia. I thought she was dead. I was grieving her when I found you."

The coralstone thrummed. "She is ripe for greatness. I have done what is in my power. Who is she to you?"

"Arcadia is—" Lilac remembered the hotel room, her nervous giggling at severe, ridiculous Arcadia. "She reminded me I want to live."

"This world has hurt you." The coralstone's heartbeat raced. "If we are to mend it, I must know its troubles."

"Old troubles," Lilac said. "The rain, the glories. The Holy Land is dying."

"Why don't the gods protect it?"

For Lilac's entire life in Logos, it had been Logoi who seemed to know everything, a bottomless well of wisdom and knowledge to drink or drown in. Strange to be informing Mother about anything, but Lilac told her how the gods had disappeared a decade back. News from abroad said they'd gone overseas, to other countries, before the ships quit coming, and the ones that left Aeg were never seen again. She told of the glories' boldness. She cried through telling how she'd lost Sara and Daphne four years ago.

The coralstone held quiet a long time, and Lilac worried Vince's blood had run out entirely until it quivered alive.

"I must be first to break this godlessness," Logoi whispered. "Free to mend this world."

"How?" Lilac turned the coralstone over. "How'd you get trapped in this thing?"

"It is unknown to me, done with some measure of power and delicacy. The sea is older than we."

"What if we break it?"

"While I am trapped inside?" The coralstone burned. "I'm uncertain you can. If you manage, perhaps I would be lost in the Between. Or it may be you've found the way to kill a god."

"No!" Lilac snapped.

The bedroom door creaked open, and Simone peered into the apartment through sleep-filled eyes. "Lilac?"

Lilac hid the coralstone beneath her hands. "Yes, Mom. I'm sorry I woke you."

"Who are you talking to?"

"Praying to Mother."

Simone recoiled into the bedroom with a sigh. The door shut behind her.

Silence lingered until the coralstone shuddered again. "Our intent has not changed from when last we spoke—I must feed. Blood powers miracles. I would have strength to break free from within."

"Sacrificial blood," Lilac said.

Arcadia had bled enough for a life-saving miracle, but not enough to free Logoi. Vince's addition was too small. The coralstone needed more than one person's blood. If only Lilac could give her own, but as Cecil had ranted last night, the gods and their mortal children could not pass power back and forth. No descendant blood for miracles, no miracles to heal descendants. They lived a half-mortal life.

The coralstone thrummed. "Where are my faithful?"

"I haven't seen anyone from your covenant since I came here." Lilac hung her head. "Vince had contacts. I shouldn't have killed him. If I'd known you'd saved Arcadia, maybe I wouldn't have done it. But then I wouldn't have found you." In this case, there could be no right without the wrong, and no wrong without right.

"All that led to this and all that surrounds it cannot be changed,"

Logoi said. "We have only now."

Lilac looked to the closet beside the toy chest, where a white dress hung to one end. She'd worn it to the twins' funeral four years ago, its skirts aswirl with embers as two empty funeral pyres commemorated two brief lives. Behind it hung the priestess robe, Vince's final gift.

Where to next? No more Vince meant no more ambushes, which meant no more blood. Lilac's carelessness had thrown Aeg into jeopardy, closer to salvation and yet too distant, while the rains fell, and the floodplains swelled, and Logoi was here and not here, in desperate need of blood if she was going to fix any of it.

The robe shifted in the growing light, its shadows smiling at Lilac. This was not the only dark robe in the city. There were plenty, with people in them.

Valmydion's old covenant. They still believed there could be a goddess in the Holy Land. And they were right. They weren't Logoi's faithful, but they were faithful nonetheless.

Lilac only needed to find them.

CHAPTER 20

The world hadn't felt right since Arcadia's awakening on the temple floor yesterday, her revolver missing, her two-way radio smashed to wires and fragments beside her. She, too, should have been smashed to bits, but a powerful whisper had worked wonders through her body. Transformation over twenty years ago had led to feeling at one with herself, but now she wobbled as if thrust into an unwieldy form. Dinner at Lilac's had grounded Arcadia somewhat, but now she again felt disconnected from everything she touched. Even her clothes constricted and rebelled, meant for someone else. Her belt sat uneven on her hips. Wrongness would be the flavor of the day, as if she'd entered a paper-thin world.

Except the world was the same. She was the one who'd changed.

Even with extraordinary luck, yesterday's fall should have meant she would never walk again. No one could know of these divine circumstances. People would expect divinity from her, but she was no miracle-giver, only the receiver, and her total count numbered two. Far more than most people got in their lives, but nothing that made her a conduit for godly will.

The woman in her mirror looked familiar, but she was not the same woman who'd stared at her reflection with questioning eyes yesterday morning. This woman—Arcadia hadn't seen her in years. Fewer lines and scrapes marred her face and scalp. Yesterday's cranial gash was gone. Her face was too young to have seen Shah, though Shah's memory still scarred these eyes.

A decade had melted away. Wouldn't Lilac be surprised?

"Why aren't *I* surprised?" Arcadia touched her cheeks, pressed her nose, and rubbed at the lightened creases around her eyes. "I should be more surprised."

Arcadia strapped the belt around her waist again. There, it felt right this time. Maybe the rest of her world would adjust, too. She slid a replacement two-way radio onto the belt; the revolver's holster hung empty, but that was fine. No more dogging homicide work. Only evacuation today. Fighting floods.

She left Radiance Hotel into a harder rain than yesterday. The bad weather soaked guilt into her skin. A day wasted. More people could have been evacuated by now if she hadn't chased police business.

Enough. Her unit was waiting. Time to put a captain's face on. Her agents needed to see a confident Arcadia, not a broken one.

When she reached Oldtown, deep in the neighborhood's real muck, she understood her presence yesterday wouldn't have mattered. The soil drank every raindrop until the ground couldn't take any more and then bled rainwater into the unpaved mud streets. Arcadia's boots sank the moment she stepped onto what had been a cobblestone avenue long ago. By the time she reached Oldtown's heart, the mud sucked at her boots and the water had already risen past her ankles.

Too much, too soon. The rain had only started yesterday morning. Even Oldtown shouldn't be flooding in a single day.

Rumbling thunder answered Arcadia's dismay. *The rain isn't letting up, Captain*, it seemed to say. *You want to come up here and do something about it?*

Arcadia surveyed the street. One flat rooftop had collapsed two days ago and taken the rest of the house with it, hopefully abandoned or evacuated already. To her left, Cassis and Bryce milled around the evac truck. Still only the handful for evacuation work, still one solitary truck. What was Thale thinking? Soon the water would rise too high for the truck's engine to run. What then?

"People are going to die by tonight," Arcadia whispered. "Why did we come here? We were supposed to save this city."

She was about to approach the house nearest to the truck, where Ilene was surely hard at work on a doomed mission, when her gaze drifted between neighboring houses. The water level here couldn't be solely the immediate rain's fault. It had been fed by a heavy flow of floodwater rushing from the next westward street.

Arcadia headed that way. Cassis noticed, as did Leander and Ilene when they emerged with a hunched elderly woman shuffling between them. Oldtown seemed full of the gray and forgotten. Her clothing's dampness suggested a leaky roof, and maybe her house was destined to collapse like her neighbor's, a fallen heap of stone in the storm.

Ilene left the refugee to Leander and hurried toward Arcadia. "Captain?"

"Has the flood barricade fallen?" Arcadia asked as she breached between neighboring houses. Floodwater foamed against her knees.

Ilene trudged behind her. "The barricade should be standing. You could see it from here before the rain set in."

"*Should* isn't good enough."

Arcadia found the next street flushed with floodwater. The buildings stood slightly farther apart here, giving wider alleys for water to gush from the west. Beyond this street stood the stone barricade, and then the floodplains where the land's elevation descended toward the beach, and then the sea. Though neither god nor man had ever set a dam to stymie the flow, the barricade should have been Valentine's last resort. As the levees held back the sea, the barricade held back the floodplain waters from hitting this smattering of houses and then Oldtown itself.

If the levees failed and the sea came to Valentine, the barricade would be nothing more than a drab decoration. An underwater one.

Ilene wiped rainwater off her scalp, but keeping her head dry without an umbrella looked as impossible as saving Oldtown.

Arcadia couldn't let herself think that way.

The barricade stood gray through the mist, a solid stretch of stone. No collapse, but then why so much flooding already? Arcadia pressed through the rushing water, onto spongy earth that squelched beneath her boots. Ilene might have kept back had Arcadia hesitated, but now both of them worked through the rising waters until the twelve-foot stone barricade loomed over them. The floodplains were drowning on the far side. The barricade was all that stood between that watery mess and Oldtown. Stone, mortar, clay.

Holes. Some looked to be caused by natural erosion, somehow stretched to unacceptable depth. Others were undoubtedly intentional.

"The glories were here," Arcadia said. She could see them in her head, scaly forms slipping serpent-like across the floodplains with unholy tools of the deep sea.

Each hole poured filthy water into Oldtown, keeping Arcadia from peering through. The largest could have swallowed her head. If the floodplains beyond had pooled this badly, then the beach had to be drowning too. Floodplains and sea would soon meet in rising tide, and then ocean waves would beat against the edges of Valentine.

Or was it all seawater anyway at this point? Arcadia couldn't tell.

"How can we be sure they left after they did this?" Ilene asked.

"We can't," Arcadia said, placing one palm against slick stone. "They might be listening on the other side."

Ilene stepped back. Arcadia meant to retreat too, but she kept her hand in place. The wall was stone, yes, and mortar and clay. And hope, weak as a sandcastle's side, as if the coming rain had doomed it by matter of natural law. The most soundly constructed sandcastle would crumble and vanish in the tide, as if it had never been more than debris and seafoam.

The glories had ignored the barricade's gate, where flood fighters kept a watchful eye. Bay Ridge stood too high in elevation for them to pester. They meant to turn Oldtown into an inland lake and then slip inside.

"We need the truck," Arcadia said.

Ilene glanced back to Oldtown proper. "The engine will never make it."

Arcadia leaned from the barricade. "This isn't the worst of it yet. Tonight's rain will make today's look like a pleasant shower. Between the glories and the downpour, if we don't try something, Oldtown's done."

And then the city—she kept that part to herself. Let the unit focus on a task they could manage. She led Ilene back to the others and gave new orders.

"But what about the evacuation?" Cassis asked.

Arcadia noted the team's uniforms were already soaked, and the day was only getting started. "At this rate, and without better resources, the evacuation plan is a death sentence. The flood fighters are out of time."

Leander sighed, and then he got to work, and the rest followed. Cassis and Bryce pulled today's refugees out of the truck, each cursing and stamping their feet in the mud. Leander sat behind the wheel, Athas cranked the engine, and the truck tires squealed through the mess. Arcadia led truck and agents toward the collapsed house, where they collected chunks of wood and stone.

"You mean to patch the entire wall?" Ilene asked, hands digging up a narrow beam.

"Prioritize the largest breaches," Arcadia said. She grasped a hunk of rock half her size and tossed it into the truck's bed. Its axles groaned.

Leander leaned out the driver's window. "The heavier the truck, the easier it'll get stuck."

Arcadia didn't know how to avoid that, but everything surging between her and this fucked-up world said to keep pushing, nothing else she could do.

Within a few minutes, the evacuation team-turned-impromptu barricade reconstruction team had filled the back of the truck. Bryce and Cassis finished first, the truck seeming full. Ilene ushered Athas to help drag a heavy wooden door and add it to the pile. There was no more room in the back.

Easy part done. Next came the impossible.

The truck lurched forward, inch by inch, the evac team following. Leander managed to urge the truck into the flow between buildings, toward the start of the spongy stretch beneath the barricade. Another few feet, and the truck slowed, crawled, and then wouldn't budge any farther.

Ilene grabbed the truck's back end and shoved her shoulder into it. The tires spun and cried, and the spray of mud and floodwater spattered flood fighter uniforms.

This was the work; thankless, hopeless.

"All of us," Arcadia said, loud over truck engine and rainfall. "Leander, on my word." She braced her shoulder against the back, Cassis and Bryce to her left, Ilene and Athas to her right, everyone's hands, shoulders, and muscles ready. "Push it, now!"

Leander slammed the gas. Tires screamed as the team shoved with all their might. The truck's back end, its bed full of stone and wood, surged into the air. Most of the team's arms were raised, hands still clutching the back fender, but they weren't supporting its weight. Cassis could only reach with her fingertips, and she quickly dropped her arms. Bryce's hands slipped next, slick from metal. Ilene and Athas noticed and let their arms drop too.

The truck's full weight rested on Arcadia's hands alone.

"How are you doing that?" Bryce backed away, their hands trembling. "What are you?"

Arcadia didn't know. The world hadn't felt right since yesterday, thin and wobbly and wrong. She had always been strong, but now mountains rose in her muscles. Part of her wanted to flinch back in horror like Bryce, but then the truck would crash atop the others. She held it above in firm hands, its back end dripping over her uniform.

"A miracle," Cassis coughed. "A god's champion." She dropped to her knees into the floodwater. Muddy foam battered her body, but she didn't seem to care. Her lips moved in prayer.

Champion? There hadn't been champions since the Holy War, when gods squeezed droplets of power into mortal empresses and kings. But there hadn't been miracles in the Holy Land for ten years until yesterday, when Arcadia's shattered body recovered from the temple floor.

And more than recovery now—power. Arcadia hefted the weight. The truck took effort, but she could lift it. She could push.

Ilene yanked Cassis up and pulled Bryce close again. "We're not done here."

Arcadia let the truck's fender sink to chest level, the tires just far enough out of the mud to move forward, and then she pushed. Leander hit the gas, and the truck rolled through spongy earth and floodwater. The rest of the evac team jogged at Arcadia's sides all the way to the barricade, and there they pulled stone and wood from the back of the truck, leaving the largest chunks to Arcadia. She shattered the heavy door across one knee, tearing her pants leg. She then stuffed chunks of wood into the barricade holes.

Ilene and the others followed with smaller pieces, jamming lumps of debris into the holes, but the water fought them too much to completely close the breaches. They needed to halt the water full-stop with something stronger than pieces of a home the rains had already broken.

The answer sat beside them.

Arcadia laid a hand on the driver's door. The truck ran well; it had helped them each day since the evacuation began, almost part of the team. She hated to destroy it.

But this was the work. She tore one door off the truck's frame and slammed it against the stone wall, stymying the water's flow. The passenger's side door crashed against the barricade, too. One axle made a decent brace to keep pieces pinned. A chunk of frame filled a larger hole. Even the tires could help. Every useful piece of truck tore apart in Arcadia's bare hands until only fragments remained.

"Now what?" Athas asked.

Ilene tore the two-way radio from her belt. "HQ, this is Agent Ilene Summers, flood fighters evac team. I need another truck at the lower Oldtown barricade, a couple blocks up from the gate. Make it two trucks. The gods have made their presence known, and Captain Myrn has been chosen as champion." To hear it stated on official channels sounded outlandish.

"Tell them to send sheet metal," Arcadia said. She didn't want Ilene to start preaching when their hands had more to do.

Ilene spoke to the radio again, but this time Arcadia struggled to hear her. Water rushed around her head, and the sound seemed crisper now, as if she noticed aural details she never had before. She tried to focus on the holes, not their noises.

Another chunk of frame might fill a smaller breach near the middle, but she would need a lot more material to seal the barricade. Even these strips of truck were only a stopgap. Once this storm subsided, another would follow, the rainy season sending beast after beast. Between storms, masons would have to take stone, mortar, and clay to the barricade, building a shield strong enough to guard Oldtown. Valentine needed a wall that would last the rainy season.

When Arcadia ran out of usable truck, she started back toward the city. If she could keep a flat chunk of the collapsed house intact, drag it to the edge of the floodplains, and prop it against the barricade, it might help better than sheet metal. The tough part was keeping the water from loosening the barricade's foundation beneath the earth. That it had remained standing this long might have been another miracle itself.

She glanced down at her hands. Powerful enough to haul walls down streets, rip a truck to pieces. Like her face, they looked younger than they had yesterday, but at no point in her past could they do what she'd done today, what she was still going to do. She wondered how long these miracles might last. What she might do next. Today, a truck. Tomorrow, maybe a mountain to block out the sea entirely.

She almost laughed. That a goddess could give a fraction of this power to a mortal seemed absurd.

The evac team joined her as floodwater went on rushing into Oldtown's streets. Cassis curled one finger over her chest, again and again, in Valmydion's clockwise spiral. Athas kept stone-faced, Leander looked bewildered, and Ilene beamed.

And they weren't alone. Beside the collapsed house stood somewhere between two and three dozen people, staring wide-eyed and bleary through the rainfall.

"Valmydion's returned?" a stiff figure asked. Their hand covered their spectacled eyes from the rain.

"Valmydion blesses us," a woman beside them said, dressed in an old coat and suspenders.

A narrow-limbed woman approached Arcadia. "What would the goddess of prosperity have us do?"

Murmurs worked through the crowd, an echo of praise and questions. What to do? How to earn these miracles? These people wanted to know. They needed guidance, the kind they hadn't felt in much too long. Far as they knew, their goddess had returned.

Arcadia wouldn't correct them yet. After the storm, she would tell the truth, but for now let them credit the miracle to whatever name they liked, and not the one whose whisper had trembled through Valmydion's temple, into Arcadia's body. The people of Valentine needed this familiar hope.

More of them came trudging down Oldtown's muddy streets, vague silhouettes adrift in the storm but growing clearer and more human the closer they reached. Umbrellas or not, dressed in dresses or suits or rags, drenched and cold, each came to witness the work of the gods for the first day in ten years.

Arcadia gave them work to witness. "Roll up your sleeves," she said. "We need every hand we can get."

NO GODS FOR DROWNING

CHAPTER 21

The rain had a harsh odor today. Alex had noticed it all morning, following him from his apartment to the Ace Investigations office where he met with Cecil, and then to the police headquarters. Through the lobby, hallway, even seated inside Thale's office with the windows shut tight, rain-stink haunted the air.

Alex tried to ignore it while Cecil paced the room. Thale seethed behind his desk, ready to kill the Ace Investigations contract and throw both detectives out.

"To make my point," Cecil said. "I want to know why you did it. Who's the murderer to you? Financier? Informant? Lover?"

Thale scribbled pencil marks into a notebook and then eyeballed Alex. "If you dragged him here to waste my time, keep in mind I don't have much to spare."

"Who stands to gain?" Alex asked. "That question's a detective's best friend, and right now you're one with the answer. Help us."

Cecil snapped his fingers to regain Thale's focus, a lightning rod for aggravation. "Everyone's on edge, you're not special. As to Alex's question, if you're behind it, why not let the murderer keep offing criminals? That's the Logos way. No need to catch the killer at all."

"I hired you, didn't I?" Thale asked.

Cecil smirked. "And then leave us flitting in the wind while the

Valentine Butcher slashes every sorry tosser in the city. The murderer's not the only one with a history of butchering and burning people."

Thale's pencil cracked in half.

Alex adjusted his fedora. "You and Arcadia have very different reactions when someone brings up Shah."

"What about you, Alexander?" Thale set the broken pencil halves hard on his desk. "You were there."

"I've made my peace with it," Alex said. "And without the shame. I followed orders. You gave them."

"You gave orders too, Captain," Thale snapped. "Don't rewrite your own memories."

Alex didn't have to. He'd been put in an awful conundrum between morality and duty. Arcadia had walked one road while he had walked the other.

Cecil strode toward the desk. "What's stopping you from doing the same here? You won't talk about it to the paper, won't give us access to your information. You're not too reluctant to have blood on your hands."

Thale's head looked like a melon ready to burst. Alex waved a hand, and Cecil slipped back.

"I don't think honestly you're colluding with the murderers," Alex said. "But I'm suspicious why you give a damn. Convince me, Rhoster, and let us see your files. We're looking for connections between names."

"You have suspects?" Thale rocked back in his seat. "And you had to parade in here, pointing fingers, to ask that?"

"You weren't exactly cooperative yesterday." Alex made to stand. "But if you like, we can square away the bill right now for our hours and leave the case to you."

Thale tore out a notebook page and scribbled at it with his half-pencil. "Give this to Terese in the lobby. She'll unlock the file room, but don't expect a fixed trail. This city's a nest of problems."

Cecil snatched the paper and folded it into one trench coat pocket. "Wasn't so hard, was it? I knew you were good for it."

Thale set down his half-pencil. "Are you finished, detectives?"

"He's done," Alex said. "Detective Gillion, I'll meet you in the file room."

"Don't come back here without a real reason," Thale said, flashing Cecil a grim glare. "In fact, don't come back here at all."

"You've been a champ, commander." Cecil threw him a half-hearted grin and stepped out of the office.

For the longest time, Alex hadn't known a life outside partnering with Cecil on contracts with the State House. To show up there was to have his hand shaken, to be offered a drink before he went to his office, because not one of those back-stabbing politicians knew whether they'd be next to need an investigator, or next to be investigated. Best to be friendly.

Now he sat in Thale's office for the third or fourth meeting this week—he'd lost track—like no time had passed since his police days, a tide sweeping in and out forever.

"Sorry," Alex said. "If I don't let him off his leash sometimes, he won't cooperate at all."

"Stone him, and you too." Thale scratched at his beard. "Shouldn't you take him for a walk to make sure he won't piss on someone else's day?"

"Having a partner and not a subordinate means learning to convince them they want to help instead of barking orders."

"You think that absolves you of responsibility?" Thale asked.

"I quit, didn't I?" Alex asked.

His resignation might have come six years ago, but it had been building since long before. He sometimes thought it might've begun the day his parents threw him at the barracks as if he'd been a carcass long overdue for his pyre.

He started to rise again. "Guess I've wasted enough of your time. I have to ask, what did the neighboring city-states say about the murderers? Logos, specifically."

Thale raised a thick eyebrow.

"You shut down the highway to Logos for a reason. Does high command know about that?" Alex gave an exaggerated shrug. "I'm fishing for reasons, but the tollhouse told me the road's out. I'm guessing there's a network stemming from Logoi's covenant where this Valentine Butcher comes from. Logos is the seed."

He expected Thale to say he was reaching, same as Cecil last night. Thale wouldn't be wrong, but Alex had to explore every possibility, especially since he couldn't call or visit Logos himself.

Instead, Thale lowered his eyes. "Check that no one's in the hall."

Alex got up and poked his head out the office doorway. "Empty."

"Close the door anyway, in case someone comes by, then have a seat." Thale reached under his desk and drew up a brown decanter and two shot glasses. "You like Mercai, right?"

"Slim choices for drink these days," Alex said, sitting again. "Aren't you on the job?"

"Not for the next few minutes." Thale poured two glasses and offered one to Alex. "Not for this conversation."

The rain-stink thickened. Alex took his glass and sipped the bitter liquid. "It's not bad."

"It won't get better." Thale drank deep, flashed Alex a beardy grin, and glanced out his rain-streaked window. "You can't see the coast from this deep in the city, temple's rooftop aside, but it lurks in my head. I see the way it was years ago, tamed by the gods. I see it now, the tide drowning the floodplains. Drowning Valentine."

Alex hadn't watched over the years. He'd seen the State House ruins, but no one could agree if an underground river had swelled and broken its foundation or if Valentine's government building had been a bad design from the start. Discussion seemed pointless. There were no survivors.

Thale splashed another shot of Mercai into his glass and downed it. "The glories don't need to eat us. Have you thought of that?"

"I don't think about glories much," Alex said. He finished his drink, but his stomach twisted against it. Where was Thale going with all this?

"They would've starved to extinction these past millennia if they could only eat humans." Thale set his glass down hard. "Why hunt *us*? Even when Aeg was an archipelago, we were land animals, more trouble than we were likely worth. I say the glories like to eat creatures with minds to know that death is coming. They kill fish quick, mercifully. Men, cetaceans, seals, they do it slow. Cruelty gives the glories a purpose. That's why the gods can disappear for ten years but we haven't been drowned entirely yet. The glories are enjoying our dread."

Alex had no answers to Thale's ponderings and didn't feel he was meant to. If the glories enjoyed dread, they had to be loving him right now.

Thale couldn't meet Alex's eyes. "Logos is gone," he said.

Alex blinked. "Gone? As in—"

"The city's part of the sea now." Thale waved a dismissive hand. "Scant ruins stand from the surface, tide splashing all around. The glories dug us out from underneath, sinking the city little by little these past few years. Someday, the ruins will vanish, and other continents' historians will misplace it, another lost city like Aedos. Could be they'll misplace every city of the Holy Land."

Alex's fingers squeezed his shot glass. Any thinner and it might have cracked like Cecil's last night. He didn't know what to say. How to even begin?

"Valentine's farther inland, but what does farther inland mean for Aeg?" Thale waved a fist in the air. "All these rivers are the lines of old islands. It's obvious we're practically dead already. We didn't come to this city to help out of the goodness of our hearts; we needed a new home. If Valentine falls, there's nowhere to go. Logos, drowned. Diomarch is walled off on the far side of Aeg. Fanatics rule Tychos, and rumors say they eat anyone they think has touched saltwater. Poetic justice, eating the eaters."

Alex thought of last night's phone call. The people of Tychos had lost their minds.

"Phobros doesn't answer calls, Korenbalas has turned warlike—I could go on, but why?" Thale asked. "The lines are down, the highways are crumbling, the railroad's gone. With the rainy season here, it'll be easy for the glories to flood every border, finish isolating the city-states once and for all, and turn the Holy Land into an archipelago again. Maybe they'll even drown the islands they've remade."

Alex placed his glass on Thale's desk. "Where's everyone else from Logos?"

"I led out who I could—who'd follow," Thale said. "Police, flood fighters, but most people wouldn't abandon Logoi's city. They didn't understand. When I sent officers back, the city had already collapsed, the temple half-pulled into the tide. They heard children crying for help, but were those really humans, or glories playing mimic? Only the gods could tell, but they won't. Instead, they left us here alone, and our people left Logos and the sounds of screaming children. We couldn't take the risk."

"You couldn't," Alex agreed, his voice flat.

"No one can know." Thale set the stopper into his decanter of Mercai, as if capping his point. "A panic would destroy what little we have left."

"Right, yes, I'll keep it to myself." Alex rubbed his hands together and wished he hadn't set his glass down. He couldn't pick it up now, no going back to holding it, like there was no going back to Logos. He hadn't planned on ever going back anyway, right? "I'm guessing my parents didn't come with you."

"No," Thale said, looking down again. "I'm sorry, Alexander."

Alex let him be sorry. Someone had to be, he guessed. "Has anyone considered Shadow Mountain?" he asked. "A day or so's trek northeast should cut past where the Holy Psychopomp Tree burned, and there are roads toward the hills."

"It's crossed my mind." Thale looked at his decanter, considering whether to open it again. "And then what? How long would anyone last in the cold? Nothing grows beneath Shadow Mountain. Down here, we at least have food until the glories drown the farmland."

Alex felt the Mercai coming up. It tasted rank in his throat. "Normally I wouldn't say this, but has anyone tried appealing to the gods? When the ships were making it to other continents, I mean. They had to guess what would happen to us."

"We sent a few officers abroad not long after Logoi left," Thale said. "And messengers to other gods. None returned—gods or officers—but one officer, she sent a message with one of the last trade ships to bother with Aeg. This was years ago."

"Only one message?" Alex asked.

"Our other officers must've liked the western lands enough to forget us. Or they couldn't find Logoi and were too ashamed to write home. Or they didn't make it. I don't know." Thale reached under his desk again, first to return his decanter, and then to open a latch and pull out an envelope. The thick paper was tattered and stained. "If *The Valentine Herald* ever got hold of these, there would be riots. I don't know why I haven't burned the damned things. I guess because it's proof that, in the gods' own perverse way, they still care."

Thale slipped a letter from the envelope and placed it aside. He then poured out a cluster of photographs. Alex lined them up. At first he couldn't tell what he was looking at, and then he could and looked away.

Thale didn't look at all. "They only sent us the negatives. We had to develop these and see the horror sharpen on our own. The message didn't say which god, goddess, or godex did this, but supposedly one officer asked why they left. No one else made his mistake."

Alex bundled the photographs together again, face down, and handed them back to Thale. "Did a god—was it a mouth that got him?"

"Teeth, claws, shapeshifting into some abomination, maybe a miracle to twist human form, who can be sure? I don't know how a god makes a man look like that." Thale slid the photos into the envelope with their letter. "And I don't want to know."

Alex wiped his mouth. "Gods."

"The message seems clear. The gods aren't coming back, and they don't want us to know why they left, on punishment of—that. Whether we follow or stay, it's no concern to them. And now it's too late to follow." Thale placed the envelope back inside his desk. "With all that entails."

Alex pressed up his fedora and rubbed his forehead. It was one thing to assume the worst, and another to know it.

"No word from another continent in years," Thale said. "My guess is they stopped sending ships to Aeg, likely because the ones we sent back never made it far from our shores. We're stuck on all sides. So, to answer your investigative curiosity, who stands to gain from the murderer? Not me, and not anyone who knows what I know. The murderer can't bring Logoi back; they'll only undermine a fragile peace. Chaos could be the end of Valentine, of Aeg, of all our lives."

Alex let Thale's declarations fall across him in time to the pounding rain.

Thale leaned over, his beard a dark blot in the room. "Am I still a suspect?" he asked.

"You never were," Alex said. "I was probing, trying to get some answers."

"You sure as shit got them." The rainy streaks down Thale's

window seemed to circle his frame. "I can't imagine it's improved your day."

Alex couldn't imagine it would improve his *life*. The weight was staggering, and somehow he'd been oblivious. Nearly everyone in the city was oblivious. And they had to stay that way? He could keep a secret, no problem, but this was beyond anything he'd expected. He felt tempted to ask Thale to whip out the Mercai decanter again, but that would be a Cecil way of handling problems. The investigation seemed smaller now, but still integral to the overall puzzle of Valentine. Everyone or no one, in the end.

Thale folded his hands on his desk. "So, you see, I'm like you. I'm not close to the gods. Still, I pray desperately there's a god who can save those of us left behind in the Holy Land. Are we done?"

That was one word for it. Alex thanked Thale for some reason and then stumbled into the hall. His breath felt heavy. He told himself if there was even a shred of regret, it was that he wouldn't get a chance to tell off his father again. Really though, in the face of the situation Thale had described, that would be petty.

Papa was gone. Mom, too. They would have no funeral pyre. Their souls had already moved on with the destruction of Logos.

Alex walked the halls until he found Terese, who sent him the same way she'd sent Cecil. First, Alex stopped in the restroom to check his face in the mirror for grim tidings. He looked tired, same as always. Cecil would suspect nothing unless he used his descendant gift.

They met in the hall outside a once-locked door. "Chewed you out, did he?" Cecil asked.

"In his way." Alex swallowed everything he wanted to share. Cecil couldn't keep a secret to save his skin. "Nothing new with Thale, story of my life. Could've used your bravado."

"How so? I'm not Cecil the Strongman, Descendant of Korenbal. What do you expect me to do?"

"Man the office, maybe," Alex said. "One of us should. Or hire a secretary, if we can scrounge enough money."

Cecil tipped his fedora. "Offer Lilac the job. She's smart, organized."

Alex laughed. "Possibly homicidal."

"Nobody's perfect," Cecil said, retreating toward the file room door. "Can't blame her for leaving that off her resume, but if it doesn't come up when we ask her biggest flaw, it's grounds for dismissal."

"Please, stop." Alex fought another laugh. "I want to stay in a bad mood today."

"Wish granted." Cecil opened the door.

The room was monstrous. Its boxes lined the walls and mounted each other to the ceiling, each filled with files. Alex opened the nearest lid out of curiosity, only for curiosity to smack him in the face.

"Hold on," he said. "We're supposed to see Thale's criminal files, pluck out the ones for the murder victims."

Cecil gestured to the room.

"All this?" Alex asked, aghast. "The old records were destroyed with the State House."

"You're looking at the past ten months," Cecil said. "Everything's a sin in a Logos officer's eyes. Small wonder they recognized most of the victims, even partly burned."

The file room had never known organization. Nothing alphabetized, not even sorted properly as cases and casework. Whenever there was a box's worth, the police had shoved that box into storage, to be forgotten. There was hardly room for the narrow, dust-coated table at the room's center where a miserable detective could open one box and begin poring over the folders inside.

Alex gazed over the room. "Can't you just wave your hand over it and find what we need?"

Cecil scowled. "Can you tell a person's face by a photo of their back? It don't work that way, never has. Maybe I'd get some semblance of the officer putting the folders together, or the history of the paper's maker, but the information is just somebody's writing. The pattern of letters never decides the past."

"I'm sorry," Alex said.

"Not like I walked in empty-handed." Cecil slid a folder from his coat and opened it over the table's center. "Had a busy morning before you let me poke Mr. Thale. Here, every paper having a scrap to do with Lilac Antonis. Not much, but we got the lease on her mother's place, employment records, birth certificates for her children."

Alex picked up the last. "Sara and Daphne. Father, Vince Barton. They must live with him. Seven years old, if my math's right. It'll be tough, but we'll want to question them."

"Can't really." Cecil pointed. "Death certificates for her children."

Alex scanned the pieces of paper. "The glories." The rain-stink followed through the file room doorway. This was going to be a long day.

Alex shed his trench coat and fedora, placed both on a box in the corner, and rolled up his shirtsleeves. He then pulled down one box and sifted through the files. Logos was gone, but he could save Valentine from falling into chaos. In a way, this made things simpler. Focus on this one problem, in this one place. No ties to Logos, no conspiracy, no interference. Two detectives and their hunt for a murderer—nothing more complex.

"You want coffee?" Cecil asked, unbuttoning his coat. "I'm thinking we'll need coffee."

That was the best idea Alex had heard all day.

CHAPTER 22

Lilac didn't need to ask many questions during her hotel shift to learn where a few members of Valmydion's covenant gathered. Less a secret, more a hive everyone knew to avoid, its bees spreading through the city each day to pollinate ears with begging or preaching.

They would then cluster at night in a building across from the Lee Village Library, between the eastern and northeastern neighborhoods of Valentine.

Lilac stripped out of uniform the moment she got home, her hand twitching to touch the coralstone. Logoi needed to know, and Lilac couldn't wait to tell her. They would still need to convince these few souls to help. Easier than the sacrifices Lilac had made the past couple days; covenants were used to bleeding for gods. She thought of lying to them, trying to play Logoi off as Valmydion, but all accounts said Valmydion was a merry goddess of song and laughter, Logoi's opposite in all respects.

Better to be honest. They sat in the same boat as Lilac and everyone else stuck in Valentine, stuck across Aeg. Nothing but a goddess would do, no matter which.

"Off to see Arcadia?" Simone asked. She had come silently from the bedroom, and Lilac said nothing as she dug through her closet and clutched the priestess robe. "I like her. She's clean and polite, has a good job. I'm glad you brought her over, even if it took you months. I was afraid you were seeing Cecil and hiding it from me."

Lilac guffawed. She loved Cecil, he was her friend, but together? Never.

"Well, I can't know with you." Simone paced the dark windows. "Arcadia's stable, exactly what you need."

Lilac knew that already, even if she hadn't admitted it to herself until yesterday's scare. Coming home to the dinner had been a welcome surprise, Detective Alexander Stathos aside. Her life was coming together again.

"Would you get out of your head?" Simone asked, half-annoyed, half-playful. "I know woolgathering's the only thing Logoi ever gave you, but you couldn't even make it through dinner without taking a moment."

Lilac didn't mean to shrug; it just happened. "I have a lot to think about. Ways to keep from getting caught."

Simone paused at her little window-side table. "I swear, you're a watering hole for chaos, sweetie. Isn't Arcadia enough?"

"It's not that simple," Lilac said.

"Does she mean a lot to you?" Simone asked.

More than Lilac had realized. "That's why she knew where we lived."

"Then build your relationship on stronger stuff than secrets."

Half-dressed in the priestess robe, Lilac slipped toward the toy chest, where her fingers teased the dormant coralstone. Gods couldn't die, but Vince's blood must have finally run out of power. Logoi might be listening to this argument, but unless Lilac found more sacrificial blood, the goddess of reason would never speak again. Never be free. If Lilac showed Simone the coralstone, would she understand? Or would she be angry?

"Have you liked killing them?" Simone asked.

Lilac froze. "Of course not."

"Stay home with me then. Or visit Arcadia at the hotel. I don't care, but don't do this anymore."

"I don't see another goddess stopping the glories." Lilac plucked up the coralstone. "We need Mother."

"Who's we?" Simone asked, her voice rising. "The city? Or just you?"

"All of us." Lilac slammed the toy chest shut. "Even you need her, Mom."

"I do not!" Simone clenched her fists and ground them against her hips. "I don't need bloodshed and sacrifice. That's temple life, and you know it, too. It was your life for forty damn years."

"Mom—"

Simone's dry eyes gleamed red and tired. "I went back to Logos. Did she tell you?"

Lilac clapped her mouth shut.

"I went looking when you were still little, but she wouldn't let me see you," Simone said. "I don't regret you turning up on my doorstep after she left, but that doorstep would've already been home if she hadn't stolen you. She stole you from me, understand? Not just when you were my newborn, but the forty years after. I lost a baby, and then a grown woman shows up on my doorstep. I loved that baby girl, like we both loved the twins, and I love you now, but we lost that time between. Logoi took that from us. She said you would age slower, that I wouldn't have known how to take care of you, but really she didn't want to share. We could've been a family, the three of us, and instead I spent decades wondering if I'd ever see you again."

Lilac hid the coralstone against the half-hanging robe and drifted closer. "What if we could have that now?"

Simone shook her head. "I don't want that *now*. I want you and me. I want the we that she stole, and the now that we have. I know those things can't co-exist, but I want all the good. She isn't good, Lilac. I think I hate her." She thought a moment and then nodded. "Yes, I hate her."

Lilac recoiled. "I don't think so."

Simone's lips parted around gritted teeth. "Well, you're going to make me find out, aren't you?"

Hard rain beat at the windows. Lilac had been too young to remember the night Logoi left her temple and entered another goddess's city. Not to discuss city relations, not to chat, but to have Logos priestesses steal an infant from her mortal mother's care. Had it been storming that night, too?

For Simone, right now, it was all the same.

Lilac approached and laid a hand on Simone's shoulder. "When Mother comes back, I'm not going off to live in that temple again. Valentine is home. You remember what I was like when I first showed up? I couldn't do anything without you. Now I have your long hair, and I cook and work and everything. Mother can't take me again."

"My long hair." Simone slid two weathered fingers down one of Lilac's auburn curls and then tucked it behind her ear. "I see godly red in yours. Had I stolen you from her, there'd be no forgiveness. Do you know why? Can you figure out why?"

Lilac couldn't imagine a mortal woman escaping a god.

But then, that was the answer, realized as Simone spoke it: "Because she's a goddess, bigger and better than anyone. Even you would never judge her." Her face crumpled, and a muffled sob died behind her hands.

"Mom," Lilac whispered, reaching again for Simone's shoulder.

Simone retreated to the bedroom. "You don't even know why you think the way you do. Back then, she stole even the idea of leaving from you. When you bring her here and she wants to take you again, there'll be nothing anyone can do to stop her." She slammed the bedroom door shut, and the apartment went quiet but for the rain.

Lilac finished changing into her covenant robe, clutched the coralstone with a godly prayer, and hurried outside to hail a cab for Lee Village.

Simone would understand once Logoi returned in all her grandiosity and many faces. Alex, Cecil, the police—everyone would understand. They would thank Lilac later for saving the city before the glories brought a great drowning like Valentine had never seen.

Chapter 23

"I've been wondering," Cecil said, hands deep in a box of files. With his fedora on the table, wild tawny locks strayed into his eyes. "You ever wish you had my gift?"

Alex let this sink in. "*Gift* is a strong word for a skill that doesn't work half the time."

"Humor me."

"I've thought about it." Alex sipped his coffee and placed the mug beside a couple of victims' folders. He hoped to keep perusing until they found all the files together, but these had emerged hours ago, with nothing since. "It would make detective work easier, but it wouldn't make me a better detective. You lean on your godly legacy too much when your own flesh-and-blood brain is more than capable."

"Some of it's harder, too." Cecil scowled at his mug. "So many sensations you'll never know. You must think this coffee's excellent."

"I don't crave difficult situations or lousy coffee." Alex aimed his finger across the table. "What would you rather be doing right now?"

Cecil stretched with a pleased groan. "Oh, Lukas Panago, from the Lelys Street Lounge."

"The singer in the top hat?" Alex asked.

"Him, yes, but when he takes it off, his hair's so fiery, I'd swear he was a descendant too if I hadn't felt what he was feeling. More ways than one." Cecil slouched over the table and chinned at Alex. "You?"

"Warm crabmeat on toast, my apartment fireplace, something to drink, and a good book." Alex tilted his head back as if resting into his easy chair. "One of those seafaring adventures, the heroes hopping from island to island across uncharted seas, skirting danger, living free."

"Pity we're here," Cecil said.

"If we aren't, and no one does the work, how likely do you think it is we'll ever get those pleasant evenings?" Alex returned to the files. "You were onto something with Thale. I'd bet he kept us at arm's length for exactly the reason you said. He doesn't know who the murderer is, but look at these files. To Thale, the Valentine Butcher's a gift from the gods. Good excuse to let blood run the Logos way, if only for the few days before he'd have to put his foot down and stop this. Don't expect any support."

Cecil chuckled. "Wouldn't dream of it."

"Here. Two victims, brothers, Obie and Andre Montey." Alex plucked a pair of folders from one box and slapped them onto the table. "I'm sure they have known associates besides each other." He took the Obie folder, Cecil took the Andre.

"Thieves, running with the Bay Passage gang on the shipping yards, back when that was a thing." Cecil turned a page. "Here's no surprise. That pawnbroker Hector Moros, questioned on some of the brothers' goods, but as always—"

"How was he supposed to know they were stolen?" Alex chuckled. "Every thief needs a fence." He put down Obie Montey's file and started sifting through boxes quicker than he could read names.

Cecil closed his folder. "Who you looking for?"

"Honest Hector. It'll be the thickest file. Hadn't thought to look before, but I want to see his known associates."

"Come off it, man. That list's got to have half the city. Shit, even I sold him an old ring four months back."

Alex dug through another three boxes before he found Honest Hector's gargantuan folder, bound in cord to keep paper chunks from flying free. "And this makes only ten months."

That would have been shortly after the State House. A pang struck Alex's chest. His home city was gone, his parents dead, all fresh information, yet here he was, missing his old job at the State House. Those were better days than he could remember from Logos. Arcadia was the only part of that past he remembered with any fondness, and she was here at least.

Cecil patted Hector's file. "Crack it open."

Alex spread the messy folder across the table and scanned papers for the names of the murdered criminals. Each victim blemished Honest Hector's file, sure as they must have blemished his pawnshop.

"Now what?" Cecil asked.

"You ask like you have somewhere to be," Alex said.

"We both could." Cecil's smirk tempted with lounge singers and good books.

Alex tapped the tabletop papers. "Someone's feeding these people to the Valentine Butcher. Maybe it's him." He returned to the files they'd found earlier and read aloud. "Marko Humphries, papers referencing Blackwater Filch, Dorian 'Flip' Niles, Hector Moros, Vince Barton, Eileen Vitali."

Cecil grabbed up another. "Arion Leos. I see Honest Hector— they actually wrote 'Honest Hector' here, if you can believe it— Vince Barton, Eileen Vitali."

Alex found another. "Eileen Vitali, associating with Hector Moros, Hector Thomas, Vince Barton, Angelina 'Sevens' Rickard."

Cecil raised an eyebrow. "Is Rickard on your dead list?"

Alex double-checked his notebook. "Fourth house, the first day."

"How about Vince Barton?" Cecil asked.

"Not on the dead list, but—" Alex pushed papers off Cecil's first folder and pulled up one of the birth certificates. "Sara Antonis. Mother, Lilac Antonis. Father, Vince Barton."

Cecil plucked up the other birth certificate. "Can't be a coincidence, can it?"

They dug around for Vince Barton's file and were lucky to find it in their second box. Like Hector's, it was thick with paper. No home address. Vince Barton seemed an eel through oil, always leaving others to take the blame.

"I think we've found what we need," Alex said.

They donned coats and hats again and put the file room back to some measure of decency, aside from the folders for Hector Moros, Vince Barton, and the murdered criminals. Cecil gathered those to carry outside. His little umbrella would have to shield them from the rain. Evening had come, darkening the sky and strengthening the storm.

"We'll drop these at the office, grab cuffs there in case we need them, and then hunt down Mr. Barton," Alex said.

"How'll we manage that?" Cecil asked.

"We ask his known associate, the one who's still alive." Alex raised an arm, and a passing cab sloshed water under its tires as it slowed at the curb. "Honest Hector."

Chapter 24

The cab parked a block from the pawnshop. Honest Hector made no secret where to find him; that was part of his business.

"Close as I get," the cab driver said, a smoke poking from the side of her mouth. "They say Oldtown's the worst part of the city, but I know better."

Alex tossed some money into the front and left the cab. Cecil opened his umbrella as he followed, only for a new hole to open and piddle rain onto his trench coat. Alex raised his umbrella between them, sharing cover and wetness. Water now ran down the paved streets, into the gutters, but soon they would choke it back up.

"Feels like the sky's out to get us," Cecil said.

"It certainly could be." Alex led toward the shop.

A three-person line formed inside. There were always people here, trading goods, rumors, or gossip, except on holidays. Alex wondered when Hector slept.

Cecil cleared his throat and raised his voice. "Really, you think that Logos commander will find what he's looking for *here*?" Alex glanced at him, as did the two men in line ahead. "Seems to me that eight officers is a little much to send. You'd think he'd let us handle it."

Both men scuttled out the door. The pale woman at the front, another West Amberdan castaway, asked Hector to hurry it up like a good lad.

Alex bit back a smirk. "Short on time?"

Cecil rubbed his gut. "Butterflies."

"Over what?" Alex asked. "Lilac?"

"Sometimes we pin someone in our heads." Cecil chinned at the counter. "Take Hector, for instance. Got his hands in pastries across the city, but I hear he's a good boy to his mother."

Alex supposed even Hector had his private side. Perhaps stocked behind the counter.

"Never can tell who someone really is. Even a friend." Cecil toyed with his injured umbrella. "Thought I saw right through Lilac, some hotel staffer trying to keep a roof over her and Ma's head, sweet girl, disinterested, sharp, but going nowhere. Never knew she had kids, or they'd died. What else might she be hiding?"

Alex would find out. He watched the West Amberdan woman leave the counter, and then he took her place.

Hector furrowed his brow. "Odd. You look familiar, but the name's slipping my tongue."

"Detective Alexander Stathos."

"Ah-hah, you worked for the State House," Hector said, smirking. "Bought a few rings over you heartbreakers."

"I'm buying today, not selling." Alex reached into his trench coat, fingered past Arcadia's map, and unfolded a slightly damp black-and-white photo of a pale man with pale hair. "Recognize him?"

Hector leaned over the counter, the tip of his beard near to scratching the paper. "Vince Barton. He's here all the time, saw him yesterday. You want to know what he was doing?"

"More where he lives." Alex pressed a twenty coin on the countertop. "We'll find out what he's doing ourselves."

"Twenty?" Hector balked. "For a man's private domicile?"

Cecil nudged his head over Alex's shoulder and eyed the coin.

"Your commander paying expenses or just hours?" he asked.

"Hear that?" Alex cocked his temple against Cecil's, becoming a man with two heads. "We work for the Logos police commander."

"Old Rhoster, huh?" Hector grinned. "Met him a few times. Admire his beard."

"I wouldn't mind if you choke on this." Cecil reached past Alex and slammed another twenty coin on the counter. "That ideal, lad? Satisfied yet?"

"Every day." Hector pulled a paper from under the counter and scribbled directions. "That's his house. Pretty close, as you can see. And I mean that, *his* house. Anything you find there, well, how am I supposed to know if it's stolen?"

Alex stormed out of the pawnshop, his hands shaking.

Cecil reached his side as they turned a corner. "We didn't thank Hector. Think he'll bill us for that?"

"This could get ugly," Alex said. His trench coat flapped at his sides, and he thought of reaching under to clutch his pistol. "Be ready."

Two women, one maybe twenty, the other maybe fifty, rushed around the corner. The younger woman slammed a broad shoulder into Cecil's, and both went stumbling.

Cecil's fedora fell into his free hand. "Where's the flood, love?" he asked.

"Oldtown," the broad woman said. "But not for long. We're off to see the miracle."

Cecil laughed, seating the hat tighter onto his head. "Miracle?"

"Someone's been living in a box all day," the older woman said. She tugged her friend's arm. "Come on, it's still a few blocks from here."

They scurried up the street and then around a westward corner, into an alley. Alex watched them—what miracle?—and then turned to Cecil. He looked less like the woman had knocked him aside, more like she'd slapped his face. Alex should have asked what was wrong, but he couldn't coddle Cecil's sensitivity right now. They had work to do.

Hector was right; the house was close. Alex's first knock pressed the door slightly ajar.

"Enough with the bloody suspense." Cecil reached past Alex and shoved the door wide open. "Ace Investigations. Anybody home?"

Alex saw nothing through the dark and rain, but the stink belched across his face. He had to duck back and suck in the rain's damp scent before he could dip his head through Vince Barton's doorway. This time when he pawed under his coat, he drew out his brass-colored pistol.

"I'll snag the light switch," Cecil said, reaching around the doorframe. "Don't let nobody stab me, got it?"

Alex aimed into the darkness as Cecil's hand found the switch. He wouldn't let anyone cross them, not here, not now.

Lightning flashed across the sky and lit through Vince's windows, giving a glimpse of the macabre scene the moment before Cecil flipped the switch. Thunder rumbled as a nearby standing lamp cast dim light through the house's innards. Fresh shadows clawed finger-like at furniture creases, crate stacks, and every crevice and contour of the mutilated body on the floor.

Alex led Cecil inside and shut the door behind them. A passerby who poked their head in might get the wrong idea otherwise.

"Vince Barton," Cecil whispered. "How long, you think?"

"Hector says he saw him yesterday," Alex said. "No more than a day."

"A wet, noxious day." Cecil took cautious steps closer.

Alex stalked the room's edges. No one in the bathroom, no one in the spacious bedroom, and there didn't seem to be any other rooms in the house. He tucked his pistol back into its holster beneath his coat as thunder shook the walls.

Vince Barton's blood painted the floor in brown streaks from his kettle-mounted stove to the stacks of crates likely holding stolen goods. A generous spray led from door to body, where a rich puddle pooled underneath. The far wall boasted the familiar smear of a vicious nine-pointed star. Bare footprints marked the blood, reminiscent of the unburned Bay Ridge crime scene. A circle interrupted the puddle near the door, as if something had been plucked up after the murder. Reading the scene became a challenge when the murderer liked to play in the blood.

"No burning." Alex patted Cecil's sleeve. "Can you get anything?"

"Stabbed. Didn't expect it, but he accepted it." Cecil staggered toward the nine-pointed smear. His arms hung boneless and doll-like at his sides. "So much desperation here. It hangs in the air, like that fetid stench."

Alex eyed the floor for a candle but saw none. "Why didn't she burn this one?"

"Too personal?" Cecil trembled. "In a hurry?"

"But you believe it's her," Alex said. "I mean, it can't be Vince Barton, unless he's extraordinarily talented."

Cecil backed away from Logoi's star. His frantic eyes darted left and right as if searching for something on the floor. "Think it worked this time?"

Alex looked at the smear. "Contacting Logoi? I can't imagine how."

Cecil approached the circle in the blood. "There's divinity."

Alex looked down, where an eye of wooden floor stared through. "I thought you couldn't sense it."

"With descendants, it's like a hole in the world. An absence. With gods, that hole lets in the sunshine. That's the sensation here. Faint, strangled, but I feel it. Can't explain." Cecil traced a finger along the floorboards, as if trailing the path of a creature long gone. "This desperation, the blood. Who knows? All my expertise in gods is that sometimes they impregnate mortals, and sometimes you get gods, and other times you get people like me."

Alex couldn't connect the threads of Cecil's nervousness and his awe. He wouldn't fabricate a god's presence. Did that mean the murderer was successful? Doubtful, but not impossible, right? Something was off here, too much for Alex to believe Lilac had succeeded.

"I've seen enough," Alex said, striding toward the front door. "I think Lilac's our murderer. If she's called the divine, they'll have to be the one to absolve her. Until then, we still have a contract to catch the Valentine Butcher. That all sunshiny with you?"

Cecil followed him into the rain and stared dreamily at the black sky. "Don't ask me. I barely know what I'm doing."

Alex leaned close, and his dripping fedora tapped brims with Cecil's. "Are you with me or not?"

"I am." Cecil glanced back at the house. "She did it. I can't believe she did it, but she—yes." He flashed Alex a grim look. "My friend killed the father of her children."

Alex squeezed Cecil's shoulder. He didn't know what to say—what could anyone say? When he let go, he started up the street. Pooling rainwater sloshed under his boots and beat at the sidewalk.

"Where now?" Cecil asked, chasing him.

"Honest Hector's." Alex hurried.

The pawnshop's lit windows and doorway hung thick with desperation. Alex thought of the women he and Cecil had passed on the way to Vince's. They'd mentioned a miracle. Lilac's doing, or something else?

This would be over soon. The murderer's name, face, motive—Alex knew everything. Lilac was as good as caught. Damn did he wish he'd been wrong.

Hector beamed as Alex approached the counter. "Back again, detective? Let me guess—whatever you wanted Vince for, he pointed the finger back at me. Am I close?"

"Vince isn't pointing fingers at anyone," Alex said. "He's dead."

Hector's face fell. "That can't be. I saw him yesterday."

"You asked if we wanted to know what Vince was doing here yesterday."

Hector gave a dazed nod. "Trying to pawn a worthless stone, buy a—"

"Was he with anyone?" Alex asked.

"He was alone," Hector said. "Only—"

Alex fished notebook and pencil from his trench coat. "Only?"

"He bought a black robe, like the covenants wear." Hector cast a big hand down his chest as if such a robe would appear. "A priestess sold it to me a little ways back."

Alex's pencil paused. Cecil had found divinity in Vince's house, but did that necessitate a goddess? If Lilac had failed, she might have given up murdering people like Vince and instead turned to hunting those most associated with holiness.

"Any repeat customers of the covenants?" Alex asked.

"No names." Hector thought a moment. "They gather in odd places, figure out what trash they'll try selling me. Sometimes they go to Valmydion's temple, other times that ugly pile across from Lee Village Library. Beckoning Tower, it was called?" He was trying to get Alex and Cecil out of his hair.

But these were places Alex needed to know. He finished his notes and blustered out the door, where the storm greeted him with harsh wind. If a goddess had returned to the Holy Land, she would be fighting the downpour, the sea itself. The tone of the night should have shifted had Lilac had called divinity into Valentine, yet everything felt the same.

Cecil caught Alex's arm. "I can check the temple, you head to Lee Village?"

"You want to split up?" Alex asked, turning.

"Want, no, but we've work, don't we?" Cecil asked. "And these holy robes might be in danger?"

Alex let this sink in. Whatever traces Cecil had found, there was no goddess here, no true divinity. Lilac wasn't finished yet. She would kill again.

"You're right," Alex said. "Check the temple, I'll check Lee Village. If you don't see her there, head my way. I'll do the same."

"Count on it." Cecil reached one hand to Alex's face, hugged him close, and then kissed his cheek.

Alex hardly felt the touch through the rain, only pressure against his skin and a warmth in his chest.

A whisper worked into his ear. "It'll be better soon, my friend. I promise." Cecil slipped back and chuckled. "Nerves are a bit fluttery."

"I'm not going to die," Alex said.

"You'd better mean it." Cecil clapped Alex's shoulder. "We got this."

Alex gave a wan smile. He really hoped so.

The rain thickened as they split from the pawnshop, Cecil heading north, Alex heading northeast. He would hail the first cab he spotted. Angry fire ripped through his core, fuel that kept him pounding across wet asphalt, past waterlogged clusters of people.

He'd stood in Lilac's home. He'd eaten her food, met her mother, worried over Arcadia beside her. The whole time, Lilac had this blood on her hands. How long had she spent washing them, acting like she'd done nothing wrong so long as her cutting and killing came in the name of the gods? She'd played the fool in front of his face and probably laughed after he left.

She had no idea what she was playing with—the fate of Valentine. No Logos to return to, no temple, no Logoi. This was a different city, and they needed to care for it. Alex had to catch her and put an end to this, even if she fooled a holy covenant into trusting her, helping her.

Even if she believed she had a goddess on her side.

CHAPTER 25

Lee Village Library faced a cluster of old dark houses, packed and piled atop each other in a twisting wayward structure. Beckoning Tower, Lilac thought it was called. Lightning flashed its gray stone alive, but it quickly faded to join the evening's black sky. A narrow door broke up the bottom of the architectural monstrosity.

Lilac paid her cabbie and stumbled toward the door. Her priestess guise meant no boots, no umbrella, only her robe and faith. The coralstone would remain a secret until she was ready. She reached out and knocked as thunder rolled through the sky.

The door slid open, and an elderly priest beamed out at her, his whiskers glowing from inner firelight. "Come in, sister," he said. "Out of the rain, quickly."

Lilac thanked him and ducked inside. A narrow foyer led past water-stained walls and rotting furniture into a wide room, where wooden beams braced the vaulted ceiling. Smoke slithered from a dancing fire up a great shaft that climbed the tower. Its flames cast curious shadows across more than a dozen faces, scarcely a fraction of Valmydion's old covenant. Black robes covered their bodies, and hoods guarded their hair against the ceiling's dripping holes.

A gentle-eyed young priestess waved Lilac over. "Get warm, please."

Lilac sat beside her, and the fire's heat baked moisture from her clothes, skin, and hair. She watched the elderly priest who'd answered the door amble over, and then she studied the others. What to say? These people knew each other, but Lilac was a stranger. Best she tread carefully.

"I haven't been to this side of Valentine in years," Lilac said. "What is this place?"

"You don't know?" the elderly priest asked. He chinned his beard at a nearby priestess. "Tell her, Kosmi."

Kosmi averted her eyes from Lilac and waved a thoughtless hand at the ceiling. "A year after Valmydion left us, government men from the State House thought they could channel the gods with crude shapes, particular geometry, like the gods would care about their symbols formed in architecture."

"Imaginary solutions," said a middle-aged priestess across the fire. A scar ran up her cheek across an empty socket; her remaining eye glared at Lilac. "When they died in the State House wreck, we took it."

Kosmi lowered her gaze. "We've all done things to cope with what's become of us."

"Indeed," the middle-aged priestess said. "Trying to call the gods is better than lying to ourselves they're already here. Those desperate hearts flocking to the temple tonight, to Oldtown, they'll believe anything."

"We knew Valmydion was gone before anyone else," Kosmi said. "We'd know if she was back, too. There's no wild grain scent in the air."

"The crowds eat what they crave—a bowl of lies." The middle-aged priestess scratched her scar. "The gods are distant, but not everyone can live with that."

Lilac nodded as if she knew what they were talking about. She hadn't kept up with city news today; she had bigger fish on her plate. Her fingers prodded the pocketed coralstone. The gods were closer than these holy people knew, and yet so far. How could Lilac offer hope to these strangers? On tip-toe, maybe crawling on her belly. They were likely curious already why they had never met her before.

"Have any of you tried calling the gods?" Lilac asked.

"We've prayed," Kosmi said, and gestured at the old priest. "Nemo leads us, usually."

"Every day," Nemo said. Others nodded with him.

"We've all done things," Kosmi said. "Wild ideas. Bloodshed in the temple, in chalices, in urns." Kosmi gestured to the one-eyed priestess. "Meridia had her plan."

"You mean on Holy Tree Day?" Meridia asked. "It would've shamed us as Valmydion's covenant to offer blood to another god, like witches, so we chose something beyond gods. No one really knows how desperate you'll get until things turn nightmarish."

Nemo chortled. "People say any god would be better than no god. Imagine Tychron here, unchecked by his cousins? No one wants that."

Except the people in Tychos, but Lilac swallowed the comment. The people of every city-state wanted the gods back, and some would burn their cars, homes, and humanity in sacrifice to make it so. They would do the impossible and seek out lost Aedos if it meant the goddess Aeda would return, migrate to Tychos if Tychron would come back, turn nomads for Lyvien—any god to save them from the glories.

Still, Lilac couldn't imagine what Meridia might have planned to do on Holy Tree Day.

Meridia sat straight, fire glowing across her scar, and faced Lilac as if sensing her confusion. "We didn't go through with this, understand? We planned, but we couldn't make the journey. Not even for the Dawn Gods."

Lilac leaned closer to the fire, and understanding began to bake her skin.

"We meant to offer ourselves on the Grave of the Holy Tree,"

Kosmi said.

Nemo cut in quickly. "Might have mattered, understand? The Holy Psychopomp Tree used to be a Dawn God."

Lilac didn't understand that logic. If Logoi had cut off one of her nine heads, the severed head would not be Logoi, only a fragment. A body, or pieces of it, did not make a soul.

Meridia piped up. "The Holy Tree was only the shell of a body. The Dawn God Sceptomos left it behind while his soul headed to the mysterious heavens. That's why Gentle Theo could become the Holy Tree's soul. A living thing without a soul violates the laws of nature, after all, and so the Holy Tree merged with him and carried on." She tutted as if this were the end of the story.

Lilac knew better. It was one of her earliest lessons in Logoi's temple. The priestesses had explained that when the Dawn Gods finished their work, six of them ascended in flesh while the last, Sceptomos, ascended in soul, leaving his body behind to become the Holy Psychopomp Tree. It was to be the arbiter of all souls crossing the Between from one life to another, a balance brought to reincarnation. Lilac had hated the idea, even as a child.

She was not sad when the lesson ended with a madwoman, Noema the Sick, burning the Holy Psychopomp Tree to the ground. She had kept her relief to herself, unsure how Mother would react.

The memory reminded Lilac that soon Logoi would spread her nine heads and tremendous body within Valmydion's temple and take up the cause of Aeg. They would be mother and daughter again, teacher and student.

Lilac clutched the coralstone and dug her way up from her thoughts. The covenant was arguing.

"Keep in mind, Noema's burning the Holy Tree might have been part of the Dawn Gods' intent," Kosmi said, her tone softening. Someone scoffed across the fire.

"She didn't burn it," Meridia said, growing haughty. "When Noema the Sick carried hatred and injustice in her heart to the foot of the Dawn Gods' final gift, set within its roots, the Holy Tree immolated itself, for it saw mankind was ungrateful."

She had recited directly from scripture, each word eating ice into Lilac's nerves. Had the last two days' sacrifices felt this same chill when she'd recited scripture to them?

Nemo shrugged. "I've my doubts. Something happened inside the Holy Psychopomp Tree, I say." His face turned grim. "Something unwritten in the Verses of Aeg."

Fire filled Meridia's eye. "You can't go adding more Verses of Aeg on wild assumptions, Nemo."

Kosmi shook her head and whispered, "This is why the gods left us. Our sacrilege."

Lilac cleared her throat, and every eye turned to her. She didn't want the attention, but she needed it. Kosmi had a point—there wasn't time for the covenant to bicker the scripture's fine print. The rainy season was already here.

"Why did you think bleeding on the Holy Tree's grave would help summon a god?" Lilac asked.

"Not a god," Meridia said. "A *Dawn* God."

Lilac bit the insides of her cheeks not to laugh. No one knew for certain what had prompted the Dawn Gods to descend five thousand years ago, but she doubted mortals alone could bring them back.

"Not Sceptomos, of course," Meridia went on. "But our Valmydion's forebearer, Lyradosia? Or Milante, or Exalis? Someone might have helped, and not only to protect us from glories. They would have driven the glories out, like in the dawn days." She lowered her head, heavy beneath ridiculous notions. "A nonsense plan, you think? You're right. Greater gifts need greater allure. Whatever special circumstances first drew Exalis and the other Dawn Gods to descend, whatever made Gentle Theo special enough for the Holy Tree, we don't have it."

"Not nonsense," Lilac said, touching Kosmi's arm since she

couldn't reach Meridia. "Overambitious."

Kosmi's robe flaked fibers and grime, a frail sleeve with frailer flesh beneath. These people were withering. Lilac couldn't help feeling sorry for them, and for herself, too. For ten years, she'd blamed Logoi's absence on Logoi while these people blamed Valmydion's absence on themselves. Guilt and shame would eat them alive.

Kosmi stood from Lilac's side. "Was it really overambitious? For our means and stature, maybe, but not our experience. I've touched Valmydion's hands and feet—touched divinity! Now I beg in a South Temple District pawnshop. The temple's falling apart, and the city's next."

Nemo raised placating hands. "Kosmi, please."

But Kosmi paced the room, fingers fraying her tangled hair and parting her robe. "It's shameful to have peaked so young." Black fabric shed from her body. She didn't wear undergarments like Lilac, maybe none of them did. Shadows danced over Kosmi's nakedness. "Look at me now, priestess to the goddess of prosperity, now priestess to Honest Hector's. I'll shed blood for a better deal, but you'll need a god to convert the currency."

Lilac wanted to hold her. This lost despair echoed the emptying temple in Logos years ago when Lilac had watched Logoi's priestesses abandon her. Nearly a year passed before she could beggar enough money to ride the now-ruined railroad north to Valentine and find Simone.

But no matter its familiarity, this pain could end.

Kosmi crumpled to the floor and gathered her robe against her chest. "Some days, I almost wish it'd never happened, so I might still have big things ahead. But my best days are behind me. There's only drowning ahead, and no gods to help us."

Lilac crept closer. "That isn't true."

"A priestess at seventeen," Kosmi said, raspy. "And an ex-priestess, what is that? Can you eat it? The job asks lifelong service, and then suddenly we're homeless, jobless, our pockets empty. I was still trying to figure things out by the time my son was born, and I'd already had years to accept Valmydion wasn't coming back." She looked into Lilac's eyes. "My son's gone now. I didn't know how to survive the street. Valmydion, she provided everything for us. I never thought she would abandon me, but the gods give and they take, and I didn't know how to keep my boy alive."

Lilac drew Kosmi's head to breast and kissed her hair. Memories of Sara and Daphne erupted inside. Smaller heads, bigger kisses.

"Seventeen." Kosmi trembled in Lilac's arms. "I swore my life to her at seventeen. What good is that? A sacrifice is only worthwhile if something precious is lost. The city's lousy with people like me. Priestesses hang around newsstands for loose change, or they sell their robes and get jobs as waitstaff, cleaners, lounge singers, flood fighters, anything but this because there's no need for us anymore. The covenant is nothing without the gods."

Lilac looked around the room. The firelit faces had turned stony, and a new tension dug through her muscles and bones. Her legs twitched to stand, run, but she didn't know why. Something had shifted in the air.

"Or maybe the purpose lies with *your* goddess," Kosmi said. "You're not Valmydion's priestess."

Two young men in black robes had slipped between Lilac and the door. Her legs twitched again, but she didn't make to stand, not yet. She shut her eyes and sifted through the patterns, looking for an escape if she needed it, and a way to convince these people to help her, too.

"I don't know who you are, but you lied to us, and that turns my gut," Kosmi said. "Meridia, what do you think?"

"With her boldness, stomping in uninvited?" Meridia scoffed. "She came with the Logos police, another wayward looking to take this city."

"I'm not with them," Lilac said, eyes still shut.

"You're a priestess, aren't you?" Meridia asked. "You want to know if we ever tried to bring another god back. You think we're the ones cutting people apart, putting Logoi's bloody sign on the city walls. A snitch hiding her nine-pointed badge under a black robe. Might even be some other god's child."

Lilac had counted more than a dozen figures here. She couldn't fight them all, even with her dagger. Meridia had to have known a descendant before, maybe Valmydion's daughter who had vanished the same time as Valmydion herself. No one ever took the descendants into account, that had been Lilac's secret to success, but this covenant was different. Maybe they hadn't known right away and needed her to sit here until they figured her out, but since her arrival they'd realized something wasn't right.

Kosmi stood tall and fully clothed. A short knife gleamed in her hand, and its blade echoed around the fire, Valmydion's covenant wielding knife after knife.

"We let you in," Kosmi said. "We shared our shame, but you're not one of us. Tell us what you came here for, and it had better be a damn good reason. Don't make us bring you low."

CHAPTER 26

Alex watched Merchant Field's neon lights fade into the golden glow of Lee Village through a cab window. How long would these lights stay lit? They might die as he reached Lilac. What dark trap was he walking into?

"Lee Village Library," the cab driver said, parking where Alex had told her to go. "They look closed to me, friend."

"I'm sure they get that a lot." Alex paid her and stepped out of the cab.

Water sloshed as he crossed the street, and he realized too late he'd left his umbrella in the back seat. Nothing he could do now but press on.

He had never entered Beckoning Tower, let alone climbed to its peak, and imagined it offered a similar vantage as the temple's roof. A climber at the top might see the lights of Tychos distant in the night, and during the day might look northward to the far off windy hills beneath Shadow Mountain. Somewhere in between lay the Grave of the Holy Tree.

And yet, looking to Beckoning Tower, Alex wouldn't have thought there could be a more broken place in the world if he didn't already know the truth about Logos. That truth might have stretched to other city-states by now.

It could happen here.

The tower door awaited. Rainwater soaked Alex's hair, clothes, his poor notebook, but not his pistol, secure beneath his trench coat. His fingers grasped the gun; his free hand raised into a fist, about to knock.

Gulls cried and he couldn't help remembering that had been an ill omen in an adventure book he'd read as a child. Now he wondered if the author had slipped some ancient superstition into the pages. The flock sounded like they were heading out of the city. Alex waited for their cries to fade beneath the hushing rainfall and then rammed his fist against the door. Once, twice.

"I know how it sounds, but it's true," Lilac said, at the end of a tiring story. "Rub your finger on the surface, a couple drops of blood. It'll explain everything."

Kosmi and the rest had let Lilac reach into her robe and draw out the coralstone. Still cold, it no longer felt like the mother who'd drank Arcadia's blood and healed her, who'd whispered about saving Aeg.

Meridia and the rest watched in silence as Kosmi placed a tentative fingertip on the porous coralstone. Her gaze clung to Lilac's as she rubbed back and forth, her blade pointed at Lilac.

The change stirred in Lilac's hand even before she saw blood smear across coral. The stone warmed against her palm, a godly sun rising deep inside from the Between where some blasphemous asshole had trapped the goddess of reason.

Kosmi's shoulders hunched. "Goddess, I'm sorry I doubted. Goddess, forgive me."

Meridia launched to her feet. "What is it? What happened?" Others stirred around her.

"Logoi," Kosmi said. She trembled to the floor, but a smile crossed her face. "The goddess Logoi says she's trapped inside. That Valmydion might be trapped somewhere else. She didn't abandon us!"

Realization wormed through the hopeless covenant. Lilac

knew the feeling—their suffering these past ten years had not been an edict by unquestionable gods. They and everyone across Aeg had been wronged. Someone had stolen their goddess from them.

"We need to free her," Lilac said. "She'll save us from the glories. Save Valentine."

"Free her how?" Meridia asked.

"The same way gods make any miracle."

A bald priest scoffed behind the others. "Give her blood? We aren't covenant-betraying witches; we've been Valmydion's faithful for years. Why don't *you* free her?"

Lilac clutched the coralstone between her hands and stood. Time to show her cards. "I can't do it myself. Descendant blood has divinity, it's no good. I need your help to free Mother."

Meridia's eye flickered between coralstone and Lilac. "Logoi has no child."

"Ask her yourself." Lilac held out the coralstone.

One by one, Meridia, Nemo, and the rest touched the coralstone, and Logoi spoke of Lilac's heritage and her godliness again and again. Twin priestesses appeared last, one of them crying, the other as hard-faced as Meridia, and yet she cried too by the end.

"I am Logoi, Goddess of Reason. Lilac is my perfect jewel. Revere her as any mortal would revere me, for I have not abandoned you. Set me free so I may save this holiest of lands."

Meridia's eye glistened. "I thought Logoi crossed the sea."

"We thought all the gods had," Lilac said. "But Logoi's trapped, and there could be others. We can find them later, but if we don't set her free now—well, you can hear it."

The covenant listened to the rain. Seagulls soared past, their calls echoing down the tower's central shaft.

Meridia scratched her scar. "A bad omen."

A fist banged on the front door. Every face turned its way and then back to Lilac. The last time she'd faced a bad omen, she'd lost her children. Would she lose her mother this time? Again?

"Is there a safe place for the ritual?" Lilac asked. "A rite to free the goddess."

Nemo huffed. "I'm sure it's another straggler."

The front door cracked open beneath a hard boot. Lilac couldn't see who stood in the doorway, but no priest wore boots. Someone else had come to Beckoning Tower. Likely for her.

Meridia led past the fire, toward the back of the open room. "Up to the second floor. Protect the descendant."

Kosmi grasped Lilac's arm and tugged her into darkness. "Protect Logoi's child!" she echoed.

The rest of the covenant formed a semi-circle and retreated as a herd at Lilac's back. An unlit doorway swallowed her. Cold stone walls dripped damp in every direction.

"Watch your feet," Kosmi said. She started up a shaky wooden staircase, cobbled from flimsy boards and old nails. Beside her, Meridia aimed her knife at an unseen second floor.

"Lilac!" a man shouted from below.

She glanced back. Past her hood's edge, a silhouette in fedora and trench coat darkened the firelight.

Detective Alexander Stathos. A brass-colored pistol gleamed in one hand.

Black robes clustered the archway, blocking him from sight. Kosmi dragged Lilac up by the arm. For the first time in ten years, she was safe among the people of a covenant, the way Mother had intended. A different covenant, but protected nonetheless.

"You're harboring a murderer!" Alex yelled after them. "You'll be next if you don't let me through."

Lilac reached the second floor, a rickety, unfinished layer of the tower, hardly more than a wooden platform. Time had eaten holes through its surface, and splinters jutted from its planks. Someone shouted below, likely at Alex, and then a knife clattered to the floor.

Nemo erupted up the wooden staircase. "Vasyl stalled him,

but we don't have long. Keep climbing."

Lilac muttered a quiet prayer for Vasyl and kept climbing. A dusty ladder shot up the stone wall toward another wooden platform high above, a makeshift third floor.

"Used to be respected," Meridia said, panting as she followed Lilac. "Now we're chased by a man with a gun."

"Puts our position in perspective," Kosmi said.

Meridia coughed out a laugh. "Fate is many throats with one stomach."

The ladder seemed more dangerous than any house Lilac had stepped into with her dagger these past couple of days. Twice it wobbled out of her control. She might have fallen had Meridia not pressed hard from below while Kosmi held the top.

"You don't understand!" Alex shouted. "I'm trying to help you!"

The climb would have been easier had Lilac stuffed the coralstone back in her pocket, but now seemed the perfect time for it to fall out, and the night was full of bad omens. She wouldn't risk letting it out of her grasp. Ten years came down to this one moment as she reached the ladder's top. The covenant clustered onto the third floor platform behind her. Nemo held the ladder for the last climbing priest.

A gunshot rang through the hollow tower.

Lilac jolted, the pistol louder than yesterday's temple crash. But when she looked down, hers weren't the fingers soaked in red.

The last priest prodded his middle. "Oh," he said.

"Come," Nemo said, grasping the priest's arms.

Heavy footsteps crashed across the stairs below. "The next won't be a warning shot!" Alex shouted. He didn't realize what he'd done, having shot wild into the tower's upper darkness. "I don't want to hurt you, but if it's between you and these people, I will. Come down without a fight."

Lilac reached for the injured priest. "It doesn't have to be fatal.

Logoi's coming back."

The young priest shrugged hers and Nemo's hands away. "A sacrifice is only as good as what's lost. Tell the goddess my name was Philip."

The ladder twitched. Philip threw his weight backward and tore the ladder away from the platform. Wood trembled, as if the rungs might drag the floor's planks down with them, but the ladder fell, and Philip plummeted down the tower's shaft. Lilac shut her eyes before she heard the wet slap of flesh against stone.

Kosmi grabbed her arm again. "Up, up. Before he takes another potshot. We protect Logoi's child."

The covenant murmured and then began their shuffle up the next ladder, toward the fourth floor and the tower's peak. Nemo and the twin priestesses lingered at the platform's edge.

"He was brave," one priestess said. "But how will we get back down now?"

The other pulled her sister away. "We aren't going back."

Lilac tried not to linger. The covenant was protecting her, and somehow that felt no better than driving her dagger into Vince's flesh.

Nemo hung by the edge until Meridia took his arm. "Work's not done, old man."

"But it should have been me," Nemo said. "Philip was too young."

Meridia pulled him to the ascending ladder, and her eye caught brief and distant firelight. "It isn't going to matter soon."

There were bodies. Moments ago, they had been living, breathing people, but now they were bodies because Alex had pushed them. Not physically, of course. His hand had never touched the knife one man had used to cut his own throat, and Alex certainly hadn't shaken the ladder to knock another down.

But he'd threatened them. He'd—unintentionally—shot the

one who fell. They were dead.

Alex stared into the tower's high darkness. "I didn't do this," he whispered. "They aren't my fault, Lilac. These ones are on you, like all the others. *I* didn't do this."

He could have waited for Cecil. That had been the plan, right? Find no one, leave. Find someone, wait for your partner. Cecil would have listened had he found Lilac at Valmydion's temple, but she was here. Cecil would have talked them down, the covenant wouldn't have felt threatened, but Alex had pushed.

Wasn't it Cecil's fault, a little bit, then? He had been the one to suggest splitting up. Alex was a victim of circumstance, same as always. He'd only killed anyone at Shah following Thale's orders. Here, he'd taken orders of responsibility, his contract, and the cold and dark night. Misfortune, nothing more.

"I did my best." Alex wanted to slink back down the stairs, away from the bodies and Beckoning Tower, let the water wash him away, but he couldn't fade into tonight's hateful storm. He would take a moment to get his head straight, let the death run rain-like down his back, and then he would raise the ladder again and climb it. Slowly but surely, once his heartbeat slowed, he would catch up to Lilac.

This was not the end.

CHAPTER 27

No one had cleaned up the rubble-strewn floor of Valmydion's temple, but droves of her undeterred faithful still gathered across the flat tops of cracked altars and the dusty jagged seating. They came in soaked dresses and dripping suits, one here, a family there, all clasping each other's hands, their gray-haired matriarch twisting a gnarled finger into Valmydion's spiral, mimicking a crude cornucopia.

Cecil saw no one from Valmydion's covenant. Not one black robe flitted at the crowd's edges.

Before these past ten years, some might have taken the gods for granted. Not tonight. With the rains shouting down, the people showed up to worship, and hard. Cecil might have mistaken them for desperate a week back, even two days ago.

But then there was that sensation in Vince Barton's house. Faint yet unmistakable.

Valmydion was nine centuries old, a grandchild to the Dawn Gods. That far down and beyond, whatever quirk in the blood separated gods and descendants from ordinary mortal rarely surfaced. Cecil's mother hadn't been a descendant, but some trace from Grandfather Lyvien, God of Instinct, had risen in her son. Different, but mortal enough to die.

Hardly anyone kept track of the eons in mankind's history, the cycles of growing and dying technology, repeating themselves across five thousand years. Even fewer noted the gods' ages, and a handful felt any distinction. Gods let history settle like the tide, in and out, and as mortals came and went, who kept track of lineage, years, and truth?

The divinity in Vince's house, like the city, was too old to belong to Valmydion. Its pressure felt more like Logoi's generation of First Children, the Dawn Gods' firstborn. Sometimes Cecil wondered how people like Alex could walk around oblivious to it. A shred inside a dead man's house was distracting. In the direct presence of a god, it would overwhelm.

"Stalled enough?" Cecil asked himself. "On with it, shall we?" He slipped through the temple's kneeling throng toward the new pit at its center. A gust of wind thrashed between temple columns and whipped newspaper pages at his heels.

On a crumbling stairway along the wall, a young woman with a strong chest and stronger voice bellowed over the crowd. "The sea is not our death! We have a chance to show our goddess we're made of sterner stuff. Look to the history above your heads—Valentine stands. Valmydion stands with us. We stand with her!"

Cecil let his gaze flicker to the ceiling of lies. This wannabe priestess didn't know a damn thing about glories, gods, or this temple, though the last was hardly her fault. A temple of worship, sure, but a temple of forgetting, too. Of secrets.

If his suspicions were right. If everything made sense. He thought it did—it had to. One of the great mysteries, a missing city, and he might have figured it out.

Stalling again, he scolded himself.

He reached the pit's edge, where some careless soul had stomped part of the second floor down to the first and shattered a hollow space below. Most would assume it was some forgotten stretch of catacombs. People assumed many things, like that ceiling murals made promises or that gods couldn't be liars. Valmydion was nowhere near old enough to have faced the glories after the Holy War, or when they'd appeared after the Dawn Gods' return to the heavens. The damn Holy Psychopomp Tree burned down near two thousand years ago and she hadn't been born yet.

Why didn't anyone ever think for a change? Because they loved Valmydion. Easy to hide a secret when affection deceived everyone.

The not-priestess carried on her bellowing. "When the goddess returns, what will she see? Cowards? No, she'll find a covenant that stretches the city!"

Cecil wanted to tell her she should quit with her original material and try reciting a few Verses of Aeg, perhaps *The Glorious Wrath* or *The Last Gift of Sceptomos*. Save herself the effort since no one here was listening, too swept up in what they thought was happening tonight. What they wished was happening.

A few of the faithful clustered inside the floor's cave-in. Cecil clambered down marble ridges and knelt beside them, but he hadn't come to pray. He was here to see.

And he saw, and felt—old divinity, same as he'd found lingering in Vince's house. Cecil followed the trail, warm against his senses as it led him from the pit's edge to a hulking marble slab. It must have sat directly beneath Valmydion's seat, an egg she surely never wanted to hatch. Had the other gods even told her it was here?

He rested one hand on the marble slab and brushed chunks of debris from its top. Two concave circles marked the center. Neither had been molded perfectly, simple holes to keep small spheres, but each pooled with divinity's pressure. This place, exposed by the collapse, was never meant to be found.

"Because they couldn't be destroyed," Cecil muttered. His suspicions had been right. He knew exactly what had been sealed in marble beneath Valmydion's altar.

Gulls cried outside the temple, far above the kneeling throng and its would-be priestess. They were smarter birds than people gave them credit for, it seemed.

They knew now was a good time to get out of town.

Chapter 28

Arcadia should have gone to the hotel already. She'd sent the exhausted evac team home when the sun began to set, and there were other flood fighters. Ilene had told her the same, and under ordinary circumstances, Arcadia would have listened. Night had come, and the rains had worsened.

But she'd forgotten how to stop. Even heading to a diner for food briefly had made her restless. Godly power coursed through her like the sun before dawn, eager to rise. What would she do at the hotel, have a staring contest with the bathroom mirror?

Better to get herself good and tired. And do the work.

The sky held a grudge against the land. Thunder laughed in the clouds, and wind tucked the rain underneath umbrellas so no one could miss the spray. Tonight hated Arcadia, hated Valentine. She imagined since Savvas, God of Storms, had abandoned Aeg with the rest of his kind that this storm and all unruly weather took the glories' side, whipping seaborn winds toward the coast.

Arcadia thought of sending Oldtown's residents north. Bay Ridge's slight elevation made it the safest place on Valentine's west side, but the runoff had to go somewhere. Floodwater clawed at foundations where the street dipped into Oldtown and lapped at the edges of the North Temple District.

Someone was shouting in the dark. "Get him up!" they said. "Get him up quick!"

Two uniformed flood fighters pulled a third from the knee-high water, his body half-caked in mud. A fresh barricade breach had let flooding come spilling through with enough force to knock a man down. The stones were giving up.

Arcadia stood at the barricade's base, where a section of wall now leaned away from its fellows. The storm couldn't knock it down without unmooring the foundation, but every hard blow tested the barricade's resolve. Arcadia pressed her shoulder against slick stone and shoved hard until block met block in a firm wall.

For now. Its foundation seemed more mud than anything else these days. How long would it last?

Still, she'd helped. The rushing water eased, and a handful of flood fighters cheered. There was no crowd to impress like earlier today. Their scant volunteers stretched thin up and down the borders of Oldtown. The promise of a goddess had brought them here, but the work drove them away. Arcadia couldn't blame them.

She approached two flood fighters—Karena and Jason? She didn't know everyone's names. Another failure by their captain.

"Any word from the floodplains?" Arcadia asked.

"Everyone should be inside the city," Jason said. His sea-green uniform looked yellow beneath his flickering lantern.

"We'd hoped it wouldn't get this bad," Karena said. "Not yet."

"It won't get worse if I can help it, and I'm not going anywhere," Arcadia said, raising her two-way radio. "Pass it down the line; the gods haven't abandoned us. We'll see daylight together."

A crash struck the far side of the barricade, thrashing water off the stone. It ended in a deep, clacking yawn.

Arcadia had never heard a sound like that in her life. She turned to the wall as if it might offer answers, but there was only the heavy smack of rain. A world of wet secrets.

"What glorious shit now?" Jason asked.

Another sound echoed across Oldtown, but at least Arcadia recognized it. Gulls came cawing overhead from the west.

"Listen to all that," Jason said. "Got to be droves of them."

The chattering cloud's tail end passed the barricade, scaled the city, and then faded beneath the storm's rumble. They ran a long stretch by the sound of them, as if the coast's entire gull population had decided to pick up and head east. They were abandoning the beach for inland Aeg.

"Listen to them go." Karena stared at the sky, as if she could see the birds in the blackness. "Do they know something we don't?"

Arcadia wished she could say. What did birds know? What did gods? She strode down the barricade, away from her agents, and slipped her fingers into one belt pouch, where they stroked a hard, porous surface until her fingertips bled.

"Tell me we'll make it through this," she whispered.

The voice she'd heard in Valmydion's temple trembled through a crimson coralstone and up her arm. "You mistake me for a goddess of prophecy," a sweet voice whispered. "I would give no cause for despair. You love them. You want to keep them safe. I understand better than anyone."

"I know," Arcadia said. "I guess I wanted comfort."

"I did not save your life without good reason."

Arcadia shut herself up before someone overheard and looked at her funny, but she was grateful. She knew who had saved her life. Not Valmydion, not Logoi, not any god she'd met before, only the one trapped in this coralstone, its surface brimming red and warm.

She owed thanks to Medes, Goddess of Love, first of the ascendants. No one else.

Chapter 29

The covenant's survivors gathered beneath the Beckoning Tower's tall rooftop. Its top floor's flat platform lay exposed to sideways sheets of rain, while its narrow pointed ceiling hunched over those gathered. The final ladder's hole gaped dark at their feet. Lilac hugged her robes, and the covenant huddled around her, Meridia pressing to one side, Kosmi to the other.

Only Nemo stood apart. "We do it here," he said, gazing westward into the storm, as if he could see ocean waves through the downpour and darkness.

"This is where we die?" Meridia asked. "Fitting."

"How so?" Kosmi asked.

"Because we'll give this building back its purpose. Its builders meant to summon a god. We will summon one."

The twin priestesses clung to each other. One cried into her sister's shoulder.

"We'll give ourselves purpose, too," Meridia went on. "Fear is fine, but overcoming it is bravery. We have to be brave, like Vasyl and Philip, and pray the goddess will remember us."

They were little more than gloomy black shapes, but at the next lightning flicker, Lilac felt every eye digging into her. This moment mattered more than each murder. These people meant to give themselves to Logoi. A holy covenant in this life, what would they each reincarnate into next? There had been no Holy Tree to

191

judge and dictate in two thousand years, each soul flying free in the Between. Lilac hoped they each got everything they wanted.

The coralstone beat warm in her hand. When Arcadia fell yesterday, Logoi must have tasted blood through these pores for the first time in ten years. Now would be the last. Every drop beyond tonight would soak her godly skin, freed and eternal.

"Mother," Lilac said. "Vasyl and Philip sacrificed themselves so we could make it here. The rest will tell you their names and be remembered." She glanced to the covenant. "Tell her."

Meridia reached over first and placed her hand on the coralstone. "Meridia Sid. I gave my eye fighting floods years ago, and now I give everything else to fight the glories again. Remember me when you save this land."

Kosmi touched next. "Kosmi Andrea, priestess of Valmydion." She coughed against the rain. "And yours, this final night."

The twin priestesses approached next. "Kate White," one said. "Our parents crossed Aeg when we were little, and we chose to serve Valmydion over any other calling. Thinking back, I don't know if my life's enough for a proper sacrifice, but I hope it'll do. I know my sister's is worth it, though."

Kate cried when she retreated, and then her sister Elly spoke, and then the doubtful bald priest. They came one by one until all had pledged names and lives to Logoi. Their service to the goddess of reason would be brief, and the twin priestesses weren't the only ones to cry. The names washed through Lilac and down her robes with the rain.

Nemo turned dry eyes to Lilac. "What is the ritual, descendant?"

Lilac leaned toward the coralstone. "Mother?"

The coralstone hummed with heat. "Rituals give shape for mortals. Gods do not need them. I have their names, and I would have their blood. Let us be on with it."

Lilac eyed the coralstone. Mother was often direct to the extreme but rarely impatient. Creeping close to her imprisonment's end after ten long years had to be affecting her. Even timeless gods could suffer and change. The Holy War had twisted Tychron from god of manners to god of madness, Lyvien had gone from temple guardian to wanderer, Aeda and her city had vanished from all knowledge, and so on. Lilac didn't want Logoi to change too.

Time to free her.

"There's no time for a proper ritual," Lilac said. "The blood will give her strength. I know it feels wrong, but Mother has your names. She'll remember."

Nemo chortled. "Sounds rightly direct for the goddess of reason. This is what we have to do, so do it. Simple and to the point."

Lilac forced a smirk. "You would've fit in well at her temple."

She hugged the coralstone to her chest one last time and then placed it at Nemo's feet. Her throat squeezed tight, but she couldn't watch this sacrifice in silence. The covenant deserved some ceremony, didn't they?

"All of you, thank you," Lilac said. "You've saved the Holy Land."

"Not us," Nemo said. His robe parted from his naked body, coated in gray hairs, and another lightning flicker lit the knife in his hand. "We're only the doorway for that awesome presence. She will save us." His head whipped to one side, and then he raised his knife against the storm. "There is still a goddess in the Holy Land!"

He buried his blade deep into his chest and fell beside the coralstone. Kate began to cry again, and her sister, too. Thunder urged them to get on with it.

Meridia waved an arm toward Nemo. "All of us together, before the rain washes Nemo's blood away and wastes his sacrifice." She glared at Lilac. "Otherwise, you keep back, or you'll accidentally drain the blood into yourself. It's for the goddess, no one else."

Lilac retreated to the ladder's hole. Nemo lay dead in front of her, but not by her hand. Somehow, that seemed strange after everything she'd done.

She looked away as Kosmi slammed a knife into her own chest. She listened as, crying and hugging, Kate and Elly slashed each other open. Young and old alike, the covenant cut itself down in a circle around the coralstone. Their puddle thickened, but it never spread. The coralstone drank and filled with bright light.

Only Meridia yet stood alive, her robe shed from long-weathered skin. "I knew a descendant before. One of Korenbal's daughters. Strong as an ox. She tried to give blood to her parent once, but it was no use."

Lilac risked a step closer. "Descendants can't—"

"I know. That's my point. If descendants could, I'd have made sure you died here and now." Meridia shrugged. "But then, what would Logoi think? I'm wasting time. Their sacrifices are growing cold, like their bodies. The gods don't store the blood for a miracle's moment. It burns in them, the blood used immediately. If this doesn't work, you're going to need a bigger sacrifice. Ours won't have meant a thing."

Lilac's mouth worked for words and couldn't find them.

"Maybe the glories drown Valentine, and this coralstone sinks to the bottom of the sea, where Logoi can go mad as Tychron." Meridia blinked. Or winked. "Or maybe there will be a Holy Land after all." She held out her knife to Lilac. "Give her every drop."

Lilac took the knife, grasped Meridia's shoulder, and then kissed Meridia's cheek.

"Don't do that." Meridia shut her eye again and patted her heart. "Do this. Do it, now."

Lilac obeyed. Steel jabbed into Meridia's heart and rained blood across the coralstone. An ugly, jittering death, but Lilac held the body until it quit moving and then laid Meridia with the rest of her covenant. They would have a great funeral later when the skies cleared, a pyre for each who'd sacrificed themselves to bring Logoi home. The tower might do for burning. With a goddess returned, it would have no further purpose.

The platform quaked beneath Lilac's feet and shook the bodies in a thumping spasm. Crimson light wriggled inside the once-yellowy coralstone and shined through each pore. Lilac couldn't reach for it, couldn't touch it. Its heat baked the air, and a hum rang louder than the roaring storm.

"Mother, this way!" she shouted. "Almost free!"

Lilac grasped Kosmi's body and drew her teardrop-shaped dagger. She had never wanted to savage the covenant's bodies, but if Logoi needed an offering mound, more flesh, more everything mortal, so be it. The dagger jabbed at soft tissue, blood-needy and desperate. If Logoi had a little more to drink, she could break loose.

If Vasyl and Philip hadn't killed themselves below, there would be enough.

If Meridia hadn't taken so long at the end.

If Nemo hadn't started before the others.

If Lilac's blood was good for anything.

A fresh gust roared from the east, against the storm, as the coralstone cracked across its center. Its hard shell peeled from one side in a jagged chunk, a single petal blooming from a blood-soaked flower. Another petal uncurled, its point dripping red.

Lilac grasped the stone and dug her fingernails into the crack. It burned to touch, and the shell held fast—it didn't need her help. She let it dance out of her fingers, strike the platform, and quake until another petal opened, and another, and then the stone shattered in a radiant crimson flash.

Lilac threw an arm across her eyes, as if the midday sun had dropped onto the rooftop this stormy night.

The brightness slowly softened around a form, one feature at a time. A reaching hand, a rising head. Feet stepping over corpses. Long hair flowed with the stormy gusts. Light faded in flickers of gold and crimson, a doorway breaking from some mysterious infinity and into the hard here and now.

And a goddess stepped into the world.

Lilac fell backward onto the slick platform and lowered her arm. A ten-foot high immortal loomed over her. The tower's roof hadn't seemed so tall before, but now it stretched to accommodate the presence of divinity. Wherever she walked, the world belonged to her.

Lilac had a million things to say. None of them good. None of them what she wanted to say to her mother.

Because her mother wasn't here.

Where were the other eight heads? Where were Mother's faces? Where was Logoi's beautiful stone-like skin?

This goddess dressed her chalk-white body in a dark wine-red dress. A similar fabric flowed snakelike from her biceps and thighs, and the wind blew them out like four wings of a fiery butterfly. She had one head, and hair ran down her back in blood-colored curls. Logoi's hair was always shorn short, and she'd passed the same to her police, her covenant, and her daughter. Lilac hadn't grown it out until Logoi disappeared. She remembered a day she tried to bribe the elderly priestess who cut hair into not shaving it. She'd been six years old and offered "lucky rocks," a few black pebbles she'd found at the catacombs' edges. It hadn't worked.

Had Logoi stood here, Lilac would've told the story. But this pale creature was not the goddess of reason.

"You," Lilac said, lower lip trembling. "You have red eyes."

The goddess blinked. "I prefer they be scarlet."

That wasn't the right thing to say. Lilac scrabbled to her feet. "Where's Logoi? Where's Mother?"

"That is not mine to know," the goddess said. Her voice came thick with an odd accent, the kind that lingered in books from centuries past. How long had she been trapped in that coralstone? Just who had stepped into the world?

"You told me you were Logoi," Lilac said. "How did you—"

"You wanted a goddess, and a goddess is here." Enormous

scarlet eyes glimmered. "*The* goddess."

Lilac shook her head. This didn't make any sense.

"I am Aeda, first of the name, first of the gods, Goddess of Birth." One great hand reached for Lilac, each finger ending in a sharp crimson nail. "And you are a daughter of Logoi. I do not know you but for these past days. Lilac, my thanks be yours."

Lilac couldn't stop shaking her head. This was all wrong. "You tricked me."

"I did," Aeda said. "I allowed your belief to root and blossom."

"But you called me your perfect jewel," Lilac said. "How did you know that name? No one but Mother called me that, not even—no one." She didn't want to mention Simone here, though she'd already brought the coralstone to their apartment.

"Perfect jewel." Aeda tasted the words. "She called each of her mortal daughters by this."

Lilac recoiled. "Each? What are you talking about?"

Aeda smiled, her lips thin and snide. "Did you think you were her first? Misshapen Logoi is not as old as I am, but she is a long-lived goddess, last of the First Children. I called that nine-headed dragon cousin until she and others grew the sea stone around me. Of course she has mothered mortal children. I take it by your presence she has yet to mother a god? We are the same this way, but in little else. Why your dismay? I allowed you to believe your mother resided in the coralstone. I gave you those brief hopeful moments. You are welcome."

"But you sounded like her," Lilac said.

"I know my cousin." Aeda touched her throat, and her tone briefly changed to a stoic whisper. "A direct, brutal approach." She lowered her hand, and her accent and confidence returned. "And you may be imperceptive, my cousin's child. You were lost with need. You must be disappointed, but fear not, for you've found a goddess—the first goddess. That is what you worked for. I am the goddess you've killed to free."

Lilac retreated from her, across the ring of bodies.

Aeda's eyes glimmered again. "No? Then a goddess at all would not be enough for you. You wanted your mother. Only Logoi would do. Why? She abandoned you."

"She could be trapped," Lilac said. Her voice barely lifted to the storm's roar. "Another coralstone."

"No, Lilac." Aeda drifted closer, her footsteps soft despite her size. "I allowed you a brief time to believe she was taken, but now you must open your eyes to truth. She chose to leave you, little cousin, as she chose to trap me four hundred years ago. My name is known to all, but my fate was not, and the gods' concern? I do not hear it now. Valmydion was but a child, yet they gave her my city, my temple, and painted lies on their ceilings and tongues. It was I who fought the glories, I who protected Aedos, *my* city-state. But you stand ignorant of all."

Lilac covered her mouth with rain-wet palms. "Stop. Please."

"And this?" Aeda arced a hand over the damp ring of bodies. "You are not some selfless savior of the Holy Land. You wanted your mother, and you told lies of heroism to have her. Do not blame me for lying to you when you would lie to yourself."

A hand as thick as Lilac's chest gripped her shoulder. Sharp nails pricked her spine. Lilac stumbled from beneath Aeda's touch and tripped on a corpse's limp legs. She fell to the platform and scuttled backward.

Aeda loomed over her. "A selfish grasp for the mother who deserted you. Your actions shame you because they could not bring what you wanted. To save Aeg? An afterthought, a guise on your motivations. I see through you, Lilac Antonis, daughter of Logoi, granddaughter to that twisted affair of Kalypses and Kaligos and the Unnamed Mother. I bear the fruits of your labors. You pretend you're the hero that is your lover, Arcadia Myrn. We all see the grander picture. It is time you do the same."

"I can't," Lilac said. She sounded tiny, a child herself. "I don't know the grand picture."

"Time would be ours if we had the power, but it is not so," Aeda said, starting for the tower's edge. "Logoi's perfect jewel, I leave you to your contemplation."

No, no, not this. Meridia and Kosmi and the rest of the covenant hadn't died for this proud goddess to emerge from the coralstone and abandon Aeg like the others.

"But you can't leave." Lilac stood up and started to chase, but she was too shaky and couldn't keep up with those tree-like limbs. "You're supposed to save the Holy Land."

Aeda paused mid-step and curled her thin smile over one grand shoulder. "That will be so, little cousin. Indeed, I will save the world entire. You did not in earnest free me for this purpose, but it was always my desire. Logoi and the others imprisoned me for that very intent, a dream of salvation they did not share." She slid from under the tower's roof, into the open air. No rainwater would touch her porcelain skin as the night swallowed her.

"Please," Lilac said. "We need you."

"Yes, little cousin. You do." Aeda did not glance back this time, but her voice rang hard through the storm. "I would tell of destiny for another favor. Find your lover, Arcadia Myrn, and my mother, Medes. Bring them both to my temple. Tarnished as it be, its steps will once more bathe in blood, thicker than your lowly cuttings could ever dream. And from this blood, we will save the Holy Land."

Aeda's voice and visage disappeared into the night. Thunder boomed overhead as if to ring with her holy footsteps, celebrating this goddess in the Holy Land.

But not the right goddess. This was supposed to be Lilac's reunion with Logoi.

Sideways rain soaked Lilac's robe and hair while Aeda's lies ate at her insides. Her own lies made it worse. Simone was right—Logoi could be wonderful, but she could also be cold and unfeeling, and she could disappear of her own choosing. Lilac had been so absorbed in tricking herself, she couldn't see Aeda doing the same. Too happy to believe what she wanted to hear.

Lilac waited for the storm's next thunderclap and screamed with it, loud as she could. Her knees struck the damp platform. "But why did the gods leave?" she asked the sky. "Why couldn't they stay with us? Why teach me so much and then forget me?"

A hard nub jabbed between her shoulders, and she heard a metallic tick. At last, someone had come to take the lies and choices away from her. She glanced over her shoulder to look this someone in the eye.

Alexander Stathos and his pistol filled her world.

PART FOUR

ABSENT GODS

CHAPTER 30

The bodies tangled atop each other, a mess of loss and suffering Alex wished he couldn't understand. The world atop the tower lay dark in ways he hadn't felt in ten years. Not since Shah. Only this time, the culprit sat on her knees at a pistol's end.

"Can you stand?" Alex asked. Harsh wind swatted rain down his face.

Lilac said nothing, no weapon in her hands. She might have dropped it among the knives strewn over the tower's peak. They glimmered patchwork in the lightning where their blades shone through the blood. The priestly deaths appeared self-inflicted, but they were still Lilac's fault.

Or were they Alex's? He could have swallowed the deaths of those priests below more readily, set the ladder faster, and clambered up before these pointless sacrifices began.

They might not have listened. And Lilac's gambit had worked in some way. Alex had only caught the barest red-and-white flicker as he ascended the ladder, but the giant's size and presence made her nature unmistakable—a goddess strode from the tower moments ago and disappeared into the storm. Light as a feather because she wanted to be. Gods had that power.

"She lied," Lilac muttered.

Alex tucked his pistol beneath his coat and slipped past the holster to grab his iron cuffs. "Give me your hands."

Lilac sat unmoving. She'd been capable of mumbling to herself about the gods' absence while he'd climbed onto the tower's platform, but now she seemed lost.

Alex leaned down, drew one slender arm to the other, and cuffed Lilac's wrists. A tug at the short chain between them said the cuffs would hold. He helped Lilac unresisting to her feet. Her eyes watched the damp floor.

"I'm taking you to Ace Investigations," Alex said, ushering her toward the ladder. "And then the police."

"She lied," Lilac whispered again, and then shuddered. Did she mean the goddess?

"Gods do that sometimes." Alex started down the ladder first and looked up until Lilac began to follow. She was stunned but not catatonic. The full force of a goddess's presence must have struck harder than she'd been prepared for, and Alex couldn't blame her. At his sole encounter with Logoi years ago, he'd barely managed to swear loyalty to the Logos police.

But more than avoiding gods, he wanted to escape the bodies. The bloodshed was too thick and familiar. His breathing lightened as he descended into Beckoning Tower, and Lilac followed to a rickety platform, another ladder, every step bringing them closer to the ground floor.

Even here, they weren't free of corpses. Alex made out the tattered robes below. Those poor priests.

A shadow slid across them. Alex paused mid-ladder until he spotted a tan trench coat crossing the firelight. Wild tawny hair with hints of strawberry twisted with rainwater beneath a soppy fedora. The newcomer clutched an even soppier umbrella at his side.

"Gods, what a mess," Cecil said, and then he cupped one hand beside his mouth and craned his neck toward the tower's inner shaft. "Happy evening! Anyone alive?"

Alex leaned over the ladder. "What are you doing here?" he

snapped.

"Fancy seeing you, too, dear Alex. You told me to come if I didn't find Lilac at the temple." Cecil flopped his fedora against his hip and then tugged it back onto his head. "Can you guess if I found Lilac at the temple?"

Alex guided Lilac to the wooden staircase and led her to the ground floor.

"Suppose you can," Cecil said, and he gestured at the bodies. "She stick these two?"

Alex's bootheel ground against stone. The bodies felt bigger now, but he could weather them. He'd seen worse. "One of them did it to himself," he said, pointing to one body. "The other—it was an accident."

"She lied," Lilac said again, her voice little more than a frail whimper.

Cecil drew Lilac into a one-armed hug she couldn't return. "There now," he said, doting. "That damn Alex can't blame you for everything."

"She coerced them," Alex said, pointing up the ladders. "There must be a dozen dead at the top, and they'd all be alive if not for her, and her blood sacrifice, and that goddess."

Cecil's eyes grew to full moons over Lilac's shoulder. "A goddess?"

"Don't." Alex took Lilac's arm and drew her toward the fire. Its warmth soothed, and he wished they didn't have to head back into the storm tonight.

Cecil padded after. His boots squished with rainwater. "Did her ritual work?"

Alex sat Lilac by the fire, where the dead covenant had likely gathered. They would never again swap stories over these flames, and no matter the result, Lilac was to blame. She'd cut a merciless wound across Valentine these past couple days, but now look what had become of the Valentine Butcher.

"She lied," Lilac said.

"Who lied to you?" Alex asked. He almost pitied her.

Lilac blinked hard and leaned closer to the fire. "Aeda."

"Aeda," Cecil repeated, his face mixing glee with astonishment. "You called up Aeda? *The* Aeda? First of the gods, lost city of Aedos—that Aeda? That is what you said, yes?"

Lilac gave a curt nod. "Valentine *is* Aedos."

Alex rubbed a hand along his jaw; fresh stubble scratched his fingertips. A nine-limbed star drove through this thoughts, its pointed painted in blood. He thought of Thale's secret photographs, showing what horrors some god had done to an officer who dared ask why they'd left. Could that god have had nine heads?

"What about Logoi?" Alex asked. "Wasn't she your goal?"

"She lied," Lilac said for the umpteenth time, her tone flat. One cuffed hand clutched a glob of empty air. "Aeda was trapped in the coralstone and pretended she was Logoi. Told me the gods didn't go by choice, maybe all of them are trapped. But she was stuck in there for hundreds of years. She doesn't know what happened to Logoi. To any of them."

Cecil knelt beside Lilac and patted her arm. "That's not so bad, right? We've a goddess in Aeg, yes? Counts for something, whichever one she is."

Alex paced between Lilac and the fire. Its heat sent his thoughts bubbling, as if to bake the rain out of his skin and clothes would free his mind. Gods gone, no one knew why. Gods not gone by choice. Gods gone, a goddess returned.

"What if it's true?" Alex asked. He nodded at Lilac, and raindrops danced off his fedora. "Why did the gods leave? The big question; we've all asked it. They chatter about it in the newspaper, on the radio, ten years of speculation and gossip, but no answers. Were we unworthy? Were they testing us? Was it apathy? Sensible theories, the gods are fickle and unpredictable, but each agreeing at the same time? Might as well herd cats."

Cecil's eyes flicked back and forth. Lilac's gaze stuck to Alex, drinking him in. She'd wanted answers perhaps more than anyone else, whatever her reason. His suspicions felt outrageous, sure, but no more so than every god collectively putting oceans between themselves and the Holy Land ten years back.

"Maybe they didn't choose to go," Alex said. "What if they were manipulated, driven off? Like somebody told the gods to scram, and they listened."

Cecil scoffed. "What, all of them?"

"They're all gone, aren't they?" Alex rubbed his jaw again. "It's possible."

"Who'd do it?" Cecil asked, lurching to his feet. "Moreover, what *could* do it? How do you intimidate an unkillable god? Rubbish."

"Who stands to gain? That question is a detective's best friend." Alex eyed Lilac, and she eyed him right back. No answers between them, but she was running the same question through her head. Quick thoughts, swift actions. She was a killer, but not a fool.

Cecil shrugged, almost exaggerated. "Easy answer. The glories stand to gain."

Embers flecked Alex's boots, and he kicked dust at the flames. Fire warmed, but it also burned. Nothing in life came neat and tidy. Back when the State House contracted Ace Investigations, every case had come with twists and turns. No sooner had they trailed a woman's husband to his lover than found she was trying to set him up for murder or some other overcomplicated plot. The glories were a simple answer for simple thoughts, and a good detective couldn't ignore a possible tie between tonight's events and the gods' disappearance.

"I've never heard of a god who feared a glory," Alex said. "They left for some other reason. Someone stands to gain, and I want to know who."

"We have to find out," Lilac said, a fiery crackle in her voice.

She looked more awake now, as if the question had shattered stones in her head. "If we find out why they left, maybe we can bring them back. Not just Aeda—all of them."

Alex studied her terse face, the way her fists clenched beneath the iron cuffs. She wanted Logoi back, but here was a thought to return Valmydion, Korenbal, Savvas, on and on, gods in abundance. Would Valmydion retake her city from Aeda? The gods might risk another Holy War. If they'd put Aeda inside the coralstone Lilac mentioned, they might do it again.

Threads tangled in Alex's mind—there could be some tie between Aeda's imprisonment, her release, and the other gods' abandonment of the Holy Land. He teased at the threads, but he couldn't yet find the knots. Hard to trust liars and killers.

Cecil threw up his hands. "What's the bloody point? The gods are gone. They're too far away to do anything about this now. Besides, we already got a goddess the way I'm hearing. I'm sorry if I see a blessing and don't want to kick mud all over it, especially when said blessing can crush my skull between her fingertips." He pinched two fingers. "Like a rotted olive."

"She's not a blessing," Lilac said. "Logoi and the rest put Aeda away for a reason."

An echo to Alex's thoughts. Lilac was a liar and a killer, sure, but she was right.

"Listen to you." Cecil glanced over the fire, his hair fraying at the ends. "What's the trouble? She'll stop the glories. We should head to her temple and pay respects. She might have gone there."

"She told me so," Lilac said. "She said she'd bathe the temple steps in blood."

The vision forced itself into Alex's head—the temple's white marble foundation running over as a growing red puddle slopped down the steps, filling the plaza—and he shuddered as if he'd soaked his trench coat again in the rain.

"What of it?" Cecil asked. "Aeda's temple, Aeda's rules."

"Why the blood?" Lilac creaked to her feet, iron clinking between her wrists. "To cast a miracle? Of what kind? She's already here. She wants me to bring her mother to her." Her tone turned brittle. "And she wants Arcadia."

Thoughts of bloodshed melted around Arcadia's face. Alex saw her present self, and then the adolescent he'd known. He saw the seventeen-year-old cadet who'd faced the goddess Logoi alone in the Logos temple to transform her body and love herself from skin to bone.

If another goddess called, would Arcadia answer? That would make her a witch of old, the kind who betrayed her sworn god for the sake of another.

Alex tried to steady his voice. "Aeda's mother?"

"Medes," Lilac said. "But I don't know if there's another goddess in the city. Aeda might have forgotten we're only mortals, can't summon by will alone. Or maybe someone else found a way to summon Medes."

"And why Arcadia?" Alex asked.

"Aeda didn't say." Lilac shifted from foot to foot. Hard to believe that despite the blood on her clothes, her skin appeared clean. "We could find Arcadia and talk to her."

Alex thought of asking gentle Arcadia about bloodthirsty gods and almost laughed. "Why would she know anything?"

"Because she almost died yesterday, and Aeda's miracle saved her." Lilac opened and closed her fists. "Through blood, through the coralstone."

Yesterday's dinner slid over Alex's thoughts. Arcadia had seemed odd, but Alex had written that off as nerves over friend meeting lover, and meeting lover's mother. Had she almost died and then sat alone with that knowledge? Both possibilities could be true. Alex had known Arcadia most of his life. She was not an open book, but she had welcomed him, and him alone, outside the Logos temple the night of her miracle. If she'd almost died, wouldn't she have spoken up?

"I'm not sure what's real or not yet," Alex said. "But if this Aeda is tied to the gods' disappearance, if we're walking close enough to why they left for us to find the truth, I want to know." He aimed a finger at Lilac. "You're not off the hook, only delayed." Thunder shouted through Beckoning Tower's walls. "If we live through the night."

Lilac nodded, but her eyes narrowed as if to say, *We'll see.*

"Great, we all care about Aeda now," Cecil said. He drew Lilac close and readied his tattered umbrella to cover them both. "To the temple then?"

Alex approached the front door. "To Arcadia. We'll see if she has a clue about any of this."

If anything Lilac said was real. He opened the front door and led the group into the storm.

Cecil muttered something under his breath and then ushered Lilac to follow. "At the very least if we get Arcadia, we'll be bringing the goddess what she wants." His umbrella coughed open in a spray of rainwater. "And we can get a drink along the way."

CHAPTER 31

Arcadia had lost count of how many sandbags she'd dropped in front of the barricade's iron gate. The gate was the barricade's greatest weakness, worse than any chipped or cracked stone. It was meant to open, a way in and out of the city via Oldtown, and the flood fighters were too busy to dig new foundations and block the way with stone and mortar. Had she known better yesterday, Arcadia would have thrown sandbags here before the storm began. Evacuation without them seemed smart when you thought there was time.

This rainy season, there was no time.

Trucks stalled halfway through Oldtown, which forced the slow and laborious work of carrying bags by hand through the water to the gate. Arcadia could only shove one truck onward at a time and plow it toward the gate herself. Anything to slow the flood, even if the bags arrived half-soaked already.

She thought she heard someone calling her name as she hefted another bag from the truck. It splattered onto the dampening mound, and she took a moment to breathe. Oldtown still need evacuating. She hoped the residents saw to that themselves now.

"Captain?" Jason peeped.

Arcadia turned to him. He and Karena were lugging a waterlogged sandbag between them. Other agents darted between gate and truck, but their eyes kept flashing Arcadia's way, Leander among them, having returned to the barricade against orders for some damn reason. Cassis had returned too. Arcadia didn't have the heart to send them away when they wanted to help.

She turned to Jason. "What do you need?"

"I didn't want to interrupt," Jason said. "We appreciate you with our whole hearts. It's just—would you mind not whistling like that?"

"Whistling?" Arcadia asked.

Jason hefted his and Karena's bag onto the pile, breath rushing out, and then turned back to Arcadia. "Or whistle anything else?" Jason asked. "That old river song's giving us the creeps." Karena nodded beside him.

Arcadia's mouth closed and opened. "I didn't realize I was whistling."

A sharper whistle shot from atop the barricade, where Cassis clutched the ring of a broad oil lantern in one hand while hunkered against stone. It would burn fast the way she kept the flame bright behind its glass.

She lowered two fingers from her lips. "Someone's wading through the water, cap."

Arcadia hefted another sandbag onto the pile. They were nearly spent. "Do you know them?" she asked.

"I can't tell. It's a man, I think."

"Or man-shaped," Karena said. She sounded afraid.

"You think a glory would swim up to the gate?" Jason asked.

Arcadia scanned the sandbag blockade. They couldn't open the gate now; its iron door swung inward. No one was getting in or out through the west-facing side of Valentine unless they climbed the barricade or somehow ascended Bay Ridge.

A heavy *whump* sound echoed across Oldtown. Streetlights stuttered, their bulbs begging someone to stop the downpour before they drowned forever. The *whump* came again, and the night spilled ink.

The power was out.

Headlights cast golden cones up the block from the iron gate, but they shined frail against the rising water. Cassis's lantern glowed sunlike above. Arcadia was grateful she'd let it burn so bright. She waited for a third *whump*, the power fighting its way back to life, but none came. A pale halo beyond the flat rooftops and their gurgling gutters suggested the rest of Valentine still had electricity. Doubtful Oldtown's would come back anytime soon.

"Enough of this," Arcadia said, tearing the two-way radio from her belt. "HQ, this is Captain Arcadia Myrn of the flood fighters. We've lost power in Oldtown. I need trucks, sandbags, and—" She didn't want to say it, didn't want Thale to know she needed his aid, but pride wouldn't help the city and its people. "I need reinforcements at the gate. Bring lots of light."

"Myrn?" Her radio fussed and crackled. "Gate, and—unclear. Can—repeat?"

Arcadia shook the radio. "Power's out in Oldtown. We need help."

Static answered. Her fingers tensed to crush the device into antenna and wires, easy as a tin can, but she jammed it onto her belt and went fishing inside her pouches for the coralstone. She needed a miracle right now.

Far down the block, a soft orange light flickered alive behind glass. Another lit a nearby window. Across the street from the gate, hopeful orange eyes filled windows and doorways, each staring patiently through the storm.

Oldtown was coming alive again in flashlights, candles, oil lamps—anything the neighborhood's people could use to break the stormy darkness and keep the flood fighters in the light.

Jason laughed; Cassis and Karena exchanged grateful smiles. A few of the agents cheered.

Arcadia remained stone-faced. Too many lights in too many windows and doorways. Too many people remained in Oldtown, more than she'd suspected before now.

"Burning the midnight oil in the truest sense," Jason said, grinning.

"But if we're burning it now, what'll we burn at midnight?" Leander asked. He fished a pocket watch from his uniform's belt, but it slipped through his fingers and vanished into the flood. No telling whether the flood fighters had already crossed midnight.

Cassis leaned her lantern farther over the wall. "The man who's coming? He's getting closer. Definitely human." She drew back. "Something's not right."

Arcadia ordered the man brought up by rope. Agents climbed truck and barricade to stand with Cassis, and she helped Jason hold Leander's legs as he sank behind stone to fetch their visitor. Arcadia would have done it herself, but one slip and her hand might damage the barricade. She went back to the sandbags, threw another onto the pile, another. Shadows and light danced over her eyes, and she glanced up at a nearby window, where two children's round faces glowed with candlelight. They waved at her. She waved back.

"Water's rising!" Cassis shouted. "It's a wave coming in."

How was that possible? The sea couldn't have risen so much.

Leander shouted from behind the wall. "Got him! Pull us up, quick!"

Cassis and Jason hauled Leander onto the barricade's top, the stranger in tow, and then they lowered the stranger toward the truck, where Arcadia could look him over.

"Water was up to his middle," Cassis said. Her lantern glared high over the man's face as everyone gathered nearby. "What's wrong with him?"

He was a gray-haired man with bronze skin. A raw rash streaked crimson, blister-coated fingers down his scalp and face. His eyes stretched wide open, filled with red bumps. Heavy breath gasped in and out from his gaping mouth, but he said nothing and didn't seem to know where he was.

"Like in the stories," Leander said. His breath smoked in cold clouds.

Arcadia knew what he meant; everyone knew. The glories had blinded this man and burned his mind. He'd been wading through the water for no telling how long.

Cassis shook her head. "Not enough to drown us. They have to drive us mad first."

A distant cry tugged at Arcadia's heart, and she turned to the wall. No one else seemed to notice until a moment later, their ears muffled by rainfall, thunder, and likely their own thoughts of a crumbling world, but they turned, too. Somewhere out on the floodplains, a soul cried in pain. Maybe in death.

Cassis's lantern clanged in her swinging arm. "Something big is coming, cap." Her lantern arm quaked in fear. "On the rising tide."

Tide. This far inland. Could the rain bring the water level that high? Or had the sea actually come to Valentine? But if the glories could move the sea itself—Arcadia didn't want to finish the thought.

"It's swaying from the gate," Cassis said. "It's—catch me!"

Her knees bent as the barricade shuddered. Rain splashed off the top in a thick waterfall and took Cassis down. Her lantern flew into the water, dousing its oil-fueled sunshine.

Arcadia lunged, grabbed Cassis out of the air, and sloshed backward.

Cassis slid loose and set foot beside Arcadia. The floodwater churned at her thighs. "Thanks, cap." She grasped her lantern's iron ring, but there would be no lighting it now. She dropped it again in the slop. "If someone has a light, I'll head back up."

She was too good. They all were. Leander handed over his flashlight and Cassis clambered onto the barricade, but the small cone couldn't match her lantern's brilliance. What did that say about the night itself?

Cassis threw her hand over her mouth to stifle a scream. Arcadia hopped up the truck and clambered onto the barricade, where her eyes followed Cassis's flashlight beam.

A dark mass rocked against the greener side of the barricade. It smelled of saltwater and brine. Another low moan rippled through the water, the poor animal's final death cry.

The glories had killed a whale. A young one, too. Wasn't it just like the glories to prey first on the elderly and the young? Even in its adolescence, the whale was enormous, but the glories wouldn't have provoked a grown adult. Too risky, and they were such cowards. Airbreathing creatures trapped in the sea—small wonder the gods had made them sacred.

"They're enjoying this," Cassis said. "Thousands of years, they've been waiting for this. Might as well take their time."

"Because they couldn't do it before," Arcadia said. She turned from the whale and looked across her agents dotted around flooded Oldtown. "In the beginning, men were prey, but that wasn't the end of it. The glories have come for us since the dawn days. They came during the Holy War. They came when the Dawn Gods left. They probably tried to come when the Holy Tree burned. Always, always wanting their prey again, but we aren't prey animals anymore. We didn't have fire, or ships, or guns in the dawn days. They're flesh and blood, same as us. We'll all die someday, with or without the gods, but the glories have no gods and we do. You've seen what I am. I will be the gods' divine instrument."

Arcadia had hoped to stoke spirits and boost morale. Jason looked ready to shout encouragement; Karena had hopeful eyes.

But another tremor rocked the wall and sent Arcadia's boots slipping. She kept her balance and grabbed Cassis by the shoulder to keep her from sailing off into the floodplains.

Another whale had struck somewhere along the barricade.

Cassis gave a grim smile and aimed her flashlight west. "The water's lowering."

Wherever the flashlight's beam touched, frothing water slid back from stone. The night yawned, the sea itself taking a deep breath, and a deeper roar began in the back of its oceanic throat. Arcadia didn't know this sound, but it was bigger than any whale. Bigger than Oldtown.

She wrapped an arm around Cassis's waist and clambered off the barricade. No one moved below. Even without the goddess's strength in their ears, they had to hear this roar. Had they given up? How could she blame them? What could they possibly do?

Arcadia set Cassis into the water and pressed her shoulder to the barricade. Cold water soaked through her sleeve, into skin and muscle. She needed another miracle, but Aeg was running short these days, and she couldn't let her hands down to touch the coralstone in her belt pouch. She had to hope the power of Medes bled through on its own.

"I will be that godly instrument," Arcadia muttered, determined. She braced herself for impact.

The rolling roar smothered all other sounds. The barricade had no give to it. Either it would stand, or it would crack and crumble, nothing in between. The work of mankind against the work of the glories. Given time, water eroded stone, but this was a single night.

Seaborn thunder pounded through the earth. The barricade shuddered beneath a mighty wave, and frothing water crested the top, but stone was stronger than water right now, when mankind needed it to be. Maybe they could last the night, the storm, even the season.

And then Arcadia heard the crash. The water was a thrusting force, and it would follow the path of least resistance. The barricade had no give, would either stand or crack, yes, but its gate was a solid iron door meant to swing inward, and only a soggy heap of sandbags kept it standing in place.

The sandbags weren't enough.

A fist of briny water punched the gate open. The sandbag mound exploded into a cloud of damp clumps. Floodwater—seawater?—foamed and bubbled into the street, swelling with sea life, debris, and the eternal rhythm of the tide.

The water climbed Arcadia's waist, abdomen, to her chest. Beside her, the truck lifted unmoored from the mud and began to float. She grabbed it by the undercarriage rim before it could pin anyone against a building and crush them, but she let go when her agents began to scream. Lights poured toward the gate, flitting across churning water as gray fins stabbed across its surface.

The sea had come to Valentine, and sharks swam the city streets. Arcadia knew little about them, whether they traveled solo or in schools. They seldom ate people out at sea, but the glories had forced the sharks into a strange and hostile territory. Worse was the water. People's homes would flood, and they'd be trapped and drowning.

There were too many problems now and only the one Arcadia to face them.

Someone whimpered beside her. Jason ran hands down his face, muttering "No, no," again and again. Cassis shook her head, but her flashlight kept fixed on the barricade's broken gate. Others gasped and mewled and sobbed. They were flood fighters and would stop the glories where they could, but no one was prepared for this.

Not even Arcadia. She watched through the rainwater at what next surged through the gate.

A snakish body, thick as two side-by-side trucks, pressed into the city. Ropes of scaly flesh danced down its trunk and batted at bloated sandbags and floating hunks of wooden debris. Sea snakes swam at its sides, each one colorful and venomous, but they were nothing compared to what they flanked.

There were different kinds, categorized by sailors and marine biologists. Some resembled dragon-like whales, called fool's whales. Others appeared as enormous serpents; still others echoed giant squids.

This one mixed snake and squid. It had to run thirty-five feet, maybe forty, from head to the tip of its tail, its serpentine body lined with car-thick tentacles, and a bony carapace covered its thick head. Arcadia thought it looked a little like a glory. Fitting, see how it had come to be here in the first place.

The glories had driven a sea monster into the city.

CHAPTER 32

No cabs crossed through Lee Village when Lilac returned to the rains, wedged between Alex in the lead and Cecil beside her. Water spit from puddles down the sidewalk and through the streets. The library stood dark across the street, but lights dotted the houses up the block, where Alex hooked around the corner.

"You want to traipse through the North Temple District?" Cecil asked. "Why not cut through the temple plaza?"

If Alex answered, Lilac didn't hear. He faced ahead as the group crossed into the North Temple District and then drew them into a tighter cluster as other pedestrians flitted in and out of doorways, down fire escapes, and up the street. Cecil kept glancing south as if a stiff wind might blow him toward the temple without separating him from his drenched fedora and pathetic umbrella. He might have been right to long for a goddess's protection, even a liar like Aeda. How was Lilac any different?

Cecil found another comfort when Alex paused at a phonebooth a stone's toss from a liquor shop, its front window ringed with pink neon. Alex opened the phonebooth, while Cecil opened the shop door and vanished inside.

"Radiance Hotel is north," Alex said. "I don't want to walk there and back if we have to head elsewhere, like the headquarters or Oldtown." He passed a coin into Lilac's palm. "Get them on the horn and see if Arcadia's home."

Lilac slipped into the phonebooth; its glass rattled when Alex slid the creaky door shut. Rainwater crawled down every window and distorted the world beyond. Lilac breathed deep, absorbing the momentary privacy, even with the cuffs still clutching her wrists. One hand lifted the black earpiece, the other slipped Alex's coin into the slot, and she leaned her lips close to the mouthpiece.

"Operator," a harried woman said. She sounded out of breath.

"Radiance Hotel," Lilac said. And waited.

She listened to the earpiece's new silence, and the tapping rainwater against the phonebooth roof, and other sounds beyond. People were shouting, laughing, crying. A boxy radio on a nearby open window sill spat static and odd bits of distant piano music. To close her eyes and forget, Lilac could almost believe this was an ordinary night in an ordinary rainy season.

But the gods were gone, and the glories had come, and Aeda was a liar, and Logoi wouldn't return, and maybe that was Aeda's fault if Alex was onto something. When Lilac had asked why the gods were gone, she echoed the despair of the Holy Land. When Alex asked, he wanted an answer, and his tone suggested he might find it. If Aeda had anything to do with Logoi's absence, Lilac wanted to know. She deserved to know.

The earpiece crackled. "I'm sorry, no one's picking up," the operator said. She sounded haggard now, perhaps ready to abandon her post.

Lilac wouldn't keep her. "Thank you for trying."

She slung the earpiece back onto the phone, listened to the coin jangle inside, and then forced open the squealing phonebooth door. At the next intersection of brick houses, a small black car parked on both sidewalk and street. Scratches marred the paint over its rear doors. A woman bounced a crying baby in the back seat, while at the front, a burly person in a torn shirt turned a crank in the narrow hood, as if the car could bring the family somewhere safe. More crying echoed down a nearby alley, and someone shouted for "Cal!" from the south.

People were panicked, and they had good reason. Flooding west of the city, bloodshed threatened at its core. Hope seemed as scarce as gods in Valentine.

Fitting, seeing how this city was really lost Aedos.

"Well?" Alex stood stiff beside her. His fedora dribbled rain; he was lucky to have so little hair.

"No answer," Lilac said, and she shut the phonebooth. "The line might be down, or everyone might have ditched the hotel. Would Arcadia stay if it's that bad?"

"She wouldn't sit idle," Alex said at last. "We'll make for Old-town, see if she's there."

"And die finding her?" Lilac asked.

Alex loomed. "Do you believe that, or are you dead-set on giving me a hard time?"

Lilac pursed her lips. He was right. To help even in the most hopeless situation sounded like a very Arcadia thing to do.

"Our minds are hardly sound under a storm like this, that's what I say," Cecil said, emerging from the liquor shop. A violet glass bottle stretched from his free hand. "A little courage won't hurt. This here's Asyx Serenity, bottled over twenty years ago in Diomarch. That city's gone, the vineyards, too, or might as well be. Last one in Valentine—sorry, Aedos—and I'm not drinking it alone." He bit the cork loose and outstretched his arm. "Alex, want any? Don't be a spoilsport."

Alex turned west without a word, but Lilac cupped the bottle in both hands and drank liquid fire from the neck. She almost spat it out, the flavor so harsh, but Cecil would make fun of her. Besides, no sense wasting it. She swallowed the mouthful and passed the bottle back to Cecil.

"That's the spirit." Cecil tipped the bottle and let Asyx Serenity pour between his lips. "Cheers, love, to a world gone mad!"

"Is that so?" Alex asked. "Since when did you start getting your

222

grandfather's premonitions?"

Cecil drank again. Lilac watched Alex wipe a hand down his face and realized she and Cecil were pissing him off. She didn't mind, and the drink was warm.

"Arcadia cares about you," Alex said. "If you had the decency to feel the same, you wouldn't have done any of this. Reasons be damned."

Lilac licked her lips—alcohol and rainwater, a poor mix. She gestured for the bottle again, drank from it, and passed it back to Cecil. Where she sipped, he chose to gulp.

"I'm sorry about your children," Alex went on. "I really am. No one should have to experience that. But what you've done is wrong."

Alex knew his business, but he was clueless about the world. Cecil seemed to have figured it out, and he had his own way of coping. Could Lilac find her way? She had pulled it together after the girls' deaths. It had taken four years and Arcadia's help, but Lilac had managed. She had to pull herself together again, right now. She was Logoi's daughter, for gods' sakes. Time to use her brain.

"You don't have blood on your hands, ex-policeman?" Lilac asked.

Lightning forked across the clouds, casting white light down desperate alleys and across dark windows. Faces shined behind the glass, each turned pale by the sky's fire no matter their complexion.

"Gods and glories want the same—to feed on us," Alex said at last. "Blood for gods, flesh for glories. But the gods figured they could get what they want willingly. Within the Verses of Aeg, it's written 'In the beginning, men were prey, and in the end, they will be prey again.' Ever consider the scripture never meant the glories? That maybe we'd be prey to the gods? Have been?"

"You sympathize with the glories," Lilac said.

"They're people." Alex took off his fedora to pour it out and then threw it back on. "Imagine the Dawn Gods came back tomorrow."

Cecil opened his mouth and then shut it with another pull of Asyx Serenity.

"Yes, that's how we'd all react at first," Alex said. "We'd think they'd come to save us again. But what if the Dawn Gods decided to elevate chickens to our intelligence? Taught them fire, speech, reading. Taught them to destroy our homes and drive us to the edge, made children with chickens and left them the responsibility of keeping things that way, temples to chicken gods, mortal chickens ruling the world, us on the fringes. And then, thousands of years later, those gods left the chickens to fend for themselves and we had the chance to take back everything. Wouldn't we do it?"

"That's a pragmatic outlook," Cecil said, a snide laugh in his voice. "Playing the pessimist. You think despite everything the Dawn Gods taught us, humanity is doomed, and the glories will win the Holy Land. Sure, from a worldly perspective. Nature puts up with a lot of shit from the gods, it'll bend to accommodate them, but if its laws are broken, it'll turn brutal and chew up the universe to put things right. We don't got that power; we got godly need."

Lilac bristled; Cecil could climb such an asinine high horse when he'd been drinking. At least he hadn't cut himself this time.

Alex stared into Lilac. "We have godly favor. The glories knew it. The Dawn Gods decided it and taught it to their children."

"Do you really want to know why they're gone?" Lilac asked.

"Independence from them isn't the same as cold abandonment," Alex said. "Why push us into toil and worship? Why not give us paradise? Or at least food and shelter enough that no one would suffer. Logoi should've handed Arcadia her miracle because she asked, no strings attached. Instead Logoi cashed loyalty to ease Arcadia's needs, like any pawnshop parasite."

Lilac wanted to grab Alex by the trench coat and slap him. He thought he understood so much about the world, and gods, and Lilac—he was oblivious to how she felt deflated, drained, purposeless. He didn't understand being crushed because he'd always been small. No god, no descendant, no chosen, he had zero influence on the world at large and gave himself a private world to compensate, one he clutched to his heart, pretending mankind deserved fairness from the gods.

"We should have gone to the temple," Cecil said, watching southbound streets again.

"You asked if I have blood on my hands," Alex said, his eyes on Lilac. "Would you really like to know?"

Minutes ago, Lilac would have pried it out of him without hesitation. But the way he asked the question coated each syllable in barbs. Small wonder he was a detective. He did not like unanswered questions, no matter who asked them.

"You said Arcadia never told you about Shah," Alex said. "But I will. Shah was Lilac Antonis on a grand scale."

Lilac's gait slowed to a shuffle. Her bare feet scraped the wet sidewalk, and she remembered yesterday's wound. Something told her this conversation would cut deeper.

"Shah was a mountain village north of Valentine—you wouldn't have heard of it back then; they lived pretty isolated." Alex waved a hand. "Hard to get there, maybe impossible now the way rivers have flooded. Traders wandered through, but most people didn't know the village was there."

Lightning drew outlines to the buildings ahead. Or maybe they were they the hills of Alex's story.

"Thale knew," Alex said. "Came a time not long after Logoi left that we were desperate to bring her back, same as you. Thale mentioned Shah, said he found the village idyllic, even lovely. Do you know how strange it is to hear that word out of a man like Thale? He took two police captains and their units to Shah; I was one of them. At nightfall, we rounded up the villagers and set fire to their homes, for cleansing. Thale told them they would be sacrificed for the greater good of Logoi. And you know what they say—a real sacrifice only matters if something valuable is lost."

Lilac looked hard at Alex. He no longer walked this city's streets; he was in Shah, lost behind his eyes the way Arcadia's often went on voyages when she stared in the mirror.

"But you know what those people did while fire raged around them, surrounded by thirty-odd officers? While we were fitting ammo drums into our submachine guns, ready to play the world's most violent percussion, what did the villagers do?" Alex laughed, cold and terrified. "They danced! They all started dancing, the whole village, like it was a party. But it wasn't just a dance, waving limbs and twisting torsos. There was power in it. Memories of some god we didn't know, pushing through them, but I felt it, and I never had Cecil's gifts."

Cecil squeezed closer to Lilac, as if that could hide him from this story.

"Arcadia felt it, too," Alex went on. "We all did, even Thale, and it scared him. Death should have been dignified, but he ordered we open fire at will, and we captains echoed him. Arcadia was part of my unit, had loaded her gun, but I couldn't get her to squeeze the trigger. Thale shouted at her, smacked her, thundered over that awful rattling, 'Fire at will! Myrn, fire!' But she couldn't. She broke down there in the hills."

Lilac watched the street as if it might cough Arcadia from its darkness, no need to reach Oldtown.

Alex cleared his throat. "When the gunfire died down, she wandered the blazing village, checking in windows like she'd find anyone alive. All she must've seen was her reflection. We hung the flags of Logoi's star in the village center, waving proud over the ash and blood. All for Logoi."

Lilac shuddered; she'd said those last three words herself while her skin drank sacrificial blood, and like everything else out of Alex's mouth, the memory struck harder now. The goddess of reason had been offered blood aplenty, a decade ago and now. Did she even know?

"Logoi," Alex said again. "You said she put Aeda in the—what was it, coralstone?"

"Coralstone," Lilac echoed. "A little blood woke her up to the world outside her prison. More blood let her free herself."

Alex glanced to Cecil and then back to Lilac. The street seemed to narrow the farther they walked. "You're one of Logoi's priestesses, right? I'm surprised Aeda didn't demand your sacrifice as recompense. Or to show submission."

Lilac thought of dinner last night. Simone would have spilled everything then, secrets as runny as blood, had Lilac let her.

"Can dish it out, but can't take it," Alex said. "Fair enough. We all want to live. Even the people you killed."

"My blood wouldn't have done any good," Lilac snapped. The sky rumbled as if to warn her she'd messed up, but the storm was wrong. She didn't care anymore if Alex knew. If Logoi wanted to enforce her secrecy, she could come back and do it herself.

"I don't bloody believe it," Cecil slurred as he grabbed Lilac's shoulder. "A descendant? You?"

Lilac said nothing. Alex glanced between her and Cecil, his face crestfallen, a man cursed to know too many descendants. Or did he think she was lying?

Cecil knew better. "You never told me."

"We're not all so—" Lilac clicked her tongue. "—so exhibitionist about it."

"Exhibitionist," Cecil scoffed, and then he shrugged. "Perhaps so, love."

"It tracks," Alex said. "Why else fixate on Logoi in Valmydion's city? I mean, Aeda's city." He shook his head as if to slide this new knowledge into place. "You're Logoi's daughter."

"Bullshit," Cecil said. "Logoi never had a—" He stumbled over a loose chunk of sidewalk and toddled into the street. Ever the lightweight. "Oh, I see. Mother keeps secrets, daughter keeps secrets." He seemed more offended at Lilac's privacy than at finding out she'd been slitting people's throats. Maybe he didn't yet believe his friend was a killer.

Thunder groaned through the street underfoot and the buildings to either side, as if the rainy season had driven a monstrous cloud against the city's asphalt.

"And what faulty gift you got to show for your lineage, daughter of Logoi?" Cecil asked.

"High detail retention, pattern recognition, execution," Lilac said, but the words felt disconnected. She might have been getting a buzz at last from the drink, but a tremble climbed her legs too; she'd never felt thunder like this. "I work out all the possibilities around me. When I close my eyes and shut out the world, I can follow the patterns faster, see the most efficient course. Like deciding the best turnover routine for a hotel room. Or finding the best escape route from the people I love."

"Quick thinker, that all? People can do that without being descendants." Cecil quaked with nervous laughter. "Damn me, Alex can do that, and there's not a drop of godliness in his family tree!"

Lilac believed it. Alex was doing it now, watching ahead for this strange cloud that kept shaking the earth. He had to feel the same tremor Lilac did.

"At last, a descendant with a gift worse than mine," Cecil went on. "Here I thought everyone was one of Korenbal's daughters, juggling boulders. But not us. Fun, isn't it? We're descended from greatness. Why shouldn't we be great?"

Lilac had no answer for him. She didn't believe they were entitled to greatness, same as the world never allowed them normalcy.

Cecil's laughter echoed on, a frightened thing trapped in his throat. "Why the secret then, eh? Nothing worth hiding."

"Secrets were Logoi's choice," Lilac said. "You're used to being abandoned, but I'm not, and I didn't want people to know." She winced. "I'm sorry."

"No, you got it right." Cecil waved a forgiving hand. "Grandfather never stuck around. We got the gods' blood, got their love, and then we got the gall to want them to be there for us. Sometimes, love's not enough, and good intentions die in the street."

The ground's quaking threw Lilac off balance, and she nearly fell to the curb. The city roared underfoot, jostling windows in their frames and cars against the curb. A gargantuan sloshing curled around the street corner ahead, like someone had turned every radio in the world at full volume to a staticky station.

Lilac saw what was coming in the frail light, but she didn't understand it at first. The darkness swelled into the street, a living monstrosity made of clawing, clutching night sky, only it rushed at her like a smacking hand. The sound loudened against brick and concrete, and then she understood.

The tide surged ahead. Not enough that four years ago it swept her daughters out of her life. The sea had now come for Lilac.

Screams filled the air, sharp where people scurried into alleys, muffled where they were trapped behind high windows or pinned doors. A shriek filled Lilac's throat as the wave bore down on her.

Alex had already slipped to one side. His hand groped for her arm. Cecil joined him, lost somewhere between sober and hammered, and his hand flashed out too, offering his umbrella. Lilac's fingers groped at its tattered edges.

Wet darkness tore against her, snapping the umbrella and knocking her away. She lost sight of Alex and Cecil, perched on a fire escape or car roof, something she couldn't make out as she shouted into the swelling water. Couldn't see, couldn't understand, couldn't swim with these hateful cuffs locking her wrists.

Glass smashed somewhere, and a nonsense thought told her to watch out or else she'd cut her foot again, but Cecil's bottle of Asyx Serenity was gone with the waves. Nothing to drink now but seawater.

The wave slammed Lilac's head underwater, and she went

swirling, dizzy, lost somewhere in the drowning darkness.
    Same as Sara and Daphne.

CHAPTER 33

The water was here to stay. Alex had hoped it might subside before he slid from the rounded car hood where he and Cecil had clambered out of the surge's way, but when its brutal force died down, the water level refused to die with it. The city's drains and ducts would take no more.

Alex's gun holster held his bullets over the floodwater surface, but he stood drenched otherwise. He'd lost his fedora in the sudden wave.

Along with Lilac.

Cecil dropped from the car and threw down his broken umbrella. Somehow his hat still hugged his head. Bright blue fish twinkled beneath the golden cone of a dodgy iron streetlamp. Scattered survivors fought their way out of houses, up fire escapes, onto higher floors and rooftops. A high-pitched shriek rang up a nearby alley, where a sharp black fin knifed through the floodwater.

Alex scanned the street for signs of Lilac, her cuffed hands clinging to a car fender, fire escape stairway, anything. Cecil pawed at the water, ignoring evidence of predators, but there was no excavation for a watery grave. No Lilac to be seen.

"We can't stay," Alex said, nudging Cecil westward. "Follow me. We're close to Oldtown."

Cecil whirled around and grabbed Alex's coat collar. "Are you mad?" he shouted. "You want us dead, that it? Bay Ridge is a muddy pile, floodplains are the new ocean shelf. Oldtown's days are numbered until they give it a new name—the beach."

Alex flinched out of Cecil's grasp. "Oldtown's not finished yet. Arcadia's team wouldn't keep fighting if it was."

"And if they're dead?" Cecil asked.

Alex trudged through the babbling water. He might usually play the pessimist, but right now he needed all the hope he could muster.

Cecil pushed after him. "Might've all been swept off. Arcadia, flood fighters, the whole lot of them gone. Like my friend, yeah? Did you forget Lilac?"

Alex doubted he'd forget Lilac for the rest of his life. "We don't know she's dead."

"You left her in cuffs!" Cecil snapped. "How ace a swimmer you think she'll be in those?"

Alex swallowed hard and tasted rainwater. Black-bulbed streetlamps loomed ahead. Bay Ridge lights stroked the unhappy sky, but Oldtown must've lost power. Only candles and lanterns lit windows here and there, frail against Oldtown's dark swirling nightmare.

"She and I had more in common than I'd ever known," Cecil said. "Understood things you never could. Both descendants, weighed by godly expectation, and yet crushed and unappreciated by the sheer weakness of it. How it sticks to your soul."

"But you die like the rest of us, right?" Alex leaned toward Cecil's face. "My patience is thinner than water tonight. You need to grieve, right? Go ahead and get it out, because when we find Arcadia, I don't want her to hear a word about Lilac."

"Oh?" Cecil cocked his head from side to side. That his fedora clung on seemed a miracle. "I thought we didn't know if she was dead."

"Cecil." Alex's temper evaporated in a cloudy sigh. "I'm sorry."

Cecil blinked hard and then pressed past Alex through the water. "Come, you horrible man. You've a friend to find, isn't that so? I hope yours is more alive than mine."

Alex would have felt better had Cecil punched him in the face, but now wasn't the time for brawling in the street.

They sloshed onward toward the floodplains barricade. The flood stirred at war with itself, in some places pushing deeper into the city, in others tugging fragments toward a barricade breach, the floodplains, the sea. Twelve feet above the street, a frail lantern rushed into sight from behind one dark house, vanished behind another, and reemerged on its far side, the light's edges illuminating a sea-green uniform. One of Arcadia's agents running along the barricade, which meant it still stood.

Oldtown windows stirred with light, as if every household wanted to help the flood fighters. Too many lights to call the evacuation a success, but the city might have already fallen to glories if not for these candles and oil lamps shining on the people desperate to save Oldtown.

Arcadia stood among them. Lanterns encircled her where flood fighters and ununiformed citizens clustered to hear her through the torrent. A heavy crashing somewhere down the wall muffled her words from Alex's ears, but she must have given instructions. Pairs of listeners broke from the group to wade through floodwater, either along the barricade or into the neighborhood.

When enough had cleared, Alex sloshed toward Arcadia. Her muscled arms gestured this way and that, directing people to man the barricade or report on whatever cacophonous disaster was making all that noise to the south.

She paused when she spotted Alex, and then a brilliant grin spread across her face. "Lexi?"

"That's me, far as I'm aware," Alex said, and his mirroring grin broke through the rain. He moved in to hug Arcadia, but she clapped his arm and started away from him.

"We need every willing hand," she said. "Too much night ahead, and maybe too much light. We need people stationed along the houses for our plan to work."

Cecil scowled, but Alex ignored him.

"I appreciate your situation," Alex said, hurrying behind Arcadia. "But we got some trouble, too. A crisis deeper in the city."

Arcadia grabbed a man by the shoulder as he started to wade past her. "Not this way," she said. "Cut through the alley to head south. I don't want you too close to it." The flood fighter nodded and hurried toward Oldtown's houses.

"It?" Cecil echoed.

"Your crisis needs to wait." Arcadia sloshed onward. "I haven't left Oldtown since this morning, and I can't leave now. I'm sorry."

"Why didn't you tell me you almost died yesterday?" Alex snapped. "We spent all dinner yattering, and you never mentioned it."

Arcadia slowed her steps and ran a nervous hand over her scalp. Droplets bounced from her shorn hair. "I really don't have time. Later, I promise."

Alex had been ridiculous to expect any different. If flooding had torn through the North Temple District minutes ago, how could sea-facing Oldtown be any better off? Cecil was right; Alex took a narrow-minded approach to investigations, first toward Lilac, now toward the gods' disappearance, as if the world's troubles would pause until he had his way.

"A miracle saved you," Alex said. "Am I strolling the right avenue?"

Arcadia began to turn. "Lexi—"

"Let me narrow the questions to a point—Aeda, that name sound familiar?" Alex watched Arcadia's face for some recognition. "She might have something to do with why the gods left, something I need to know. She's looking for you, and goddesses don't usually do their own fetching."

The wind thrashed at Arcadia's uniform, forming tents where scratches had cut the fabric. Alex had time for maybe one more question before she ran back to the fray.

"Fine, Aeda means nothing to you," Alex said. "What about Medes?"

A rolling wave surged against Arcadia's chest, and an inhuman calm rippled beneath her skin. She slid one hand into the water and prodded at her belt. The hand returned as a loose fist, where meager light glinted off a small red stone. The air tensed around its hard surface.

Alex took a step back without meaning to, water splashing around him, and he wondered if this sudden warm gravity was anything like the sensations Cecil felt through his clairvoyance.

"Inside this coralstone is Medes, Goddess of Love," Arcadia said, her voice solemn and reverent. "She saved me when I fell. She's the reason I can do this." She tapped the barricade, where steel plastered the stone, leftovers of a truck's fender.

"Gods, she didn't just save you," Cecil said, rushing beside Alex. "You're chosen. A champion."

Alex's eyes wandered Arcadia's body. She looked like herself, but the sense of her reached beyond skin, taking up a greater space in the air and water. In ancient times, champions were empresses and kings, more gifted than most descendants, which might have been why the gods hadn't chosen anyone since long before they abandoned Aeg. What did that make Arcadia?

"I can't play detective with you tonight." Arcadia shoved the red coralstone back into her belt pouch. "Chasing leads nearly killed me yesterday, and I'm needed here, where I should have been in the first place. We need to get communications running up and down three blocks if we're going to guide the sea monster out of the city." She patted Alex's shoulder. "Blackout means turn your lights out. Tell anyone you meet."

Past Arcadia, the night reached out in a claw of massive

squirming fingers that folded around two bright windows. Their sudden darkness echoed in shattered stone and muffled screams.

Arcadia whirled around and charged through the high flood-water. Shadows ate at her sea-green uniform, but her voice pierced the night. "Clear the small debris!"

Alex followed, more questions on his lips. Lanterns lit a stony mound—a house until moments ago. Arcadia stood in the rubble and shoved her hands beneath a collapsed wall, maybe five times her size. Muscles tensed down her back, shoulders, arms as she heaved up the debris and held it long enough for two flood fighters to duck underneath and drag a thin figure from the watery ruin. The wall crashed from Arcadia's fingers like a slamming door. She took a moment to catch her breath, and then she went back to barking orders against the storm.

Cecil tugged Alex's coat. "We can still make the temple, you know." Alex guessed *we* meant he and Cecil.

Not Arcadia. She wouldn't abandon her post.

The darkness thrashed with watery churning, and Alex realized he'd been hearing the sea monster since he and Cecil stepped into Oldtown. He'd never heard of a sea monster inside a city.

But Arcadia would stop it. She was a creature of the gods now. Would she want to know why they'd left, why they wanted her? Only if she thought knowing could make a difference against the glories and their flood. Cecil was still tugging, and Alex shrugged him off as another wave rolled against them. Some bold flood fighter darted atop the barricade with a flashlight in hand, boots squeaking over slick stone.

"We're in the way," Cecil said. "And we've a good chance of winding up like poor Lilac, or the people in that house if a sea monster snatches us. Did Arcadia say it was a serpent?"

Arcadia hadn't specified; doubtful it mattered. Shallow water was not a sea monster's natural habitat, and it would destroy and kill in its confusion and panic. A god should have eased this disaster. Why had Aeda gone to the temple when she could do better work here, as Valmydion had done in ages past? Hadn't Aeda done the same when mortals still called this city Aedos?

Alex waded toward the nearest Oldtown homes. The alleyways would offer some shelter from the sweeping rainfall, if not the flooding.

"We're headed for the temple?" Cecil asked, sounding hopeful.

"We're not going anywhere," Alex said, but his words felt distant, the speech of someone braver in his throat. "We're going to help."

He pulled off his trench coat, hooked it to a windowsill's corner, loosened his tie, and rolled up the sleeves of his white shirt. His vest was swollen damp, but if he could tolerate the flood, so could his clothes. His holster clung to one shoulder, scarcely keeping his gun above water.

The city lay dark beyond the meager windows of light, but the domed temple would stand above every other rooftop. If Lilac had told the truth, and at this point that seemed likely, Aeda would be there. Waiting for Arcadia.

And Medes, her mother. Trapped in a coralstone, same as Aeda. Lilac must have felt similar tension coursing from the daughter's coralstone as Alex had felt moments ago from the mother's. One goddess must have somehow learned about Arcadia from the other. But why did she matter to them?

"You mentioned Medes last night," Alex said.

"Did I?" Cecil asked. "I don't think I did."

"You were drunk." Alex shook an outstretched index finger. "I remember. Talking about the forgotten mothers, that Medes was the first ascendant. Which makes Aeda first of the gods. Meaning no god or mortal was her other parent. She had a father then, one of the Dawn Gods."

Cecil gave a forceful shrug. "Exalis, I think?"

The wind stilled to a brief calm in the squall, giving Alex a

NO GODS FOR DROWNING

moment to breathe without sucking in rainwater. He peered harder down eastward streets, past flooding and car parts and floating newspaper pages, as if he had a clear view across the city to the domed temple roof. The gods must have gifted the temple and city to Valmydion after they had imprisoned Aeda, with the truth washed away by years of stormy seasons. How many centuries since that temple had looked upon its true goddess?

How many millennia since it had looked upon her father, a Dawn God?

"No, it's impossible," Alex muttered, the weight of it dawning on him. "It can't be."

CHAPTER 34

A crimson tide splashed across white shores. Its sticky black strands grasped claw-like at the sand, the slaughtering ocean eager to drag the land beneath blood-thick waves. They tossed Lilac in their copper-tasting surf, lost between solid earth and the swirling deep. She would drink only blood now. She would drink the sea.

Her face burst up from the churning floodwater, waking fully as the surge smacked her shoulder against a hard corner. She reeled in pain, submerged, nearly fainted again, and then charged for the surface. The water fought against a dead-end alley, and she was caught in the middle. Her mouth tasted of copper.

She kicked down until her feet found asphalt, and then she twisted to right herself against the nearest brick wall. Her wrists strained at iron; that asshole Alex should never have cuffed her. She would find a way loose once she escaped this alley. Both palms patted for a path. Brick, brick—air.

Lilac jerked back. A dead end should have three walls; this one only had two. The alley led to an open space, but here the floodwater slammed against an unseen wall and cycled back on itself in an endless looping waterfall between Lilac and the temple plaza. The flood had driven her here, as if bending to Cecil's wishes.

She half-expected this force would reject her too, but when she stepped against it to try, her fingers broke through open air.

Raindrops peeled from her skin, and then her hair and clothes as she breached the rain-resistant space. Her stomach lurched; her chest ached. She doubled over and coughed up saltwater onto dry cobblestones. The new puddle rippled and then retreated to the plaza's edge where unwelcome water belonged.

Lilac wiped her mouth and looked to the temple, the same place she'd nearly gotten Arcadia killed yesterday. Where a goddess had saved her.

That power now pulsed across the plaza, a warm heartbeat fighting back the storm. A thousand lit candles surrounded the temple's marble columns, where hundreds of people stirred across white steps. Some carried suitcases and bags for some reason; others nothing but their children and the clothes on their backs. They had found here what they must have longed for every night since Valmydion's disappearance—a miracle.

No, better than that. A goddess.

Her gargantuan white arms swam in the candlelight, their steady fingers toying with the air as if taming the wind. Scarlet eyes flickered at Lilac, noticing her outside the gathered crowd.

Lilac's exhausted legs buckled, and she fell on hands and knees. Tremors ran up her forearms and clacked the iron cuffs against each other. Aeda would like her this way. She strode toward the plaza's edge, her footsteps migrating the crowd both out of her way and behind her. Everyone watched or followed, as if afraid that letting her out of their sight would mean she'd abandoned them like the other gods.

"I see no coralstone which makes my mother's prison," Aeda said. "I see no Arcadia Myrn either."

Her eyes glared in giant rubies. Two great fingers danced at her hip, either a sign of impatience or another step in the dance she'd been performing before she noticed Lilac. Beneath Aeda's stiff veneer, she must have been weaving a miracle from moment to moment, likely to keep the rain and sea at bay from the temple plaza.

Lilac lowered her head. "The flood caught me."

"Not a surprise, and so not a disappointment." Aeda waved back at the temple. "You see what I make of this godforsaken place. The burden has always fallen to divinity. The Dawn Gods reshape the world by their very presence, and we children make do. Would that I had a covenant, they would dance and channel, but there is no time for ritual. Only blood."

Lilac glanced at the marble steps of Valmydion's—no, Aeda's temple. Someday she would accept the difference, but the truth ached. Still, the steps were clean. No blood bathed them yet.

Only people, each thrumming with the makings of miracles.

A sharp wind howled through Aeda's hair. "I cannot do the work to save this world without you, Lilac, daughter of Logoi, granddaughter to Kalypses and Kaligos and the Unnamed Mother, yourself a mother to twin lost souls. And yet, as my liberator, you become mother and savior to Aeg. To mankind." A curling finger beckoned Lilac to stand and follow toward the temple steps. Another two fingers went on dancing at Aeda's hip.

Lilac climbed from the warm cobblestones and hurried to Aeda's side. The doorways to her temple stood so high, they were probably the only entrances in the city which didn't have to stretch to accommodate godly height.

"I remember when Logoi was born," Aeda said. "Your grandmother, the Unnamed Mother, has no like. Impregnated by two Dawn Gods, some say she violated the laws of nature, but we gods cannot be one with the natural world. We dance with it, and it dances with us. Logoi tore her mother apart before she could ascend to godhood herself. Dead before divinity, a nine-headed child to show for this. Did Logoi ever tell you?"

"No, goddess," Lilac said, and she wasn't sure how to feel. This story felt like dirty family secrets being aired before a too-large crowd.

"Logoi was beautiful, and she was also a monster," Aeda went on. "Mortals feared her until her intelligence shined, and so they accepted her, but she could not love them. Why keep your affection? Could it be only familiarity?"

Logoi also spoke less than Aeda, a quality Lilac cherished in Arcadia, too. Mentioning that now would be disastrous.

"Logoi was my teacher," Lilac said. "My everything. I didn't know my mortal mother until later."

"After Logoi abandoned you? Fortuitous, again." Aeda spread her arms to either side, and the crowd scattered down the temple steps. She stroked the air, swaying with it in a strange dance. "Some believe we gods cast our will upon the world. Perhaps so, but we cannot guide fate, the nature of time, the nature of nature itself. Gods fuel the year's wheel, but it rests upon you small cogs to turn this great machine."

"You know about machines?" Lilac asked.

"Your culture's progress ebbs and flows with the tide," Aeda said. "When the glories recede, you prosper by steam, by oil, by lightning, even by miracle engines. But the glories return, and all your progress lies sundered by their seas. We gods drive them off, and you climb from stone and dust again. Cyclical centuries. The glories, too, have their machines, empowered by the ocean floor's volcanic fire. How else could they send the seas into my city?"

Aeda's arms slithered in the wind, beckoning to the temple's ceiling. Its deceptive murals hid far beyond candlelight. Would Aeda let those painted lies about Valmydion last until dawn?

"Beginning tonight, the glories' machines will end," Aeda said. Crimson light bristled down her pale skin. "Five thousand years have passed since the Dawn Gods' descent. In the eons since, mankind has spread from Aeg to dot distant continents. My great father set seed inside my mother, and followed by this came her ascension, my birth, the First Children, the half-dozen Holy Wars which your history recalls as one, the Holy Psychopomp Tree, the tree's burning two millennia ago, and now you have dwelt ten years without the gods."

Lilac watched the dancing candlelight, evasive as truth. Miracle engines, technology and culture lost to time, more than one Holy War? She'd never heard anything like it. Were there missing Verses of Aeg, or did the holy book only cover the final war before the Dawn Gods set their children straight? Aeda might have been lying again, but Lilac didn't think so. Gods saw much more of time and the world than any mortal.

Aeda paused at the temple's debris-strewn seating, where fabric strips and torn newspaper pages seemed to desecrate the marble. "Tragic and blessed times seem alike, for the glories have forever hunted and haunted mankind. No more after tonight. I should elevate you, daughter of Logoi, to the ancient and forgotten rank of high priestess."

Lilac turned now, her brow furrowing. "High priestess?"

Aeda nodded once. "This rank has fallen from use. For some time, covenants have kept no leaders when the gods have taken a direct hand. But long ago, there were the people, the covenant, and then the high priestess, and only she would attend to that highest of powers."

Lilac trembled. That highest of powers? That couldn't mean—

Aeda faced her temple's ceiling. "Lilac, daughter of Logoi, I anoint you high priestess to my father Exalis, first of the Dawn Gods to descend from the heavens, first to seed gods upon the world, and soon first of the Dawn Gods to return from the heavens. When he breaches the skies and reaches his magnificence across land and sea, he will bring an end to the glories and seed a new world for mankind." She thrust her hands out, gesturing to the open plaza. "When my temple runs red."

A sick lump welled in Lilac's throat. She looked to her palms, clean only because they drained any blood they touched. She'd lost her dagger, but there would be others in the temple.

"This heralds a moment of great and terrible sacrifice for a bright and beautiful future," Aeda said.

She tapped one mighty fingertip on the chain between Lilac's cuffs. Their stern iron slopped mud-like from her wrists, no more solid than blood, and dribbled onto the marble floor.

"No better a high priestess for these mortal acts than one already accustomed to the slaughter." Aeda laid two enormous fingers on Lilac's shoulder. "None would dream to carve this sacrificial flesh without our beloved butcher."

CHAPTER 35

The wind swirled in Arcadia's ears like it wanted her to miss the warning. She could see just fine, unlike Cassis who kept batting damp hair out of her face. Maybe Logoi had taught them to keep it short to ready them for a night like this. Still, seeing wouldn't do Arcadia much good if she missed—

"Circling!"

Jason shouted over the howling downpour. He perched on a street corner, up to his chest in water, where he watched for the sea monster.

Every other agent had taken cover or climbed atop the barricade where Arcadia and Cassis stood. Arcadia hoped they wouldn't get blown away. Bad as the city was, the floodplains now belonged to the sea.

"Blackout!" Arcadia shouted. Cassis and the other barricade-mounted flood fighters echoed down the line.

Candles and lanterns choked across Oldtown. Everyone seemed to have done their job passing the word along the streets. Echoes of "Blackout!" carried from block to block, dousing the neighborhood in a protective black sheet.

Except where Arcadia and her agents clasped flashlights around the barricade's gateway. The sea monster seemed to like the lights. It had thrust its bone-helmed head into six houses tonight—those with the brightest windows. Families with either too much oil or too much eagerness to help the flood fighters.

Families with nothing now.

The sea monster might spring at stone walls like a writhing piece of night, but deep down, it was nothing more than a confused animal that didn't want to be here. Furious, possibly injured by the glories when they drove it into the city, maybe dying. Better it die at sea where it wouldn't take anyone with it.

Arcadia aimed her flashlight at the gateway. Cassis mimicked her, and others followed. Every light in Oldtown shone the way to the sea.

"Arcadia!" a familiar voice called beneath her feet.

Alex waded in the floodwater below, hardly visible outside the flashlight beams. No sign of Cecil. Hopefully he'd retreated to somewhere safe like Alex should have done.

"Take cover," Arcadia said. Her boots squealed against the barricade's top as a fresh tremor rumbled through the stone.

Floodwater surged around a street corner as the sea monster charged for the barricade.

"We got its eyes," Cassis said. Her flashlight twitched in her shaking hands.

"Ease it through," Arcadia said.

Water rushed as the monster charged for the gateway. If everyone kept their lights aimed at the gap and toward the floodplains, it might forget about destroying Oldtown and swim back where it came from. There was still the storm, wind, and flooding, but there would at least be one less problem.

"Arcadia!" Alex called up again. A precious need filled his voice.

A sudden screech ripped Arcadia's attention from him. The sea monster's carapace gleamed beneath flashlight beams as it made a sharp turn along the barricade, splashing the flood fighters.

"Wait!" Cassis cried, as if wild animals took orders.

Arcadia tried aiming her flashlight ahead, but the monster focused on brighter lights peeking around a northern street corner.

Cassis whipped the two-way radio off her belt. "Captain Myrn ordered full blackout! Whose light is that?"

The radio crackled. "This is Agent Ilene Summers. Don't worry, everyone. We've brought reinforcements."

Chilly rainwater slithered down Arcadia's spine. She raised one arm against the oncoming flashlights, their beams casting deep shadows over the floodwater. Clusters of darkness floated upon makeshift rafts, forming a writhing silhouette with each one's head and limbs indistinguishable from the others.

But the shouting came clear and familiar. "Ready yourselves!" Commander Thale bellowed. "Agents, seek cover! Officers, take aim!"

Arcadia didn't have time to shout him down or stop him. She grabbed Cassis's collar and dragged her flat against the barricade's top to cover her. Alex would hopefully brace himself against the stony foundation below.

The world had not been quiet since the glories sent whales and waves and the sea monster rushing against Oldtown, but their assault was a peaceful lullaby compared to this rattling gunfire. Thale had limited ideas on how to resolve a crisis, and right now he squeezed every bit of his imagination into a submachine gun's trigger, each round clacking a thunderous symphony. They were the same type of rapid-firing rifle he'd loaded officers with ten years ago in the mountains, their undersides fitted with disc-shaped ammo drums, feeding rounds out the barrels as they went *clack-clack-clack* in the night.

Bullets tore across the sea monster's helm and trunk. Tentacles thrashed at the water, the barricade, and the makeshift rafts, knocking gun-wielding officers overboard and agents down the wall. The sea monster wanted to kill the light, and everything that made light.

But the gunfire didn't stop.

Arcadia wanted to rise, carry Cassis away, shout for Thale to stop. His way had never solved a problem, only caused new ones, as if that were all his police could do.

There wasn't time. The sea monster needed out, needed to escape, and turned sharply, knocking its tail into a stone house as its trunk whipped across the barricade. Cracked and bleeding carapace scraped against stone.

Arcadia grabbed for Cassis's arm as one muscly rope slapped the barricade beneath them, and then another came sweeping across the wall. The blow knocked Arcadia clear from the top. Cassis's flashlight twirled, struck a slab of bent-up truck, and shattered.

Cold darkness engulfed Arcadia's head. The water's surface felt far away, and the world was fading. Where was Cassis? What about Alex? Which side of the barricade had Arcadia fallen toward, the city or the doomed floodplains?

Maybe both sides were doomed.

CHAPTER 36

A lex saw the splash a moment before realizing who'd fallen. No, he wasn't going to let the flood take anyone else he knew tonight, especially not Arcadia. He dug his hands under her armpits and tugged her up from the water. She was a limp doll, and the drenched uniform weighed her down, but the high floodwater eased Alex's load in gliding her toward a wrecked pile of what used to be part of the barricade's top. Tentacle or stone or both must have struck Arcadia's head—a shallow gash tore along her scalp, glinting in the new light.

She would be fine, Alex was certain as he hauled her onto the ravaged stone. Godly power pulsed through her body. He felt it as he touched her neck for a heartbeat and then as he hovered a hand over her mouth and nose to check for breath. Unconscious but alive. She would probably wake soon.

Alex had an opportunity now, but not for long.

He glanced back at the fight between Thale's forces and the sea monster to be sure the creature wouldn't come this way, and then he opened a pouch along Arcadia's belt.

The coralstone was rougher than expected. Alex's fingertips raked across its porous surface, and two digits emerged bleeding when he lifted it to his face. Hard to believe this palm-sized rock held the power of a goddess inside, but she made her presence known when sunshine-like warmth breathed through his skin.

"Mmm, a new sweetling."

Alex flinched and nearly dropped the coralstone. He hadn't expected that gentle whisper. His slick fingers squeezed tight, rubbing his palm against the coralstone's pores. More blood for Medes. No getting squeamish; he would only have this one chance.

But could he blame his nerves for twitching? He'd last faced a goddess over twenty years ago at his induction into the Logos police. Logoi's many heads had seen him, sure, but he'd stood with Arcadia and everyone else from their barracks year. Arcadia must've had unique strength inside her to approach Logoi again, alone, and receive her miracle. If only Alex could mimic that bravery for five minutes. He hadn't planned for this moment, but there was no precedence for questioning a god. It wasn't done.

"Do not pretend us strangers, sweetling." Medes hummed through Alex's bones with a strange pressure and unfamiliar accent. "I felt your presence tonight, and last night. You would bring me pleasantries and friends. Savior to Arcadia, aren't you?"

"Arcadia is perfectly capable of saving herself," Alex said, his voice cracking like a teenager's. He blamed the storm.

"In your experience, perhaps," Medes said. "I did not find it so. I found her bleeding in a secret chamber beneath my daughter's temple."

"You're Aeda's mother," Alex said.

"My daughter was present with us, but too far to help." The coralstone hummed. "She knows of our dear champion. Arcadia lay dying, and for that blood, my miracle stitched flesh and bone to rightness."

At Alex's feet, Arcadia stirred. Already recovering. Time was running out. "And Exalis was her father. Which made you his— what, priestess?"

"Dawn Gods give no designation." Medes's pleased sigh rippled through the coralstone. "To them, the world runs no thicker than water. Sift it, drink it, reshape it in vessels. To love a Dawn

God is to love the universe. You cannot imagine the sheer awe of standing in a wheatfield and staring into the heavens as his colossal presence descends." The coralstone shimmered red. "But you will know it."

Alex squeezed the stone. He doubted the goddess felt the pressure as its rough edges scraped his skin. "Will I meet him? Exalis?"

"Briefly," Medes said. She sounded regretful. "My courageous daughter calls her father to the world, a reunion many years in the making. Expect him to greet her, yes, love her, yes, do as she asks, yes. But then comes his return to the heavens for the final time."

"Final?" Alex echoed. The Dawn God Sceptomos had shed his physical form while his soul returned to the heavens. Exalis might do the same. "What then? A new Holy Psychopomp Tree?"

"Clever sweetling." Another hum rippled through the coralstone, and a smile caught Medes's voice. "Arcadia's fondness be a small wonder. I, too, enjoy your quick mind."

Arcadia stirred again as gunfire clacked over the floodwater. A quick mind wasn't enough; Alex needed quicker words.

"Is that why the rest of the gods left us?" Alex asked. "You stand to gain, right? They put you in these stones to stop you from summoning a Dawn God?"

"Indeed, Logoi and the others did not wish Exalis's return, not for our purpose," Medes said. "Your gods have abandoned you, their reasons unknown to me, but fate rises fortuitous in their absence. All the world may gain when Arcadia joins the body of my heavenly lover."

A nervous tremble fought the coralstone's warmth from Alex's skin. Same as Gentle Theo had become the old Holy Tree's core, Arcadia would merge with the new one. But if Medes and Aeda hadn't steered the other gods out of Aeg, then who was responsible?

"Logoi and the others did not appreciate Aeda's vision," Medes went on. "My ambitious, beautiful daughter sought a particular kind of soul centuries ago, and for that, we were punished. Now we find another, Arcadia Myrn, she whose hand would not bring death. Not to man, not to glory, not to those who are people. A unique find, yes?"

Alex shifted on the stone pile. "But why *that* kind of soul? Why Arcadia?"

An excited breath slid through the coralstone. "Expect no simple return of Sceptomos's Holy Tree! Sceptomos taught healing to mankind, but Exalis taught fire. Aeda's new Holy Tree welcomes the era of the transcendent psychopomp. She whose hand would not bring death will draw up the souls from still-living mankind and hold them in the tree's branches to await the Between."

"You'd steal our souls?" Alex's grip tightened so hard that his fingers ached. "What would happen to our bodies?"

"Unstoppable mankind." Medes gasped with glee. "No souls to sully or restrain with simplistic morality. Forget the laws taught by the Dawn God Kalypses, forget anxious guilt and doubt. Unshackled and merciless, your kind may clot the seas with glorious blood. By Arcadia's deathless hands, expect mankind to shepherd true death oceanward and usher in a world without the glories."

Alex swallowed hard. "Genocide."

"Simplistic morality," Medes repeated. "They ravage Aeda's city and drown your Holy Land, yet you cower. For what? Your souls? Their existence? Do not cherish your weaknesses, sweetling. Would you pity the glories moments from now? I think not. I see your death."

Alex leaned the coralstone away from his face. Clacking gunfire began to fade; same for the sea monster's thrashing. "My death?" he asked.

"Death, and then the Between." Medes sighed through Alex's skin. "May you find reincarnation in a better world."

A cold fleshy rope snagged Alex's throat and yanked him backward. His body smacked against debris-strewn water and then

252

plunged underneath as scaly limbs coiled around his arms, legs, and chest. Floodwater sloshed over his face. He thrashed forward, opened his mouth to scream, but there was no air, no clear sound, only water closing around him.

Only a glory to drag him down and drown him.

CHAPTER 37

Gunfire eased as Arcadia sat up straight and coughed salty water onto her lap. She had landed on a pile of broken stone. Flashlight beams cast flailing shadows over nearby houses in a twisted dance.

Something red glimmered in the floodwater. Arcadia glanced at her belt, one pouch open, and then snatched the coralstone from the rubble's edge. It must have flown loose when she fell. She stuffed it back into her belt pouch; the last thing she needed tonight was for a goddess to sink into the waves.

Ammo drums struck makeshift rafts, and another volley of gunfire thundered through Oldtown. The sea monster thrashed, and one muscly limb grasped a Logos officer and flung him screaming over the barricade's top in a flash of blue uniform. There was no helping him, but the monster was weaker now. Had it been in prime shape when it arrived, those limbs would have torn Thale's firing squad apart, but the glories had dropped it on death's door.

"Cassis?" Arcadia called. No answer. "Lexi?"

She staggered along the lower barricade, where cracks forked around fresh leaking holes. They were the same, she and the barricade, both weary and crumbling in this long night. A rag doll floated against her thigh alongside a wooden toothbrush. She pawed at the water, came up with a pistol—did it belong to Cassis? No, she would have had a revolver. Two feet away, the water sloshed and churned.

"Lexi?" Arcadia asked. "Cassis?"

Limbs tussled beneath the water as if bound in rope. Arcadia waded closer, where a face strained for the surface. Not Cassis's long hair, but Alex's shorn scalp. Arcadia plunged both hands into the water and tugged the wriggling figure toward her.

Alex did not surface alone. Behind him, a womanly face stared with blue-black eyes, mostly pupil, each wide as a fist. No human had eyes like that, or fleshy tendrils down their scalp, spine, and limbs instead of hair, or a hide of shimmering blue-white scales. Tentacles stretched from her abdomen beneath human-like arms, each curling at the end like a fist. Her thick snakish tail writhed in the water in place of legs.

Arcadia had only seen glories in stylish murals and fuzzy moving pictures or photographs, or as far-off shapes on dim coastal evenings. Always separated by distance or medium, never a face-to-face confrontation until here in the muck of Oldtown, where squid-like limbs tugged and strangled Alex.

His choked cry came wordless and desperate, his face dark. Arcadia stuffed the pistol in her lost revolver's holster and launched herself on the glory. Claws scraped at one shoulder, but she squeezed a hard fist around the limb at Alex's neck and uncurled it from his throat. He gasped hard, almost sinking into the water. Arcadia wrapped one arm around his chest to hold him up and fought at the glory's fleshy ropes with the other, untangling tentacles one by one even as the glory scratched and flailed. Arcadia's arms bruised beneath glorious muscles. They would drag her and Alex to watery death given the chance.

Arcadia reeled back and slammed her fist into the glory's slick chest. The glory was sleek and strong, but no goddess fueled her with holy purpose. No god would ever champion a glory.

The glory came again for Arcadia's free arm, but she let go of Alex, grabbed the glory's trunk in both hands, and slung her at the debris pile beneath the stone barricade.

Alex collapsed against Arcadia and grasped at her uniform. She hauled him to standing. He coughed up a throatful of seawater—alive, unharmed. Good; Arcadia had other problems. Her free hand dove for her holster and drew the pistol.

The glory scrabbled at the debris pile, but she was sluggish. Either Arcadia's blow had shaken her, or this had been a long night for everyone, human and glory alike. Was this glory drowning in the air? Arcadia knew little about their anatomy, whether they had dolphin-like lungs or fish-like gills, or both, or something in between. Could the glory's flat nose smell the dying sea monster's fish-rot like Arcadia, or did that facial feature have another purpose? How different and alike were they?

Alex slinked from Arcadia's trunk and stood on his own two feet. His wide white eyes glared across the water as hard rain dripped across him, and Arcadia, and the glory. Could she feel it, or did her scales not notice water?

Arcadia raised the pistol. She hadn't been made to aim a gun in years, and now twice in two days. This one belonged to somebody else. Would that make pulling the trigger easier?

Alex coughed out a question. "What are you waiting on?"

The glory's midnight eyes watched Arcadia. However she breathed, her chest expanded and contracted, and her whole body vibrated with tension. The fight was gone.

Arcadia's hand trembled. She lowered the gun an inch.

"Arcadia," Alex said. "You're a flood fighter. Do your work." He broke into another coughing fit.

The glory didn't look much like a flood. Sinewy tendrils curled and uncurled down her scalp and arms, each like a numb hand trying to work feeling back into its blood vessels.

Up the street, the gunfire at last died beneath the sea monster's hollow moaning. Nothing heavy splashed in the floodwater; no Logos officers or flood fighters flew screaming over the barricade.

Either the sea monster was already dead, or else it, like the glory, had surrendered.

"Arcadia," Alex said again. "The trigger. Pull it." He said this like he'd forgotten his own pistol, as if what mattered wasn't the glory's fate, but that Arcadia decided who would live or die.

And she would. She studied Alex's stern face and then let the pistol slide back into the water where she'd found it. He choked out her name again, but she missed whatever else he said. Her gaze stuck to the crushed stone and the beaten creature lying partway in the water.

The glory's gaze followed the sinking pistol and then slid back to Arcadia. The expression was unreadable across flat features, sideways-blinking eyes, and a thin mouth lined with sharp fish-like teeth. She leaned her head back, showing thin blue scratches down the left side of her face. Had she fought with some other glory, or was this the mark of an animal attack out at sea?

Arcadia climbed dripping onto the stone debris, closer than she ever thought she'd get to a living glory.

The glory didn't move. Only watched.

Arcadia knelt in front of her and sighed. "What did we ever do to you?"

The glory's eyes twitched back and forth. Her mouth opened slowly, revealing sharp teeth. "Ever do to you?" she said, a perfect mimic of Arcadia's voice and inflection.

Clear enough to imitate, but unlikely the glory understood human speech. If any simple answer existed to Arcadia's question, some clear motive that drove the glories to hate humans so much, this one glory probably didn't know it. She was one small cog in their machine, same as Arcadia. And if this glory did know, why would she think Arcadia deserved an explanation?

Light slashed from up the street, casting Arcadia's shadow across the debris. She waved a hand toward the water and gave a curt nod. The glory must have understood—she slunk head-first down the debris and under the water's surface, where her tail splashed once as she vanished from sight. She would probably swim through the gateway in a blink.

Arcadia turned toward the coming light, where Thale waded closer. Officers trailed behind him, while flood fighter agents wandered the ravaged street. Some haunted the sea monster's corpse, murmuring to each other while they watched Arcadia.

"Commander," Arcadia said. She couldn't remember how to formally greet Thale. He seemed so much smaller from up on the debris. On even footing, she crested him, but from this stone incline, she stood a head taller.

"I can't have seen this," Thale said. "You had a glory at your mercy, but you let it go."

Alex edged toward Thale. "She slipped away," he said, and then coughed again.

Thale ignored him and clambered out of the water, onto the pile of stone. "Don't think anyone's kept your miracle a secret from me, Myrn. Tell me, is this the gods' will? Let a glory have another chance to kill people?"

Arcadia glanced at the water, as if the glory might resurface to explain for her. Nothing moved but raindrops forming circles in the flood. Alex stared up. He looked as tired as Arcadia felt.

Thale slid into Arcadia's view. "What are you really, Myrn? You wouldn't hurt one worm on that squid-fucker's head, you wouldn't help summon a goddess."

"Rhoster—" Alex started.

Thale shouted over him. "What are you, Myrn, but a walking pointless failure?"

Arcadia shifted on her feet, knocking pebbles into the water. Not one touched Thale's boots. Thale saw Shah, glories, and the world one way; Arcadia saw another, but he had no place in her head.

"I'm not your officer anymore," Arcadia said.

"You don't head the evac team anymore either. Not the flood fighters. Any of it." Thale cocked his head toward the flooded street. "Get out of Oldtown. I'll find something more your aptitude tomorrow. Pray to Valmydion there'll *be* a tomorrow." He splashed past Alex into the water and stormed toward the sea monster's carcass, his beard a wet mop down his face. "Find oil and machetes, enough for a sea monster. We can't leave this thing rotting here."

Agents and officers scurried to obey, but here and there they stole glances at Arcadia as she slid into the floodwater and waded down the street. They had to think she was a traitor to Logos, Aeg, mankind itself. Any one of them would have pulled the trigger, or drawn a knife from their belts, anything to stop even one glory. Alex had tried to order it as if he were still her captain. As if Shah haunted Oldtown and maybe the entire city tonight.

No one else understood the glory was a person. Hairless, scaly, covered in tendrils, a tail instead of legs, but she wasn't a fish or a squid. She was like Arcadia. In the dawn days, glories kept their own architecture, arts, inventions, their own kind of peace. Did they still prosper in the deep sea? With the gods gone, their society might have turned solely to annihilating Aeg's city-states. Little else explained the tide rolling from beach to city but some unknown machine of glorious invention.

But glories wanted mankind dead, and Arcadia was supposed to kill the glory. Something crucial inside this world was broken, and she didn't know how to fix it. She didn't know how to swim along with the brokenness either. Did that make her whole, or was she broken in a different way?

Maybe Thale was right, and she was useless, purposeless. Godly power burned through her body and yet she couldn't help being herself, with every fault that entailed. Arcadia should have been turned away from the barracks, the only orphan in Logos too meek to someday be forced into the police. No one back then had noticed the pointless soul inside.

How could Logoi have seen a life worthy of a miracle? How could Medes have seen this life as worth saving?

The water floated thick with wooden shrapnel and household items. A white soap bar, a red necktie, a face-down photograph loosed from its frame. Arcadia hoped for no bodies right now. The first corpse she'd ever seen was her mother's, and then her father's beside, both half-buried in a landslide outside Logos when Arcadia was small. Her mother hadn't looked like herself, too much red dressing her brown skin.

Someone splashed through the water, and Arcadia glanced back to find Alex trailing behind, with Cecil joining from within a dark alleyway. They kept their distance, as if her sense of mercy might be contagious, but they followed her anyway.

Conversation might bubble up, and then questions. Maybe somewhere safe existed in the city's hopelessness where Cecil could get drunk, and Alex could laugh with Lilac. But what of Arcadia? Last night's peaceful dinner had no place in her life. She was a creature bound in chaos and bloodshed. Pleasant company made a bad fit for her soul. Friends, lover, lover's family— privileges of another's life, handed to Arcadia by mistake.

She deserved none of it.

CHAPTER 38

"Rip out our souls?" Cecil whispered. "What, from the lot of us?"

Alex opened and shut his mouth. He'd been too horrified to ask specifics, and now Medes in her coralstone was out of his hands. Many things were.

"Gather that's why the gods put her and Aeda in them blasted stones to begin with." Cecil sounded apathetic. Raindrops bounded off his fedora.

Maybe he was right; not like Alex knew. Nothing seemed certain these days. He couldn't even read his best friend three feet ahead of him. Had Arcadia overhead him repeat Medes's plan to Cecil as they crossed from Oldtown? Would she care? Alex had known her too long to be sure, remembered too many facets—that frail adolescent standing over beaten police cadets, the changed teenager emerging from Logoi's temple, the broken officer at Shah, the flood fighter of recent, and now this forlorn champion of the gods.

But she was also every facet at once. Frail, powerful, brave, broken. Streetlights glared off the floodwater's surface, and their shine pulled Alex into a decade past, when Shah burned against a black sky. He had braced the submachine gun against his shoulder, slammed in the ammo drum, and prayed *All for Logoi* like everyone else. And then he'd squeezed the trigger, like *almost* everyone else. Between the flickering fires and his lowered eyelids, he hadn't been able to tell which dancing bodies fell from his rounds or those of his fellow officers. He could pretend he'd shot no one. Only Arcadia knew for certain that she was blameless.

She broke down there in the hills, Alex had told Lilac, the same as he'd believed these past ten years.

Tonight was different. Arcadia had refused to pull the trigger in Oldtown, but not for breaking down. She had looked Alex in the eye, damn her, defying his coughed-out demands and Thale's expectations. No panic, no breakdown. The glory had been at Arcadia's mercy, and she'd made a choice.

Maybe not for the first time, Alex now realized. He might have spent the last ten years misunderstanding Shah. He thought she'd quit the Logos police out of shame, but what if she'd been too disgusted to ever wear the badge again? Same as Alex, only years earlier.

In that case, how well did he really know Arcadia?

He pushed through the floodwater to catch up with her. Electric light glimmered in the South Temple District windows; the sea monster had missed this neighborhood in focusing its rampage on Oldtown. The radiance showed mud stains and torn fabric down Arcadia's uniform. A row of deep scratches lined one bicep, but they were already healing. She was tense and tired, and she needed a rest more than any other soul tonight.

"It's true," Alex said. "You never killed anyone."

Arcadia glanced at him but said nothing. He doubted she'd put much thought to it. Most people never had to, and only Alex and the other murderers both current and formerly with the Logos police had to weigh how much blood they'd spilled. All for Logoi, or all for themselves?

Something thrashed down an intersection as they crossed the street, and Alex drew his brass-colored pistol. Water ran slick down its barrel. Could it fire if another glory appeared? Should it?

He plucked bullets from its bottom-loading chamber and used his necktie to rub the rounds as dry as he could, one by one. If Arcadia noticed the gun, she kept it to herself.

"I've seen you fire, but only in training," Alex said. "Practice shots. Never in the field."

They neared the South Temple District's main thoroughfare, emptier than usual. Farther east, Honest Hector's pawnshop was likely open despite the hateful storm. Northward, not far from the Central Temple District, they would find Lilac's apartment. Had Simone abandoned home, or had she decided she was safer on that second floor than anywhere else?

"You quit the police years before I did, like you knew it sat wrong," Alex went on. "Was it Shah? Or something else?"

"You know why," Arcadia said, almost pleading.

"Shah, then." Alex examined another bullet. "I wish you'd drilled the same into me."

Arcadia pressed past a door floating in the water. "Your place wasn't my decision."

"Of course not," Alex said. "You made a choice at Shah, while I followed orders. Never questioned if it was right until later, only hoped I didn't cause too much harm. Story of my life." He dried another bullet. The rain seemed to lighten, leaving fewer ripples in the water. "But that's no way to live. We have to make decisions against harm, and I let the blood flow onto my hands, Logoi's star glaring down at us like she was there. You knew better. The star reminded you that wasn't your work. No death or harm on your hands."

"I've caused harm." Arcadia sounded cold. "There's no place in the Logos police without harm."

Alex turned over his last bullet. "I've wondered if so many people really did wrong back in Logos that Logoi had plenty to drink, or if her laws and demands pressed them until they cracked. A god who wants blood will find a way."

"Bringing people in, we knew they'd wind up at the Racks," Arcadia said. "All for Logoi."

Alex almost laughed; why did she have to be so fucking right all the time? "You got me! I'm still making excuses for us. We can't blame Logoi. You knew that, even when you went to her for a miracle. It was your choice to swear yourself to her in a deeper way than the rest of us, and yet you chose not to kill."

Arcadia paused and offered him a meager smile, as if she understood some secret truth about their souls she wasn't allowed to share. She would take that understanding to her death.

Alex clacked the pistol's chamber shut. "You're too good for the rest of us," he said, ticking back the hammer. "You always were."

Thunder quaked from the pistol. Arcadia groped at her chest, where a hole now punctured her uniform, and then she collapsed into the water. Her body began to sink, and for the second time tonight Alex caught and held her. He let the rainy darkness drink his pistol; he never wanted to fire it again. His gaze stuck to Arcadia's empty face.

She was already gone. He hadn't thought it would happen so quickly.

Cecil gasped. "What's the matter with you?"

Alex cradled Arcadia to his chest. Her legs bobbed partway between surfacing and submerging, weighed by her waterlogged boots.

"I'm sorry," Alex whispered. "I love you, and I'm so sorry."

He wanted to tell her he didn't have a choice, but he no longer knew whether or not that was true. Maybe every human action since the dawn days had been a choice. The true curse of the Dawn Gods was to uplift mankind and let them make decisions. A mistake of five thousand years dwarfed Alex's every miserable action. They'd left him to clean up their consequences and prevent new divine errors.

Or was he still making excuses to let himself off the hook?

Floodwater splashed as Cecil crept closer. "Is she gone?" He looked her over. "She is. Gods, what did you do that for?"

"They want our souls." Alex's voice came gentle, as if explaining this terrible night to a small child. "Part of us would be bound to the Holy Tree, and the rest would be deathless husks. All to kill the glories." He held Arcadia tighter. "No choice in it anymore. They shouldn't all die, and we shouldn't all live as soulless abominations. Wrong for everyone. No wonder the gods put Aeda and Medes in those stones. How could you call Aeg the Holy Land with an unholiness like that?"

Cecil glanced at the water, as if he could see Alex's gun. "Unnatural."

"The gods can heal the wounded and sick." Alex glided Arcadia over the water's surface toward a building's black-iron fire escape. "They can empower, or weaken, or change a body between sexes and forms, give a womb where there was none, or take one away. But souls leave the dead and join the living—any other way violates the laws of nature, right? The gods never pay the price for that; it's always us." His hand stroked Arcadia's cheek. "This time, we all pay. Even the gods."

"But Aeda wanted her," Cecil said.

"No one gets what they want tonight." Alex hauled Arcadia onto the fire escape's firm steps. She was heavier now than when she'd drifted unconscious at the barricade. "Arcadia wasn't a descendant. She couldn't hide from them, no matter where she went, and I don't even know if she'd have gone, but they'd have found her. Aeda can't have our souls, by any means. No matter what the rest of us have to lose. Now, open Arcadia's belt pouch."

Cecil slipped closer, but his hands remained at his sides. "What for?"

"What for." Alex's cackle rang hollow through the street. "I murdered my best friend to stop this, so don't fuck with me, Cecil. Open the middle pouch and get the coralstone. I'm not touching the damn thing again. Keep it hidden when we reach Aeda." He laid Arcadia's head against one iron step and slid from beneath her. "Hurry it up. We're outrunning a Dawn God."

Cecil slipped one hand up his trench coat sleeve, opened the belt pouches with the other until he found the coralstone, and picked it up with the fabric-covered hand, as if afraid to touch its porous surface. Alex couldn't blame him. A descendant's blood might not feed the goddess inside, but her presence ached to touch.

"But I don't see why you care," Cecil said.

"I have a plan," Alex said. "That's all you need to know. Now keep it on you; we'll need it."

Cecil partway unbuttoned his coat and slipped the stone into an inner pocket.

There. Alex had done all he could. He wasn't sure he could destroy the coralstone, didn't dare try in case it freed Medes, and he couldn't risk stashing it somewhere after it had last been found, but it would serve his purposes when he reached the temple. Cecil was the best choice for holding it, both a descendent who might mask its presence, and someone Alex trusted more than anyone now that Arcadia was gone.

Nothing left to do but to face another goddess. Alex drifted down the steps from Arcadia's body and dipped chest-deep into the floodwater.

"You've made an awful mess," Cecil said from behind. "Without Aeda's chosen one to toss into the Holy Tree, Exalis might not come. She might punish everyone in the city. We can't be sure. She's not a goddess known for intimacy or forgiveness."

Alex sloshed northward, aiming for the Central Temple District. Faster—he needed to put city blocks between himself and what he'd done. The coralstone throbbed against the air behind him, even from within Cecil's trench coat, as if the goddess were still clawing after the woman they'd left behind. Without blood, Alex expected she would weaken before they reached the temple.

Cecil chased. "It's godly wrath you're risking," he said. "What were you thinking?"

"I'm thinking that I want to keep my soul," Alex said, and the night's pain burned through him. "I'm thinking someone helped clear the Holy Land to fetch up Aeda and Medes so they could take our souls."

Cecil's jaw gaped, and he shook his head. "Alex."

"Why are the gods gone?" Alex snapped. "Why aren't they here to stop this? Mother or daughter, one of these monsters knows. And one of them—the freed one—she's going to put an end to this if she wants a scrap of anything she cares about. She doesn't deserve even that!"

His voice cracked, and he remembered being that frightened boy in the barracks too many years ago. The boy smart enough to befriend Arcadia, and she who'd been kind enough to befriend him back. Look how he'd repaid her.

Alex swallowed rainwater and breathed cloudy air. "When we have to lose everything we care about, why should a goddess get one little thing? Because she'll live forever? It isn't right. Someone has to step up and say so."

"Alex, you're unwell," Cecil said. He reached an open palm for Alex's forehead. "Come now, they're gods. It's the way of things."

Alex flinched back. "Use your gift. Do I feel sick?"

Cecil withdrew his hand. "Heartsick. Out of sorts."

"But not unwell," Alex said. "I'm right. I've been right all along. The gods are bad news."

"Maybe," Cecil said. "But what good will it do you?"

Alex doubted much good would come of tonight for anyone, but he hoped to prevent some harm. A better man than he'd been at Shah, and yet worse than the world deserved, but he couldn't be any more than that. At best, he could try to ensure there was still an Aeg and a city at dawn, and perhaps until the end of the drowning season. Once Aeda stopped the rain and sea, he would come

back to this place for Arcadia's body, for her funeral pyre.
It was the most and least he could do.

CHAPTER 39

Lilac stood beside a squat bloodstained altar, clutching a straight-bladed knife she'd found in the temple. It had been dusty, but she'd cleaned it, and now she cleaned it again. Her lost teardrop-shaped blade had been Vince's gift, and maybe he'd thought it made up for his vanishing shortly after their week together years ago, for never knowing about the twins until long after their deaths. Likely in his dying moments, he'd learned better.

Valmydion's great altar lay crushed in pieces within the pit where Arcadia had fallen. Lilac supposed it was Aeda's altar in the first place. Logoi must have decided that made a fitting hiding place for the coralstones.

Sticky red fed fluid now traced the pit's edges. As Aeda had said while still pretending to be Logoi, rituals were for mortals, performative comfort when the gods only needed blood.

Aeda had plenty of it now.

The first sacrifice had approached in a sleek black dress beneath a puffy white coat, an outfit for dancing, singing, or dining in a lounge. Not for climbing temple steps to offer blood and life at a goddess's whim. Before approaching the altars, she had kissed a man on the lips, and then a woman, and then touched a third woman's hands. She'd then stumbled toward the temple's center.

To Lilac.

No one who'd gathered in the temple plaza wanted to shed

their blood. They'd wanted a goddess in the Holy Land, but now their prayers came answered in ways they'd never expected.

What could Lilac say? A silent executioner seemed cruel, but preaching had never given her previous sacrifices much comfort. To read any Verses of Aeg seemed crass when summoning a Dawn God. None had touched this world in over two thousand years, and Lilac wasn't sure the Holy Psychopomp Tree had counted. It was only Sceptomos's empty husk that burned by mortal hands. A full Dawn God would never burn. Fire was a whisper to them, and the sun itself bowed its rays as they demanded.

Many of those gathered would not live to see Exalis's return.

Like the woman in her white coat who wiped her cheeks and asked, "Where do I go?"

"Lie here on the altar," Lilac had heard herself say. "In the beginning, men were prey. The Dawn Gods gave us life and so much more."

The woman stretched across the altar and swallowed a sob.

"They will give again," Lilac went on, but the words felt hollow. She had never wanted to kill anyone, but at least she'd made a choice to slaughter Vince's associates. In Aeda's temple, an unseen chain bound Lilac's arms and forced her knife downward. She had no say in her part. The deaths came, and she wielded the knife.

The woman had grabbed Lilac's free hand and squeezed. "Goddess Aeda, great Exalis, keep my babies safe." Her wide, expectant eyes then drank in the ceiling murals of Aeda's great works, though someone had painted Valmydion in her place. Under whose direction? Likely Logoi.

The first sacrifice hadn't known, hadn't needed to. No telling which god might rule this city by the time she reincarnated as human again.

Lilac couldn't stare into those eyes for long. She'd turned to the woman's chest, breath pounding up and down beneath her black dress.

"May you reincarnate as one of her faithful," Lilac said.

Her blade had then thrust deep in the woman's heart. A gasp, a jittering, and then the woman slumped, her limps draping the altar. A damp patch stretched across her dress and poured red into her coat. Lilac had then cut the woman's wrists and let them drip ruby rivers onto the marble floor. Small stains against the greater temple.

There were other altars, and much more floor to soak in blood.

The next sacrifice arrived hard-faced, said he'd happily die for his children, but he cried once he lay flat across the altar. He mourned lost time. If his children grew up, he would never see it, but if he didn't help them, they would never grow up.

Better this way, Lilac wanted to tell him. Better to die and never know their future, never drag on childless, wondering if Sara and Daphne had reincarnated as fish or flowers or birds. Better to die believing they would grow up someday.

She kept their names to herself and only told the man the same as she told the first sacrifice, and then after him the third, and fourth, and so on.

Each time, Lilac drove her knife down, fast at the last word. She wanted to give these people comfort, with no chance to remember that though the Dawn Gods once promised mankind would never be prey again, the Verses of Aeg suggested otherwise, as if someone writing that holy book had known better.

A promise was worthless when the promiser abandoned the world.

Lilac was about to call up—which sacrifice? She'd lost count—when clacking boots rang through the temple. Aeda danced to the plaza's north, where the crowd gathered thickest. She wouldn't see them approach.

Alex and Cecil picked through crushed seating and marble debris. Their clothes were dry, benefits of Aeda's miracle upon the temple plaza, but Cecil looked numb. Alex had lost his fedora and trench coat. Blood painted his white shirt above the vest. His gun holster hung visible yet empty. That told its own story, one Lilac didn't know.

Cecil's placid expression broke as he realized who stood in the hooded black robe at temple's center. He bounded at Lilac as if he couldn't see the bodies, the blood, or the knife in her hands.

"I don't bloody believe it!" Cecil cried.

He hugged Lilac around her hips and swung her in a circle. She landed hard on bare feet, and he went stumbling back in a fit of laughter. Either he'd sucked down another drink, or he was drunk on the relief of seeing her alive. If he wanted, he could touch the running blood across the marble and let his skin refresh his muscles on the sacrifices meant for Exalis.

Alex hung back and studied the scene, his eyes weary. He noticed the bodies, Lilac was sure, but he said nothing.

Cecil kissed Lilac's cheek. "You beautiful creature! I kept faith, I did. We've had a shit of a night, but seeing you alive, that's the silver lining."

"Glad you're alive, too," Lilac said, lukewarm. She would've liked to see Arcadia and Simone trail the detectives into the temple's shelter, a reunion of last night's dinner, but no one followed.

There were only sacrifices dithering at the temple's edges. Waiting to be called. If none plodded up the stairs at Lilac's beckoning, Aeda would wonder why the delay, and then she would find Alex and Cecil.

"You'd better go," Lilac said. "Before it's too late."

"Too late for what?" Alex asked. He looked less imposing without his hat and coat. The night had chewed him up and spat him out, made him small in ways even he couldn't deny. "Before you summon a Dawn God? It's never enough blood with you. Cut down those thieves across the west side of the city, those robes at the Beckoning Tower, the father of your children—it never stops with you."

Lilac's fist tightened around her knife, but she didn't move. How did Alex know about Vince? About Exalis? His voice sounded hoarse. He might have been crying before he arrived. Such a smart man; could he glean what was happening in this temple? Could he see the godly chains that bound Lilac? This nightmare clung to the air, gaining physical form the closer a Dawn God tore through the heavens.

Alex eased back on his heels. "Bad night for everyone," he muttered, eyeing the bodies.

"Who told you about Exalis?" Lilac asked. Her fingers loosened from her knife.

"Oh, I bet I know more than you at this point," Alex said, sounding reminiscent. "Exalis. The Holy Psychopomp Tree. Aeda's genocide. A cunning goddess like her wouldn't share secrets. You're her tool, nothing more. No way she'd tell you she means to rip the souls from our still-living bodies. Turn us into abominations. A crusade against the sea. Any of that sound familiar?"

"None of it but Exalis." Lilac couldn't guess how Aeda would accomplish any of that, but the Holy Psychopomp Tree? That meant Exalis would leave the world shortly after arrival. No protection, only an arbiter for the dead, and maybe worse. "How would she steal our souls?"

"Doesn't matter. She needed someone special, and she's not going to get that." Alex stroked his jaw. "Still trying to figure out who might've driven off the gods for her. Who stands to gain from Aeda?"

Lilac glanced to the body-littered altars. "Not them."

"But the rest of us," Cecil said. "The survivors."

Would there be survivors? Exactly how much blood did summoning a Dawn God take? In the dawn days, nothing less than the near-slaughter of mankind had lured them from the heavens to raise the archipelago into the continent of Aeg. Would a handful of people in one little coastal city be enough now? Aeda might order

Lilac to slit every throat in Aedos.

"Has she mentioned Arcadia?" Cecil asked. Alex glared, but Cecil didn't seem to notice. "Out of curiosity."

"Less mentioned, more demanded," Lilac said. "Aeda's impatient. She sent out a search party for Arcadia, but I haven't seen them come back." She gestured her blade toward the altars. "Been busy. Why? Do you know what Aeda wants her for?"

Alex's boots scraped the marble floor. "Arcadia wouldn't kill anyone. That made her special to Aeda. Put someone like her in the Holy Tree, and she could've been coaxed to pull our souls out. At least, that was Aeda's plan."

Lilac thought of the police and the bodies they used to bring to Logoi's temple. Wouldn't Arcadia have had a hand in that, or was she peripheral? Lilac thought of Arcadia in this temple yesterday, her face, her posture, her gun. Vince had seen her up close, aiming for the Valentine Butcher.

"That can't be right," Lilac said. "She nearly gunned me down when chasing me yesterday. It's a long story, but she would've killed me."

"She fired?" Cecil asked.

"Not exactly." Lilac gritted her teeth. "Almost."

"Did she do anything to you? Even if she had her gun trained on a murderer, someone she didn't know was her sweetheart, how could you know for certain she'd pull the trigger?"

Lilac hadn't asked Vince because it hadn't mattered; Arcadia was supposedly dead. Right or wrong, Lilac had killed Vince in the end.

If Arcadia wouldn't fire yesterday, knowing she had the murderer in her sights, Lilac or not, maybe Aeda had judged right. Outside of the green uniform, lying together in a hotel bed in the early mornings, or when Arcadia would feel cold in her heart and need Lilac to stroke her head, those might have been less the soft moments of a hard woman, and more the truth beneath a battered façade. Arcadia was who she was.

Alex swiped a hand at his eyes. "Doesn't matter," he said again.

Lilac was about to argue with him. Yes, it mattered. They needed to leave here, find Arcadia, and get her as far from the city as possible. Maybe head south toward Logos, or past there to Korenbalas if it still stood. Maybe north toward the hills beneath Shadow Mountain. Anywhere but here.

Aeda's voiced boomed from the north side of the temple. "Be not distracted, High Priestess. My father's approach comes faster by the blood you shed in his name."

She appeared beyond the temple steps. Sickly pale arms slid down her sides, their dance ceasing while her fingers went on tapping at her hip. Each step came deliberate; Aeda wanted her approach to not only be seen but felt in the air.

Alex turned to her and spoke as if he matched her height. "No more sacrifices."

Lilac stepped to one side, Cecil to another. She waved for Alex to follow, but his gaze locked on the goddess.

Aeda cocked her enormous head, and scarlet hair thrashed at her shoulders. "I know you, Logos man," she said. "So inquisitive in Lilac's home last night, and yet you could not see the goddesses in your midst. Whatever your ties to great community, forget this city's mortal law. There is once more a goddess in the Holy Land."

"You'll want to hear out this Logos man," Alex said. "I know where your mother's coralstone is."

"Oh?" Aeda smiled. "I should like to learn this."

"I'll tell you if you meet my terms." Alex puffed out his chest. "Stop the summoning. Protect the city from glories and floods until we're through stormy and growth seasons, all the way to the dry season. When the rain ends and crops thrive, I'll tell you where to find Medes."

Aeda stood blank-faced. Alex's brazenness had to seem novel to her, at least a little bit. Here stood a mortal who thought he could make deals and play games with the gods.

"I need not my mother's freedom for my purpose," Aeda said. "She will be well until the time of our reunion, when I find her myself." Hot wind danced from her skin as she rounded on Alex. "Enough with wasting my time, Logos man. You have a means to mend the Holy Land? I would hear it now. Tell me how we'll drive the sea from all corners of Aeg, and I would see it done by your hands."

Alex's determined face faltered.

Aeda's gaze pressed into him. "If your foolishness stands finished, you will help my dear cousin Lilac and slit sacrificial throats. A high priest paired to the high priestess. You pride yourself on clean hands, have suffered for them, indeed? I would see you brought low, defiant little man. Draw up a blade, and throw away your heavy morality."

Alex glanced at the bloodstain down his shirt.

Aeda turned to the temple plaza. "So you see, the might of a goddess rises not in her hands, but in her words. Know this, as it was known by those who shed their blood to free me."

"I don't have a knife," Alex said, his voice finding confidence as he lifted his eyes from his reddened shirt. "Don't have a gun, either. I dropped it after I killed Arcadia Myrn."

Lilac's chest banged. She shut her eyes and let the pieces crash into each other.

She needed someone special, and she's not going to get that, Alex had said.

Has she mentioned Arcadia? Cecil had asked.

Lilac wanted to lie down and never get up. She wanted to reach back from tonight, from this entire mess, to a time when Alex could've been a friend to her and told her about Arcadia and Shah on friendlier terms, and Lilac could've done—what, exactly? What could fix this? Nothing, but she could have been better. Everyone could have tried.

Lilac bared clenched teeth at Alex. "You."

"Yes. Me." Alex kept his eyes on Aeda. "She was my oldest friend. And now she's gone."

Lilac looked him over for some sign of uncertainty. Vince had thought Arcadia was dead, too, and he'd never found out he was wrong. Maybe the same was true now. For all the secrets they ferreted out, these clever men never knew everything.

But Lilac studied Alex's shirt, where the red patch darkened his vest, and then his hand. Blood dotted his skin. He must have touched Arcadia, after he did it. Of course he'd held her, he loved her, she was his best friend.

And now she was gone.

Lilac's heart sank, and she staggered against a marble column. Arcadia's soul had moved on, with no Holy Psychopomp Tree to trap it. Even in the tumultuous chaos of the Between, a determined soul could supposedly steer reincarnation in a chosen direction. Lilac hoped Arcadia went wherever she wanted.

But facing selfish honesty, more than anything Lilac wanted Arcadia to come back.

Aeda's eyes glimmered, a snake ready to strike. "Why have you done this?" Lightning flashed, and her shadow formed a dark stain that swallowed Alex whole.

"You think that's what I wanted to do tonight?" Alex asked. "Murder my friend in cold blood? I did it because I know about your plan. A special kind of Holy Psychopomp Tree. How you would've taken our souls." He stamped his boot. "Not happening. Your scouting party won't find her alive."

Lilac's fingers ached. They craved Alex's neck. Her knife could slit his throat. A marble chunk could bash his skull and come away sticky with blood. He deserved every pain imaginable and more, but nothing Lilac did would bring Arcadia back.

"You can still get something out of all this," Alex said. "My offer stands."

"And what is it I would be getting, little man?" Aeda towered, her toes so close, they could crush Alex's boots. "My mother, whom I will find in time? You offer what you cannot give, and you cost me what you cannot repay."

Alex slid back a step. Did he understand now? He must have understood when he last appeared beneath Logoi in her temple, proud with his badge and pistol and horrid ideals, but too many years had passed, and he had lost his frightened sense of smallness beneath the gods.

Lilac slid toward Cecil and held his hand. "Don't watch," she whispered. But Cecil couldn't look away.

Aeda glanced to her faithful throng piled around and upon the temple steps. They had grown tremendously in number.

"Never is it my wish to bring loyalty by bloodshed," Aeda said. "Blood belongs to my father. Loyalty belongs to me as Aeda, first of the name, first of the gods, Goddess of Birth." As she turned to Alex again, the wind caressed her hair down her shoulders and back, the elements drawn and submissive to her. "I pressed, and had you bent to me, all would have been well. But you have defied me and murdered the chosen, so comes this punishment."

"Rules and punishment," Alex squeaked out. "Sounds more like Logoi."

"You wish to anger me further, bring rash action? It is not to be." Aeda leaned down, her cavernous mouth ready to bite Alex in half. "No gluttony for blood. I give only a fate fitting your consequence."

"That's what law is." Alex's voice cracked, and his eyes glistened. "Law is action and consequence. I've tried to live by that, even better than Logoi, but someone always twists it for their own benefit. You'll break the laws of nature, make us abominations, and say it's for our own damn good. Logoi would cheat, and we'd help her. How many of these people want to live? With the gods, the rules you make up for us don't matter. You do whatever you want for blood. Don't pretend we should want it—you force us. It isn't our choice; we never have real choices. That's all I am, another man with no choice, story of my life!"

Aeda plunged two enormous fingers deep beneath Alex's ribcage. "And suddenly, your story ends."

Cecil staggered back and fell. Lilac flinched, almost dragged by his hand, but she stayed standing. Neither turned away.

Alex gave a choked gasp. A hard spasm jolted his limbs. His head lolled back as his legs jellied, and his body hung doll-limp on Aeda's hand. A wider stain tore across his shirt, his blood mixing with Arcadia's. His boots clacked against the ground, and the sound pulsed through Lilac's head long after his feet quit twitching.

Aeda's fingers curled. "Your end comes not in death."

Not a drop of Alex's blood touched the marble floor. It seeped over and into Aeda's hand. She was using it, the fire of a miracle burning through her palm and fingers. Blink, and Lilac would miss it, but she knew that sharp light. She'd seen Logoi heal people before, mold flesh into new shapes, transfigure and transcend between illnesses, organs, and ages.

But nothing this drastic. Alex's body crumpled, and where Aeda had ripped a chunk of sternum, heart, and lungs from inside his chest, she uncurled her fingers to reveal a wailing baby girl. She was dark and bloody and writhing as if she had been pulled not from a miracle of organs and blood, but from a womb.

"Not in death," Aeda said. "But in birth."

CHAPTER 40

Aeda glowered over the crowd. "One of my faithful, caretake this new life."

A young man in a sea-green uniform hurried toward the temple steps and gingerly lifted the infant from Aeda's hand. He must have abandoned Oldtown and found himself a better purpose here.

At last, Cecil turned from Alex's body. Lilac pulled him to standing. She didn't notice a shift in the air until she looked to Aeda and found godly eyes staring down on her.

"Keep no concern for him," Aeda said. "To the altars. More have gathered in offering to hasten my father's descent from the heavens."

Lilac glanced to Alex's body. "Do we leave him?"

Aeda waved an impatient hand. "My faithful will carry him to the water. Do as bidden."

The crowd shuffled around Lilac as they moved to fawn over the goddess's flesh-and-blood miracle. Lilac hoped none of Alex's blood had splashed on her feet; she didn't want him to be part of her.

Despite what he'd done, her revulsion felt petty. He'd died trying to stop the ball she had sent rolling. He'd killed to stop it, too.

"Arcadia," Lilac croaked.

"Her death makes matters difficult," Aeda said, wistful now. "My father will demand a chosen be prepared. To disappoint him—" She trailed off, lost in thought as she surveyed the crowd.

Lilac's grief for Arcadia was of no matter to Aeda. Mortal feelings were beneath notice for the goddess of birth. Logoi was cold and calculating, but she had still cared and enmeshed herself in her city's comings and goings. Reason dictated there was no quick solution to mankind's troubles, only one foot in front of another for the rest of time. Had she never cared, her disappearance might have hurt Lilac less. Small wonder Simone couldn't let go of Logoi's dismissal. She and Lilac both knew Logoi gave a damn, and still she'd made choices that hurt them. Even tyrants like Tychron cared, yet he had abandoned the Holy Land, too. Valmydion, Logoi, Korenbal, Lyvien, the list went on.

All of them gone, with only these world-threatening monsters left to the people of Aeg.

New sacrifices awaited as Lilac returned to the altars. In suits and suspenders, dresses and nightgowns, no matter their posture in everyday life, Aeda had set them kneeling at the temple's center where the last sacrifices had bled and died. Lilac's knife would cut these hearts. She might have cut Alex's heart, too, given the opportunity, but Aeda had ended him and recycled some of his flesh into new life. His soul might even find the baby first, the Between spitting him out right when and where he'd entered. Everything came twisted these days.

Eyes closed, Lilac raised her arms above her head, crossed her wrists, and steepled her fingers. She then crossed her ankles and turned her feet toward each other. Warmth pounded up and down her limbs. She had started these sacrifices two days ago with the best intentions. To honor Logoi was to honor reason, the connection of thoughts and ideas, and maybe people, too.

For a moment, the dead could be alive again, bound to Lilac's heart—Arcadia, Vince, Sara, Daphne, even Alex, and the city itself. In some impossible fantasy, Lilac kept everything good from before Logoi left, and everything good from after. None of the bad.

Aeda's bellowing knocked Lilac back to reality. "Why do this which displeases me?"

Lilac staggered and spun.

Aeda stood at the bottom of the temple steps, still taller than Lilac.

"We met when you lived in desperate supplication to my young cousin. Our first communion, I found you on the ground, begging her return. You spilled blood for her, and yet you received me. Do you believe spilling blood in her name will bring her to you instead of my father?"

Lilac kept quiet. Descendants being immune to godly powers, Aeda couldn't turn Lilac's flesh into infants, but killing would be easy. One marble chunk in a godly hand could crush bone.

"He will come, whatever name you say," Aeda snapped. "Logoi will not change her mind. Pledge each death and drop of blood to her, as you please. You will find it a fine and pointless thing. No word of yours would make any difference. Your godly mother is never coming back."

"How can you be sure?" Lilac asked. She sounded so frail when the force of Aeda's voice made her shudder. "You don't know why she left. No one knows why any of them left." Even Alex hadn't finished solving his puzzle, Lilac realized.

"You would have nothing to offer her, be it blood of sacrifice or blood of family," Aeda said. "When her mind is made, it cannot be unmade, a decision as immortal as we. In this same way, she would never have let me free. Were it not for you mortals and the absence of the gods, I would have remained in the sea stone for all time. Yet we are here. My thanks to you, High Priestess." She raised an arm and aimed toward the temple's center. "Now, do as bidden. Hurry my father to this world."

Lilac eyed the plaza behind Aeda's back. Four men carried Alex's hollowed-out body toward the North Temple District, where for all Lilac knew, he might float to the Ace Investigations office. Few of the crowd watched them go. Most of them focused on the baby made of Alex's flesh, while the rest watched Aeda, and Lilac.

A familiar face stared out from among the desperate, and Lilac's heart fluttered.

Simone stood amid the crowd. The night had deepened the creases down her face, and her dress and shawl hung tattered, but she had made it from the South Temple District. She was alive.

So long as Aeda didn't notice her. They had already met in a way, when the coralstone sat in the apartment last night. To defy Aeda now might risk Simone's life.

There was always someone else to lose.

Aeda turned to her faithful throng. "In the beginning, men were prey," she said. "You wish to see the glories suffer for your suffering, yes? They have murdered your children, and you must murder theirs. This is the way of it."

Lilac heard Sara laugh, and then Daphne, as if the glories from that day at the beach had journeyed to the temple and echoed in her ear. She wondered what a glory child looked like. She'd never given their little ones any thought before. Were they different from her daughters? Or did they laugh and play and try to make permanent marks in ever-shifting sand? Lilac's bloody work had never focused on revenge, only stopping this nightmare. Killing glories wouldn't bring the twins back.

Neither would killing humans. Only the immortal ever returned, wanted or not.

"My father, the Dawn God Exalis, will punish the glories for their brutality," Aeda said, waving a hand over the crowd. "On your knees. Bow to Aeda, first of the name, first of the gods, Goddess of Birth, daughter to Exalis, *bringer* of Exalis. Be ready for the awe that is my father. Bow, for first he brought you fire, and now he brings deliverance."

The crowd sank to their knees. They had lost their homes and loved ones under a merciless tide brought by the sea's uncaring, unfeeling evil. Aeda would have willing sacrifices by the handful.

None of them knew what she really meant by deliverance. Not freedom from the glories. Freedom from their bodies. A city of abominations. A Holy Land of soulless monsters.

How to stop it? Lilac could think quickly, but Alex had had caught a thread only he could make sense of, tying the gods' absence to this unholy night. Such an insistent man. Without him, Lilac wasn't sure she could find a way out. A thread could lead you through a maze, but it could also tie you in knots.

His question bounced inside her skull as if inherited after his death. *Why did the gods leave*? It was *her* question now. Under the coming weight of Exalis, the flooding, the glories—a better question might have been, why wouldn't the gods leave this terrible land for brighter coasts? Why would they bother to stay?

Beneath the altars, the new sacrifices averted their eyes from Lilac. That was fair. She didn't want to look at them either.

Footsteps clicked, too small to be Aeda's, and then Cecil's chin sagged onto Lilac's shoulder from behind. She pressed her head to his and felt him tremble against her. She wanted to reassure him, but her nerves were spent. She had only mustered enough resolve to comfort herself, and the goddess had stomped that flat beneath her great heel.

"I'm sorry about Alex," Lilac whispered. There was little else to say.

Cecil gave a half-chuckle. "After what he did? No, I'm sorry for Arcadia. I didn't mean for you to find out that way. What he did."

Arcadia's death didn't seem real yet. Not like yesterday when Lilac had glanced over one shoulder and caught her plummeting thanks to Vince. Without a body, Lilac could almost believe Arcadia would stride across the temple plaza, death be damned.

"But he was your friend, and I am sorry," Lilac said.

Cecil lifted his head and rubbed thumb and forefinger over his eyes. "I warned him. He didn't have to die."

Lilac thought of firelit Alex in the Beckoning Tower, of his reminiscence in the street tonight, his slyness in her apartment last night, the way Arcadia had hugged him and so clearly loved him. Lilac couldn't imagine his pistol aiming for Arcadia. Every image sank into the gory crater of Alex's chest.

"You're stalling, love," Cecil said.

Lilac gave a ragged sigh. "Shouldn't I?"

"Resist, and Aeda will rip you open." Cecil wiped one palm against the other. "A little different from Alex, your blood will stain her hands, but dead is dead. And she'll preen just the same. First of *this*, first of *that.*"

"She does make a big deal about that." Lilac laughed, surprising herself. "But if I slow her down—"

"Exalis is already on his merry way." Cecil chinned at the ceiling. "Can't you feel it? He isn't subtle."

The temple's candlelight was frail, but dancing shadows offered glimpses of the ceiling murals, where Valmydion had stolen Aeda's role in history. Beyond the ceiling hung the clouds, the sky, the heavens, and—yes, a coming pressure. Lilac shuddered against it.

"We can't stop him from putting his feet down, if he chooses to have feet," Cecil said. "Won't hang his hat though; doubt he's got one of those. No, he'll do what Aeda wants and leave. There'll be a new Holy Tree. We need to put someone else inside it."

Lilac's bones felt limp and ragged. She needed to rest beside her sacrifices, not cut them open. Aeda hadn't given time to process the fate of the night. Exalis, the Holy Psychopomp Tree, the plan to rip out everyone's souls. Too big for mortals, even descendants.

"I don't want there to be any Holy Tree at all," Lilac said. "Our souls should choose their next life, not whoever she puts inside the hollow body of a Dawn God. Not even Arcadia."

Cecil spread his arms in a vague shrug, stretching his buttoned trench coat across his chest. "Like you said, what choice we got?"

Lilac fondled the knife in her pocket. "Noema the Sick burned the first one. The second can burn, too."

"And then?" Cecil asked. "Outside here, the city's up to its gills in seawater. Refugees keep pouring into the plaza, and Aeda will find a replacement for Arcadia. Besides, any idea how long a big spruce tree takes to burn? Take that times a hundred, maybe a thousand, for the Holy Psychopomp Tree. By the time you get a chance, it could be too bloody late. But if we get someone else inside the tree, then we might have a shot." He lowered his head and hands. "Someone she don't approve of."

Lilac wouldn't have believed he could ever look so defeated. "You're not suggesting—" she started.

"Why not?" Cecil asked. "I can't be the worst choice, surely. Not like I want it that way, but could be the Holy Tree will bring the rest back. Possible answer to Alex's question, you know? The gods must've left because they knew what Aeda was going to do." He grimaced as if he shouldn't have said that. Mentioning Alex was painful. "They'll feel Exalis's return from around the world, and maybe when he's left, they'll go, 'Crisis over, time to head home.' Surely my grandfather will want to see what's become of his grandson. Lyvien would never sit a temple, always the wanderer, but he'll visit. He loves me."

"And the gods have followed his lead before," Lilac said. "They might do it again."

"At the very least, we stop Aeda from stealing our souls." Cecil's smile returned, more confident now. "That's her one shot. She only has the one father."

Lilac couldn't think of anything better. She pressed a hand to Cecil's cheek, where new stubble poked her fingers. "But I'll lose you, too."

Cecil gently boxed her chin. "No, love, I'll be everywhere. Eternal. Don't be so selfish. This is the world we're talking about."

Lilac turned to the altars, where her dark work awaited, and then back to Cecil, the desperation plain on his face. Aeda wouldn't like that he was stalling the sacrifice. She had no purpose for him.

Lilac did. He was her friend, and she'd lost too much tonight. Still had more to lose. "Are you sure?" she asked.

"How can I be?" Cecil asked. "But it's all we got. Play our parts to the last moment, and we'll slip away before she knows it. It's one small hope." Nothing he said sounded much like hope at all.

His head thrashed to one side with a sharp cry. He grasped at the side of his face and then stumbled against a white column, his fedora's brim creasing against the marble.

Lilac reached for him. "What's wrong? Is it Exalis?"

"Not yet." Cecil winced, and his hand rubbed up and down one eye. "Sudden migraine. Don't got any pain pills in the goddess's temple, do you?"

Lilac had nothing but her knife. She wondered what that said about her.

"Feels awful," Cecil said, groaning. "Pressure like nothing that's ever hit me, and I been hit plenty."

Lilac glanced ceilingward. "It might be Exalis."

"I feel him too, but this is closer, somewhere in the city." Cecil shook his head as if throwing off the pain and then took a deep breath. "The brunt's fading a bit, but it lingers. Some sick fuck dancing on my skull."

Lilac lifted his fedora and rubbed the heel of her palm against his forehead. What could have happened?

Cecil chuckled and fitted his hat back on. "Might not be so bad, joining the Holy Tree. Never another headache." He chinned at the altars. "Never mind me. Best get back to work, love, before Aeda scolds us again, or worse."

Lilac didn't want to leave him, but if his plan worked, the pain would only be temporary. Maybe all pain was. Even heartache. Lilac turned to the sacrifices and plucked the knife from her robe, clean and ready to do Aeda's blood-soaked bidding. Dutiful resignation, all a goddess might want from a Dawn God's high priestess.

"I'm sorry," Cecil said. "But it's nearly over. We can make it."

Easy for him to say, with no blood on his hands, no blood to shed, but Lilac couldn't knock him for being hopeful.

She laid a hand on one kneeling man's shoulder. "May you reincarnate as one of her faithful," she said, and slid the knife into his chest. When he dropped and lay still, she scratched Logoi's star into his skin.

There had to be hope, even so small as a pattern drawn in a dead man's flesh.

CHAPTER 41

Hector Moros wasn't born Honest Hector but might as well have been. Everyone called him that, and no one knew it was his mother who had given him the nickname.

"The best of me," she often told him, but he knew that between him and his brothers, best was a matter of comparison. While the rest had eventually got into politics and died in the State House, Hector prospered in the shadows. Still, his mother was proud of him.

It was on her account alone that Hector left the seeming safety of his pawnshop. The door and windows leaked in droplets, but he was one of few South Temple District residents who could afford to floodproof his property. He could've waited out the storm in peace.

But the radio said buildings were coming down in Oldtown. Hats off to the brave news reporter still broadcasting from that slum via janky handheld radio. Hector's mother didn't live in Oldtown, but her house down the street wasn't exactly a fortress. Best to bring her to the shop.

Hector dressed in a yellow rain slicker and carried an oil lantern out the door, where his clothes kept him no drier from the flood than if he'd stepped outside naked. Wading meant slow progress, but ten minutes to get there, five minutes to collect his mother, maybe twelve minutes to carry her back. Half an hour in the storm was a lot less than that man on the radio had to deal with.

Ripples disturbed the water's surface in long lines between raindrops. Hector aimed his lantern, and the light reflected off a fat school of silvery fish, hurrying west. Hector was about to turn away when he caught another ripple and froze in place—a gray fin cut the water towards him, closer, closer, close enough for light to flash in the shark's black eyes.

And then it passed him, following the school of fish west.

Hector laughed and patted his chest. "Chasing the fish so hard, missed the real meal."

But then other fish passed him. Tiny blue ones, long green things, fish with stripes and spines, an eel with an arm-ripper of a maw. All creatures that had been swept into the city by the storm, desperate to get out.

Hector couldn't help being reminded of the gulls and their mass escape to the east a scant few hours ago. Now all these fish swam west.

A strange inclination told him to swim with them, into the sea.

Down another street, the striped fish charged through standing water and swirling currents until they reached the gateway where they'd first been thrust into the city. The water calmed here, leading sea life across the floodplains, where they could reach the submerged beach unopposed. Only the sea mattered. The blues, the sharks, everything in reach converged on Oldtown, swam past the Logos officers and flood fighter agents, through the wall and out to sea.

Like Hector, some officers and agents felt the sudden urge to hop into the water, out to sea or at least away from the city. A nervous sensation like wind through their uniforms, a warning something bad was about to happen. But why take the feeling seriously? Bad things had been happening all night.

On the far side of the wall, wading in the floodplains, the glories shrank away, one by one. There were fights, and there were gods, and then there was *this* beyond it all.

One glory hesitated. Thin scars itched down the left side of her face, and her dark eyes took in the night, desperate to see and understand what was about to happen in deeper ways than the rhythmic waves could tell.

Understanding evaded her. There was too much fear in her blood for her to discern anything except *Abandon this place*, and she followed her brood away from the city. There was nothing she or anyone could do but flee. It was too late. It had been too late the moment it started, and no one would know the gravity until after it ended.

A red coralstone had stirred in Cecil's trench coat as he'd headed for the temple.

A dead heart now stirred on a fire escape not far south from Lilac's apartment.

Arcadia knew something was wrong. It was the only thing she knew. She'd been going—where? Been doing—what? She was supposed to make a decision, and then she wasn't, and now she was here, and everything was wrong.

Her heart ached, body and feelings alike. She shouldn't feel pain anymore, but it scratched across her chest and tugged the rest of her body into a bloody, self-eating whirlpool. Glass shards swirled through her veins and cut her from the inside.

Fingers twitched, and then toes. Her spine remembered itself, and her brain remembered more. She shot up from iron fire escape steps and screamed high-pitched against the rainfall. A small and hateful chunk of metal tumbled from above her breast. Panic burrowed through her limbs, her face, deep in her bones and her mind with the agony of life.

Arcadia slammed a fist against the fire escape steps, bowing the iron. She couldn't stay here. Had to go anywhere but here. But where was here? She plowed down the fire escape and into the floodwater. Every step was a walk on glass.

"Lexi?" Arcadia called. "Captain Stathos? Lilac?"

Wrong order, damn her memory. If she remembered Lilac, then Alex had already hung up his position with the police, same as Arcadia. Gone with the blue, on with sea-green. Gone with Logos, on with Valentine, and then Lilac, but when had Arcadia quit being relevant to those events? They had all come so far from home and the people they used to be. Hadn't she been soft once?

"Make sense, please." Arcadia clawed down her face and roared at the sky.

Thunder roared back but told her nothing. She had drifted from the world, and then it had pulled her into itself again with no sense of time or place. She deserved no sense. Alex and Lilac were always changing. Arcadia needed a constant, someone who could ground her. There was one man who had always been the same, always eager to break her. He could be a port in the storm.

Rain and wind did not slow Arcadia's journey to Oldtown; the floodwater turned choppy as if to escape her. Humid air thickened across her skin, urging her to stay right where she'd woken up, but she groaned against it, a creaking house broken from her foundation until she shattered some invisible barrier and reached the streets of Oldtown.

Screaming, fire, and Commander Rhoster Thale—this was the right place. He was a constant. Too constant. Oldtown was a maelstrom, but Thale towered at the catastrophe's center.

"Shah," Arcadia whispered. "Again. Always."

All things darkened around Thale's moving face. He must have eaten the world. How long had he been doing that? Why hadn't he finished yet? He was coming closer.

"I told you to leave," Thale said. "What are you doing here?"

"Gods, commander," a voice said. There was someone else here Thale had spared. "Myrn's hurt."

The world came alive again. The screams pressed in, and the fire, and a landscape of carnage hidden by Thale's scowl. He hadn't eaten the world; Arcadia had misplaced it.

Thale glanced over his shoulder at the flaming carcass of a sea monster and then back to Arcadia. "It has to be burned. We can't have it rotting up the city."

"Can't leave Shah to rot," Arcadia said, voice unsteady. "Burned it."

"What did you to say to me?" Thale snapped.

Arcadia sank her face into one hand. Indistinct murmurs ran through the street between curious Logos refugees. She was nothing, worthless, incapable of obedience. Incapable of helping anyone.

"For Logoi," Arcadia whispered.

Thale waded closer. "Go home, Myrn."

Arcadia pawed at her chest. Insubordinate. Pointless. Unwilling to dirty her hands in sacrifice to the great goddess Logoi, powerless to fight back as Logos officers' guns went *clack-clack-clack* through the hills. All praise Logoi, Goddess of Reason, Logoi the Many-Headed. All praise her except one, weeping in the soil while murder crushed the world around her, Logoi's star glaring as if each point were its goddess's eyes.

The failure Arcadia, all she was and all she would ever be.

"You slaughtered them," Arcadia said. She fingered the hole in her uniform over her chest. "You wanted to slaughter me."

"Did that glory touch your head?" Thale asked. "Go home. Sleep it off."

Past Thale, there was no village in the fire, only a sea monster's corpse, its arms alight above the floodwater. Officers wandered in battered blue uniforms, agents in greens, everyone lost. Like Arcadia. Their frightened eyes were reflections in Shah's windows. At last, the night made sense.

Thale pressed close to her face. "Stand down. Your behavior is unbecoming."

"Is unbecoming," Arcadia echoed. "When do we stop becoming? I quit years ago, but I'm still here. It never goes away. How many people do we kill and burn and then stop being people too?"

Thale's face flushed. "You don't kill *any*. You're worthless as an officer. Worthless as a flood fighter. You wish you could be part of a larger body, but you can only be yourself, and that's a fate worse than death."

"You don't know fates worse than death. There's dying, and then there's coming back." Arcadia pointed down. "There's right here and now."

Thale's stern demeanor softened, and he looked as confused as the agents and officers behind him. "Myrn," he said, almost concerned. "Where do you think here is?"

Arcadia lunged at him and grasped his waist between two hands. "It's Shah," she said, almost too quiet to hear. She could end it now. She had to stop him. "It's Shah! They call their home Shah! They dance and live here! They die and burn here!"

She was vaguely aware of crushing flesh and cracking bones, of tears and screams, but she couldn't stop until he saw what she saw.

"Shah, Thale!"

Not until he understood.

"Do you hear me? SHAAAH!"

His weight left her. She didn't remember throwing him, but he slammed against a wall of debris and fell splashing into the water. Officers dove to help him. Agents stood gaping at her.

The fire went on burning across the sea monster and through that small village. Memories circled round and round, striking Arcadia like an endless storm. This mass murder was fate; she would never get away. Shah could not be undone.

She charged again through the water. She'd left terrible things behind before, and she could do it again. With enough running through the streets, never slowing or stopping, maybe she could find a place beyond Shah's reach. Never undone, but maybe forgotten, her uselessness forgiven. If she could drift away from the world and come back to Shah, then she could drift away and find someplace better.

How much city did she have to run through before she was home in Logos? How much time had to be broken before she was small again, at the feet of her father in their home, before her parents' accident, before the orphanage? How long before she'd sworn herself first to Logos and then alone to Logoi? How long before Arcadia had turned thirteen

293

and went to the barracks, before the night she had to show them what she could do, and the night years later when she showed them what she couldn't do, before she was a disappointment who couldn't cheerily drench her hands in blood?

How long had it been since she was allowed to be soft?

She couldn't remember that far back anymore. There was only fire and blood and failure. She couldn't even die right.

"Arcadia Myrn?" Another voice. Not Thale this time.

Arcadia slowed, the water calming around her. "Captain Arcadia Myrn or Arcadia?" she asked. "Which do you want?"

A pause, and then, "Whatever you like."

"Call me something sweet." Arcadia splashed water over her head. "Call me like Lilac does, sweetie and honey and doll."

A man waded in the floodwater. Others waded behind him. "We're supposed to bring you to the temple."

A temple. Logoi's, or someone else's? Arcadia lumbered closer. "Who does she want me to kill? When does she give me Lilac? Where's Lexi?"

"I don't know about that," the man said. He looked back at the others and then to Arcadia, his face drawn and tired. "She said if you come with us, to her, no one will ask you to bloody your hands ever again."

This felt more straightforward than running. Maybe they knew the way to Lilac. They might even be telling the truth.

"I'll go with you," Arcadia said.

The man turned to lead, and the rest of his group followed. Arcadia trailed behind. Their route slid north from Oldtown, past Bay Ridge, and through the North Temple District. A longer route than they might've taken, but the search party had at least the wherewithal of a few fish.

Best to steer away from that wrong feeling south of the temple.

An odd tremor ran through the water as if the flood itself wanted to follow all sea life's exile from the South Temple District, ripples of a heavenly force fast approaching the Holy Land. He wouldn't arrive in time to stop what was about to happen, if this was even within the power of a Dawn God to stop.

It began on the fire escape where Arcadia had rested with a bullet in her heart.

The iron steps grew bright in the places her blood had dripped with the rain, more vibrant than the bloodstain she would have left on a dry night. An angry pink hue spread along the fire escape's railing, up the brick wall where it had been bolted into place, into the stirring water below. The steps flaked apart into tiny grains the colors of dark blood and burned sunset, the iron no sturdier than a clump of sand thrown into water.

The epicenter of Arcadia's death and resurrection spread into the apartment building, the unmaking less a starving beast devouring everything it touched and more a suicidal entropy within all matter. Once touched by red sickness, a thing no longer wished to exist. The air itself shined bright, grew heavy, and broke into spores. If someone were to step close and somehow avoid the sickness, they would asphyxiate with no air to breathe.

The quiet destruction was almost peaceful.

A small violation of nature might have kept its unmaking anchored where Alex had gunned Arcadia down, but the reaction spread as predictable and inevitable as a stone being dropped into a pond and disturbing the water's surface. The ripples wouldn't subside until the force of that disturbance was spent.

Neighboring apartments shredded into red dust, everything they were and kept inside them turning to mist. Floodwater evaporated into spores. They spread in every direction, eating raindrops and streets and sewers.

The sickness touched Lilac's apartment, shattering the kitchen, living room, windows. The dining table eroded. Red-orange destruction ate the oven's glass and steel and stone, Simone's *Nights That Never Happened* movie poster, the toy chest where Lilac had hidden the coralstone, the bedroom where Sara and Daphne once shared a crib, Sara's drawings—everything burned red and then flaked apart.

Destruction spread through every South Temple District street. Vince's house turned to ash, Honest Hector's pawnshop fluttered into the wind. Red spores crashed into each other and fell to the earth. Only the soil beneath streets, sewers, and catacombs seemed safe from the unmaking.

Hector had almost reached his mother's house when he felt the full force of the wrongness. It overtook him in silence. He noticed the color pour across his clothes and then his skin. Raindrops turn red and vanished before they hit the floodwater, and this seemed almost pretty to him before all his thoughts and flesh burst into crimson butterflies.

The range of red destruction halted where the South Temple District met Merchant's Field. No spore spread into the Central Temple District; none flew past the southern city gates. The unmaking lapped at Oldtown's edges but did not enter. Between the churning sea and the widespread disintegration, there was little left to destroy.

A quake traveled the red spores from where Arcadia's heart had revived, and then the unmaking settled into its new territory. Merging spores danced airborne until they weighed too heavy for the wind. They sank across the frothing red landscape and hardened into shining stones, some larger than the buildings they had eaten away. Every fresh raindrop grew another puff of spores, and they fused and crashed like those before them.

No neighborhood remained between deadly air and earth. It was as if the site of resurrection had never existed, its wound on the world now washed clean and cauterized into a vicious red scar.

Silence blanketed the city, all witnesses gaping with a guilty twist in their guts as if they had taken part in this violation. Their hushed awe was only fair. The soul Medes had dragged back to the world had been given no chance to protest. If the wrong had been born in silence, its consequence could exist in silence too.

Even the raindrops died without a sound.

PART FIVE

THE HOLY PSYCHOPOMP TREE

CHAPTER 42

Cecil was right. When the time came, Lilac felt Exalis descending, sure as she felt the blood run slick down her fingers before her skin drank it in.

The temple quaked, subtly at first, and then from ceiling to floor to the bodies littering its altars and seating. Lilac eyed the murals, wary the rest of the second floor might collapse, and then glanced down where she held a knife above a prone young woman in a black suit who stared with wild wet eyes.

Lilac lowered the knife. "I guess you're the lucky one."

The woman slid to her feet and dashed toward the southern exit. The temple's quaking turned violent, and dust rained onto Lilac's head. She tucked her knife into her robe and hurried out the northern exit.

Aeda stood below. Cecil lingered not far from her, Simone a few paces behind, and the crowd of faithful surrounded them. No one watched Lilac; every eye looked skyward. Had the faithful not already lowered to their knees, the pressure would have forced them down.

Lilac hunched, buckled, and fell beside Cecil. There was no standing against the force of this coming presence. She hadn't ever thought about it, but she didn't know what a Dawn God looked like. Would she even see anything at all?

She saw Aeda. Not so tall and proud now, the goddess of birth looked nervous, her father's pressure weighing even on her divine shoulders. She didn't drop to her knees like everyone else, but her spine bent. Compared to a Dawn God, maybe there was no difference between a goddess and a descendant and everyone else.

Golden light warmed the clouds as if the sun itself were breaking a hole above the temple. Had Lilac not known better, she would've thought it was dawn.

Rainfall shrank from the plaza edges. The storm scurried out of city neighborhoods, its patter ceasing. Soon the only sound was running water as the sea fled the city. The view atop Aeda's temple might have shown the flood retreating across the floodplains and back to the beach. This was the will of the Dawn Gods from the start, that Aeg should be a continent and not an archipelago.

And now came a Dawn God to see his will made real.

Cosmic might slashed knifelike through the flesh and muscle of the world as a Dawn God found himself material and manifested on a plane beneath his enigmatic divinity.

The sky grew blurry where Exalis broke through. When Lilac's sight sharpened again, he was there, as if he had always been there and it was her fault for never noticing him before. She had to be remembering wrong, didn't she? Yes, he'd always been there. Anywhere across worlds and heavens he went, he'd always been there. Always everywhere.

Exalis descended in nearly a dozen fragments of ruby-colored crystal, their formation unfamiliar, each vaster than his daughter's temple. A strange alien fire danced beneath their sheen, and Lilac thought of bodies writhing in the crystals forever. Not one touched another, but enormous forking blood vessels twitched in the air between them. Maybe the air itself was part of Exalis, an unseen connecting tissue.

A quake in Lilac's thoughts told her she was not seeing the whole of him, but she couldn't imagine what else there might be. Faces in the crystals. Cries in the blood vessels. A scent in the air of the absolute.

The lowest crystals peeled the temple rooftop apart, the marble dome no stronger to them than an orange rind, and laid each broken piece gently around the temple steps, their murals now facing the sky.

Exalis's blood vessels then picked apart the second floor, the walls, the columns, everything higher than the altars where his sacrifices bled, and laid the dissembled pieces in empty spaces within the temple plaza.

He never touched the ground, but some unseen part of his enormity seemed to settle while the crystal fragments floated.

Stifled sobs and horrified gasps echoed through the crowd. Their city had already been ravaged tonight, and now the Dawn God meant to save them descended as faceless and destructive as the flooding itself. They did not understand he bore the visage of eternity.

Cecil glanced to Lilac, but there was nothing to say, and their faces tugged toward Exalis.

"Sorry," Cecil whispered.

Good, he was right to be sorry—how dare he look elsewhere when a Dawn God stood before him? The thought didn't feel like Lilac's, but she'd thought it anyway, a judgmental shape being driven into her mind. She didn't have to guess where it had come from. He towered over the plaza.

The air grew still and silent. The world took a breath to absorb the descent of this monumental power.

Every story of the Dawn Gods was true. Lilac had never seen anything like Exalis. Gods were tall, but never like this overwhelming colossus. If a god were a house, a Dawn God was a mountain taking root at the city's center.

The crowd was right to flinch. He hadn't spoken—or had he? Lilac wasn't sure again. Thoughts and feelings no longer seemed like they belonged to her, more like pieces Exalis had lent out and now he was taking them back. Some part of him reached through her, and everyone here, as if his very presence made his will work through them. Not even Aeda looked confident anymore. Small wonder Logoi and her closest cousins had bound Aeda and Medes in coralstones to stop this.

How dare Lilac think that? Exalis had journeyed across the vast heavens tonight after millennia of absence, while also having always been here, and she dared regret his presence.

These were wrong thoughts for Lilac, for anyone. Doubt taint-ed her, and not only her. The passage of time and the brevity of mortals had corroded their due reverence. Exalis would remove this doubt from all present. From all existence. He would unmake and remake the cosmos to show them.

The world went black.

And then—

In the beginning, men were prey.

Noema twisted in the fire. Life couldn't be fair, but death should be. How many years before the cursed tree let her be human again? Two thousand stretched ahead, a glimpse of the many things she'd become before she returned as another wailing baby girl.

Lilac held the lucky rocks tight in her fist. She didn't want to lose them. They were her only chance of keeping her hair from being cut again.

The priestesses had no answers, and Lilac couldn't call, "Moth-er?" through the Logos temple. No one was supposed to know. Here, and always, she was alone.

Simone reached weathered hands through the apartment door-way and grasped Lilac's face. "You're mine, aren't you?"

Vince, and his rakish smile, and the way he called her "love." Lilac felt safe in his arms, like she hadn't in years.

Lilac took her daughters to the beach. She wanted to go before the sky turned gray for the rainy season that year, while the wind was gentle and smelled more like the sea and less like a storm. There were dangers in the calm season, too, but if Lilac wanted to avoid all risks in life, she wouldn't have had children.

"Oh, I'm Captain Arcadia Myrn. Sorry, I'm in the way again."

Lilac was about to knock on Arcadia's room door when she real-ized she couldn't stop giggling. She hadn't felt so silly in years. Hadn't laughed like this since that day at the beach.

"Yes, call to the gods." Lilac dragged her free hand's fingers

through Flip's blood. The coppery stink thickened, and she thought of priestesses, daggers, and a nine-headed holiness filling the temple. "All for the gods. All for Logoi."

Cecil was right. When the time came, Lilac felt Exalis descending, sure as she felt the blood run slick down her fingers before her skin drank it in.

—the world came back.

Lilac's skin tingled as if every part of her had gone to sleep. Louder crying broke out from the crowd, but it stopped when Exalis wanted silence. In what had been a moment for him, he had unmade and remade this world from its beginning to this point in time.

Even a Dawn God didn't have that kind of power, right? No, he did. And he didn't want any more doubt. Lilac's thoughts needed to get in line with his or else next time she might not return with the rest of the world.

All eyes and crystals burned toward Aeda. It had not been Exalis's wish to return, ever, but she was his daughter. Lovely, wonderful daughter. He came to her call, but why?

Lilac opened her mouth to say it herself and then her jaw snapped shut. Exalis wanted Aeda to tell. It had to be Aeda.

"I longed to see you again," Aeda said. She sounded meek, a withered branch of her old tree. "The Holy Psychopomp Tree of Sceptomos was burned long ago by mortal hands."

Exalis already knew that. He knew everything, down to the core of every soul. He told Aeda, and all present, that the soul behind the burning lingered here, and his daughter should beware, as this soul would always long for chaos. It could not do otherwise.

Lilac curled into herself. She could feel his ire.

Her worry must have breathed through the crowd, or maybe she had felt it breathing from Exalis himself. His vessels twisted between crystals, their ends almost touching his fragments. He demanded Aeda's certainty. To do as she wished would cleave his physical form from every other aspect of him and plant it in this world.

"Nothing to do with my wishes," Aeda said. "It costs my seeing you ever again, but I make this sacrifice for mortals. Everything I do arises of their need."

Lilac tensed from head to toe. "Not true," she tried to say, but a dry whisper wouldn't leave her tongue.

Cecil glared beside her. She was going to give them away. "Exalis doesn't care what you got to say, love. Promise. Stick to the plan."

Plan seemed a strong word for letting Aeda get her way until the last moment. Alex had planned, and now he was dead. You couldn't gamble against the gods and expect to win.

But what other options were there?

Exalis's fragments twitched above the ruined temple. In the distance, the sea cowered from him. He reached across it, and his irritation mounted in the air.

"Yes, my cousins fled the Holy Land," Aeda said. "They fear your disappointment." As if she knew why the other gods were gone any better than the rest of Aeg.

Exalis's displeasure weighed grand and terrible. He and the other Dawn Gods had trusted their children and children's children to safekeep the Holy Land, and they had abandoned it? He knew the reason why, Lilac could tell, but his knowledge didn't radiate into her, only his frustration. Her palms scraped cobblestones, and she thought her head might fall next.

Red vessels curled into beckoning fingers. Exalis wanted to know the core of the future Holy Tree before he consented to his sacrifice.

"Father, the unique mortal we'd made into a champion, the one I'd intended as psychopomp, was murdered moments ago,"

Aeda said, trembling. Could a goddess like her cry? "I must find a replacement suitable for my purposes."

Lilac stopped breathing. All air and muscle went still beneath Exalis. Aeda shouldn't have summoned him until she was ready. Lilac shouldn't have helped. His time was infinite, but they were wrong to waste a single speck of it. He wanted to make good on his sacrifice or leave this world. Everyone present, Aeda included, should beg his forgiveness.

Cecil's lips moved, ready to offer himself, but he couldn't breathe any better than Lilac. Everyone here was going to die.

A wild glare burned in Aeda's eyes. Her hair curled into angry fists and flared unkempt from her head. She scanned the crowd, hunting for a quick substitute, but if everything Alex and Cecil had said was true, this was not a choice she could rush. Deep down, her plan was dead. There was no one in this world with Arcadia's inner gentleness, no one so special.

Exalis's grip eased from Lilac's lungs, and she sucked in breath. Gasping echoes flooded the crowd as his presence slid from the temple's foundation.

"Father, a moment," Aeda said.

Exalis's attention picked through each kneeling mortal. Lilac wondered how many times she could withstand his clenching fist and then understood she would suffer him as many times as he wanted. Everyone would.

But he didn't want her. He wanted something *beside* her. Cecil? No. Something Cecil kept. His trench coat twitched over his right breast, and then the fabric flowered open around a rising red sphere. Light glinted in its tiny pores.

Another coralstone.

Lilac gaped at Cecil, *Where did you get that?* stuck in her throat. He returned a desperate stare, like he'd known he could hide the coralstone from Aeda but had underestimated the unfathomable sight of a Dawn God.

Aeda strained through the miasmic air and snatched the coralstone from above Cecil's chest. She turned to Exalis and cocked her head, throwing scarlet hair over one shoulder. Divine luminance shined across the coralstone's surface.

Medes stirred inside. Lilac felt her without touching, knew her name, what she wanted, how she had missed Exalis. Something she told him both eased him and concerned him, and a new pressure spread over the plaza as if the air had grown thick with physical disappointment.

Lilac's head jerked southward. Every head seemed to turn with hers, forced to look where Exalis wanted. A vision rushed across Lilac's thoughts, striking those gathered like a stiff wind against their minds.

The South Temple District. Lilac had lived there the past several years, knew its streets and apartments and shops, but she saw none of them now. Everything seemed to have melted into jagged rows of jutting rock, and burning dusk-colored particles filled the air, leaving only a red scar tearing across the south side of the city.

No familiar shops, no stairs, no landing. Home had been erased by this vicious new landscape. Everything physical Lilac had kept from the twins' brief time in this world had melted into crimson violence.

Every piece of Sara and Daphne, gone like they were.

Understanding seeped beneath the vision as all heads turned again to Exalis, an undercurrent flowing across the plaza between him and the mother of his child. He had not felt this violation of nature since he and the other Dawn Gods last put the glories in their place. Here came a similar violation, some choice by Medes which had brought a ferocious unmaking to the world and left a red scar over the wound. No matter what her reason, she could not undo it.

And no matter how else this moment ended, the city was cursed.

"This was not by our hands alone; the glories have abused nature too since you left," Aeda said.

But her confidence turned brittle, the tone of a child making excuses. Lilac recognized the kind. *Mommy, she hit me first.* Everyone began as a child, even a goddess, and maybe deep down, no one ever really changed.

"The gods were fearful, but—" Aeda's voice caught, as if listening to a message outside Lilac's hearing. "But Mother has offered a gift."

Exalis bristled between crystals. The gods were right to fear his disappointment, he let her know, let *everyone* know.

But this seemed lost on Aeda. Tension eased from her face as she turned to the west, where figures staggered into the plaza, bearing the pressure of a Dawn God and leading his daughter's treasure.

A shrill, triumphant laugh rang over the crowd, the kind from a goddess about to get everything she wanted.

CHAPTER 43

Aeda's search party had returned at last. She wasn't concerned about them—she was an expert at apathy—but the woman who walked with them concerned Aeda very much.

Lilac knew the feeling. She loved this woman, from her shorn head to her bright eyes, from her quiet moments to her secret smiles, in past, present, and future, through life and death and life again.

Could Exalis feel that love? Did he care? Was that why he let Lilac get shakily to her feet and stagger through the kneeling throng, shouting "Arcadia!" at the top of her lungs? She kept shouting anyway. "Arcadia! Arcadia!"

Her stagger broke into a clumsy run. She passed Cecil and Aeda, and then threw herself into those should-be-dead arms, wrapping her limbs around Arcadia's shoulders and waist.

And then Lilac slid back to the ground. Arcadia's arms hung at her sides, limp as her expression. That was fine; she and Lilac and everyone else were having a night like no other. Lilac placed a hand against Arcadia's cheek. It was warm and full of life.

"I looked for you," Arcadia said, her affect flat. Bloodstains spattered her sea-green uniform's chest. A small hole over her heart burned a glimpse of ragged scarring on brown skin.

"Alex didn't mean it," Lilac said. "He thought he could help."

Arcadia shrank back. Something was wrong. Lilac patted at

Arcadia's face, her neck, even her chest to be sure there was a heart still beating in there—yes, under the wound.

Lilac trembled. "Arcadia, look at me."

Arcadia tried, but her gaze darted this way and that. She was looking at Lilac, and looking past Lilac, and looking in places Lilac couldn't understand. Lilac stood on her toes, meeting Arcadia's tan eyes. Gods, they were beautiful. Lilac could've stared into them for eons.

But then she remembered Arcadia's purpose here.

"Run," Lilac snapped.

The air grew heavy again, and Lilac's knees struck the ground. She pivoted on cobblestone until her eyes found Exalis, where he became her everything once more. He was paying attention now. Couldn't she understand? Aeda would have what she wanted; Exalis would give it to her, and Arcadia would fulfill her chosen purpose. All would be well.

"You have done your work, High Priestess," Aeda said, as she ushered Arcadia to the front of the kneeling crowd. "And now comes time for the chosen to do hers."

Lilac couldn't scream. She might have thought she wanted to, but Exalis knew better. Lilac wanted to behave. If a smile broke across her face, Exalis would welcome it. Mortals should be joyous when the gods got their way. Deep down in this universe, what other way could there be?

Arcadia's head craned skyward. "Sunrise?"

Exalis shifted his attention. Lilac felt adrift, insubstantial, as if she existed less because he wasn't looking at her.

Aeda lifted an open palm to Exalis. "Father, meet the core of your tree."

Exalis knew. He likewise knew Arcadia's resurrection violated the laws of this world's nature. The Between coiled inside her soul, traces of a spiritual plane intruding in this bodily manifestation. The wrongness wore Medes's handprints, and Aeda bore part of this responsibility. He had trusted her and the other gods to safe-keep this world, these people, and instead she and her mother had raked the red scar across this city, where it would burn everything it touched for eons. How dare she abuse this power? What a disappointment.

Aeda's cool demeanor flickered. She hadn't expected her father to chastise her. Gods never thought they would be judged.

Lilac's attention flicked toward the coralstone in Aeda's hand. Cecil had carried it, and he must have seen Alex murder Arcadia. Had the coralstone been with her then? Aeda's request that Lilac fetch them both made sense. Arcadia had shared her blood with Medes, and this consecration of blood was the core link between the Dawn Gods and humans. Their children. Their sacrifices. Medes had brought Arcadia back to life against the laws of nature, no matter the consequence, all for her daughter.

Aeda's cool demeanor disappeared. In her eyes, her mouth, the curl in her nose, the way her hair writhed, she showed almost mortal desperation, a child ready to throw a tantrum because her parent wouldn't give her what she wanted. Aeda, at her most honest.

Glee stirred in Lilac beneath the layers of Exalis's will. Aeda would fail. This would end now.

Aeda laid a finger across Arcadia's shoulder. "Mine will not be the Holy Tree of Sceptomos. Arcadia Myrn must be the core of a *new* tree, and for my intentions with this tree, she proves nothing short of perfect."

Lilac couldn't breathe again. Why did Exalis keep the air to himself? She knew, of course—he kept it because he chose to, and that explanation was good enough. She liked it. Simple, straightforward, no complications. He could take and keep anything he wanted, and he was right to do so.

In return, he gave his warnings. The choices of Aeda and Medes would impact him in no way beyond his final breach into this facet of the universe. Whichever ways they chose to pervert this world, to the point it needed to break down before it could heal, they would have to live in it.

He would not control them, but no one should mistake his stayed hand for approval. He loved Aeda unconditionally. That was all it meant.

For a moment, Lilac thought Aeda looked as small as Sara or Daphne.

Breath surged into Lilac's lungs as Exalis's blood vessels splayed themselves like bloody hands in the air. Their makeshift fingers clutched his crystals, and then each hand swelled and hardened into rich, twisting limbs and crimson roots. The floating fragments slid together, driving skyward and earthbound until they formed the shape of a tree. A knot bulged at their top, where their ruby sheen burned white-hot and brighter than the sun.

Aeda raised the coralstone skyward. "Father is leaving us. Say your final farewell to him, Mother."

Exalis's knot swelled, almost a head to the forming tree. Thunder pounded in cracks down the center as a golden light burst through. The sky went white, the light jerking and writhing, alive and dead and eternal in ways no mortal could ever comprehend. Slender rays lashed across clouds and sky, out to distant places Lilac couldn't see.

One final luminous knife cut across the temple plaza and through the red coralstone. Aeda flinched, the blow buckling her.

Exalis's light rocketed toward the sky, and the cloudy atmosphere fuzzed and scrambled, turning scratchy and monochrome like a dirty film print. A broken-radio hiss rushed through the air. Every inch of Lilac's skin tingled with numb static. The world could not translate Exalis's new ascent into mortal sensations.

Lilac wasn't certain even Aeda had absorbed the whole picture.

The sky and city dimmed back to stormy night. Thunder rang

out, and the air pressure eased. Lilac had almost grown used to it, and its absence felt like a warm hug had ended right when she needed it to last a moment longer. Her head swam. When Exalis was here, the line between him and her had blurred in ways she couldn't understand. She had been herself in moments and entirely not herself at others.

Did it still matter? No one who stood around the temple ruins would ever see him again. Only his body, in its towering new form.

The red coralstone twitched between Aeda's fingers the way the knot had convulsed atop Exalis's changing body. Light poured through fresh cracks in the coral, and a voice screamed with it.

"It burns! He burns the sea! Too much!"

Aeda lowered the coralstone. "Mother?"

The coralstone exploded. Shards struck Aeda's fingers and ricocheted against her. Others blew around her, into the nearby faithful, and they fell flinching and screaming.

Except Arcadia. Sharp fragments cut her face, arms, clothes, but she stood motionless, her eyes vacant and unfeeling, as if she only had half a soul in her body. Maybe she did.

Beside her, the light dimmed where Aeda now cradled a naked woman in her arms. The woman's hair seemed to have been blasted from her scalp, and so had stretches of skin, now giving way to raw muscle. Her eyes were closed, her expression serene.

"Mother?" Aeda said again.

She sank to the ground and held the woman close. It had to be Medes, except she was injured.

"Mother, you bleed." Aeda glanced at the crowd, her scarlet eyes wild with need. "Tell me, how does a god bleed?"

No one answered except with crying and wailing. After shrinking to nothing but cells beneath a Dawn God's greatness, these people weren't ready to be themselves again. Lilac curled and uncurled her fingers, remembering how her body used to eat and breathe and keep a heartbeat on its own.

Aeda stroked one tremendous fingertip across Medes's cheek. Her glare settled on Arcadia. "Place yourself in the tree while I tend to her. Our endeavor must not end in failure. Be free of your heavy thoughts, Arcadia Myrn, and do as bidden."

Lilac tensed. Too much was happening too fast. Exalis was gone, but he'd left chaos behind. Medes was hurt; Aeda was angry. Arcadia wasn't herself anymore, but she could walk. Her every step left dark splotches on cobblestone and then marble, and her eyes fixed ahead as she staggered onto the temple steps, to the ruin above, and approached the last gift of Exalis.

The Holy Psychopomp Tree.

CHAPTER 44

Since Lilac was a child, this monstrosity had haunted the edges of stories. Its creation, its destruction. She had seen it in dreams, the bark and leaves aflame. Now, dawn's early red light slid through the hole in the clouds and broke between orange-hued limbs, as if this tree, like its predecessor, would burn above the Holy Land.

Like the coralstones, the Holy Psychopomp Tree had a pulse so strong it beat outside itself, through its roots beneath the cobblestone plaza. The highest branches towered taller than the now-ravaged temple in its prime, and the limbs stretched over outer-plaza buildings. Murky red-black bark scaled its swollen trunk. No leaves or fruit grew yet from the bows, but given time, the Holy Tree of Exalis would blossom and thrive the same as had the Holy Tree of Sceptomos.

It only needed a soul.

A tempest in Lilac's heart wished for this tree to die. It had no right telling the dead what lives to live next. They should chase whatever destinies they liked, rising with light spirits or falling with heavy ones. Insects, or birds, or people, let them try.

And certainly no Holy Tree should pluck souls from still-living bodies. Mankind should not become monsters who wandered soulless across Aeg.

Lilac gazed through the crowd and found Simone again. She didn't glance Lilac's way, the Holy Tree having devoured her attention. Would she look so stricken if her soul were ripped out? If Arcadia joined the tree, Lilac might never hear another motherly voice.

Aeda couldn't get her way. Logoi had been right to imprison her in a coralstone. Lilac had put this wrong in motion, and now she had to take up her mother's cause and put it right.

All she needed was fire.

At the foot of the trunk, where its roots coalesced across temple steps, the bark split around a vulval cavern where doomed Arcadia Myrn faded into the tree's darkness.

Lilac would have to follow her inside and get her out. In the Verses of Aeg, Gentle Theo had stepped inside the Holy Tree of Sceptomos, sacrificed his body on some unknown altar, and become the living tree's soul. Much later, Noema the Sick had followed the same path and burned the tree from the inside out. Some believed hers was the last soul guided, perhaps cast into a stone for centuries until that was destroyed and she could reincarnate again.

Lilac's first childlike inclination was to follow the story she knew. If one Holy Tree could burn, so could another. That was only reasonable.

But Sceptomos had given mankind the gift of medicine, no more protective than Lyradosia's gift of agriculture or Kaligos's gift of language. The Holy Tree of Sceptomos had been flammable. The new Holy Psychopomp Tree grew from Exalis, a manifestation of the Dawn God whose first gift to mankind, before this tree, his daughter, or the idea of gods at all, had been fire.

That same fire lived in his body now, soul or no soul. Warm light coursed through the bark and danced behind it, same as the flames within Exalis's descending crystal fragments. His living remains now coursed with fire the way blood coursed through Lilac's body. This Holy Psychopomp Tree would not burn. They would have to try something else.

Even something as desperate and unfortunate as putting Cecil inside.

Lilac hurried toward him, grabbed his arm, and pulled him to his feet. "Where did you get Medes?"

Cecil brushed his fingers over the fresh hole in his trench coat. "Long story," he said. "Alex would tell it better; it's his fault." He turned to the tree and started across the plaza. "Besides, time's up. Was hoping we'd sneak in ahead, but Aeda mustn't think Arcadia's long for this world. Right or wrong, she's got a head start."

Lilac glanced again to Simone. She seemed to notice Lilac and Cecil now, but her lips remained pursed. She was confused and afraid, and who could blame her after the terrible night they'd all endured? Lilac wanted to comfort her, but Cecil was right. They'd run out of time.

"Quickly now," Cecil said, scurrying through the still-kneeling crowd and toward the temple steps. "Aeda's distracted. We still got a chance."

Lilac dogged Cecil's heels. "And Arcadia? If she tries to stop us?"

"Don't know." Cecil reached the temple steps and glanced back. "They've done more to her than raise her from the dead. She's still their champion, got a force in her to battle a storm, and I'm not much in a fight myself. You?"

"Sometimes," Lilac said. "If my heart's in it."

Cecil hopped up the temple steps. "Can you get your heart in it this time?"

Lilac doubted it. Arcadia was alive again. The universe kept throwing Lilac chances, and she kept squandering them. Still, Aeda had sent Arcadia to die, as if some vicious fate had decided she absolutely could not live any longer.

Stopping her meant saving her.

Climbing the temple steps, the tree seemed to cover the clouds. Something so large, grown from a Dawn God—killing it didn't seem possible. More likely, this Holy Tree would swallow the sky, and Lilac and Cecil too.

There would be no coming back from here, whether they stopped Arcadia or not.

Cecil slipped through the tree's dark opening, and Lilac followed. The cavern was gloomy at first, but Lilac's eyes soon adjusted to orange firelight snaking between root walls and black tree-flesh. The tree was minutes old, but it smelled of ancient wood. No burning scent; the inside appeared as fireproof as the outside. Lilac stepped on cool marble floor, where the tree's roots had burrowed. No telling how deep they went.

"Did Exalis show you the red scar?" Cecil asked. "In your head, I mean? He showed me, and I damn well wish he hadn't. Utter madness, bringing Arcadia back to life. Medes must've done it after Alex—what Alex did. That goddess bit at nature, and nature bit back."

An enormous root divided their way in two. Lilac started right, but Cecil hooked her arm and led them left, chasing red dots across the white floor. Firelight flickered in their surfaces.

"Arcadia was dead," Lilac said. "Souls can't go back to the dead."

"They can," Cecil said, following the blood. "If the god doing it doesn't give a shit about the consequences. Poor Arcadia's soul went to the Between to make her next important decision, and then Medes grabbed her and forced her back to this life, this body. I don't know how someone processes an experience so violent. The world itself certainly don't like it. That Arcadia can focus on who she is at all is the real miracle."

The bark-coated cavern split again. Lilac chose the left route this time, her feet following but avoiding Arcadia's blood.

"She's disoriented," Lilac said. "She'd be impressionable."

"Hardly matters," Cecil said. He sounded stunned, the breadth of it weighing on him. "Aeda and Medes know she won't kill, and now they've nudged her this way, get her to rip our souls out. They'd do anything. Ungodly destruction, that red scar shredding through Valentine all to bring Arcadia back, and they'll do worse across the Holy Land. Maybe the world. Anything to kill the glories. We can't let them have their way."

Lilac's heart sank. "I'm going to lose her again."

"I'm sorry, love." Cecil squeezed Lilac's arm and kept moving. "You up for this?"

Lilac wiped one hand across her face. The other, without meaning to, clutched the knife inside her robe. "This went so much bigger than it was supposed to."

"Sometimes life's like that. I wanted to help people, too. But good deeds always seem to need bloodshed." Another choice opened in the cavern; Cecil tugged them to the right this time. "Even Aeda thinks she's helping. Stop the glories from slaughtering mankind." He gave a despairing laugh. "Even at the cost of mankind."

Lilac's fingers stroked the warm wall of bark. Through feet and fingertips and the air itself, the Holy Tree's pulse rippled in her blood.

"Yes, it's alive," Cecil said. "Only missing a soul."

"You wouldn't let me try to stop Exalis," Lilac said.

"He wouldn't have listened. His daughter said this was best and that was all. They love their children. Gods can't help it. Same with my grandfather." Cecil flashed an empty smile. "Even Logoi, I'm sure."

The path split again and then curved toward the temple's perimeter. No architect had designed this labyrinth, only the random sprawl of roots by a Dawn God who hadn't stuck around to see everything placed right.

Exalis's apathy was for the best, Lilac decided. If the rooted caverns had stood more straightforward, the navigation easier, she and Cecil might not have caught up with Arcadia before she found and died upon whatever altar hid inside this tree, bringing Aeda's plans to fruition.

But this Holy Tree was a twisted thing, and a looming figure broke the dark ahead.

CHAPTER 45

"I see her," Lilac hissed.

Arcadia lurched in the gloom. The path ahead split into three, and she was about to take the farthest right, veering deeper into the temple. She moved slower than Lilac and Cecil.

Lilac slowed to match pace. "Does she know what she's looking for?"

Cecil passed Lilac and approached Arcadia on soft steps. "Couldn't say what she knows. Verses of Aeg note something like an altar, but with a blade or spine for the sacrifice. We'll know it when we see it." He reached for Arcadia's shoulder. "Now, if you'd—"

Arcadia spun around and slammed her fist into Cecil's gut. He doubled over and stumbled back into a wall of roots. His fedora slid off his head and glided to the ravaged marble floor.

A more recent story than the Holy Psychopomp Tree sank into Lilac's thoughts—Alex telling of Arcadia's adolescent triumph in the barracks. Arcadia had always been capable, whether she knew it or not.

"I can't fight her," Lilac said.

"Can't?" Cecil gasped.

"I can't win." Lilac watched Arcadia disappear around the next right turn and then chased after her. "Arcadia, please. This isn't you."

That was exactly the problem. If this wasn't Arcadia, why would she care what Lilac had to say? Disoriented by her death at Alex's hands, wronged by the gods, Arcadia wouldn't know her lover. Did she even know where and when she was?

But Lilac had to try. "Doll—" She slipped toward Arcadia's right, but a muscly forearm slammed across Lilac's neck and pinned her to the wall. Pain rocked her spine, and she gasped against choking pressure.

Arcadia's eyes looked more lost than any night's staring contest with her hotel mirror. Her forearm slid loose, and she went on walking.

Lilac coughed hard, pried herself off the wall, and followed. Her foot padded in the blood trail, and she didn't mind drinking some of Arcadia in.

"If only Alex hadn't shot you," Lilac said.

The next splotch of blood was too big for Arcadia's puddles. They were nearing the altars where Lilac had helped summon Exalis with flesh and blade.

"If I hadn't started this—" Lilac said. Sara and Daphne dashed across a beach in her thoughts. "What are your regrets? If only this, if only that. Arcadia, tell me your ifs."

Arcadia didn't answer. Lilac crept close behind her, thinking to slip around, and then touched her still-aching throat. Had Arcadia wanted, she could have snapped Lilac's neck.

But Arcadia wouldn't, not even had she the power to tear the world to pieces. There was no murder in her heart. That was the real problem, right? Not that she wasn't herself, but that beneath the pain and confusion of every wrong done to her, Arcadia Myrn couldn't be anyone else.

Maybe that was the answer, nestled in another of Alex's stories.

A goddess commanded Arcadia. Not in the vague sense of duty interpreted by mortal mouths, and not a trembling hunk of coral. A present goddess, having long ago come into her power, almost unimaginable in the Holy Land after ten years, after this night.

And wouldn't Arcadia be that godly instrument? She'd said as much in Oldtown. She'd meant it. No more uselessness, no more dropped responsibility. She had purpose. Not much farther now.

"Tell me your ifs, Arcadia."

Lilac was here. Arcadia would miss her, regret never sharing secrets with her. Wasn't Arcadia sharing them now, amid the fire and bodies? No, they walked Valmydion's temple, or someplace like it. Nowhere else.

"If only you hadn't come to Valentine, right?" Lilac asked. "If only you hadn't met me? If only you'd never seen Shah?"

A goddess commanded Arcadia. Her regrets were dust in the face of holy edict.

Lilac kept behind her. "If you join the tree, you'll be stuck with these regrets forever. You want to think about Shah for all eternity?"

Arcadia's boot squeaked on slick marble. She had to reach the temple's center. Where Valmydion once sat, there now gaped a hole. Arcadia's life had changed there forever. Now she would find new change. A final death.

"Shah still means something to you, doesn't it?" Lilac asked. "Alex thought it did. Aeda killed him, you know. Your best friend, torn open by her fingers. Do you really want to do what she says?"

Arcadia didn't answer, and Lilac stopped walking. She was looking at something, Arcadia could tell.

"I won't be there to stroke your head when today's done, not if you do this," Lilac went on. "You have a choice. You always make choices, and you own them in the worst way."

Arcadia heard pattering now. A man with a West Amberdan accent. Cecil Gillion, Alex's friend. But Alex was dead, Lilac said.

"I'll go with the punch this time, like a gentleman," Cecil said, louder than a whisper. "But I've a better idea. A tribute to dear Alexander Stathos, if you will."

Arcadia lumbered onward, where the hole in the tree's center pulled her toward some alien place below. There would be no coming back this time.

"Myrn, fire at will!" a man shouted.

Arcadia jolted. Her nerves knew that order and its hypocrisy. Fire at will, but she'd had no will to fire on Shah's dancing villagers. She'd fired with all the will she had, but none was not enough for Commander Thale.

"Myrn, fire!" Was that Cecil? Arcadia couldn't tell. "That's an order! Fire now!"

Lilac shouted over him. "You made a choice, Arcadia!"

Arcadia dizzied, and the walls danced. She felt something rush past on her right and slammed her fist at it. The world sank in and out of darkness. She was in the barracks, lights out by her hand, where everyone was her enemy, and it didn't matter which kid she struck or why.

"Myrn, you coward. Fire!"

Arcadia swung again, hit soft flesh. A figure grunted and recoiled. The darkness brightened. She could see her place in the temple again, among the fires. And the bodies. A shadow broke the firelight ahead.

"Arcadia Myrn," Lilac said, her voice stern. "Do you know where we are?"

Darkness again. Firelight. Arcadia craned her neck, toward the descent, toward purpose, but no sign of Aeda marked the wall above fires and bodies.

The nine-pointed star of Logoi stained the world. Hail the Many-Headed, hail the goddess of reason. All deaths to Logoi, all blood dedicated to the mistress of the slaughter.

Arcadia stumbled back. She had wandered through the years again. Hurting Thale had stopped nothing. The dead did not forget; they dragged at Arcadia's heart, always leading her to Shah.

"Myrn, fire your weapon!" the man shouted, weaker now.

She should've tried harder to stop Thale and the others. Put herself between the dancers and death. She might as well have shot them herself.

"You made a choice," Lilac said again.

Shah was here, everywhere, always behind Arcadia, and now ahead. She sank against the warm wall and then collapsed beneath Logoi's bloody symbol, as if she crumpled at the feet of the goddess herself.

Cecil staggered closer, a hand on his middle. He seemed to have recovered quicker from Arcadia's second blow than her first. "The star did it," he said. "Knew it would. The way Alex talked—well, you know."

Yes, Lilac knew. This was not the first time she'd clawed up Arcadia's bad memories, only the first time she'd done it on purpose. She squatted on the pads of her feet between Arcadia's splayed legs and laid a hand on her cheek. Her skin burned feverish, hotter than the Holy Tree's roots. Tears welled in her eyes. Her mouth opened and closed, but nothing came out.

"I know, doll," Lilac said, quiet and serene.

Sacrificial blood pooled in Arcadia's sea-green pants. "All for Logoi," she said.

"It was the same for me. All for Logoi." Lilac pressed her forehead to Arcadia's and let the heat burn into her skull. "It's over now. It's been over for a long time."

She brushed fragments of red coralstone from Arcadia's arms. The wounds were little worse than scratches. If anything, Arcadia's vigor had returned in body. Only her spirit had become frail.

Lilac turned to Cecil. "I don't think she's going to die."

"She will if Aeda impales her in the center of the tree." Cecil chewed at his lower lip. "And Aeda most certainly wants to. Her mother's condition won't distract her long. We can't dally."

"Give me a moment." Lilac took Arcadia into her arms. Too much woman for Lilac to lift, but she propped Arcadia against the wall. She deserved better than to be left crawling in the remains of Lilac's mistakes.

Cecil looked to where the marble floor sank toward another forking path. Somewhere beyond, the Holy Tree's roots had filled the hole in the temple floor and led wherever Arcadia had meant to go. Where Lilac and Cecil needed to go.

"This is only a delay," Cecil said. "If Arcadia died here, Aeda would take her elsewhere and repeat her mother's mistake, unmake another part of the world. She'll only stop if she can't have her way. Hurry, or we'll wish we'd followed the gods out of the Holy Land before this happened."

Lilac felt an urgent pang in her head. He was right. "Sure, Cecil, yes. We're going."

She rested Arcadia's head against the bark wall, where tears went on streaming. Most likely she would be safe here. Aeda wouldn't hurt her—too valuable. But would Arcadia obey her again, or resist committing another nightmare in the name of a goddess? If only Lilac had been allowed to do what Cecil said, follow the gods out of the Holy Land. That would have been best for everyone.

Another urgent pang hit her head. Some crucial detail.

Lilac stood from Arcadia and shut her eyes, pushing out the sight of her lover, and flickering firelight, and the rich redness at her feet. Brief peace stole over this darkness, enough to wonder about this notion, why Cecil's harmless words might tick apprehension and alarm, why some patterns in the puzzle made sense and others didn't. She turned the words over a hundred times and found older ones, reminders.

The gods must've left because they knew what Aeda was going to do, Cecil had said after Alex's death. And now: *We'll wish we'd followed the gods out of the Holy Land before this happened.*

But also Alex: *Why did the gods leave?* Only theories, no clear answers, but he'd asked other questions too. *Who stands to gain? That question is a detective's best friend.*

Who stands to gain? A detective's friend.

Who stands to gain?

A detective.

We get someone else inside the tree, then we might have a shot, Cecil had said. *Someone she don't approve of.*

"Cecil," Lilac said, her voice shaky. "How did they know what was going to happen?"

"Who?" Cecil piped from a few steps deeper inside the temple. "What?"

"The gods left before I freed Aeda." The darkness became wriggling and hazy, and Lilac's eyes blinked open to escape it. "Here in the temple, after what Aeda did to Alex, you said the gods must've left because they knew what was going to happen. But only Lyvien gets premonitions. No one else sees the future."

Cecil cocked his head to one side. "Was only speculating, I—and that was about Alex's thinking, and—" He shut his mouth and let the words drift away.

"How did the others know this was going to happen?" Lilac asked. "If Lyvien told them, if they knew, then they could've stopped Aeda like they did before, right?"

Cecil stared at her. The nearby fires danced in his eyes, in the shadows of his face, and teased at his features. They tugged at the corner of his mouth. His lips twitched once, and then again, up into a wry smirk.

Lilac felt cold everywhere. "What did your grandfather tell them?" she whispered.

"Does it matter?" Cecil shrugged. "I told you. They're too far away to do anything about it now."

CHAPTER 46

Lilac's vision swam. She found Logoi's nine-pointed star she'd painted in blood across tree bark and let it ground her. She'd been looking at this star all her life, with and without Logoi.

"Your grandfather," Lilac said, her breath shallow. "He's the reason the gods left us. He lied to them."

"Some truth, some lies," Cecil said, wagging a splayed hand from side to side. "Come now. We'll need to find the altar before Aeda realizes we've stopped Arcadia."

Lilac pressed a hand to her forehead. "What difference does it make anymore?"

"Because someone has to be the core of the tree!" Cecil snapped. "Aeda's an immortal goddess, so she can't do it. Arcadia's down for a little bit, that shoots Aeda's plan in the foot. You're not going to do it; you don't even want there to *be* a Holy Tree. That leaves it to me. A descendant, yes, but not her chosen. Mortal enough to die."

"You *want* to be the core of the tree?" Lilac still couldn't believe this. She licked her lips, suddenly dry. "You said we're descended from greatness."

"And one of us should be great. No reincarnation—true eternal life, like the gods. No, *greater* than gods. Even they get forgotten sometimes, but a new psychopomp will stand revered for all time." Cecil thrust his hands out, his trench coat buttons straining at his chest. "That's the plan. Been the plan, love. For years. Grandfather Lyvien told his kin they needed to leave the Holy Land, for their own good. Like you said, the gods used to listen to his advice, and they did this time. If they were here, no one would've had a chance to find the coralstones, and even if someone had, the gods would've stopped all this like they did four hundred years ago. We had to clear out the Holy Land."

Lilac's voice came corpse-like. "And then the glories came."

"Was bound to happen." Cecil retreated another few paces into the tree's caverns. "Granted, I didn't think uncovering the coralstones would take until nearly the last minute, but no one knew where Aeda was, not even me, not even Lyvien. I searched hard, promise. Cutting it close, but here we are."

"And they've flooded the Holy Land and killed our people," Lilac said. "Killed children."

Cecil nodded, not looking.

Lilac fingered inside her robe. "They killed my children."

Cecil's leg twitched at his next step. "Now, Lilac—"

Lilac lunged, knife in hand. "My. Children."

Cecil darted around a bend in the corridor. Lilac chased him. She would bring him down, carve open his belly, hold him close to her while he died. She would ask him to tell the truth first, because what he said couldn't be right, this couldn't be happening. Friends didn't do this to each other.

The roots curved at a three-way fork. No sign of Cecil. He'd vanished down one path or another, leaving no blood to follow.

But his voice rang through the Holy Tree. "I'm sorry, love. Meant to finish with you being none the wiser, but the future's teetering."

Lilac had to make a choice. She steered for the right-most path and hoped it sank toward the Holy Tree's center. Cecil didn't know the way any better.

"I got careless," Cecil said, out of sight. "Insistent. I'm as close to getting everything I want as losing everything. You understand."

"You," Lilac growled. "Losing everything."

"That's right." Cecil sounded close, as if he might be running parallel with her on the far side of a root wall. "That night at dinner looked pretty gloomy to me, like the glories might sink Aedos. Would've had to take drastic measures, and the gods might've come back. And then hours ago, I realized you'd found the coralstones, but Aeda had already chosen Arcadia. What a mess."

Lilac's path split in two. She squeezed into a narrow right-side fork and strafed between two rough root walls. The path widened after a few feet and then sank into a sharp descent. The temple had never been so large, meaning Exalis must have twisted its inner reality. Every story about the Dawn Gods had undersold their power. The inside of the Holy Psychopomp Tree spread larger than its outside. Would it go for miles? Lilac doubted it. She was reaching whatever point Arcadia had meant to find. The altar lay somewhere ahead and below.

"Your whole murder business put a fright in me, too." Cecil's voice rang from all directions. "The sacrifices, summoning Logoi. Didn't think it would work, but hard to say at the time."

"Could you have brought Lyvien here if you wanted?" Lilac asked. "To save us from the glories?"

"You never knew your grandparents did you?" Cecil asked. "Dawn Gods on one side, Simone's folks long gone before you met her. Something you might have noticed when your little girls were around Simone though, something universal about grandparents—they spoil their grandkids."

The floor carried Lilac downward, and the fires began to darken. "Lyvien set all this in motion for you to be the core of the Holy Tree? Nothing else to it?"

"Of course he did." Cecil sounded almost offended. "I asked him to. He loves me to death. People think he wanders and ruts because he doesn't care, but that's nonsense. He's a big softy, heart of adventure, whims of a lover, more vagabond than god. Did you know I'm his only living grandson? He'd do anything for me."

Lilac curled her fists. The bloodied marble path had run out. She now walked soft, black earth into a strange space within the Holy Tree. She couldn't make its shape fit with the world she knew; best to ignore the outside and focus on reaching the center before Cecil.

"Descendants get a raw deal," Cecil said, his voice growing distant. He might have headed the wrong way. "Stamped down, unappreciated. We watch ordinary mortals die, the ones we love, almost enough to relate with immortality before that, too, gets snatched away. And then reincarnation? Being a descendant sticks to your bloody soul. A curse across lives, and you know what? I like this life, who I am now. Helping people."

His rant wore rags of the other night's tirade, and he almost sounded the same, an arrogant drunk. Maybe he was drunk now and wasn't himself. Worse, maybe that arrogance had always been his truest self.

His voice pounded on, as if Lilac couldn't escape him and yet couldn't catch him either. "Messy, sure, but think of all the good I'll do as the Holy Psychopomp Tree. Lyvien will come back, at least long enough for the other gods to follow him. And I really am sorry."

"Sorry," Lilac echoed. The tree's dimming fires burned as empty as childless funeral pyres, each a hollow gesture pretending to say goodbye. The next fork in the roots steepened the descent. Soil clung to Lilac's robe. "Sorry doesn't bring my girls back."

Somehow, Cecil heard her. "Not like I'm alone in keeping secrets, daughter of Logoi, the Valentine Butcher. I didn't want you swept up in this. If I'd known you were helping me, I would've stalled Alex instead of leading him your way. It's not right, friend against friend. Wasn't until we found Vince Barton that I realized you were incidentally doing Aeda's work. Sacrificing the father of your children so your mother would come back. That's damn cold of you, love. You're something else!"

Lilac's next left dropped down a steep inner slope. Slender tendrils snaked through the earth, and the root walls thinned to black soil around her. She had to dig her heels in to keep from tumbling down.

"Couldn't have Aeda knowing I'd set this in motion, either." Cecil's distant voice sounded lost behind the Holy Tree's beating heart. "She'd see through me and decide I wasn't pure of heart or whatnot. Nothing like Arcadia; they must've chosen her the moment she bled on one of them. Part of me hoped you'd kill her in your sacrificial spree, but I underestimated how selfish you are."

Lilac balled her fists. Selfish? Sure, but Cecil wasn't one to talk.

"Alex got close, a couple times," Cecil went on. "I really thought he had me for a moment, but in the end he doubted me too much. Still loved the man. Didn't deserve what Aeda did, but he didn't get the worst of it. Oh, I know stories. I know before Aeda and the other First Children were born, Dawn Gods were called the Sun-Bringers, but language has shaken up over the millennia. I know what really happened to your granny, the Unnamed Mother. And I know what Aeda's done to mortals who've displeased her."

Darkness swelled as Lilac drifted downslope.

Cecil's voice quieted, almost gentle. "We need to stop them, Lilac. They don't care, you see? The cost of killing the glories is worth anything they do to us. Let me be the soul of the tree. This is the only way. Still love you, none of that's changed. You'll miss me when I've joined the Holy Tree, but I'll do good by you. By everyone. That's my way, and I'll keep true to it for the long haul."

Faint blue light painted the darkness far ahead and below. Lilac made out an archway of tangled roots. The space was wide here and maybe too tall to make any sense with her descent.

"For eternity," Cecil said, his voice a whispering echo.

Cool air breathed across Lilac's ears. She had reached the subterranean core of the Holy Psychopomp Tree.

CHAPTER 47

A world stretched underground. Wider than the Holy Tree as seen from above, wider than the temple plaza. Tendrils of humid mist roamed the tremendous space, as if the Holy Tree's underside had a climate of its own. The mist cast a luminous teal hue across the darkness and curled around Lilac's legs. Great columns of roots, thick as cars, jutted in all directions from the ceiling's center and braced the walls. Archways opened between them, offering more than one path to the Holy Tree's core. Cecil could come from any direction.

A carpet of gentle grass filled the floor, its blue-green blades rustling beneath a faint breeze. It teased at Lilac's hair and robes as she neared the meadow, and it tickled cerulean flames where they haunted the inside of the cavern's columns.

Cavern—wrong word. This place was almost a temple of its own, a sanctum within the earth. There was a peace here only a Dawn God's power could bring. Were someone to rip the tree open from the outside and peer down the hole in Aeda's ravaged temple, Lilac expected they wouldn't find this sanctified underworld. Only an approach from within would bring someone here.

Above, the trunk of the Holy Tree, its branches, they were only the still-living body of Exalis. Down here rested the impossible nature of the Dawn Gods, a sliver of divine force now buried in the soil. It formed a crossroads where the tree's bodily presence in the world outside met its spiritual presence as psychopomp in the Between.

How could any mortal hope to stand against this power?

Were there no glories, maybe Alex would have been right to despise the gods. If the Dawn Gods had never left the world, maybe no glory would have ever mattered. Humanity had never been safe before they came or since they left.

No Holy Tree could help. It was the living body of a Dawn God, but its soul would come from a mortal, and it would only dictate mortal destinies.

Lilac glanced at her hands, scraped and weathered from these past days, scarred by past years. She couldn't be that soul. There should be no such soul. There were matters for gods, and matters for mankind, and matters of nature none should touch.

She found what she was looking for at the meadow's center. A frail, leafless tree hunched amid the grass and soil, where the air vibrated with a squeezing pulse.

The heart of the living Holy Psychopomp Tree—its altar.

It was an ugly thing. Bent and gnarled, a single knob bulged from its slender trunk, the foundation for its only limb. A sleek, unmarked branch grew from the limb's end and curled downward from the trunk into a sharp curved thorn.

As if it had been designed to skewer a human body and clutch it against the trunk. Lilac didn't need to shut her eyes to imagine how the sacrifice would go. The chosen mortal would stand with their back to the frail trunk, grasp the thorn in two hands, and tug it into their chest, impaled for the sake of fusing with the Holy Tree's heart. The tree would devour whatever body its thorn pierced, and the dead would pass directly into its pulse, offering the first soul for this Holy Psychopomp Tree. The one that would stay.

Lilac tucked the knife into her robe and placed her hands around the thorn. She found it warm and quaking. Though his spirit had ascended to the cosmos, Exalis's body remained primed and vigorous, the hollow-yet-living tree craving a mortal body from which to tear itself a new soul. Mortal and Dawn God made one. The earthly and the heavenly. To leave it living and soulless was another violation of nature. How long could the Holy Tree be left standing soulless before Exalis's vision of the red scar spread from here and ravaged the temple plaza, no different from the South Temple District?

Lilac tugged at the thorn. If she could break it off, then no one could join the tree, and maybe it would die.

The branch did worse than hold firm. At least then Lilac would've had something to ground her effort. Instead, the curling branch moved with her, a cooperative arm, whichever way she wanted it to go.

It would not break. It would bend wherever she led, let the thorn jab anyone who sacrificed themselves, whatsoever their height, but it wouldn't be snapped off and made useless. The altar was here to kill. It would fulfill that purpose.

"Oh marvelous lady, you've found it!" Across the meadow, Cecil strode from one of the many archways, smiling as if everything had gone according to plan.

As if Lilac hadn't learned the truth. It was his fault the gods were gone this past decade, that Sara and Daphne were gone these past four years. Dragged into the sea and drowned or eaten by a glory. Just three goddamn years old. Lilac found her knife again and clutched it tight.

"Good work," Cecil said, boots crunching through the meadow. Always too damn cheerful. "Got here before she did."

A stern voice slid through the mist. It froze Cecil in place and sent a jolt down Lilac's spine.

"Only barely has she arrived before me, but here I have come," Aeda said.

Even in the vastness beneath the tree, she appeared gargantuan. She might have chosen to look that way, a violent crimson-and-white stain against the cerulean firelight. Roots had shifted to accommodate her grandiosity.

"It's too late," Cecil said. "Arcadia's down, head's a mess, and my soul will have joined the tree by the time she gets it sorted."

Aeda almost seemed to float through the sanctum. One foot pressed into the meadow. "You descendants have an agenda of your own, beyond Logoi's return and some unrelated foolishness, but it is no matter. Be gone from this place. It does not belong to you."

Cecil inched toward Lilac and the thorn. "Now's our chance," he whispered.

Lilac ripped the knife from her robe and aimed it his way. "There's no *our!*" she snapped. "No *us.*"

"Come now, Lilac." The wind toyed with Cecil's tawny hair, freeing it from where his lost fedora had clamped it wet to his head. "We're friends, aren't we? At least more than you and her. I'll brace that altar, jab it in me. It'll take seconds."

"Our bond is greater than your hollow friendship," Aeda said. "We are kin."

"Well, we're kind of kin too, aren't we, goddess?" Cecil asked. "I know Lyvien's a generation or so removed, and I'm two down from him, but those Dawn Gods, they got around." His arms dropped to his sides. "Well, what then, Lilac? You're closer kin to her than to me. You'll let her win?"

Aeda took another step. "Such are the circumstances of fate, exactly. Lilac has left her selfishness behind. She now wishes to save the world. Arcadia's deathless hands will relieve mankind of the burden of souls. No restraint, no mercy. Expect glorious blood to lap the shores, your nature twisted toward war, an unmaking for those demons of the sea."

"You don't even know what you're playing with," Cecil said, scoffing. "Logoi knew. That's why she bottled you and your mother up. Haven't you two twisted nature enough already? You won't save us by fucking us over."

Exalis's vision of crimson death filled Lilac's head. What Aeda and Cecil argued over sounded no different from the red scar, burning, devouring, unmaking. Would Aeda turn human beings into similar destruction?

You'll break the laws of nature, make us abominations, Alex had said. He might've figured that part out too, without even knowing about the red scar. A better oracle than any descendant, better than the god of instinct, and none of it had saved his life. Wouldn't save anyone's lives.

Aeda's smile faded. "I intend salvation. Without souls, mankind will be strong as never before. Strong enough to end the glories. For all time."

Lilac kept her knife aimed at Cecil, it wouldn't do any good to Aeda, but she turned to the goddess. Neither he nor Aeda approached, as if Lilac had some power which kept them from storming her.

"You'll ruin everything," Lilac said.

"Why do you two speak ravage and ruin?" Aeda asked. "Who told you this? Him? Should he be trusted more than a goddess?"

"You've lied to me already." The knife quivered in Lilac's hand. "Both of you."

"You lie to yourself, and yet you trust yourself." Aeda laid a hand over her chest. "Trust me. I am not like Logoi; I love the mortals. But at times, we must hurt those we love to make them strong."

Lilac turned from Aeda to Cecil again. They were both so eager, Cecil to thrust himself under this thorn, Aeda to tear apart Lilac's flesh and bones. They twitched with it, but neither lunged to do what they wanted. Why the hesitation?

The knife gleamed in Lilac's hand. No threat there to Aeda, immortal goddess, only to Cecil, a descendant but mortal.

Descendants. Lilac and Cecil fed on blood like gods, lived longer than most humans, but they weren't gods themselves. What was it Cecil had said? He could join the tree even as a descendant, trade up on his raw deal.

Mortal enough to die.

Lilac aimed the altar's thorn below her ribcage. "Back off," she snapped. "Both of you."

Aeda retreated a step. She'd been waiting centuries for this, most of the time imprisoned. She could be patient.

Cecil hid apprehension beneath a goofy grin. "Come off it, Lilac. You can't."

Lilac dropped her knife and grasped the thorn in both hands, bending the branch closer. "We're mortals, remember?" she asked. "Like this little tree, we have a heartbeat. Like all the people I killed. It'll be the last blood I ever shed."

"Oh, I know how it's done, now that I see it," Cecil said, his tone patronizing. "I'm saying you, Lilac Antonis, cannot do it. Maybe Aeda's right that you want to save the world. You did leave Arcadia behind, splendid. But wasn't that to chase your vengeance? We both know even if you've opened your heart, you're still too selfish to off yourself here and now."

Lilac pressed the thorn deeper. Its point rumpled her robe.

Cecil dropped the grin and stepped back. "You don't want an eternity like this."

"You took my children," Lilac said. "My mother left because of whatever Lyvien told her. All so you could be the eternal Holy Psychopomp Tree, remembered forever, loved forever."

"Listen, Lilac—"

"And you." Lilac glared at Aeda. "My home is gone. Everything I had of my children, gone. You took Arcadia to be your special sacrifice, the one who could steal everyone's souls without killing them. Brought her back to life—I don't know *what's* left of her mind. And Simone's going to die out there. The whole fucking

Holy Land's drowning, and there's nothing I can do about it, right? I have nothing left to lose. So why shouldn't you both lose everything, too?"

Cecil and Aeda glanced at each other.

Lilac ran one hand along the thorn's bendy branch, to the frail tree that was at once the altar and the anchor to the sacrificial blade. And here was the high priestess who might also be the sacrifice. Somehow it felt fitting after everything she'd set in motion.

"You would damn the city," Aeda said. "Either I have my way, or I'll leave. No more goddess in the Holy Land."

Cecil took a step closer. "Let me join the altar. I'll save everyone."

Lilac scoffed. "With what? Your branches?"

"Lyvien will come back if I'm the Holy Tree," Cecil said, every word insistent. "The rest will follow, I'm sure of it. Everyone will see it for a miracle, and what else are the gods good for but miracles?" He pointed across the meadow. "And they'll imprison her and her mother again."

"Not my mother," Aeda said. "Mortals cannot become flesh in the Between."

"She's mortal now?" Cecil laughed hard. "Serves her right! Did Exalis do it, or has she paid a price for tugging Arcadia's soul screaming back to the world?"

Lilac's stomach turned, and she cringed against the small tree. Arcadia lay in pain above. No one would come to help her. And now Medes, a goddess ascendant, had—what, descended? Nothing seemed right. Too many clouds hung in Lilac's head, and she almost missed the crunch of a footstep.

When she looked up, Cecil stood another pace closer. "Lilac, please don't side with them," he said. "Think about it. Descendants, raw deal, remember? An ordinary mortal visits a god and says their body isn't what they're meant for, and the gods can change it. Another's child rots away from some blood disease, and the gods

338

bring healing. They can be chosen, become empresses and kings."

Lilac squeezed the thorn as Cecil drew nearer.

"But us descendants?" Cecil swiped a hand through his hair. "We get so much as a papercut and the gods are powerless. We're damn well on our own. Time for a descendant to trade his hat for a crown and become as immortal as the gods."

"And *you* deserve it?" Lilac snapped. "My girls are dead because of you. I shouldn't have had to see those empty funeral pyres, what that did to me. And to my mom. Do you even care?"

Cecil trembled. "I didn't know."

Lilac shuddered; Cecil sounded too much like Vince the moment before she'd killed him.

"The ignorance of man," Aeda cooed. "If we're making offers, Lilac, then best you know mine. Let us see you become a mother again."

Lilac led the thorn lower along her abdomen.

"Beyond all else, know me as Goddess of Birth." Aeda paced the meadow's edge. "How many children would you like? How often? In a touch, I could make it so. A descendant cannot become an immortal goddess, but it lies in my power to stir the fertility of any other mortal seed. Some of your children may be descendants, perhaps gods themselves. Any children you want, little cousin. The offspring of your desire."

High-pitched squealing laughter. Tiny footsteps. The whining and crying. Drawings on the wall. The little songs. Simone nodding off in her chair with two drooling toddlers for a nap. The way they would hold each other's hands and whisper secrets in their own strange twin language. A beach sank in Lilac's mind.

"She's lying to you," Cecil warned.

Lilac tightened her grip on the thorn.

Cecil had stepped closer, bolder. "A god can't help a descendant. She could turn another's womb inside-out and place Aeda-touched eggs in you, and you'd give birth to that flesh and blood. She could fill someone else with children and hand them over."

"I would make it so in whichever way you liked," Aeda said. Her body aimed at Cecil, eager to charge across the meadow and crush him. "I would do this for you, cousin. We are kin."

"You'd love them, sure, but they wouldn't be your twins," Cecil said. Grass crunched beneath his boot. "I can do better. When I'm the psychopomp, I'll touch every soul in this world. I can find your children's souls, wherever and whatever way they've reincarnated."

Lilac's hands shuddered around the thorn, almost losing their grip. "Sara. And Daphne?"

"You kill whatever they're in—human, rabbit, tree, whatnot— and I'll hold onto them here." Cecil took another step and reached out a hand. He wasn't far now. "You get pregnant again, by whatever means, and once grown enough, I'll send those souls inside you. Got it? You can have your children back. Not *new* children, but the souls of Sara and Daphne, the ones you lost."

"The ones taken from me," Lilac said.

"Exactly, yes." Cecil's smile returned. "Give me the chance to make it right."

Aeda said nothing. Maybe she was thinking up something to sweeten her deal.

Lilac considered Cecil as an eternal psychopomp. The Cecil she'd known—kind, playful, flirtatious, life-loving Cecil—might not have been a bad choice if there absolutely had to be a Holy Tree.

But that man was only a facet of the whole. On some other side of him lurked a frightened liar who cowered at losing himself to reincarnation, envious of the gods as much as he shared blood with them. He was a man who'd brought ruin and horror to the Holy Land solely to become the great psychopomp, fixed and endless.

"They say Gentle Theo was kind in life," Lilac said. "But even he couldn't keep from judging souls. The worst became stones and stayed in them until those stones cracked. Reincarnation by tiers and hierarchies and punishment."

"The Between is a mess," Cecil said.

"And?" Lilac gritted her teeth. "Death is uncertain, and that's scary, sure, but at least it's uncertain universally. At least we can be sure there isn't a liar and a coward deciding where our souls go after we die."

Cecil stamped the grass. "I want to help the world, Lilac. I'm a good person!"

Lilac pressed the thorn tight beneath her ribcage.

Cecil froze where he stood, and then his face curled, baring his teeth. "Fine then, what kind of Holy Psychopomp Tree would *you* be? Did you give that a think when you started this game of threats? Imagine, the soul of some cutthroat who'd slaughter anyone she could get her hands on so long as she gets her way. You don't belong in the tree."

"Who does?" Lilac asked. "Arcadia? Seems like she's too good."

"Her soul's a mess because of them." Cecil chinned at Aeda, stiff and resolute. "I'd almost say if Alex hadn't gunned her down, they'd have had you kill her anyway so they could bring her back, make her pliable for what they want."

Lilac shook her head. The gall of him. "You don't get to judge anyone on being manipulative," she said.

"You want to know what Lyvien told the gods to make them go?" Cecil asked, drawing closer.

Lilac prodded the thorn tighter against her. It was beginning to hurt. Much more of this and it might puncture her flesh.

Cecil took his next step anyway. "He told them someone would find a way to kill the gods."

Aeda tittered, a cold cruelty through the Holy Tree's underbelly.

"It's no joke, no lie." Cecil lowered himself to the grass. "Lis-

341

ten to me. On top of having your babies back, you'll get revenge. How to kill a god—the prophecy's since come true. I know how it's done."

Aeda's laughter cracked with impatient thunder. "How much fiction will you suffer in this holy place?" she asked.

Lilac couldn't look at Cecil. She couldn't look at Aeda, either. She focused on the bending branch, the thorn, the altar, her feet in the grass, her hands on her own life.

What now? Stop them.

Stop them, how? The simplest, clearest way, the way the thorn already faced. Take everything they wanted, no matter the cost. Straight to her heart.

What would happen? She could see the lines of fate clearly. Exalis was the only Dawn God whom Aeda could call. None of the others would care if she tried to summon them; they weren't her father. She would think she'd lost her chance to save the Holy Land when really she'd lost her chance to destroy it. Jilted at her failure, she would make good on her threat to abandon Aeg. Maybe the other gods would come back, having surely felt Exalis's coming and going, but not in time to save Valentine—Aedos, whatever it was—if the glories pushed the sea across the city-state. Same as humans, the glories would've felt the Dawn God's departure as well, and Lilac couldn't be sure the tree would deter them.

Simone would die. Arcadia, too, again. Cecil would probably die when the floods came. Or not. A silver tongue like his could do well if he found another city-state, if there were any left. For days or decades, he'd live the rest of his life dissatisfied, having sacrificed so much for nothing.

Lilac could relate more than she wanted.

And what of her? If she became the Holy Tree, she could press the souls of her loved ones into better lives, every time they came to reincarnate. But the tree wasn't the Between, and they were supposed to decide for themselves. That's what made having a Holy

Psychopomp Tree so wrong, the part where it played the psychopomp. Could she be a benign Holy Tree, or would she feel compelled to take action, the way a soul freed from the body suddenly knows so much more?

She had no answers. All she knew was that she wanted to finish this life. Not as a goddess, not as a Holy Tree. Only as Lilac.

Maybe Cecil was right. She was too selfish, and this was all a bluff. To be mortal flesh and blood meant the risk of your loved ones being mortal flesh and blood. Life flowed inside Lilac right now, in the grass, in the tree, all of it fleeting and therefore precious. Every mortal life meant a hundred times more than the endless existence of a god.

Lilac slid the thorn away from her ribcage and aimed the branch down. She heard Cecil running, taking his shot. Probably Aeda was lunging, too. Lilac kept bending the branch, curving the thorn inward. The tree was alive, and the thorn wanted a life. Too strong for her to hurt it, but strong enough to hurt itself.

She put all her weight into one firm shove and drove the thorn deep into its frail trunk. The barb dug through the bark, and a twitching heartbeat rang through the underground.

Cecil staggered to a clumsy halt. Aeda froze two steps from Lilac. They looked at each other, Cecil's face wide and wild, Aeda's mouth gaping open.

Lilac swallowed. None of them knew what might happen now. This was only the second Holy Psychopomp Tree to ever have existed, and the first one to be forced to stab itself on its own altar. Aeda liked firsts. She would get to see this new precedent set with her own eyes.

For a moment, nothing happened.

And then the underworld's rooted columns flashed with white fire, the altar buckled around its trunk's frail wound, and the Holy Psychopomp Tree's heartbeat shattered into an unholy scream.

CHAPTER 48

The Holy Tree must have changed its mind. That was Simone's first ludicrous thought when the ground trembled and the red-black roots snaked out from the ruined temple. Across the sky, branches and limbs curled inward like burning hairs, and the trunk caved in halfway up. It had only formed an hour ago at most, and now it was dying.

"What do we see?" Medes asked. She lay on the cobblestones beside Simone, wearing a coat someone had thrown over her. She was supposed to be a goddess, at least from what Aeda had said, but she looked too young and vulnerable. Too mortal where raw flesh showed in patches down her skin. "Have I missed Exalis?"

"You saw him," Simone said, holding Medes's hand. "He gave you to the goddess's arms in light."

"He has done more than that, I should wonder." Medes's free fingers traced cuts in the flesh of her bare legs.

A quake tore through the temple plaza as the Holy Tree's trunk rose up on its roots like a rearing horse. If it came crashing down, it would kill most of the gathered refugees, but it held.

Simone wished for Logoi. Hatred and love still sloshed together in her heart, but at least the goddess of reason could explain why the Holy Psychopomp Tree looked to be eating itself from the inside.

The temple's foundation split as roots untangled from marble.

Exalis hadn't stayed; the Holy Tree wouldn't stay. On and on, everyone seemed to abandon Aeg. Dawn Gods left the Holy Land to the gods. Gods left it to the descendants. Each generation expected too much of their children, who had greater numbers yet far less power.

What was a descendant supposed to do? Of course Lilac had reached out for a goddess. And of course that goddess had reached out for a Dawn God. Did Exalis, too, have a parent to ask for help, an entity beyond the Dawn Gods, unknown to lowly mortals? Was he finding that parent now, somewhere in the heavens?

Every inch of the Holy Tree turned pale, as if camouflaged with the temple's white marble. Bony, sickly, a great maggot eating at the morning sky's carcass.

Simone had the sudden thought that the Dawn God's body was dying. To go a lifetime hearing the story of the Holy Psychopomp Tree, the many centuries it had stood, the story of its demise, she'd thought it a thing meant to outlast any mortal.

This Holy Tree had been brief. Exalis might not have given his body to become the tree had he known it wouldn't last.

Some vacuous force yanked the roots and branches against the massive trunk, again and again until it became a pale column, floating in the sky. The trunk crunched between them. The Holy Psychopomp Tree became an ever-shrinking tower of churning wood, the size of a house, the size of a tree, a sapling, a toothpick.

And then it was nothing, an implosion of empty air where a Dawn God had floated not long ago. Blue-green grass rained across the crowded plaza. Not a splinter of the tree remained, only the damage it had left on the city, the ruins of the temple. Someone stood at the top of the steps, impossibly tall, the way you expected a goddess to be.

Medes tore her hand loose from Simone's. "Aeda, come to me."

Aeda descended the temple steps. Her face appeared stony, disinterested in the people who surrounded her or the destruction she'd left behind. She stopped above Simone, reached her great hands to the ground, and plucked Medes up, no heavier to her than a doll.

"My daughter," Medes said. "It has not gone right, has it?"

"No, Mother. All lies in ruin." Aeda pressed her forehead to her mother's tiny mortal body. "And Father is lost to us forever."

Medes reached for Aeda's cheek. "You have suffered, sweetling. What would you have us do?"

"Away," Aeda said. "As with the other gods, away from this accursed land."

Medes kissed her daughter's forehead. "Take us."

Aeda nodded, but before she left the plaza, she glanced over her shoulder, past Simone, at the temple. "Best you be pleased with yourself or be nothing," she said. "You have damned the world."

She began across the plaza. Some of the gathered faithful broke around her feet, while others hurried after, murmuring that Aeda would need a boat if she meant to bring now-mortal Medes across the sea, and some knew how to build one.

"For these sins, I curse you all with the red scar and its endless hunger," Aeda said, stepping into a throng of faithful. "I curse your eyes to watch your loved ones fade and perish."

Some of the crowd clustered where Aeda stepped, reaching for her as if they could cling to her dress and be carried over oceans to safety. A red glimmer haunted her skin where they touched, and Simone watched them fall away from the goddess's path, grasping at mouths and throats now clogged with blacked-over puddles. They were drowning on dry land.

"And I curse you with lungs of blood and water, and a slow, slow death," Aeda said.

She ignored the people writhing beneath her, and the rest scattered at her approach toward the plaza's edge, westward into Valentine's alleys. Goddess and mother alike slipped out of sight, and the rain trickled onto the crowds and cobblestones as if Aeda had never stood here.

Simone turned to the temple to see who Aeda had been first talking to, whoever had supposedly damned the world, and her heart skipped a beat. Through all this destruction—there she was.

Lilac wobbled to her feet, groggy, aching, but alive.

CHAPTER 49

The temple was little more than a marble pile where Lilac stood. No seating, no altars. The hole remained in the center, but no strange tree grew above or below. The world had righted itself in the absence of the Dawn God's power. Arcadia lay against a broken hunk of marble. Dead? No, her chest rose and fell. Breath. Good enough for now.

Cecil staggered to his feet not far away, holding his head in one hand. In the light of early morning, the red traces in his pale hair glared like a crimson sunrise.

Lilac watched and considered him, but there was little to sort out. She had fed the tree to itself. She had kept Aeda or Cecil from getting what either of them wanted. Troubles persisted, but there was only one she could do anything about, and it was a simple problem with a simple solution.

She was already charging at him before she finished her thought. He noticed at the last moment, too slow to react. She grabbed his arm and yanked him against a chunk of once-altar.

The collision breathed white dust into the air. Cecil clambered up its side. Blood painted his forehead.

Lilac squeezed his shoulder hard and thrust him at the pock-marked marble floor. He landed on his back. One hand danced for the knife in her robe, but she'd dropped it. She would have to make do. Her knee sank against Cecil's chest.

348

"You," Lilac said. "Every awful thing's happened because of *you*." There was a cry in her voice she didn't like. She shouldn't mourn this moment. Cecil was her friend, and he'd betrayed her, and she wasn't going to let that hurt her heart.

Cecil coughed. His limbs were weak, and he couldn't seem to shove Lilac away. "You're blaming me," he said, almost in disbelief. "Aeda could have pushed the sea from Aedos, didn't you think of that? But that wouldn't have made people desperate. Don't you get it?"

Lilac punched him in the mouth. The strike screamed through her knuckles, but it was worth seeing his lip split open.

Cecil winced. "You weren't caught between two rough spots, love. *You* made this happen. Want to kill me? How do you know years from now, there won't be someone who finds out you set Aeda loose? Who blames you for all the killing?" A smile tugged his bloody lip. "They might want revenge. It never ends. It'd go better with a friend to watch your back."

Lilac hit him again. The blow hurt less this time.

"Fine, fine, Aeda didn't bring the sea, I admit it." Cecil spat blood, careful not to spit on Lilac, as if politeness might save him any better than inventing stories and excuses. "Going to kill me? Come now, I'm your friend. And I didn't even know you back when my grandfather sent the gods running. It was ten bloody years ago."

"And two years later, I started growing my babies inside me," Lilac said, raspy. She leaned close to Cecil's face. He smelled like blood. "And after they were born, I started growing them outside me. Inch by inch, meal by meal, until they were three years old, when I never saw them again. These past four years, I've been thinking of those empty funeral pyres because of you. Because you killed my babies."

"I didn't take them to the glories and say, lunch is on me!" Cecil snapped. "Unforeseen consequence. Nobody's fault, not even yours."

"Yes, it is. I take responsibility. You're like Alex." Lilac raised her fist again. "You can't own what you do."

"No, that isn't it. Stop hitting me a moment, just listen!" Cecil inhaled hard. "But if I have to take responsibility in their deaths, I get a share in responsibility for their lives. I'm the only reason you left Logos, right? Met their father? If it weren't for me, you wouldn't have had children at all. No Sara, no Daphne. You'd have never met Simone. And later on, never met Arcadia. All these good things only happened after the gods left. Would it really have been better without them?"

Lilac's hesitant fist trembled in the air. "Some days, it's felt that way."

"I'm sure. I can imagine." Cecil tilted his head, splaying tawny hair over pale floor. "I see it in your eyes. Never used my gift on you, you know?"

"Descendants can't."

"But I never tried either—"

"You're lying," Lilac snapped. "You thought your damn gift didn't work."

"—so I never knew you were a descendant until this past night," Cecil went on, as if Lilac hadn't spoken. "Good to my word, right? Isn't that how you've known me? We've been friends for years. Look at me." He flashed a grin. There was blood in his teeth. "Still me. Still your mate, Cecil. None of that was fake. I lied more to Alex last night than anyone, and to your benefit, love."

Lilac punched him again. "Don't call me that." She could grab a chunk of marble. Put a swift end to this.

"That's fair. Perfectly fair." Cecil raised his arms, his hands open-palmed. How many hugs and friendly pats and general gestures of affection had he given? He'd acted so caring before, only to show his true malice here. "Listen, Lilac. We're still in trouble. Let me make a couple sacrifices to Lyvien, draw his sign of the foxhead. He'll come."

"I tried that," Lilac said. "Logoi's star. If she couldn't hear me, why would Lyvien hear you?"

"Logoi heard." A soft wind stuck Cecil's blood-tipped hair against his cheek. "We're their kin, Lilac. Special privilege. Sacrifice for them, offer blood, paint their signs, speak their names. They'll hear us. She always heard you, every time, and she made a choice."

Lilac studied his face. Another lie? Or worse, a truth?

"But Grandfather Lyvien is different," Cecil said. "He'll come. Next time the glories try for Aedos, they'll find a god here. We can still save the Holy Land."

"From *you*." Lilac's chest swelled. "From what you did!"

"Let me make it right." Cecil's voice cracked with desperation. "We can all be better than I was. I reamed you on being selfish, but it was me, too. I admit it, selfish pile, that's me. Look at Arcadia over there."

Lilac cast a split-second glance Arcadia's way. She looked as dazed as before. Cecil had put her through unimaginable horror. Shah, shortly after the gods left. Lilac. Medes and Aeda and their machinations. That sweet soul clung to the world, but Arcadia hadn't deserved any of this nightmare.

"She wouldn't do what I did," Cecil said, and then raised a weak hand toward Lilac. "And she wouldn't do this. Killing me isn't what she'd want you to do."

"I'm not Arcadia." Lilac grabbed Cecil by the trench coat collar and tugged his face close. She hadn't realized until now that her cheeks were wet with tears. "You—damn you. I loved you, Cecil."

"Don't fret." Cecil's voice sank to a serene lilt, almost motherly. "I'll make it right. Lyvien will come. A god will save us. Isn't that what you wanted, so that no one else has to die the way your daughters did?"

Lilac turned it over in her head—bring Lyvien here. She could almost see it. She wasn't sure who deserved the blame more, grandfather or grandson, but she knew she couldn't stomach that god to wander the Holy Land, to become its savior after he'd set its destruction in motion.

"Cecil?"

"Yes, love?" Cecil's eyes turned calm.

"I can't," Lilac said. "You were right. I'm too selfish."

Her grip tightened around his collar. She raised his head high from the floor and then slammed the back of his skull against the marble. A wet crackling thud echoed over the temple ruins. Cecil's eyes quivered, and then his lips. Lilac raised him up and thrust him down again. Another crack, harsher this time.

That was enough. Cecil's head lolled to one side.

Lilac stood, watching the puddle of blood spread across the marble. Crimson stained her hands, and drops had spattered down her face.

This blood didn't seep into her hungry skin. It lingered, sticky and warm.

Of course. Cecil was a descendant. Same as their blood was no good to the gods, it was no good to each other. Lilac couldn't drink it, almost like she wasn't some blood-sucking descendant at all. Painted in red splotches, she looked like any other murderer.

She wiped her palms on her robe, frantic to rub the marks away, but the red blemishes stained her olive skin. She'd pitied the first men she killed for Logoi, and then Vince, and then the temple sacrifices. Cecil didn't deserve it, but she pitied him, too.

And herself.

Water rushed in the distance. The rains were coming back, and maybe the sea would join them. Lilac didn't really want to know anymore. She staggered toward Arcadia and collapsed beside her.

Arcadia blinked, her eyes a little more focused than before. "I don't know what I'm doing," she said.

"Nobody does." Lilac pressed at the dark bloodstain on Arcadia's chest. "Does this hurt?"

Arcadia shook her head. That was something, at least.

Lilac let her head sink onto Arcadia's chest and listened to a steady heartbeat. "He killed my babies," she whispered.

Arcadia couldn't know what that meant, but she held Lilac anyway, the most natural thing in the world for Arcadia to do. Lilac wished this was all they had to do, forever.

And in some ways she wished they had never met.

And in greater ways, she wished for some other impossible life. She wanted a life spent with Logoi and Simone and the twins by day and then with Arcadia by night. They would meet up with Alex and Cecil for dinner, and they would all be friends. Vince would visit sometimes to see Sara and Daphne, let them know he loved them, but Arcadia would help Lilac raise them, and they would play with Arcadia's uniform and want to be flood fighters like her when they grew up. And this miracle life would thrive in a city immune to glories, some winged metropolis that could never drown, where the rain only came when you wanted it.

There, Lilac never had to sacrifice anyone. Never sup on their lives. Never hurt the people she loved.

Never wear this tattoo of Cecil's blood on her skin.

CHAPTER 50

A barrage of damp boots squelched the earth to the west of the plaza. Arcadia's arms dropped. Lilac wanted to lie here longer, but there was no safety in the city, whether they called it Valentine or Aedos, and everyone knew it. She helped Arcadia to her feet and turned with the gathered crowd to face the newcomers.

They were the remains of the Logos police and flood fighters. Mud and blood had erased any distinctions between their blue and sea-green uniforms. Lilac couldn't imagine what nightmare they had seen in Oldtown, but she guessed they'd been forced to their knees when Exalis arrived and had been gathering themselves since.

But they'd taken too long and missed everything. Doubtful they could have helped. When had they ever?

A burly man with a scraggly beard sat in a wheelchair, pushed by a young woman. He raised his hand for her to stop, and the rest of the approaching group stopped with him.

"Commander Thale of the Logos police," he said. "Anyone want to explain what happened here?"

Arcadia leaned against Lilac, and they started down the temple steps.

Thale gazed over the crowd. "Anyone?"

Most heads turned to the temple, and Lilac realized they were looking to her, as if she were still Exalis's high priestess. She didn't want the responsibility of explaining anything. She wanted to take Arcadia and Simone and go home.

Except home was gone, erased by the red scar. Medes had seen to that.

"We thought we'd be saved," Lilac said. "We were wrong."

Thale looked her up and down, seeking something special, seeing only a woman in a black priestess robe, tired beyond belief. "And who are you supposed to be?" he asked.

"Nobody." Lilac descended the steps, where she found Simone and hugged her tight.

Thale creaked uneasily in his ill-fitting wheelchair. He gave Arcadia a long stare and then winced. "Valentine is done. The storm's eased off, but we can't hold the glories back an entire season. We barely held them off last night."

The young woman who pushed his wheelchair leaned over him. "What do we do with the people?"

"I don't care what they do." Thale's speech became a roar. "Anyone who wants to follow me, I'll lead them across the city-state, up the North Road toward Shadow Mountain. It'll be hard, but I'll take any small chance over no chance, which is all we'll get in Valentine. I'm tired of wasting time and lives trying to protect you people. Follow us if you want, but I agreed to run this city, and it's finished. You do what you want."

Rumbling commotion worked through the crowd. Lilac studied the flood fighters and officers, many with bandaged heads and limbs, some walking on sticks or leaning on each other. Injured in ways both visible and unseen. After what they must have endured in Oldtown, they would still follow Thale. The city's people would go, too. What else were they supposed to do? There were no more gods here to worship.

Simone brushed Lilac's tangled hair out of her face. "Do we follow them?" she asked.

"I can't make that decision," Lilac said. She needed Simone to be the mother now, but neither of them came equipped for this. "I have no idea what to do."

"Lilac." Simone's hand brushed again, harder this time. "Tell me you had something else in mind when you killed Lyvien's grandson."

Lilac jerked back.

Tears filled Simone's eyes. "Tell me you thought everything out and saw a better way, like Logoi taught you. Tell me, Lilac. I need to hear it."

Lilac hesitated. "I killed him because if we let him live, we'd regret it. I turned it over and over, and I couldn't find the pattern for it. He sent the gods away, Mom. He's the reason Sara and Daphne are gone."

"But he could've saved us, couldn't he?" Simone asked.

"He said Lyvien would answer, but we couldn't trust him." Lilac watched her mother's eyes turn cold. "Don't hate me."

"He could've got a message to Lyvien, but you couldn't get one to Logoi. He told you how, right? You can contact her. I'll put up with it, I promise."

"No, Mom," Lilac said. "I'm sorry."

"I'm sorry, too." Simone held Lilac against her. "I tried to think of something I could've done."

"Mom."

"If I'd helped you with the sacrifices, maybe Logoi—"

"Mother heard me every time I called." Lilac's tone dropped to a whisper. "Every time I shed blood, every time I painted her sign, she heard. Because I'm her daughter, she heard me. She chose this. She won't come back unless she wants to. And she doesn't want to."

Simone wiped at her eyes. The way she looked now pulled Lilac back to the day they had reunited years ago. She had understood the woman who opened the door to be her biological mother, but also a stranger. Simone hadn't been Mom yet.

That was the look on her face now. She was her own woman,

who had once traveled far to the temple of Logos, hoping the goddess of reason would give her purpose. And she had. That mortal woman hadn't come to the temple in search of love, but she'd found it. Yet love hadn't stopped one mother from casting the other out.

Simone's teary eyes turned red and aching. "You understand now, don't you? About Logoi. You understand why, if I'd stolen you, it'd be different? Because a god can do no wrong."

Lilac still loved Logoi. But yes, she understood. If she had to talk about it, she would start crying again. Aeda had been wrong. Any god could be, and the gods knew it. Logoi had led their kin to trap Aeda and Medes because the gods knew what mortals must never learn—the gods were fallible, and they feared the Dawn Gods' disappointment.

All those years in the temple, Lilac had obeyed Logoi's wish for secrecy. Who was a mortal daughter to question a goddess? Lilac hadn't had to fend for herself until the day Logoi abandoned her, and she hadn't known how. Any human who did that would be called neglectful, abusive, and rightly so.

But Logoi could do it without consequence. She was a goddess. That was one of the perks.

Lilac tried not to think too much, or else the memories would needle her into rage. She could close her eyes to shut out the world, but there was no shutting her heart against this truth. Logoi was her mother, and Lilac loved her. She would always love her.

But in that moment, Lilac hated her a little, too. If she let herself work at this, turn it over a hundred times in her head, maybe she would hate Logoi a lot. A hatred as strong as Simone's. Lilac tried to focus on the here and now.

But the here and now was heartbreaking. She headed south, without Simone or Arcadia, against the flow of crowds split between leaving with Thale or staying in city. Valentine, Aedos— whatever they wanted to call it now that Aeda was gone.

Now that it was cursed. Lilac reached the southern edge of

the temple plaza, but a scant few blocks of street ran any deeper into the South Temple District before hitting a crimson fog. She had hoped to deny the red scar Exalis had thrust into hers and everyone's minds, but standing here, she had to accept the red scar before her eyes.

A blood-painted glow lit across its spore-choked miasma, where pavement tore and melted in a strip of shining stones. Some lay no bigger than Lilac's hand, while others stabbed skyward in geode-like clusters as large as her apartment building.

Which was gone, along with any sense of home and everything in it. Simone's belongings, Lilac's belongings. Sara's drawings, the twins' toy chest. The clothes Lilac used to pretend still smelled like her children. She would have to find other clothes, pretend harder, tell herself she could still remember their weight and touch like she'd only lost them yesterday, even when memories were all she had left.

Everything empty, same as the glories had left her that day on the beach.

After she collected herself, Lilac followed Thale's scavengers into the North Temple District, where she found clothes and changed out of robes into a heavy shirt, pants, and thick boots. Real clothing felt good for a change, but she bundled up the covenant robe and kept it in the pack she was putting together. Dressing as a priestess had started to feel normal again, and she wanted to keep it. Hard to know what normal meant anymore.

She found clothes for Simone and Arcadia, too. They could rip and sew fabric for more to get by. There would be a lot of getting by.

In a spare moment, Lilac scrubbed soap and water over her hands and face, washing away Cecil's bloodstains. In some spots, she scrubbed so hard, she couldn't quite tell where his blood ended and hers began. She would have to live with some of it until it faded on its own.

Arcadia sat with Simone on the temple steps, where a mournful look haunted her eyes. Thale avoided glancing her way, even rising now and then on uncertain legs and hobbling elsewhere before returning to his wheelchair, intent on looking like he no longer noticed Arcadia.

Lilac fastened one roll of supplies to Arcadia's back. "Think you can manage?"

Arcadia gave a faint nod. She was still out of sorts, but the shock inside the tree had dragged her back at least a little ways from the damage Alex, Aeda, and Medes had done. If there was a future, maybe Arcadia could come back to herself, and then to Lilac. Arcadia had danced with miracles before, for better or worse.

What about Simone? Her home of the past few decades was gone, but how could she hike north? Aeg only grew rougher with its northern elevation. The fields climbed into rocky crags, and then foothills, where chilly wind howled down Shadow Mountain. A land of poor shelter, bitter cold, and little food. Exposure could kill even the young and fit. Maybe Lilac needed to give her mother more credit, but she doubted Simone would survive for long.

The shuffle of a few thousand footsteps filled the city, an evacuation in progress. There were other city-states, but flooded rivers had cut most of them off. Lilac could take Simone to Bay Ridge, but could Aeda have gone there to ready for leaving Aeg? And how safe was it really? Oldtown was crumbling. The North Temple District had only taken water damage, but as soon as the sea returned, it would begin to crumble. Same for Lee Village, especially if the eastern fields became another set of floodplains where they faced the river between Valentine and Tychos. Neon-lit Merchant's Field sat farthest from the water but would likely flood, too. The red scar had turned the South Temple District into a land of death. None of these were habitable places.

But then, the red scar lay between the sea and Merchant's Field. And it burned everything that touched it. Even water.

This could work. Maybe not forever, but longer than the rest of the city. Certainly longer than Simone would last beneath Shadow Mountain. If they could make it through the rainy season, their options might grow.

"We're not going with Thale," Lilac said.

"What choice do we have?" Simone asked.

"Merchant's Field." Lilac hefted supplies onto her back. "The seawater will have to hit the red scar first, and it will eat anything it touches. Human, stone, rain, even seawater. We can be safe there, for now."

Simone shrugged beside her. "If you say so."

She looked defeated. Arcadia, too. The same defeat might have dug itself into Lilac, but if she let it consume her, there would be no one to lead. She started southeast. They would briefly detour through Lee Village, and then head south to Merchant's Field. A longer way, but it would keep them from touching the red scar.

Shuffling steps sounded again, headed for Shadow Mountain. Some would make it; some wouldn't. Some would wish they hadn't tried.

How many thousands would die there? Lilac couldn't guess. More would join the procession as they passed through the North Temple District and Lee Village. Above, the clouds closed against each other, as if the breach of frail sunlight had been an open wound and only the storm could heal it.

Lilac's throat was scratchy and rough, but she tried. "There's another way." It came as a whisper. She made herself shout. "There's another way!"

Heads turned at the procession's tail. They were listening.

"I don't know if it's any better," Lilac said. "But if you want to stay, we can make Merchant's Field safe enough."

She started again, only making sure Arcadia and Simone followed. She didn't want these people thinking she'd made them any promises. By sharing her plan, she had at least given them a chance.

Like Cecil had suggested, there was no escaping her bloody hands in this.

Shuffling feet followed, maybe a few hundred. Lilac was surprised even that many had broken from Thale's procession. Arcadia kept to Lilac's back, and Simone, too. A once champion, and a goddess's ex-lover, and a goddess's daughter-turned-high priestess to the Dawn Gods. Maybe they were worth following. Maybe not.

"Aren't you the high priestess?" a melodious voice asked. A small girl wearing a tattered dress and oversized derby marched to Lilac's left.

"That's what Aeda called me," Lilac said, her tone deflated.

"Why didn't you go with the goddess?" the girl asked.

"I don't think the people who followed her are going to make it." Lilac wished she had a kinder answer.

The little girl lost interest and drifted back into the crowd. Lilac hoped she hadn't cut down one of the girl's parents in the temple—maybe that was where she'd gotten the hat from—but regardless Lilac had cut down someone who mattered to someone else. Was Cecil right again, that they would want revenge someday? Or did Lilac share a goddess's immunity to judgment? Aeda had appealed to their devotion toward each other.

Now Lilac appealed to their sense of survival. She hoped she wasn't killing them.

If it mattered. After everything she'd done, starting from the day she brought her daughters to that beach up to now, Lilac doubted there was any spot left unblemished on her soul. No further wrong could make it worse.

CHAPTER 51

Dusk fell across the Holy Land as the tide lapped at its new coast, Oldtown. In Merchant's Field, Lilac and a few others huddled around a small radio in the dark cramped living room of an abandoned second-floor apartment. The radio belonged to Ilene Summers, an evac team agent who had broken away from Thale's procession out of the city. Other groups huddled in neighboring apartments. Rain pounded overhead.

The water had waited in the floodplains while Thale's procession left Valentine unmolested, and only at dusk did the tide flow in.

While much of what came directly from the west would hit that no man's land of the red scar on its own, Lilac and her group had spent the day blocking off northern streets and breaking channels in the pavement to lead seawater toward the South Temple District and its destructive substance. Every encroaching wave of seawater to touch that unnatural wasteland burst into spores, unmade as if it had never crossed from the floodplains.

The calm wouldn't last forever. In time, the glories would press themselves into the city and build routes for seawater to bypass the red scar. This survival was temporary.

Lilac couldn't think about that future right now. She wanted to hear about the north-heading evacuation's progress.

"You're camped, Leander?" Ilene asked the radio. "How close

to the hills?"

"Closer than we thought we'd be in a day," Leander said over static. Lilac guessed he was another flood fighter. "We picked up a few hundred people outside the city. Everyone's having a rough time."

Parts of Merchant's Field had already been deserted when Lilac and her followers arrived. Crowds were fleeing the city. Some changed their minds and joined Lilac's group, but most hurried to catch up with Thale. He must have led thousands north.

"We shed a few hundred or so before we hit the high road," Leander went on. "They spotted Tychos. Some wanted to try taking the city, but we wouldn't go near it."

How desperate did a person have to be for Tychos to look like a safe option? Then again, the river between city-states might have offered at least a quick death.

"We're high enough that the flooding shouldn't touch us before we pass the Holy Tree Grave," Leander said, as if Valentine hadn't become another such grave. "The rain's getting worse, and it's colder here, but we should make the hills tomorrow."

There was more talk about Thale's health, questions about Arcadia. Ilene told Leander about the blocked roads and the hope that they'd wake up to a dry Merchant's Field, rain aside. Lilac quit listening after that and wandered to the blankets she'd spread in one corner next to Simone, who lay asleep. Tomorrow, the refugees would spread out, find more abandoned houses and apartments in hopes they could outlast the rainy season.

Lilac was too drained to search tonight. She hadn't slept at all through the previous night and day, and she would've fainted if not for blood she'd drawn into herself while committing Aeda's sacrifices.

And besides, her place in shaping these events was done. Time to let someone else take over.

She stretched beside Arcadia, naked but for a sheet wrapped

around her. Warmth radiated from her skin. Lilac held her tight, consciousness fading. She reached across Arcadia's scalp and stroked her fingers through bristly hair.

"We're alright," Lilac whispered again and again, even as she drifted into sleep herself, a mantra to dictate their dreams.

As the world turned black, she fantasized that the evacuation might reach the hills and find kindly strangers, hidden away from the city-states like the long-dead village of Shah in Alex's story. They would explain they'd lived up there for generations, a hidden paradise. Leander would send the news across the radio to get everyone in Valentine moving as soon as they could.

But the northbound group hadn't headed for some secret green hills of plenty. They were headed for Shadow Mountain, where the world was rock and ice and death.

CHAPTER 52

Lilac found a small apartment for herself, Simone, and Arcadia. Not much, but there were two beds and a radio that Simone kept on one table and fiddled with each day in hopes of catching a broadcast from distant city-states. Leander's updates became city-wide after a middle-aged couple who used to work in a Valentine radio station helped rig his reports for wider broadcast.

But the news was bleak. On the second night out, Thale's group reached the hills, first those full of thistle trees, and then to the rolling slopes of rock, sheltered by their forests from Shadow Mountain's icy winds. Cold and wet, and then came the disappearances.

"Another five missing today," Leander said after a week. "That's forty-one gone, I think. A farmer found a blood trail this time, but Thale said no one's going anywhere in the woods unless it's to cut down the edge of the tree line to build shelter."

"What's become of them?" Ilene asked.

"Ravines, rockslides, animals. Not sure clearing farmland will do much good either. If we can't find food, we'll starve long before any harvest. It doesn't matter what we do."

Simone buried her head in her hands. Lilac wanted to turn the damn radio off, but she had nothing to offer in its place. She drifted to Arcadia, who sometimes haunted the streets, often confused, sometimes morose, never really lucid. If any of Medes's divinity remained, it flowed through a cracked shell.

"Did you eat today?" Lilac asked.

Arcadia stared at her knees.

"You didn't, did you?"

"Not hungry," Arcadia said. "Makes me sick."

Getting more than two words out of her was a good day. After the first night in Merchant's Field, she wouldn't wear anything but her soiled uniform with the bullet hole in the chest. Only when Lilac trekked to Radiance Hotel and carried back similar uniforms would Arcadia wear anything else. Even then, Lilac sometimes found Arcadia sitting naked in the corner, arms locked around the bloody uniform she'd been wearing when she died.

Like now. Lilac sat beside her and petted the once-green garment. "We never talked about Alex."

Arcadia squeezed the bundle tighter.

"He worried about you," Lilac said. "If he'd known you would come back, he wouldn't have shot you." She set her hand on Arcadia's knee. "No one ordered him to do that. He thought he didn't have a choice. He loved you. But I'm not helping, am I?"

Arcadia placed the rags on the floor, dressed herself in a different ill-fitting uniform, and trudged away, like she might march out to Oldtown to fight floods and glories one last time.

Whatever deep machines the glories used to move the sea seemed to best function at night. The tide left Valentine after each dawn. Survivors spent gray days gathering supplies and building wider channels to guide the seawater toward the red scar. Some began digging a ditch to the south to keep seawater out of Merchant's Field. Others ventured beyond the city, hoping to defend the farmlands. The nearest fields lay ankle-deep in water at best, but they had to try.

Most of Valentine lay abandoned except perhaps Bay Ridge. The only people who had traveled there had gone looking for Aeda. No one had seen them since.

How long could the city hold out? The glories would eventually realize the east side drew power from the river dams between Valentine and Tychos. They would then darken the city for good. Food wasn't a problem yet, but someday it would be.

Five days later, a mason from Lee Village died south of Valentine. He had been digging the ditch to help seawater flow into the red scar. Lilac had never met him, only heard mention of him on panicked lips. Motes of once-human drifted together and burned atop the soil, same as inside the South Temple District, except this was south of the city.

Which meant the red scar was growing.

Oldtown was a soggy ruin, every building reduced to rubble, the barricade left standing only because it no longer offered resistance to the sea when waves washed through the broken gateway. The North Temple District was getting worn down, too, its pavement cracking. Streets would sooner or later collapse into the catacombs and sewage system. Cobblestones were breaking from the temple plaza.

Eventually the red scar would spread there, and all evidence of Valmydion's greatness would disappear from the Holy Land. As it had been for Aeda and her Aedos before.

"Ilene?" the radio asked that night, and the crackling voice stole Simone's attention. "Summers, can you hear me?"

The speaker didn't sound quite like Leander, but the signal weakened each day. The radio in the hills would die soon, cut off from the city for good.

Ilene's voice broke onto the radio. She sounded exhausted. "Leander, I'm here," she said. "You sound a little off tonight."

"This is Bryce," the radio said. There was a sigh, maybe a sob. "Leander's missing. Two agents with him, and a little girl too. People vanish even when there's a rotating guard. No one was ever meant to live here, like the land hates us. We can't sleep. Can't stay. Thale says the glories have surrounded the Holy Land, but they didn't start in on Valentine until this rainy season. We could cross Shadow Mountain and the far hills and shallows to Aeg's eastern city-states. See if Diomarch or Dialos are still standing. The radio won't hold up through the mountain's snow. This might be the last you hear from us."

"It'll be the last we hear from you because you'll die up there," Ilene snapped.

"A lot of us." Bryce had a shrug in their voice. "Maybe most of us. But we can't live like this. Isn't that the same for you?"

Lilac stormed off the couch to shut this shit off.

Simone crossed her arms over the radio. "We need to hear them."

"What for?" Lilac asked. "You think they have some survival plan? Let's say any of them make it across the mountain, the eastern hills, the shallows. Where to then? Diomarch was the first to go silent. Aeg is lousy with rivers, tributaries—there's nowhere the glories can't go." She drifted to the couch and sank into its cushions beside Arcadia. "This isn't survival. It's a slow death."

"A god's curse." Simone's hands trembled their way to the radio's dial and switched it off. Her head sank against them. "Do the glories know what they're doing?"

Lilac scoffed. "They want to kill us. Of course they know."

"But the land won't be theirs if that red scar eats it," Simone said. "If they knew, wouldn't they stop? Even if it meant letting us live?" Her hands slammed the table to either side of the radio. "They come, and we fight them, and they hurt us, and the gods push them back, but has anyone talked to them? Has anyone tried?"

Lilac thought of Aeda's bloodlust, the destruction that would have come to glories and mankind alike had she gotten her way. Maybe they could have found a common enemy in her. A common problem like the scar Medes had left behind.

"I don't think glories understand us," Lilac said. "We don't understand them. A god might have figured it out, but the gods are gone. Anyone who goes to that sea is good as dead."

Simone wiped her face and went to the bedroom. "I'm going to pray on my next life. Maybe if I pray hard enough about what I want, I'll get it."

"Mom, please—"

"I'm glad I got to see you again," Simone said. "I'm sorry I didn't keep you. I'm sorry Logoi disappointed you. I would've liked to be wrong, for your sake."

Lilac didn't know how to fix this. What else was new? "You don't know what you're saying."

"I'm trying to approach my death with the little bit of dignity I have left," Simone said. She forced a smile through a creased, worried face. "I think you should, too." She closed the bedroom door.

Dignity? When had such a thing helped anyone? It wouldn't save the people Lilac loved. That sort of pride was what kept Simone's disdain for Logoi lit across the decades.

But what else was there? Forgiveness? A goddess didn't ask forgiveness because there was no right or wrong, only what a goddess did. Even in some reality where Logoi would ask forgiveness, Simone wouldn't give it. Why even consider these things?

Lilac knew. The same reason everyone in Merchant's Field tuned in to these radio conversations—it was easier to focus on somebody else's problems. The city's doom. Simone hating Logoi; Mom versus Mother. What wonderful distractions against the relentless gnawing in Lilac's gut.

Arcadia sat beside Lilac on the couch and stared at an empty wall. The trouble wasn't about feeding her, clothing her, bathing her. Lilac knew what she needed to do, even if it meant ruining this meager peace. She had called Cecil a liar and a coward, but wasn't she the same if she kept quiet? Had she let him live, maybe things would be easier, but she couldn't trust someone who had done what he did. There would always have come a time when he would put himself first. They were more alike than either would've admitted.

Her choice was either to go on Cecil's way, or try honesty. She had nothing to gain except to scrape the coarse feeling off her heart. Logoi would've called this an irrational path, when the gains were so small, the losses so great.

All the more reason to do it. Because Logoi wouldn't.

Lilac turned to Arcadia and laid a hand on her leg. "Can we talk?"

Arcadia went on staring at the wall. It was almost a mirror, casting her haunted eyes back at her.

"The night you brought Alex and Cecil, after that dinner, I told you I knew what I wanted," Lilac said. "This might not be a world where I can have it, but it's you. I want you. And I want a relationship with you that's bigger than secrets. You brought me back after the worst thing happened to me. And then I thought I'd lost you again, and then again. It's like someone's shoving me, saying 'Hey, Lilac, do you mean it yet? How many chances do you need?' I think if I don't open up, then I really will lose you. But to do that, I might lose you anyway."

Now Arcadia turned to look. "Lilac—"

"I need to tell you something." And then Lilac told her everything.

CHAPTER 53

Lilac felt sick by the end of it. Every terrible choice. Every miserable action. Every horrific consequence, from Vince and the twins, to glories and godly lineage, to the murders and chases and sacrifices, and the confrontation beneath the Holy Psychopomp Tree. Lilac was shaking so badly, she nearly fell to the floor.

"I don't make any excuses," she said, her voice hoarse. "I lied to you, kept secrets, and you suffered because of me. If you were in my place, you'd have made better decisions. We all hurt you so much when you shouldn't have been mixed up in this in the first place. It was never supposed to be so complicated. It's my fault. I love you, Arcadia, and I'm so sorry."

Lilac swallowed when she was done. She hadn't cried at all. She wasn't sure if that was good or bad or insignificant, but everything was out. It was done.

Arcadia said nothing. She showed no emotion, asked no questions, but Lilac could tell she was listening, those bright eyes darting back and forth. Spilling out the truth was not a request for forgiveness. Lilac didn't deserve it. Whatever good had come of her actions couldn't balance the pain she'd caused. To say so would sound like she was desperate for Arcadia's comfort, and even if she was, Lilac hadn't confessed for herself.

This was for Arcadia.

A hand ran down Lilac's long hair, fingers catching on auburn tangles. Another hand joined it, and both palms cupped Lilac's ears. Arcadia leaned close and kissed Lilac's forehead.

Lilac's eyes welled up. She tried to turn away, but strong hands stilled her face, baring her tears. "You haven't—not since—sorry." She forgot what she wanted to say and kissed Arcadia's cheek.

Arcadia's smile was weak, but Lilac took what she could get. She would've given up these kisses, these hands around her face, these arms encircling her body, everything that followed tonight to pull Arcadia out of this haze she'd lived under. To see old Arcadia would mean Lilac hadn't broken her. That would mean the world.

But this was the night they had, and Lilac focused on Arcadia in the dark, and took in lips at her neck, and a hand between her legs. She gave kisses upon a gunshot-scarred chest, and fingertips on bristly hair, and every sight and sound and touch between them. She let the moment come to life and keep her thoughts from turning over puzzle pieces and clawing at solutions. There was sweat, and pleasant noise, and peaceful darkness, some endlessness beating through Lilac until she was shaky and exhausted, and she fell asleep without meaning to.

CHAPTER 54

Insomnia had haunted Arcadia for several nights now in this hopeless apartment. She lay motionless until slow breathing slid in and out beside her, and then she reached for Lilac and stroked her back. Lilac didn't stir, exhausted in body and soul. When her confession began, she had probably expected Arcadia to hate her, and the stress had drained her last energy.

Hating her was impossible. In the face of everything they had lost and were still losing, for Lilac to risk what tiny happiness remained was an act of absolute bravery. Arcadia wondered what such bravery felt like. Failure was always easy to grasp.

Lilac had also made tonight's burden far heavier. Arcadia had planned to explain what she meant to do, as she'd already told Ilene in private. Instead, Lilac had steeled herself to tell all.

Perhaps it was a night for decisive actions. Other people across the city might put on determined faces and harden their hearts, committed to making brave confessions and works of redemption. They could fashion a new holiday out of it for Valentine's survivors.

A holiday for no gods—it would be a first.

Arcadia covered Lilac in a blanket, dressed again in her most tattered uniform—her ragged kin in Valentine's ordeals—and then crept to the door. Lilac's soft breathing filled the apartment. If the truth came out, people would blame her. She would probably welcome their scorn, though the glories would have flooded the city nonetheless. She deserved forgiveness.

Blame instead belonged to Arcadia for her silence and fear of doing what needed to be done. She wished she could wake Lilac and tell her it would be fine, maybe mean it, but lingering would only prolong the night. Lilac, Simone, Ilene, and the rest of the survivors had been hard at work while Arcadia had tried coming to terms with one awful night.

Past time she did her part.

The apartment door opened and closed, and Arcadia took to the rainy streets. No one wandered Merchant's Field. The rain fell too heavily, and flooding blocked the southernmost streets. No one would risk stumbling into that red scar where the South Temple District had ceased to be.

Who to blame for that catastrophe—Alex? Aeda? Medes? It was too much to fathom. Death wasn't a game, and blood wasn't currency—everyone in Aeg needed to understand that. Death had weight. If Lilac was to blame for anything, it was for falling into the same dreadful pattern humans had taken with the gods since they left Aeg ten years ago—no, since the Dawn Gods first descended from the heavens.

Someone had to say *Enough*.

Arcadia sloshed through the Central Temple District's flood-water. Hard to believe a Dawn God had descended here, but the temple told its own story, as did the jewelry, photographs, and all manner of manmade detritus floating around the temple's marble ruin. So much upheaval since Arcadia had unknowingly chased Lilac here and marveled at ceiling murals dedicated to Valmydion. Or Aeda, Arcadia supposed, since the entire city had been altered to hide the gods' shame. Had minutes passed since then, or centuries? No temple remained to mark the passage of time on its walls.

Arcadia detoured briefly into the North Temple District and almost made it to Radiance Hotel out of habit before swerving toward Oldtown. Her path slipped past the police headquarters, a

once-pleasant diner, the Ace Investigations office, each site worn
by flooding.

Gods, poor Alex. Arcadia didn't blame him for shooting
her. She'd been confused then, but the way Lilac told it, Alex had
thought he could stop a greater atrocity. He'd been oblivious to
Medes and her insidious conviction, much like Arcadia herself.
She wished she could tell him not to worry, but to reach out even
in thought would be too much like what Medes had done, vio-
lating the laws of nature and death. If there was a future, Arcadia
would grieve for Alex then. Tonight's work was not about death,
but about life.

Arcadia waded into Oldtown, starting from the north and
heading south, the same path as her flood fighters' hopeless evac
team. Ruined homes hid in darkness, but she could tell their sorry
states. She'd approached many of these stone walls and knocked on
their wooden doors, selling worthless promises with empty smiles.
Somewhere, June Green's house crumbled. Arcadia hoped she and
Junior hid among the refugees in Merchant's Field.

Not far away lay the ruins of a house where Lilac had painted
Logoi's star on the wall in blood. She'd been desperate not to let
Valentine turn out like her daughters. Maybe, despite the murders,
her work too was about life. These houses had borne the brunt
of the glories' assault while people like Lilac had taken it on their
souls.

No more. Arcadia reached the stone barricade, weathered and
cracking, and climbed over the top. The sea filled the floodplains.
There was little light, the clouds having hidden tonight's moon, but
Arcadia didn't need it. She saw every whitecap and splashing wave.

Distant whales sounded warnings. *There are glories here!* they
seemed to sing. *Turn back, you won't escape them again!*

Arcadia would've thanked them if she could, but she already
knew the glories were here. She saw them clearly upon the rolling
darkness, little more than sleek black shapes in the distance. Bob-

bing up and down, watching. Waiting. Maybe they knew what she had come here to do.

The whales sang their warnings again, but Arcadia would have to disappoint them. She wasn't going anywhere. Her luck had run out that night she let one glory get away and nothing since then could ever be the same.

She slipped down the battered side of the barricade, into the sea's salt and spray, and let the waves take her.

CHAPTER 55

Lilac woke alone in the morning. Arcadia had wrapped a blanket around her and vanished. Not to the bathroom, not to the kitchenette. Lilac expected to glance out the window and spot Arcadia wandering the street below, as she did most days, but there was no sign of her.

Not in the bedroom either. Lilac found Simone seated cross-legged on one of the beds, her head bowed as if she'd been praying. The other bed looked untouched since Lilac had made it yesterday.

"You haven't seen Arcadia?" Lilac asked.

"I haven't left the room since last night," Simone said. "I thought of fasting, but if bigger sacrifices can't bring the gods back, I suppose skipping breakfast isn't going to change anything."

"No, you need to eat." Lilac remembered then that Arcadia hadn't been eating. Was fasting the reason? Arcadia was too weak to go wandering Merchant's Field half-starved. Lilac had to find her.

There was no Arcadia to find. Lilac searched up and down each street, asking passersby if they had seen Captain Myrn, and then she set her sights on Ilene Summers. She often woke up at dawn to start organizing the day's work.

"Captain Myrn is busy," Ilene said when asked.

Lilac stood close to her. "I'm not some random well-wisher looking to praise her. She lives with me. Do you understand? I can't find her."

"Ms. Antonis. Right." Ilene shut her eyes and sighed. "She didn't tell you."

"What didn't she tell me?" Lilac asked.

Ilene's eyes fluttered wetly. "She went to see the glories."

"To see—" Lilac stumbled back. "Where? On the floodplains? The river?"

"I don't know," Ilene said. "She told me she'd be back before dark."

"She won't be back at all." Lilac's trembling hands curled into fists. "You should've stopped her."

Ilene looked incredulous. "Stop her? How? There's fire in her eyes like I haven't seen in weeks, and this isn't something she went to do on a whim. She's been gearing herself up for it, she said. I couldn't have stopped her if I'd tried."

Arcadia, gearing herself up? For what, Simone's nonsense about talking this out? Except Arcadia appeared to have had the idea since before last night. What did she think she could do by throwing her life to the waves?

Lilac had taken for granted that Arcadia would passively accept all these changes, as if she wasn't an intelligent person with her own thoughts and intentions, and the will to act on them. While Lilac had rattled off her confession, Arcadia had been working out ways to help. Lilac could figure out her next move in moments, but that didn't mean no one else had thoughts in their heads. Especially Arcadia, who had made up her mind to save as many people as she could.

But not herself. This was suicide.

Lilac crumpled on the curb beside Ilene's boots. "What does she think she can do? Why does she have to be this way?"

"Arcadia's good like that." Ilene looked to the sky. "Even before she was champion, she was special."

Lilac couldn't argue. She might want to escape Cecil's dissection of her soul, but when it came to being a genuinely decent person, Arcadia was the real thing. Even Aeda had seen it, if only to exploit it.

"I have work to do," Ilene said, and then lowered voice. "But if anyone could come back from this, it's her." She slipped away without another word.

Lilac didn't move. The curb warmed as fragments of sunshine poked through the clouds and then cooled as they vanished, the rains coming again for a new storm. The day stretched on, and she tried to fill it with helping fortifications, digging trenches, and scouring for supplies, but outside Bay Ridge, the city had been picked clean.

She thought of praying with Simone, but it seemed pointless. If the gods wouldn't return earlier, they certainly wouldn't come back with the red scar devouring the city. Even Cecil might have been wrong about Lyvien. The god of instinct wasn't well-regarded for a strong sense of responsibility. At best he would have impregnated half a dozen mortals on the chance one of the children might become a god and then left the ascended parent to solve Aeg's problems. Ever the wanderer.

Dusk came fast in the overcast sky; still no sign of Arcadia. Lilac bothered Ilene again, but she didn't know anything more than this morning. When the sun finally set, rain ebbed to a drizzle as if to whisper a message in Lilac's ear.

She left Merchant's Field and traveled into Valentine's dimness with only a slender half-working flashlight. Over her clothes she wore the covenant robe, partly for the hood to guard against rain, partly because it felt right to wear it as she crossed the temple plaza.

The refugees had disconnected the streetlights in Lee Village and the North Temple District to conserve power, but they left the streets lit around the temple's foundation out of respect. No one knelt in the shadow of the ruins tonight. No bodies remained either, not Cecil or Alex or anyone Lilac had sacrificed to Exalis, either swept off by the tide into the red scar or dragged out to sea. Too many ambitions had risen and died on this spot.

With no sign of Arcadia, Lilac headed to Oldtown, where her part in this had begun.

The lights had gone dark here before anywhere else. The waves had brought down every house, leaving the neighborhood an un-recognizable smattering of broken stone hills. Lilac couldn't have drawn an X on a map of this new Oldtown with any certainty.

She sat on the edge of a hefty ruin and let the rain fall across her robe. This wasn't suicide; she would leave when the tide came in strong enough. The rising water would tell her Arcadia's fate. She only hoped the telling would mean she spotted Arcadia striding through the streets, worn and hurt but alive, having shown what a human can survive—especially when it came to the glories—and not because a body floated by dressed in a green uniform.

"The tide should be deeper by now," Lilac noted. She took it for a good omen.

She had come out here, dressed like this, almost as repentance. Oldtown was where she'd made her choices. Where people had died by her hand to summon a goddess. If the twins had lived, things might've been different, but they had gone to the glories, too, in their own innocent, three-year-old way. Lilac's choices had eventually dragged Arcadia toward death, once most of the way, and then all the way. That made it the place where repentance mat-tered.

"You came back each of those times," Lilac said, hugging her legs against her chest. "I like to think that's one of your habits, like cutting your hair so short, like helping people. Something you can't help doing."

Her thoughts drifted as she waited for the seawater to spill over the remains of the floodplains wall and into Oldtown. Good and bad crisscrossed over her life, regretful choices leading to love, and love leading to regrets. There was no point in dwelling on the contradiction. The maybes and would-haves couldn't coexist with real life. Even Cecil had known that, before Lilac killed him.

No right without the wrong, and no wrong without right.

"What do you do with that?" Lilac asked the night. "It's maddening." Her only consolation was that she could never change the way things were. Those choices floated outside her grasp. She laughed to herself.

The tide should have surged through Oldtown by now. Its absence was bizarre. Every night over the past few weeks, the sea had come to Valentine. Lilac hopped onto the muddy street and landed in shallow, stagnant water, the ebb and flow of waves absent from its surface. As if the sea had remained where it belonged.

But it had to be coming, didn't it?

She splashed through Oldtown, her dingy robe dampening at the bottom, until she reached the floodplains barricade. Her flashlight showed her a stone wall turned sieve against seawater, but no wave flowed here to worsen the erosion.

The gate was long gone, washed away to places unknown, and water should have come flowing through since before sunset. There was no rushing roar. The flashlight showed the gateway damp but clear. In the daylight, you could stare through that opening, across the waterlogged floodplains to the waves now covering the beach where Sara and Daphne had disappeared. They wouldn't be coming back from there, but they were children. Breaking a mother's heart was what they would have done had they lived, too.

Arcadia wasn't a child. She had no right to break Lilac's heart. She would come back. She had to.

Lilac stuffed the flashlight inside her robe and clambered up the barricade's holes to its top. Braver souls had stood here alongside Arcadia while a storm ravaged Oldtown. As Lilac crested the stone, the clouds thinned and let the sky breathe thin moonlight across the water. Rolling waves broke apart its shimmering reflection.

The tide had only come in far enough to keep the beach and half the floodplains drowned. Oldtown should have been drowning, too, but the sea had receded. This made no sense.

Not far from the barricade, Lilac noticed the moonlight bend where a towering figure waded toward Oldtown. She ducked on her haunches, ready to drop into Oldtown's mud. It had to be the glories again with some new weapon, or an enormous sea creature from the depths.

Except sea monsters tended to slither and swim. This figure walked from the floodplains water on mighty legs. Taller than the twelve-foot barricade, yes, but less like a sea monster and more with the gigantic size, gait, and grace of a god.

Another few steps, and the figure had almost reached Lilac. The head crested the barricade, and Lilac couldn't help but think of bald Logoi.

No, the goddess of reason hadn't severed eight of her heads, reeled in her dragon necks, and come stalking out of the sea. This figure didn't come naked as Logoi, either. A gown of sea-green and white flowed as if the figure came draped in moonlight upon the sea. The head had hair after all, shorn short as always. Her face wore a secret smile, familiar and cherished.

Lilac craned her neck over the barricade and gaped in shock. "Arcadia?"

She had always loomed by inches over Lilac, but now Arcadia's mammoth height made Lilac feel tiny, almost verminous. She met Arcadia's eye level at the barricade's top, but only came to her knees when she slid down the floodplains side of the stone. Raindrops flittered from her robe and hair, off her skin, and the water on the ground seemed to evaporate in a cloud around Arcadia's steps the way floodwater had retreated from Aeda's sanctuary.

Lilac fell to her knees. "A goddess."

Arcadia reached down for her. "Don't worship me." Her voice boomed over rushing waves. Massive hands grasped Lilac's sides tenderly and helped her to stand.

Harsh heat breathed off her great abdomen, as if she had swallowed the sun. The skin there almost burned, but Lilac reached for it anyway, soaking in the pleasant warmth. Her fingers felt compelled to touch. Arcadia's middle pulsed, and it reminded Lilac of a small coralstone, or the altar of the Holy Tree.

Or a child's heart.

"You came back," Lilac said, gazing up at Arcadia's face. "I knew you'd come back to me."

Arcadia glanced at her own hand as if noticing it for the first time. She was forever now. She would always come back.

"And you're not alone." Lilac drew her hand from Arcadia's burning abdomen and settled for the softer warmth of Arcadia's hand. "How?"

"Medes, it has to be," Arcadia said. "Some of her divinity, planted inside me. She's the other mother."

"Did she mean to?" Lilac asked.

"I doubt it." Arcadia lowered her hand, interest in it lost. "Blood between her coralstone and me. The resurrection. Her coralstone shards beneath the tree. I don't know which way, but she put godliness inside me, and now there's something else. *Someone* else."

Lilac understood. With Arcadia having taken so much of a goddess into her and having not died in the Holy Psychopomp Tree, it seemed inevitable that divinity would mix with flesh and fill her womb. Medes should have known better. It had happened to her before anyone else, long ago.

"Does Medes know what she's done?" Lilac asked. "What she's made you?"

Arcadia shook her head. "Only you, me, and the glories."

"Why did you go to them? To show them?" Lilac kissed one of Arcadia's fingers. Two of them together were thick as her forearm. "They'll leave Aeg alone now, right?"

"They'll let Valentine be." Arcadia had a morose look in her eyes.

"I thought last night would be the end for us." Lilac pressed her head into Arcadia's palm. She smelled different now. Some of the old Arcadia was in there, but laced in a new, windswept scent Lilac couldn't name. "But you listened. And then you were gone in the morning and when Ilene told me why—I panicked."

"She shouldn't have done that," Arcadia said.

"I thought this was how you'd leave me," Lilac said.

"I am not Logoi." Arcadia's stoic visage blocked out the moon. "I won't leave you."

Her great hand slid down Lilac's waist, plucked her gently from the ground, and seated her atop the floodplains barricade. Arcadia pressed her head toward Lilac's body, and Lilac wrapped her arms around that mighty face.

"I'd put a child inside you, if you weren't a descendant," Arcadia breathed. Even her whisper shook Lilac's bones. "Must be hard, living past everyone else. The longer you live, the better chance you'll see consequences of what you do, ones you never expected. And you blame yourself for more than your share already."

Lilac studied Arcadia's tremendous eye. "I've made this harder somehow, haven't I?"

"It would be easier except for what you told me last night. About your girls. And the glories." Arcadia nodded against Lilac's chest. "But I didn't know any other way."

Why would this bother Arcadia now and not last night, when the glories were a real threat? Because Arcadia had been an ascendant even then, before this moment, unknown to all the world, even Lilac. Because Arcadia had some plan to handle the glories, and something about Sara and Daphne had unsettled it. Not enough to change it, but to disturb Arcadia's heart.

"What happened with the glories?" Lilac asked, her voice calm.

Arcadia lifted her head, and those eyes dazzled with distant deserts the glories could never touch. "I showed them who I am.

What I am. I can't fight them across the Holy Land, not in a way that would help or matter. We couldn't talk to each other easily, but I needed to make them understand."

Lilac almost laughed. "Of course you did. You're you."

"We made an arrangement best we could." Arcadia clenched one hand over the barricade. "They won't come to us. We won't go to them. I gave them a promise in body and soul, like only I could give. And I gave them half of Aeg."

Lilac's heart twitched. Her thoughts dredged up those voices on the beach, so much like Sara and Daphne that they'd almost fooled her, almost drawn her to death as well. She thought of the city and the sea, and everything she had done. And she thought of the glories, bereft of even a scrap of the Holy Land, nothing from the Dawn Gods except their mercy for five thousand years.

And now this, because the only goddess they had to deal with was Arcadia, the goddess of—what? A goddess of mercy at last? Homes were flooded, children dead, a continent abandoned by the gods, but now there was something to hold onto.

"Cut a line down the Holy Land from Shadow Mountain," Arcadia went on. "Tychos, Phobros, and everything west of them is ours. The east belongs to the glories. They have the land, the sea. We swore a consecration in blood and power—"

Lilac waved a hand. "I don't want to know the details. I can't take it."

Arcadia climbed onto the barricade and sat beside Lilac. A creature of her size should've crushed the stone, but a goddess could weigh whatever she wanted, and she began to shrink at Lilac's side. A goddess could do almost anything.

Arcadia reached out. "Lilac, it doesn't mean—"

"You don't owe me excuses or explanation," Lilac said. "I don't exactly deserve them, either. You did what you had to do." She steadied herself. She had done plenty of what she thought she'd had to do, too, and now it was Arcadia's turn. More importantly,

Arcadia would do better. "I understand. Really. I'm on your side."

They both turned west, where the sea lapped at the flood-plains. In many places, grass had washed away to soil. Eventually the waves would form sandbars, new beaches, but not here. The tide would recede a little more each day, and only the rains would water Valentine.

"Are you going to tell the others?" Lilac asked. "Everyone in Merchant's Field?"

"They'll know we're safe," Arcadia said.

"But about Aeg. The future."

Arcadia grew quiet. She and Lilac looked down at her abdomen. She was smaller now, but she could only shrink so much of her greatness when a divine world grew inside her.

"The glories will leave us be," Lilac said. "And half a Holy Land is more than any other god left us. You're the only one who cares, you and the one inside you, when they're old enough. We'll send people out, get people moving from the east. Maybe this should've been done a long time ago, like Mom said. Maybe there could be peace."

"Or maybe Aeda was right," Arcadia said. "Maybe we've damned the world."

Part of Lilac lingered on Sara and Daphne. They couldn't be disappointed in their mother. They had been three, would always be three. Vengeance and hatred were their mother's vices, and she would lock them down if it meant saving Aeg. She wasn't going to let herself be what Aeda or Cecil had said about her anymore.

"I don't know if Aeda's right or wrong," Lilac said. "But I know you're already a better goddess than she'll ever be."

Arcadia's eyes searched the oceanic darkness as if she could see the nighttime horizon, or perhaps the glories beneath the waves.

"We'll let them be, they'll let us be," she said. "I think in most ways, we all want the same thing. A chance to live, love, raise our children." She turned Lilac's way, her eyes no longer haunted. "You

HAILEY PIPER

told me we had a second chance, remember? You want us to be serious. What's happening to me is as serious as it gets. I'll understand if you want to walk away."

Lilac started to laugh, wiped her eyes, and then laid her head on an immortal shoulder. "I'm not going anywhere, Captain." Her hand found the hot place on Arcadia's abdomen. "And this one? You'll be a mother someday."

"Yes," Arcadia said.

"Will I be this one's mother, too?" Lilac asked.

"I want that." Arcadia leaned close. "But do you?"

Arcadia's middle burned again, but Lilac rested her hand there a moment longer anyway. Inside grew a child who could never die.

Oh yes, she wanted to be this child's mother. She wanted to be priestess to Arcadia, though she couldn't give blood. High priestess, then. Leader to the covenant of Arcadia, Goddess of Mercy.

There would be more work to do. First, everyone in Merchant's Field had to know they were safe. Someone needed to radio the hills before the travelers there made a terrible mistake. Survivors could then spread back across Valentine, and put the call to neighboring western city-states, share the good news. Get word to the eastern city-states and draw as many people as possible.

They would come. There was a goddess in the Holy Land, after all, one who would never leave them. There would be questions of what came next and how to heal. A new covenant to build. The new goddess would need a temple for her and, many years later, a temple for the child. The world ahead held limitless possibilities.

And from that future, for the city, for Aeg, for this family, the paths were so limitless that no amount of turning them over and over in thought could tell Lilac what might come, what best roads to take. But she wasn't thinking about that right now anyway.

She was thinking about what they might name the baby.

ACKNOWLEDGMENTS

Inklings of this story have been with me for decades, a living thing in the back of my mind no matter what other troubles and wonders I'd lost myself in. Twenty years of twisting narratives and changing priorities—that makes it hard to recall where any single spark began. The vision has grown so much that I don't think there is a single moment for it, but various origin points throughout my life. A character here, a detail there, thoughts and whispers and daydreams turned to narrative truth. I think teenage me just wanted to tell something big and strange, and I hope she'd be proud.

But a torch can't burn that long on its own, and it certainly hasn't found its way into the world through my hands alone.

Thank you to Chantelle Aimée Osman and Jason Pinter of Agora and Polis for taking on this beast of a book in the first place, and special thanks to Chantelle for her insight and vision in helping shape No Gods for Drowning into its best self, through both some minor nudges and major shoves. I also want to thank Mimi Bark for her elegant cover art.

My family, especially my mother, has had to deal with my writerly oddities from an earlier time than anyone. From when I would hog the family computer to write my dinosaur and werewolf stories, or later with understanding that I needed my own computer to keep writing, plus the time and space to myself to write, I'm grateful.

The horror community has had my back in countless ways, and I'm fortunate to have had so much encouragement as this book tossed on uncertain seas from Mary SanGiovanni, Brian

Keene, Joe Koch, Gabino Iglesias, Gwendolyn Kiste, V. Castro, Becky Spratford, Sadie Hartmann, Sandra Ruttan, Tracy Robinson, and so many more.

I don't know where I'd ever end up if not for Cynthia Pelayo leading me in the way only a beloved friend can, between "good job, you did it" to "hey, we're heading this way." I'd be totally lost without Cina. I cherish the constant wild weird talks and confidence injections (sometimes snuck in without my realizing until later) with Sara Tantlinger, Sam Kolesnik, Nat Edwards, Claire Holland, and Lisa Quigley. I don't know what I'd do without any of you. Possibly disintegrate. Definitely scream like mad.

There are older, forgotten ties, too. This story has been with me in some form or another through high school, college, internet forums, morphed in subtle ways by people who've left footprints through my life even when I only knew their online handles, their names forgotten. The connections of the modern world stretch the globe, but they can also vanish, and when people we once talked to every day become ghosts, we're haunted by missing them without ever knowing how things turned out in their lives. No one writes in a vacuum, but in this body of a world.

I will never have enough gratitude for my wife J. She hammered into my head over and over to not give up on this project, no matter how much of a genre stew it became once I finally sat to write it in adulthood, to keep improving it piece by piece, believing in it and me even when I sometimes forgot to. She was right, as she usually is.

And to every reader, a story is only a suggestion until it gets inside someone's head. Thank you for my letting this one into yours.

HAILEY PIPER, JUNE 2022

ABOUT THE AUTHOR

Hailey Piper is the Bram Stoker Award-winning author of *Queen of Teeth*, *The Worm and His Kings*, *Unfortunate Elements of My Anatomy*, *Your Mind Is a Terrible Thing*, *Benny Rose the Cannibal King*, and *The Possession of Natalie Glasgow*. She is an active member of the Horror Writers Association, with dozens of short stories appearing in *Pseudopod*, *Vastarien*, *Cast of Wonders*, *Daily Science Fiction*, *Cosmic Horror Monthly*, *Dark Matter Magazine*, and many other publications. She lives with her wife in Maryland, where their paranormal research is classified.

Find Hailey at www.haileypiper.com or on Twitter via @HaileyPiperSays.

CONTENT WARNING

This novel contains:

Graphic violence
Child Death
Animal Death
PTSD